COCKIEST SUITS SERIES

ALEX WOLF

ALEX WOLF

Publisher © Alex Wolf June 9th, 2018
Cover Design: Lori Jackson
Editor: Spellbound
Formatting: Alex Wolf

I'm a devil in a suit.

I don't play nice.

It's not my style.

I'm the best attorney in Dallas and I have a reputation to maintain.

If opposing counsel smells weakness, they walk all over you.

Not on my watch.

Life was good until I met her—Brooke. I had more money than I could ever spend. More power than one man should possess. People respect me and it's for a reason. I demand it.

Brooke's nothing but another encounter.

She'll end up beneath me. They all do. I'll keep it casual. Nothing more.

I don't do relationships. I don't do love. It's counterproductive to the lifestyle I lead.

But, no matter how hard I fight it, I want more. Brooke doesn't take any sh*t and she gives it back twice as hard. She turns me on in ways that can't be explained with her tight body and snarky mouth.

I'll take whatever I want from her and then some.

Because I'm Weston Hunter, Attorney at Law.

Chapter One

BROOKE

I f ever there was a day for some bullshit, this one takes the cake.

I throw up my hand in frustration. "Oh, come on!"

Some jerk just hopped in the cab I was waiting for. His dark eyes meet mine through the window as a cocky grin spreads across his face. Rubbing his chin, he says something to the driver.

Asshole.

I'm tired after my flight, and all I really want to do is get home and crawl into bed. My one-bedroom studio apartment is my sanctuary. God, how I've missed the comfort of living on my own after spending Christmas with my folks and our extended family in Vermont.

My Aunt Susan and her divorce was all everyone wanted to talk about. Depressing is what it was.

I look down the line of cars hoping another cab is mixed in there somewhere. Traveling during peak holiday season is a real bitch and right now so am I. I could've called Misty to pick me up, but she's perpetually late for everything.

My flight was terrible. I was seated next to an overweight man who kept sniffling and blowing his nose, coupled with excessive coughing. Every time he went through the motions he elbowed my right tit. I probably have a bruise, and the last thing I need is to get sick with the caseload I know is sure to be waiting for me on my desk when I return to work. I would've asked to switch seats, but the plane was full.

When I pull out my cellphone to get an Uber, a deep voice calls out to me. "Wanna share?"

His tone vibrates through me, and he smirks when I look up from my purse.

My first inclination is to flip him the bird, but I want to get home more than I want to tell him to shove his head up his ass. "Oh, gee. Thanks." I roll my eyes as I tug my luggage behind me.

The cabbie hops out, takes my belongings, and places them in the trunk.

The back passenger door hangs open, held by the cab thief and his charming grin he seems to wear with pride.

I stop by the door, waiting for him to move out of the way so I can get in. His gaze travels up the length of my legs, not stopping until our eyes meet when I slide into the seat next to him.

The first thing I notice about him is a small dimple in his left cheek, next to his well-groomed beard.

"You're welcome."

I scoff, unable to stop the shocked smile turning up on my face. "I think what you mean to say is, 'sorry I jacked your cab.'"

He holds out his hand expecting me to shake it. "Weston."

I accept it to be nice. His grip is firm and swallows mine. He's definitely muscular, but not bodybuilder huge.

"Nice name for an asshole." My tone is half-joking as I release his hand.

The annoyingly attractive man's jaw ticks as he loosens his tie. I suck in a breath as the intoxicating scent of his cologne invades my senses. It's a smell that I can only describe as pure male—woodsy and natural.

His tailored suit tells me he comes from money. The gray jacket hugs his biceps. I spot a hint of a tattoo under the collar of his shirt and I can't help but wonder what it looks like.

The cabbie closes his door and turns to me. "Where to?"

"Village apartments. North side."

The man nods and pulls into the traffic leaving DFW.

The world's most annoying ringtone sounds from Weston's pocket, and he flashes me an apologetic smile as I scrunch my nose at the whistling sound. My temples throb in warning of a headache. I'm sleep deprived.

He pulls his phone out, texting furiously.

I lean my head against the window, anxious to get home and fall face-first into my bed.

I don't know what I was thinking flying home the day before New Year's Eve.

My cellphone chirps from inside my purse.

Pulling it out I see I have a text from my mom.

Mom: Did you make it home safe? I worry about you traveling alone. Should have come with you and caught up with the girls.

Ugh. I love my mother, but I'm glad she didn't. My mother thinks my friends are her friends.

Brooke: I'm alive. Tired. Call you soon.

"Boyfriend?" Weston, the cab thief, stares at me when I shoot a glare in his direction.

His breath tickles my ear as he leans in, invading my personal space.

"None of your business." I hit send and stick my phone back in my purse.

"So, he dumped you." He chuckles to himself, clearly having much more fun with this situation than I am. His eyes roam up and down my body once more, then his eyebrows raise. "Makes sense."

This prick.

"I'm glad you had a moment of human decency back there, allowing me to ride in *my* cab, but I'm not in a chatty mood. I want to go home, take a nice hot bath, listen to an audio book, and enjoy a glass of wine."

"I prefer whiskey, but I'll settle for the wine if it's a good year. We could help get you over this man that stole your heart and left you so bitter." He has the audacity to wink at me and my traitorous body absolutely takes notice. The man is attractive and exudes confidence.

The way he stares at me seems to heat the cab up twenty degrees, and it's not from the air blowing out the vents. Everyone thinks Texas is hot year-round. But in the winter things can get chilly.

"Wow. I mean, that's some offer right there." I roll my eyes.

"I don't make bad offers."

I close my eyes and count to three, trying to ignore my attraction to the raven-haired hottie who knows how to wear a suit and press my buttons. My eyes meet his again and what a mistake that is. His eyes are like dark pools threatening to drown me. "Jesus, you're full of yourself."

"You can be full of me too, if you play your cards right." He smirks.

I look out the window, because I'm afraid he just made me blush, and I don't want to give him the satisfaction. "Jesus." I shake my head and realize I'm biting my lip.

"Just making conversation. Passing the time." He whistles and looks off out the window.

"Right. Do you normally have women falling at your feet to worship you when you turn on your charm? Your game needs work."

"Usually on their knees for other endeavors but worshiping me sounds nice too."

"You're ridiculous."

"Never said I wasn't." He grins.

The cab rolls to a halt in front of a giant high-rise building. This must be the asshole's stop.

"I'd love to continue this conversation, but this is me." He flashes me a panty-melting grin as he pulls a money clip from an interior pocket of his jacket and slips the driver a few bills. "Keep whatever's left over after you drive her home."

Part of me wants to smack the shit out of him. I know the type. Act like assholes, then play the victim. If he wasn't so damn hot while he did it, I might've.

Ugh.

Men.

Men suck.

Just ask my Aunt Susan whose ex-husband ran off with his trainer.

Before I can offer a thank you, he's out of the car and the cab pulls away.

Chapter Two

WESTON

P ounding my fist against the punching bag, I can't get the woman I shared a cab with out of my mind. Her snarky attitude had me wanting to shove my cock in her mouth. I should have known by her designer handbag and three-inch heels she'd be a snob who thinks she's hot shit. Who knows? No strings attached rough sex might've gotten that stick out of her ass. I could've replaced it with something much better.

I smile at my thoughts.

I admit taking her cab was a dick move, but my driver was stuck in traffic, and I had a late dinner meeting. It wasn't personal. But, my mother did raise me to be a gentleman and this is the south, so I shared the cab and paid for her ride home.

Getting pussy has never been a problem. Hell, I could've fucked my client's wife before I flew back home yesterday. I could've handled our meeting by video conference, but Mr. Pike insisted the meeting take place in person. He couldn't be bothered to fly back to Texas while vacationing.

Fucking clients.

I shouldn't complain really. He brings in a shit ton of billable hours for the firm. The only problem with a man like Mr. Pike is he has too much money to burn. Thinks he owns everyone and doesn't let you forget that you need him. Expects me to drop my life to tackle any legal problem that falls in his lap because he's been with my firm, The Hunter Group, since the beginning.

And he needs attention all the time because he's an asshole who can't keep his cock to himself. Neither can his wife by the count of how many times her hands found their way to my ass during my visit. Somehow, I've managed to settle every sexual harassment case against him outside the courtroom. You'd think the bastard would learn by now with the millions he's shelled out for my services and for the silence of his accusers.

He hasn't though, and it's rich pieces of shit like Pike that keep the world turning.

He's an associate of my father. A real power player who has his hands in a bit of everything. The man has gone through more assistants than I have, and that's saying something because I'm hard to work for.

I throw a few more punches before hitting the shower. It's New Year's Eve and I intend to go out, get drunk, and get laid. Three things that should be simple to accomplish.

I need to fuck that sexy woman from the airport out of my mind. If only I could stop thinking about her long legs wrapping around me and her heels digging into my ass while I go balls-deep into her sweet little pussy. She had blue eyes with flecks of green in them and I'm pretty sure she's a closet screamer. I can just tell.

That's how I imagined last night playing out in my mind, had she accepted my courteous invitation. I would've canceled my dinner meeting for her. Would've gladly had her as a meal.

I shrug. Her loss.

Yet, I still can't shake her from my mind. The chick is everywhere.

Visions of her plump pink lips wrapping around the head of my cock have me fucking my hand as the warm water cascades over me. My fist tightening in her strawberry blonde hair as I work in and out of her smart mouth.

Fuck me. I stroke myself harder.

I watch her blue eyes staring up at me. She's a hard little worker, making sure she tongues my shaft just right, trying to please me.

I should've asked for her number before hopping out of the cab. I bet she would have had another sassy remark. I can imagine her pink tongue flattening against my shaft taking me to the back of her throat.

It doesn't take much imagination to get me off when I have good material to fantasize about.

As I step out of the shower my phone pings with a text from my little brother.

Brodie: Coming out tonight? Jaxson reserved the VIP room at that new club.

Weston: I'll be there.

Tossing my phone on my bed, I finish toweling off and put some deodorant on.

Once I get dressed I head into the kitchen to heat up one of the meals Karen, my housekeeper, left before taking the weekend off. I fucking hate when New Year's Eve falls on a Sunday. It means everything shuts down Monday for the holiday and it assfucks my whole week.

Digging into my chicken and vegetables, I look at the empty chairs around my table.

Being thirty-four, most people expect me to be married—settled down in the suburbs with kids. Fuck that. I'm in my prime and love single life in the city.

Sure, I've had my share of flings, but I don't do girlfriends. I don't do love. I like to fuck, and I like them to leave. It's efficient and drama-free, usually. The arrangements work perfectly for me. I rent a room and get my rocks off. There's no talking about how our day went or sitting through shitty movies to get to the prize.

I don't have time for mundane shit, nor do I feel like doing anything I don't want to do. I don't need to know that a woman's cat has allergies or that her hairstylist is a gossip.

Unlike Pike, I know how to separate my dick from my work. Which is another reason most of my assistants hate me. They see me, a young attractive man with a stable career who is unattached, and they think they can trap me. They think working in close-quarters means maybe I'll fall in love if I just get to know them.

There's only one problem with their theory. I don't want to get to know them. All I need them to do is fetch my coffee and run my errands. Occasionally pick up my dry cleaning. It's simple.

Finishing my meal, I toss out the leftovers and rinse my plate before sticking it in the dishwasher.

Glancing at the clock, I go back to my room and fire off a text to Rick, my driver, to bring the car around front.

When I exit the building, he's waiting. Like I said, efficiency.

Chapter Three

BROOKE

"Come on. It's New Year's Eve for crying out loud." Misty screeches through the speaker on my phone.

"I can't. I'm still recovering from the vacation from hell." I stretch out on my couch with a bowl of popcorn watching a Twilight movie marathon. Jacob is about to turn into a werewolf, and I'm going to sit right here and debate which team I'm on.

I let out an aggravated huff and take a sip of my water.

"We're not even thirty. Get off your ass. You can't be a crazy cat lady until you're thirty-five, at least."

Running my fingers through Casper's fur, I laugh lightly. He looks up at me as though he takes offense to her tone.

He purrs as I scratch behind his ears. At least Casper is loyal. Unlike my ex-boyfriend, Sean. He blamed his cheating with my former roommate on my job. Said I cared more about my work than I did our relationship. Maybe he was right. I don't know.

My life seems to revolve around my profession. I love my job, but Sean was right, I don't know how to shut that part of me down as often as I should.

"I got us a table at that new club. You know what I had to do to get Mr. Pike to get me this table? Please?" She draws the word out.

Mr. Pike is her silver fox asshole of a boss.

"No, and don't tell me." Misty and her boss have a *special* relationship. Meaning she's his plaything, sidepiece, whatever the kids call it these days. I don't know why she works for the man—I really don't—but she's a big girl. She can take care of herself. Not my concern.

She can deny it all she wants but I know she's in love with him.

"Meet you there in like an hour?" Her voice is desperate, a pleading tone.

Ugh. I hold my phone from my ear and look at the time. In Misty speak that means more like two hours which would give me time to get ready, if I *was* going out.

I do have a hot little red dress I've yet to wear and the perfect shoes to match.

Hmm.

"I didn't hear a no." Her voice is nasal and singsongy.

"If I say yes, will you stop talking like that?"

"Maybe." She does the voice thing again.

"Fine. Text me the address and don't be late."

"I promise."

She's full of shit and I'll be sitting at the table drinking alone for at least two songs before she shows up.

"I'll be there."

"Yay!" She squeals in my ear before the line goes dead.

Clicking the power button on the TV off, I move Casper from my lap and put a lid over my popcorn bowl to save it for tomorrow night.

That red dress hanging in my closet screams my name.

———

When I get inside the club, it's filled with people wearing New Year's party hats and dressed to the nines. The bar's jam-packed, and the waitresses appear to be running their legs off for the private party going on in the VIP section that sits up a flight of stairs and overlooks the club. I'm twenty-eight. I should be living it up like the group up there. Maybe I will, for one night, anyway. I deserve it.

I'm married to my job because I love it. I'm an attorney on retainer for a women's non-profit. I represent women who can't afford someone on their own. I know I can't save the world, but I try.

Maybe it's time I put myself back out there again. It's been nearly six months since I ended things with Sean and moved into my new apartment on my own.

Closing my eyes, I take a moment to let all my worries go. Tonight, I need to cut loose. It's almost a new year and the air seems full of possibilities. Smiling to myself as my mind clears, I move to the music, swaying my hips with the beat.

Right now, I don't care that Misty's late. I don't care that there will probably be ten new cases on my desk when I return to the office on Monday.

Right here, right now—there is just me and the music.

"Fuck me, that dress would look fantastic on my floor." An oddly familiar voice growls in my ear and a hand slides around my waist from behind, pulling me into a solid chest.

Woodsy cologne envelops me, and I shake my head.

I know who it is without looking.

Shit. Shit. Shit.

Out of all the bars in Dallas, fate has delivered the asshole from the cab.

"Weston?" I don't look back, and hope to God it's him or I'll feel ridiculous.

I haven't been able to stop thinking about his cocky smile and that heart-piercing dimple, ever since he disappeared from the cab. I can practically feel his smirk burning a hole in the back of my head.

"I made an impression. What are you drinking?"

Normally I'd smart off, but I do need a drink. Besides, I need to kill some time until Misty arrives. "Whatever you're having."

He clears his throat, and I turn around to face him. I think he was expecting a snarky remark, and his face actually looks a little disappointed.

"Champagne in the VIP room. Want to join me?"

Is that hope I see sparkling behind his dark eyes?

"Okay."

"Seriously? That's it?"

"Nope. It's New Year's Eve and a time for new beginnings. Why don't we start over?" I smile and hold my hand out. "I'm Brooke."

He grabs my hand and electricity shoots straight to my pussy when he smiles, exposing that dimple I spent a good part of the night dreaming about. "Weston." He gives me a side eye.

"What?"

"I don't know how I feel about *this* yet." He wags a finger up and down my body.

"I thought you liked the dress?"

"I'd like what's underneath more."

And, we're back.

"I'm sure you would. I could use an errand boy to take it to the dry cleaners for me."

"That's better, cab girl." He grins.

"Can I call you Wes?" I stare into those dark eyes and everything and everyone around us seems to freeze. It's like we're the only two people standing here while the rest of the night blurs past. Only a minute has passed but it feels like forever.

"No."

"So, about that champagne you were going to fetch me?" I raise an eyebrow at him.

He doesn't let go of my hand, simply moves his other to the small of my back and leads me to the velvet rope that gates the stairs to the VIP area. His hand is like fire, just inches from my ass, and I think I might combust.

He nods at the bouncer who lets us through.

As we approach the tables where his group is seated, a few of the girls flash me nasty looks. Guess they think I took him off the market for the night. I ignore them. I'm only using Weston to occupy time until my friend arrives.

Chapter Four

WESTON

S ipping on my fourth glass of champagne, I watch as the party rages around me. Everyone laughs, dances—they're having a hell of a time. Me, I'm soaking it in, perusing the crowd in search of who I'll be balls-deep in later. Normally I'd have pussy lined up for the night, but I ended shit with Katrina, my flavor of the week, before I flew to Montana to have a sit down with Pike.

His latest fling threatened to lawyer up. Things usually never get that far. We usually throw enough zeroes at his conquests that they shut up, take the money, and disappear.

My brother raises his glass at me. He and Jaxson sit, surrounded by artificial women hanging all over them. It's a pity. They managed to pick up some hot ass, but I can smell their desperation. That's the problem with women. They don't get that you don't go to a bar to find Mr. Right. The only thing men who frequent clubs are interested in is being Mr. Right Now and Mr. Let Me Fuck You Tonight. That's it. They aren't looking to stick a ring on your finger. Maybe a cock ring on themselves if they think you're into that kind of thing.

I'm not even going to warn them—Brodie and Jaxson. They should be smarter than this by now, but they're thinking with their cocks, and you can't reason with a man's dick.

"Hold this. The future Mrs. Bass just walked in." Maxwell shoves his flute into my chest.

I look to see who has captured his attention.

Standing near the edge of the dance floor I spot a woman wearing a red dress that hugs her curves so damn tight it should be against the law.

Damn. Wish I'd seen her first to lay claim on her.

The woman spins around as her hips sway. Her head tilts up in our direction and I freeze. It's the woman I shared a cab with last night. We're too far away for her to recognize me. I do, however, recognize those long legs I imagined wrapped around me and that tempting smirk on her face.

What the hell is she doing here alone?

There's no way I'd leave her side if I went anywhere with her. For the night, anyway.

If she's here with someone he's a fucking idiot who doesn't deserve her. She belongs under me, in my bed, having so many orgasms she can't see straight. My cock hardens just thinking about stripping her out of that fuck-me dress.

"Hold your own drink. She's mine." I grit through my teeth at him as champagne sloshes over the brim and down both our hands.

"I saw her first, bitch."

I shoot him a glare that tells him to back the fuck off in a hurry. "I shared a cab with her from the airport last night. Sorry, man. I'll owe you one." I grin as he shakes his head and calls me a cock-block.

"Goddamn right I am." I mutter the words under my breath as I make my way down the stairs. If he even talks to her, I'll rip his arms off and beat him to death with them.

When I get close to her some clown in a cheap suit is about to hit on her. I jerk him backwards with a strong hand to his shoulder. "She's taken. Go elsewhere."

He holds up his hands with wide eyes. "I don't want any trouble." He melts back in to the crowd.

He got that fucking right.

Sliding my hand around her front, I tell her exactly where I'd like to see that dress. On. My. Floor.

She's like a demon sent here to torture my dick. So fucking sexy and tempting. She got lucky I let her leave last night. But not this time. No, the universe has spoken.

Her body fits snug against mine. That tight little ass of hers presses against my cock and I have to bite back a groan.

She shocks the hell out of me when she agrees to join me in the VIP room. She can pretend all she wants, but I see the look in her eyes.

When I move my hand to the small of her back, her lips part, telling me my touch affects her. I can feel so many eyes throwing daggers into my back. She's by far the hottest woman in the club.

Maxwell scowls at me as I lead her to our table.

I slide into the booth next to her, draping my arm over the back as the server pours more champagne.

Brooke brings the flute to her lips, smiling over the brim, and all I can think about is how good that red lipstick would look smeared around the head of my dick.

Fuck, I want to take her home right now, pin her to my bed, and bury myself in her for hours. Her eyes don't break from mine as she swallows a long drink.

Her gaze is almost challenging. Daring me to make a move on her. I'm a player by nature, but maybe I've finally met my match.

Her cell phone rings breaking the tension between us. "I need to check this."

"Go ahead." I down the rest of my drink and wink at Maxwell as he gives me the evil eye. I slyly flip him off over her shoulder.

She stares at the screen and her face twists like she just swallowed a lemon. Her fingers move, typing out a message. I can tell by the pout she's wearing whatever the message says it has upset her.

I place a hand on her knee, making sure to remember exactly how soft her legs are. "What's wrong?"

She rolls her eyes and her mouth tugs into a weak smile. "My friend ditched me."

"Looks like you're stuck with me. It's fate."

She shakes her head. "I don't believe in fate. I believe in choices and consequences."

I grin. "Jesus, you sound like a lawyer."

Chapter Five

BROOKE

I shrug and smile into my glass, taking another sip of champagne. He really is cute and he's charming when I ignore the fact that his dirty mouth doesn't seem to have a filter. The rumors are true. No matter how much women try to deny it, we all love the asshole in the crowd.

Misty. That bitch.

She sent me a text message to please not be mad at her. Apparently, Mr. Pike showed up on her door, home from his vacation. His wife put him out and he had nowhere else to go.

Yeah right. The guy's like a billionaire. He could easily afford any hotel in the city or stay at one of his other homes. Hell, Misty lives in one of his buildings. Rent free. She has asked me to move in a few times, but I just wouldn't feel right accepting his charity. What happens when he tires of her or they have a fight? The man is powerful, and I don't trust him as far as I can throw him. He's a grade-A prick.

He owns one of the largest chains of BBQ restaurants in all the United states, Pike's Grill. They have over four hundred locations in the US and a few international.

The world is his playground. He's a little boy with too much money and not enough to do. Still, though, Misty is my best friend, so if that's what she wants, who am I to tell her no? I clench my jaw, but then I catch a glimpse of Weston grinning and nodding at someone else he's talking to.

His hand is still on my leg. As much as I should swipe it away and leave, I just can't.

God, he's going to be the death of me.

I'm not sorry I came out tonight.

Tonight, I'm going to be shameless and flirt and have fun for one night out of three-sixty-five.

His hand slides up my thigh, adding the slightest bit of pressure. It's warm, tempting as his fingers brush closer to the hem of my dress.

"What are you thinking?" His voice is low as the words whisper against the shell of my ear. His lips brush down my neck and over my collarbone.

My breath hitches in my throat at his touch.

"I need more champagne."

He smiles next to my ear and motions the server forward again.

His fingers tug at the hem of my dress, and he whispers where nobody else can hear, "On my floor, later."

Heat blooms in my stomach and shocks of tingles fire between my legs.

"You seem pretty confident." I take another sip of champagne as he squeezes my upper thigh.

"Oh, it's gonna happen."

"What makes you so sure?"

"Because I'm an asshole. I'm dangerous to you. And it turns you on. You can't help but wonder what'll happen if you give in. You're too curious."

"Maybe I'm just being polite."

His grin widens. "You want to know what it's like to be with a man like me. And I want to know what your pussy tastes like. There's a mutual benefit there."

Fuck, if he keeps talking like that I might come right now. I can't even believe I'm thinking this, but he's right. I do want to know. I want a night of fun and mind-blowing orgasms from a rich, hot asshole who wants nothing more than to take from me. It's the same thing I want from him, to use his body, so what can it hurt?

"What happens after you find out what I taste like? After you get what you want?"

"I walk away."

"I see."

"Is that a problem?"

I study the sharp line of his jaw, and his intense eyes for a moment. "As long as you live up to the hype." I flash him a smirk of my own. "Don't waste my time, *Wes*."

His jaw clenches tight when I say his name.

The champagne is going to my brain. I'm never so forward. So —brazen.

I've never had a one-night stand, but Weston is the perfect candidate to start with. I've always played it safe. Made sure I was in a relationship, and commitments were made before falling into bed with someone. Maybe it's time to do things differently. No attachments. No broken hearts or hurt feelings.

Who needs to be tied down in a large city like Dallas? I can sleep with him, and then we can part ways. What are the chances I'll ever see him again?

Maybe he's right about the fates and all that shit. I need to get laid, and nature has provided me an opportunity.

Fuck it.

Chapter Six

WESTON

I'm two seconds from sealing the deal and having Brooke out the door and in my bed when Maxwell slides into the booth on the other side of her. I glare in his direction and he ignores my stare.

"Maxwell." He grins right at me as he says his name.

Blood rushes into my face. *This motherfucker.*

Brooke clearly sees my face tense up, and smiles, then turns to him. "Brooke."

They shake, and it doesn't escape my attention that his hand lingers on hers a moment too long.

He's playing with fire. How much booze has this cocksucker had?

He's going to catch every shitty case that walks through the door for the next year.

"So, how do you know Weston?"

She smiles between the two of us, but I know she can feel the tension.

I scoot a little closer to her and put my arm around her shoulder. Maxwell is still pissed that I fucked Katrina. She was his assistant. I fired her just so I could fuck her. I don't mix business and pleasure. She was a disappointment in bed, then wanted to talk about feelings and shit the next day.

I don't feel things. I fuck things.

"We just met."

Maxwell scowls.

Fuck.

What is she doing?

I glare at her this time.

"Fuck you, bro." He grabs the bottle of champagne and takes a hard swig.

"We met last night and watch your goddamn mouth when you talk to me."

Brooke straightens up in a hurry when she hears my tone. She clears her throat. "I umm—I didn't mean to cause tension. We met last night but tonight we decided to start over. New year, new beginnings and all that." She eyes the two of us cautiously.

My brother looks over at me from across the way and raises a brow, but I shake my head. I don't need my kid brother getting involved. I can handle my own. I was a state champion wrestler in high school for fuck's sake.

"Oh." He glances over at me. "You won't mind if I steal your date for a dance, would you?" He flashes that evil smile again. Fuck, he's brave. I don't need other people seeing this shit and thinking it's okay to challenge me. He must really be burned up about Katrina.

"We're leaving." I grab Brooke's slender hand and pull her out of the booth with me.

"Maybe I want to dance." She picks the wrong time to be cute. I don't like to be told no, and I'll be fucked with an iron spike if she's dancing with Maxwell.

"Then you'll dance with me." I give him a nice big fuck-you smile and pull her toward the stairs.

We walk down and out under the silver disco ball.

It's close to midnight and I want nothing more than to see what's under that red dress.

The music playing has a softer beat. It's a slower tempo as her body moves against mine. Her back presses against my chest as I dance with her from behind, and she lays her head back on my shoulder. Our fingers thread together under her breasts as she works her ass over my dick.

Her reddish-blonde hair lays to the left, giving me perfect access to the right side of her neck.

I lick around the shell of her ear and shove my cock up against her ass. "You're delaying the inevitable."

"Mm, patience."

"You're playing with fire, Brooke." I smile against her neck. "You're going to fly too close to the sun and end up getting fucked on this dance floor." I pull her harder against my cock when I say the last part.

"Did you just quote Icarus and somehow make it degrading? Maybe there's more to you than I thought."

I smile at her wit. There's something about this girl that scares me a little, somewhere deep inside where nobody else is allowed. "Don't go falling in love and getting attached. I might vomit."

She snickers a little, then leans harder against me. "Mmm. You know all the right things to say."

"One of us has to do all the talking while you come on my cock."

I feel a tremble of excitement ripple through her body. This little game we're playing is fun, but I'm going to come in my fucking pants if I don't get to fuck her soon.

"Mmm." She moans as her lips part.

I dive right in, claiming her mouth, taking what's mine for tonight. Her kiss is as sweet as I imagined as her tongue moves with mine. Tasting. Teasing. Licking. Exploring. There's a give and take. We push and pull, fighting for control. Fuck she's sexy. I like a woman who's not afraid to go after what she wants.

Her ass presses against my dick again. The thought of pulling out my cock and fucking her right here in the middle of the dance floor crosses my mind. Everyone else is in their own little worlds, doing the same thing we are. Nobody would know.

I rub my thumb over one of her nipples and she gasps. My cock aches, knowing I can touch her and make her sound so breathless and needy. I can't wait to hear her crying out my name.

Soon.

My hand glides down the swell of her breast and along her ribs, loving the feel of her curves as I grip her grinding hips.

I have to bite back all the pent up sexual frustration. Fuck, I want to bend her over and spank the shit out of her for doing this to me, making me want her this bad. The only thing stopping me is the scandal it'd bring to the firm when I get charged with indecent exposure and lewd conduct. I have a feeling Brooke's pussy would be worth the risk. But, I've worked too damn hard to build up what I have to throw it all away for something that's already guaranteed.

I work my way to the top of her thigh, my fingers inching up under the hem of her dress. I'm dangerously close to her pussy.

"Oh, God." She whimpers when I tug her dress up even half an inch.

"Look at you, such a naughty little bitch." I grit in her ear as she grinds her hips in an attempt to get closer to my fingers. Something tells me this is all way out of Brooke's comfort zone. She's living it up for one night. Wants one night with the dangerous asshole who isn't afraid to do whatever he wants to her. I can easily live up to that. Deliver what she needs. For her. I'm doing all of this for her.

"God, don't stop talking. Touch me."

Fuck, I love my life.

"I knew you'd be dirty. You want me to fuck this little cunt with my fingers, right out here in front of everyone, don't you?"

She gasps when I slide my hand up her dress and cup her pussy in my palm. Fuck, she's soaked through her panties for me.

"You can deny it all you want, but this wet pussy doesn't lie, Brooke." I slide her panties to the side, and glide my finger back and forth through her slick folds. I look up and see Maxwell watching us from the balcony of the VIP area.

He raises his glass to me. Asshole.

I'd wave right now, Maxwell. But I'm knuckle-deep in Brooke's hot pussy, so a head nod will have to suffice.

I remove my finger and spin Brooke around. When she looks at me, I shove my pussy-soaked finger in her mouth. Her eyes widen, and I lean in next to her ear.

The music dies down and the crowd begins to count down. "Ten, nine … two, one. Happy New Year!" Party streamers and confetti rain down on us, landing in her hair and on her shoulders. My finger is still in her mouth and I can feel her tongue working around.

"That's what my cock's going to taste like in an hour."

Despite her half-hooded eyes, and serious demeanor, I feel another tremble course through her body. I pull my fingers from her mouth, and she sucks them clean as if she doesn't want to let go.

Her arms hook around my neck and our mouths connect once more. Her tongue is needy and tastes like champagne.

"We're leaving, now."

"God, you're bossy."

"Well, I'm the goddamn boss."

"Hey." She grabs me by the arm and gives me a look that says be serious for a minute. "I don't normally do—this." Her eyes dart around. "I don't sleep with men on the first date."

"Good thing it's not a date." I haul her toward the door.

I make sure to shoot Maxwell the fucking bird when Brooke looks the other direction.

Cocksucker.

Rick's already parked up front and waiting. I wave to my brothers and the other guys, but they're all occupied. Maxwell is the only one watching, and he glares. Like I'd just let him have a go at Brooke. Even if I didn't like Brooke, I wouldn't share. He knows better.

No fucking way.

And Brooke is mine. She belongs to me.

For the night.

And maybe more than that, if I want more.

Chapter Seven

BROOKE

W hat the hell am I doing?

I'm going home with Weston. This is actually happening.

He's practically a stranger. I don't know anything about him. But then again, I suppose that's how one-night stands work. Everyone gets off and goes home, hopefully happy, and then you never see each other again.

My stomach is a swarm of butterflies and misfiring neurons. Jesus, I can't believe I let him talk to me the way he does, but I can't help myself. There's something about—him. It's like he's serious, but he's not. I definitely believe he wants to do all the things he says, but there's this swagger or confidence about him that's magnetic.

As he leads me to the car waiting out front for us, I know two things. Weston is attractive, and this feels right. I need this. I want it. I want him to take me back to his place and fuck me so hard I can't walk straight. I've gone far too long without sex, and when it's over I can call a cab and go home. Return to my life of routine. It's as simple as rebooting a computer. It'll take care of my needs for a while, give me a clean slate.

He can be the story I tell girlfriends about for the rest of my life. The one time I did so and so on New Year's, blah blah.

Maybe all the champagne has gone to my head but when we get in the car, I slip my panties down my legs and shove them in his face.

To my surprise, he doesn't miss a beat and takes them in his mouth. He pulls me onto his lap and undoes his zipper. He stuffs my underwear in his pocket as he smirks at me. "Dirty little girl." His finger finds its way inside me, and I gasp when he adds a second one. I can't believe I'm doing this. My brain tells me to slow down but my body screams fuck me right now.

He removes his fingers and I clench around the air, missing the warmth of our connection. Bringing his hand up to his mouth he licks each finger, slowly, like he's savoring the taste of my arousal.

"You have no idea how hard I'm gonna fuck you."

"Wait." I stop him as his dick presses against my slit, so close to being inside me. God do I want him, but I need to stop being rash and think for a minute.

"What?" He growls the word, biting at my lip. I can taste myself on him and my pussy fucking contracts. It's such a damn turn on.

"Condom." I barely breathe out the word.

"Nope."

His mouth latches onto mine. I deepen the kiss, grinding my pussy over the head of his cock, unable to resist.

"On the pill?"

"Yes." I hiss the word as his cock parts my entrance.

He raises his eyebrows at me. No matter how forceful or dirty he's been all night, he still waits for my reaction. There's something extremely hot about how confident and playful he is, yet he still respects my boundaries.

I nod, unable to even think straight anyway. Fuck it. Wild night out. Bad decisions. I never do anything like this.

That smirk returns to his face.

He shoves me down on his cock as he drives up into me with his hips.

I suck in the largest breath of my life at the sudden intrusion and bite down on his shoulder. Fuck, he's so thick and long. I'm so turned on that my body eagerly stretches for him, taking him all the way in.

His hand presses down on my shoulder as a guttural grunt catches in his throat.

His hands find my hips and he digs his fingers into them, then looks up at me with hooded eyelids. "God, I've been waiting for this tight little pussy."

I whimper into his neck as he hits me with fast and deliberate strokes. He angles his cock just right, finding all my hidden spots.

I don't know what it is that has me insanely attracted to this man. As I ride his lap in the back of his car, I don't have a care in the world other than getting off. My orgasm rocks into me hard. A ripple pulses through my body and I shudder.

He pulls my ear down to his mouth. "Didn't take long for you to come all over that cock, did it?"

I shake my head. It's all I can do as I clamp down and squeeze on him. "Fuck, West—" My voice cracks.

My pussy doesn't want to release him, ever.

Before long I'm bouncing up and down, riding him again. I want to make him come so bad.

His hand snakes into my hair and he balls it into a fist. He's nothing but a fury of tense muscles and hard cock. I feel him twitch inside me, and he pulls it out.

I roll off to the side, and he angles himself over. "Show it to me. Show me that pussy."

I spread my legs without even thinking, wide open and exposed. He stares at it, stroking his cock furiously. He angles his cock down and grunts, then shoots hot come straight onto it, lashing me with every spurt.

"Fucking hell." He groans and fucks into his fist a few more times.

Some of his warm load shoots across my ass, and I don't know if I've ever been so turned on in my life.

He stills for a moment, chest heaving—and the way he looks at me. It's like he just marked his territory. Something about it is very primal, raw—just a hundred percent male.

His breathing finally slows, and his gaze is still pinned right on me. He pulls my panties from his pocket and cleans me up with them. I sit there, letting him, mind still fuzzy from the ridiculous orgasm he gave me.

"Didn't need these anyway." He tosses my defiled underwear onto the floorboard.

I shake my head at him, and crawl seductively back onto his lap, straddling him on his seat.

Our foreheads touch as we both still struggle a little with our breathing.

"That was—"

"Perfect. But just a warm-up. When I get you upstairs I'm going to run you a bath and feed you strawberries."

"Careful, you almost sound like a gentleman."

"Then I'm going eat your pussy until you can't see straight."

"And, he's back." I grin and lean forward for a kiss.

I didn't even notice the car had stopped moving. I look to the right and see we're parked in front of that building where the cab dropped him last night.

As we exit the car, I feel a bit on the dirty hooker side with the remnants of his come coating my inner thighs.

The building he lives in is similar to Misty's but quite a bit nicer.

A doorman gives us a nod, telling us to enjoy the rest of our night.

Blush creeps up my cheeks as I hope he doesn't think I am, in fact, a dirty hooker.

In the elevator Weston pushes me up against the wall and slams his mouth down on mine.

He inserts his fingers in me, smearing his leftover come all over my pussy. "Fuck, I can't get enough of you."

I want to tell him the feeling is mutual but can't seem to find my voice. I wonder if that's what life is like for all of Weston's women, nothing but gasps and orgasms? I can't concentrate on much else other than what he's doing to me right now.

Shock fills me when the elevator comes to a halt and we stop at the penthouse.

I push my curiosity down. This isn't about getting to know him. This is about two strangers meeting a desire in one another. It's a sexual contract. One night. No strings.

But, I can't help but ask myself the same question over and over.

Will one night be enough?

Chapter Eight
WESTON

True to my word, I take Brooke straight to my clawfoot tub and draw her a warm bath. I don't do relationships, but it doesn't mean I don't take pride in the experience I provide. I want it to be memorable, and to ruin her for every other man.

"Holy crap." Her eyes widen, taking in her reflection in the mirror as she stands at the sink.

As the tub fills, I come up behind her and squeeze her shoulders.

"I look like a dirty hooker." She frowns, twisting her hair up on her head.

"You fuck like one too." I grin.

"Oh my God. I feel like—"

"Not yourself?"

"It's like a dream."

"Most women's dream."

"Jesus." She narrows her eyes at me. "You may be the cockiest bastard on the planet."

I shrug. "You like it."

"Not usually."

"Really?" I slide up behind her. "I could probably get you off, just whispering dirty shit in your ear."

Undoing the back of her dress, I slide it down her form, taking in every inch of skin. There's three freckles shaped like a triangle on her left shoulder and I can't resist kissing each one.

"Could not."

Her slinky dress pools at her feet and she steps out of it. I unhook her bra and toss it on the dress.

"You keep up this attitude." I shove her down on the counter with fingers splayed across her back. "And I'll have to spank this tight little ass of yours."

She gasps. "Oh my God."

She's even more gorgeous than I imagined.

I keep her bent over for a second, pushing down with my weight. I pull both of her wrists behind her, and pin them to her lower back. It's testing boundaries. Always the first thing I do. I want to take her as far as she's willing, but it's a fine line to tow.

"Have you ever had your ass spanked, Brooke?"

"N-no." She stutters a little, but there's excitement in her tone.

An amateur wouldn't pick up on these little clues, and a timid guy would shy away from what he really wants. Fortunately for her, I'm neither.

I reach up with my free hand and fist her hair. Then I lean down next to her ear as my hard cock shoves up against her bare pussy. Her eyes flutter closed, and her heartbeat speeds up on her neck. Her legs start to tremble. Fuck, she's so turned on. I can feel her hot cunt through the fabric of my pants.

I release her hair and her head nearly bangs on the counter she's so relaxed. My hand smacks against her pussy and I squeeze.

Her whole body tenses, and she jolts back to reality.

"Tonight, this is mine. Understood?"

"Yes." She nods her head.

I can't help myself and swirl the tips of two fingers around her swollen clit. Her ass instinctively shoves back against my fingers. I don't have to be knuckle-deep to know she's clenching around nothing. That'll change. But the build up to this next orgasm is going to be epic and it's going to happen with my cock shoved balls-deep.

"You don't come until I give you permission, understood?"

Her ass bucks against my hand, her slick pussy needy for attention. She's on the edge already, and I'm going to tease that shit as long as possible.

"Okay."

"Good girl."

Her body constricts again at the sound of my words.

"Let's go."

I hold her hand and lead her over to the bath. She glares at me, wanting to come already as she eases into the tub.

Giving her a moment, I walk to the kitchen to retrieve the fruit I promised to feed her.

When I walk back in and pull up a seat, she's humming to herself with her eyes closed. She hasn't noticed my return. Either that or she's ignoring me.

I take the moment to drink her in as she relaxes. The thought hits me that she looks a little too damn good all naked and soaped up in it. Part of me wants to join her, but that would be too intimate. I have limits. That would be a couple thing to do, and I'm not about to give her any wild ideas.

Plucking a strawberry from the bowl, I rub it over her lips. Brooke's eyes pop open as she accepts it. Her tongue touches my fingers and I can't help but think about her sucking me off.

I want her in every way possible, but I don't know that one night will be enough to do everything I want to her. I want her against the wall. In my bed. From behind. Bent over the couch. I want her to sit on my face. I want her to ride me. I want to stare deep into her eyes as we come at the same time. The last sudden and unexpected thought gives me pause. My hand freezes mid-air as I am about to give her another strawberry.

"Everything okay?"

I blink. "Yeah. Spaced out for a minute. Too much champagne."

"I know that feeling." She grins then splashes me with the water, soaking me.

I want to be mad but when she looks at me with that playful grin on her face I can't resist.

I shrug my shirt over the back of my head, exposing my tattooed chest. Her heated gaze rakes over my pecs as I drop my pants.

"Commando, huh?"

"Is there any other way?" I climb in the tub behind her as she scoots forward to let me in.

What are you doing? Don't get in the tub.

I've never bathed with someone before. I've watched women I've slept with shower, but this feels more private—more intimate as her head lays back on my shoulder.

We stay like this for minutes. Silence stretching between us. It isn't heavy or tense. The moment is nice, but I know I can't keep breaking my rules.

I've never felt such a raw need to claim someone in my life. The primal urge takes over. She's so soft and wet up against me. I need to be inside her, need to mark her. The thought should scare me. I barely know this chick. For all I know she could be plotting to get pregnant by a man of my wealth and status.

I trust her, though. I don't know why but I do. She feels genuine and it's been a long time since I've met someone so true to themselves. I'm in the business of liars. I tell lies for my clients every fucking day. My soul is probably tainted black for the half-truths I've served up in court to get rich bastards off the hook.

Brooke doesn't seem self-conscious or afraid to hurt my feelings. She might be giving in to my devious ways, but she knows what she's doing. She speaks her mind and does what she wants. Her actions aren't a ploy to trap me somehow. I've fucked women like that many times. Hell, most are that way. Pretending to be something they're not.

Wearing ass-padded underwear. Fake tits. Slimming wear. I like a woman who owns her body. A woman who takes pride in what she has. Brooke is toned and fit, but doesn't seem like she'd be afraid to order a burger.

I find myself wanting to ask her to dinner just to see if I'm right.

Chapter Nine

BROOKE

Once the bath water turned cool and my skin was starting to prune, Weston and I got out of the tub. He wrapped a soft, warm towel around me. The dude must be loaded to have heated towels in his bathroom. My parents have money but not on this level.

I don't care about his status. It wouldn't matter to me if he lived in a shitty apartment right now. The man has me so turned on and wanting him. He could graze my clit and I'd probably sing his name.

He sits on the edge of his four-poster bed in his bedroom. The room is huge, fit for a king. In Weston's world he probably *is* king.

His body is seriously like a sculpture you'd see in Italy. He clearly works out. He's lean and toned. Not all bulky and huge but seriously athletic like an Olympic swimmer.

Leaning back on his elbows, he's on full display for me in all his naked glory. Just the way he carries himself is hot as hell. I hadn't expected him to climb in the tub with me. I hadn't expected to be treated to a bath and fruit, either.

I figured by now we'd be wrapping things up after he got what he wanted. I don't know if I'm disappointed or excited. He's like a good book, completely unpredictable.

I've never had the urge to suck a dick in my life. I don't know, it's never been my thing. But, tonight I'm someone else. I'm fun, sexy Brooke. Not workaholic Brooke.

Staring at him, I want nothing more than to take him into my mouth and get a taste.

I figure Weston has earned a blowjob for the amazing bath.

Dropping the plush towel to the floor, I climb up on the bed next to him. He smiles at me as I stroke my fingers along the length of his shaft. His cock grows harder and longer with each touch.

The man has me licking my lips eager to please him. His fingers tweak my nipples as we kiss, our connection never breaking as he attempts to lay me back and cover my body with his.

I wag my finger in his face. "Not yet."

"Oh." He raises an eyebrow. "You look like you're about to be bad."

"Maybe I am."

"Fucking do it then. Don't be a little cock tease."

I shove against his shoulder, sending him to his back. Then I slide down, trailing my tongue along his abs.

He stares me directly in the eye, that cocky smirk on his mouth.

I want to make this night good for us both—memorable. I want to be able to look back at it, knowing it was the start of my new beginning.

Not the start of something new with Weston, but the start of something new for me.

Licking my lips, I press the head of his cock to my tongue.

He has one arm at his side, and one back behind his head.

Jesus, his cock is even bigger up close. My mouth stretches wide to take him in. I moan around him, licking and sucking as his fingers thread through my hair, gripping me to guide the pace he desires.

"Oh, I may have misjudged you. Fuck." He groans.

It only makes me want to speed up. I move up and down, gliding my lips along his length as I tease at his balls with my fingers, paying them extra attention.

He squirms a little when I cup them in my palm and massage them.

Good. It's good to know I can get to him too.

"Keep that up and I'm gonna come down your throat."

His words egg me on and heat me up at the same time. I want to bring him that pleasure. I want to feel him erupt on my tongue and take all that he gives.

After a few minutes of watching me, our eyes locked, he must lose patience and want back in control.

He reaches down and yanks me up to his face, kissing me deeply, then spins me around like I'm light as a feather. "I want something to eat while you suck that cock." He grips my hips and yanks my pussy to his mouth.

I do some kind of half squeal, half moan when he jerks me back.

His tongue parts my folds, sweeping back and forth at a leisurely pace like he's lapping at me. I bend back down and take him in my mouth, until it's almost a competition.

Right when I'm about to shudder and come all over his face he smacks my ass.

I jolt at the stinging pleasure ripping up my spine.

"Not until I say."

How the hell does he know when I'm so close?

When he adds his fingers to the mix I nearly lose it. His tongue flicks wildly over my clit, humming against the throbbing bundle of nerves. He works his fingers in and out, curling them up to my g-spot. His strong fingers on his free hand dig into my hip, keeping me right where he wants me.

When his tongue flattens against my pussy and sucks my clit hard, I'm right on the edge of shattering.

"You want to come, don't you?"

"Mmhmm." I can't even form words and realize I stopped sucking him and my hand is basically holding on to his cock like an arm rest while I moan.

"You're gonna come on my cock. Then I'm going to blow in that hot cunt."

My thighs squeeze around his head just at his words. Fuck, he has the filthiest mouth on the planet.

My whole body trembles as I climb up onto him. I don't know how I hold back, my body in desperate need of release. Precum beads at the head and I flick it with my tongue.

He growls and yanks me up so that I'm straddling him, his cock inches from where I need it. He teases the head across my clit, and my entire body shivers.

"I-I—" I can barely speak or breathe. Somehow, I manage the rest of my sentence. "I'm gonna come if you keep doing that."

He lowers me down onto him, and his cock drills up into me. "Not until I say."

My jaw clenches. "Fast, please. I need to come, please."

He smacks my ass, and it gives me a little relief. But his fingers move right back to my clit and he pinches it, hard.

"Oh, fuck."

He grips my ass with both hands and guides me up and down on him slowly. One hand moves to my hips and the other digs into my rear.

"Beg me."

My eyes shoot open and I glare.

"Beg me to come on that dick." His eyes roam down to my pussy.

I'm so close. I should come just to prove a point, but I don't. It's all a fun little game, and I know it'll be worth it if I hold out.

"Please?"

"Please what?"

"Please, fuck."

He hammers his cock up into me, that grin still plastered on his face.

"Please let me come."

Before he answers, one of his fingers slips in and teases the rim of my asshole.

I clench around him at the sudden intrusion.

"Fuck, I love the way you squirm on my cock."

It's weird at first. No man has ever gone anywhere near *that*. But the more his finger works around the edge, smearing my arousal all over it, the more I think I want him to go deeper.

His other hand slides from my hip, and strokes across my clit and I let out a breathy gasp.

"God, please let me come."

His finger speeds up even faster on my clit until I'm grinding my teeth, holding back the release with everything.

"Okay, come on my cock." Right when he says it, his finger goes in my ass and he thrusts up into me.

My entire world shatters into a thousand pieces and fireworks go off behind my eyes. It's so fucking intense, I don't even know where I am for a second. I'm in a whole other world. I convulse and shake, and my pussy clamps around him like a vise.

I seize up as wave after wave rolls through me.

He doesn't give my body any reprieve. He slides his finger out of me and grips me with both hands on my hips.

"Fuck, Brooke."

My name sounds like it's a million miles away or in a tunnel or I'm underwater. When I come back into the world, I look down at him. His face is red and tense, and he shoves his cock as deep as it'll go. Just drives up into me while he shoves me down on him.

Then I feel his cock twitch, and he lets out a growl. Hot come fills me from the inside and I damn near get off again, back to back, just at the sensation and intense pressure.

I rock back and forth on him slowly when his hands drop from my hips. He's still rock-hard inside me.

Another orgasm burns through me. I circle my hips grinding down on him, not wanting to give him a second of reprieve. I want his cock hard, and I don't want it to leave me.

Weston lifts me off him and climbs behind me. I feel like jelly and on the verge of collapse. Not him though, he seems to have enough stamina for the two of us.

Lining the tip of his cock up with my entrance, he slams into me. One hand is used to support me, holding me up and the other is on my hip, fingers digging in hard enough to leave bruises. Everything about him is so possessive. He takes whatever he wants, and I'm pretty much like a rag doll after my little moment of control.

His hand snakes into my hair and he fucks me from behind. Somehow, a burst of energy surges through me as he pushes me toward the edge of the orgasm cliff once again. This time he's really rough, and I find myself loving every second of it. I want to see how far he'll go, what he'll do.

My pussy thinks he's a god. He's one in the bedroom for sure, even if I'll never tell him. He doesn't need any extra help in the ego department.

Crack!

His hand lands on my ass, and I cry out.

"Fuck."

"Yeah, you like that, don't you?"

"Mmhmm."

"That's what I do to naughty bitches that tease me in their little red dresses."

"Oh my God." I mutter the words under my breath. I want to provoke him. This is by far the best sex I've ever had in my life. This one time I want everything and don't want to settle for anything less. I want to goad him on. Drive him as crazy as he's driving me. "Am I in trouble, sir?"

His hand tightens in my hair, and I would give anything to see the look on his face when I said that.

"Yeah. This is how I treat dirty sluts that try to come too fast." He smacks my ass again, and I jolt forward.

His hips crash into me so hard, the wet smacking and clapping sounds echo around the room. I can barely even speak, because he's fucking me so hard my words vibrate. "Oh-oh, my-my G-God. F-f-fuck."

"Yeah, that's right. Take that fucking dick. You're gonna come on it again, aren't you?"

"N-no." I try to smile at my insubordination.

He leans forward, and his hand slides around my neck. He tilts my head back so that I'm staring up at his face.

His cock continues to piston in and out of me, and I don't even know how he's doing it. I'm about to explode again.

"Are you going to come on that cock again, Brooke?" He grins at me. "Like a good little whore?"

Jesus Christ, I should be insulted at the things he says, but it only heats me up in ways I've never been heated.

"Mmhmm." The sound is a whimper as I try to nod my head at the hold he has on my neck.

"Yeah you are." He lets go and shoves my face into a pillow, his hand on the back of my head. Then he crashes into me with all his weight, flattening me on the bed until he's slamming into me with his mouth next to my ear. "You're gonna come all over this fucking cock and take everything that comes out of it."

"Oh-oh sh-shit." I release and my mind is nothing but fuzz. Fuzzy dots, fuzzy thoughts.

He leans down on my neck and bites down on my collar bone, then rams his cock into me and blows so hard it spills out around the base.

"Oh God, Weston. Weston. Shit!"

"That's it, Brooke." He grunts and fills me again. "Take it. Take that fucking come." His words come out on groans with each thrust into me.

He finally collapses against my back and rolls over. Something happens. There's touching and kissing and caressing and nothing registers. I'm boneless, weightless. At some point in my hazy state, I just pass out.

———

The next day I wake up smothered by Weston. Our legs are interlocked, and both his arms cage me in. I feel like I can't breathe, but I'm afraid to move out of fear of waking him.

Last night was perfect.

Too perfect.

I don't want to do anything to mess it up. I want to savor this memory for what it is—one wild evening between two people who were attracted to each other.

Nothing less.

Nothing more.

Unable to lay here any longer, I shift slightly to free myself.

Our legs feel like they're glued together. He's like a furnace, maybe sweating off the alcohol from last night.

When I move my legs, it's like ripping off a Band-Aid.

Weston stirs, rolling away from me.

Letting out a sigh of relief, I move to the edge of the massive bed.

I make it to the bathroom without incident.

It isn't personal. I just don't want to go through the whole awkward conversation of him asking for my number. I'll feel obligated to give it, and he won't ever text or call. I see no point in making things weird.

After washing my face, I slip my dress back on and go in search of my shoes and my clutch so I can call an Uber.

My body aches in the most delicious way. I can still feel his touch, heat, and strength in every step.

Chapter Ten

WESTON

A s I wake up, the other side of my bed is empty and cold. It seems Brooke gave me the slip. That was usually my role, but this is my place, after all. I never bring chicks here. I don't know what I was thinking. I had a hotel room reserved. That red dress and sweet pussy had me under a spell.

My head pounds and I'm disoriented as I make my way into the bathroom. I find Brooke at the vanity pulling one of my shirts over her head.

"Do you mind?" She tugs on the collar of the black shirt. It looks sexy as fuck on her, even if it is over her dress.

I shake my head, trying to push away thoughts of fucking her again while she stands there in my clothes. It's difficult because my cock aches from a combination of morning wood and seeing her tight little ass uncomfortably fumbling around for things. She's messing with my head. She needs to disappear before I break another rule and ask her to stay for breakfast.

"Have you seen my clutch? I need to call an Uber."

"My driver can take you." I deserve a kick in the balls for being nice.

"You sure? I don't want to be difficult."

"It's fine. I was about to ask you if you wanted to stay for breakfast." My hand nearly clamps over my mouth as soon as I realize what came out of my mouth. It's like there's a disconnect between my brain and my words.

She offers me a weak smile. "That's sweet. But I have plans." Her hand brushes my arm as she moves past me and out the door. "Bathroom's all yours. I'll be in there trying to find my phone."

"There's coffee. I'll call my driver when I'm done in here."

"Thanks." Her brows knit as she walks away. I don't turn to go into the bathroom until she leaves my line of sight.

What the fuck? What's wrong with me? I don't do nice. I don't do let's exchange numbers and chitchat over coffee.

When I finish up in the bathroom I find her bent over the kitchen counter enjoying a cup. I end up chitchatting. Fuck my life. I'm on course for self-destruction.

"He'll be here in about twenty minutes."

"Okay." She smiles over the brim of the mug. "Thanks."

"It's fine. Find your phone?"

"Yeah." She holds up her little red bag.

Silence stretches between us.

"You want to grab dinner or something sometime?"

She frowns and looks away before giving an answer.

Seriously?

"Listen, Weston."

Is she seriously giving me the brush off? This is *not* happening.

"You're a nice guy and last night was great."

I smile because I know there's a *but* coming.

"But I think we should leave it at that."

This is my goddamn speech to give.

"You already said you don't do the whole dating thing, and I'm not looking to start something right now. My job is demanding and I—"

I cut her off with a kiss, giving her a little reminder of what she's going to miss out on. Nobody lets me down easy. I mean, what the fuck?

Her sweet lips taste like coffee and my hand slides down and cups her ass. She moans into my mouth.

You still got it. Don't let her get to you.

Rick calls and interrupts the moment. I glare at the phone.

That motherfucker.

"I wasn't asking you on a date. I was just going to say this was fun and we should think about doing it again sometime. Just the sex. No feelings." I grin, but it's a cover. I'm lying to myself and to her. There's something there, whether I want to admit it or not.

"Text me sometime and we'll see. No promises."

I nod as we exchange phones, putting our numbers in.

"I'll give your shirt to the driver when he drops me off."

My jaw clenches thinking about her taking it off in front of him. "Keep it."

"Bye." She kisses my cheek and the word sounds so final.

It feels like I just got punched in the stomach.

Normally, after I fuck a woman so hard she can barely walk, I can't get away from her fast enough. Why is she different?

The challenge.

It's been a while since I've had one.

I watch her walk out the door and wonder what I can do to make her change her mind.

Chapter Eleven

BROOKE

"Tell me everything. What did you do last night? And don't you dare tell me you went home and rang in the new year with Casper." Misty looks at me with bright eyes eager for gossip. She tucks her hands under her chin and bats her lashes.

I roll my eyes and take a bite of my bagel, then wash it down with mimosa to cure my hangover ails.

"Actually, I ran into someone." My cheeks heat at the thought of Weston and the night we spent together. The things the man did to my body—I wouldn't mind a repeat. But I know that would only open me up to getting hurt. He's not the kind of guy you hand your heart to. He's the kind of guy that shatters it and leaves you to pick up all the pieces.

God, he really is possibly the world's biggest asshole. But there's something endearing about him that just makes me want more. He left me unsatisfied. He makes me smile, and the orgasms—Jesus.

"Who what now? When did you meet a guy? Is it a guy?"

"Yes, it's a guy." I throw a balled-up napkin at her. "His name is Weston."

"Tell me more." She leans in closer.

"You're ridiculous." I look away. "We shared a cab from the airport the other night." I leave out the part where he stole my cab. Why am I trying to paint a good picture of him?

"What's he look like? I need details, woman."

"Dark hair. You know that look that says I just rolled out of bed and I'm still hot? And he has dark eyes that are so—dominating. There's a mystery to him. He's cut, but not too cut. Lean but athletic build. He's taller than me even when I wear my heels."

"Sounds like one of your book boyfriends. So you met up with him last night?"

"That's the funny thing. He was at the club. It was totally random." I grin and finish my food.

"Sounds like fate."

I roll my eyes. "Please. Don't with that shit."

She holds her hands up. "I'm just saying."

"Well feel free to not just say." I smirk.

"Did you hook up?"

I shrug and she glares at me.

"Don't withhold information, bitch. Tell me." She pounds a fist on the table and gives me her best fake intimidating stare.

I laugh. "What about you and Mr. Pike?"

Now it's her turn to roll her eyes. "I don't want to get into it. You'll judge me like you always do."

"I don't judge you." I scoff.

"Do too."

"Do not."

"Now who's the child?" I stick my tongue out at her. This is going nowhere fast.

She folds her arms and pretends to pout.

"Okay, I'm sorry. You're a grown woman. You can do whatever you want. And I promise to listen with an open mind if you want to talk about him."

"Thank you. Because I'm dying to tell you all about last night. He showed up at my place and cried about his loveless marriage. He always wanted kids. Wanted someone to leave his legacy to, but his wife refused. Their marriage is just business. Her father would merge the companies if he married his daughter."

"That sounds sad."

"He asked me to have his baby."

I choke on my drink. "He what now?"

"I think I'm going to do it. He promised to pay for everything. And he'll even live with the baby and me. His wife doesn't care as long as he supports her financially."

"Are you kidding me?" I try to hold back my words, but it's too late.

Her face turns red. "You promised you wouldn't judge." She folds her arms over her chest.

I take a deep breath. "I know. And I'm sorry. But sleeping with him is one thing. Having his baby—that's a big deal. I just worry about what happens to you if he goes back to her or whatever."

"He loves me."

"I'm not saying he doesn't care for you. Just, this is a huge decision."

"I'm pregnant." Tears burn in the corners of her blue eyes.

I suck in another breath.

"I was going to tell you last night. I thought maybe if I got you drunk enough—"

"That I'd give you my blessing?" I take a second and try to calm myself, then reach over and grab her hands. "If you're happy, then I'm happy for you. It's just—wow. It's a lot all at once. Are you okay?"

"Are you mad at me?"

I stare for a brief second, then shake my head slowly. "No. Of course not." I get up from my seat and go around to her side of the table and hug her. "You're my best friend. I just want to see you happy."

"Pike makes me happy. I love him so much it hurts. I'd do anything for him."

I sigh and cup her head in my hand, holding her tight to me. "I know. I just worry he doesn't feel the same."

She squeezes my hand. "He gave me his black card. I need some new clothes."

When she gets up from the table I see the small bump under her bulky shirt.

"How far along are you?"

"Three months." She smiles, rubbing her stomach.

"How long have you been planning this?"

"I found out last month. I would have told you, but I wasn't sure what I was going to do."

"I wish you would have come to me. I may not like Pike, but I'm still your friend."

"I know."

"Let's go find you some hot maternity clothes that will have Pike on his knees." That wins me a smile from her.

Chapter Twelve

WESTON

"Can I get you anything else, Mr. Hunter?" Daisy stares at me from the doorway.

"That'll be all. Thanks." I dismiss her with a flick of my wrist.

She's a sweet girl but way too nice to be in this business. She cares too much. You can't practice law and allow your feelings to compromise the job. It doesn't matter if I think a client is at fault. All that matters is that they pay me enough to represent their best interest. Their personal life is of no concern to me. I avoid politics and religion in the office and make it a point not to discuss either with my friends as well. People are so damn sensitive. One sentence taken out of context can cause a fucking shitstorm.

The world is a bunch of sensitive pussies not afraid to go on a crusade.

I see my brother across the hall through the glass walls of our offices. We have blinds if we need them, but mine are always open. I like to be able to see everything, including threats before they knock on my door. I don't bring pleasure to work. He's on the phone and looks like he wants to throw something through the wall.

Glad it's him and not me.

He's got a young client who just inherited the family ranch and has no idea how to manage the business or his life. The kid's been arrested for two DUIs in six months. Brodie's growing tired of his antics, but I file that situation under *not my problem*.

It's been three days since I fucked Brooke, and I can't get the memory of her pussy out of my mind. I've picked up the phone several times, tempted to reach out to her. I can't believe she hasn't called or texted me yet. I even called my cell phone provider to make sure my shit was functioning properly.

They assured me it was. It's ridiculous.

I thought about having my driver deliver flowers to the place where he dropped her off, but that's a bitch move. She needs to stop being stubborn and call me.

I press the button on my phone and buzz my secretary. "Hey."

"Yes, Mr. Hunter?"

"Hold all calls until I tell you not to."

"Yes, sir."

Turning my cell over in my hands, I'm conflicted. Torn between my pride and wanting to see her again.

Fuck it. I type out "hi" then quickly delete it. Then I type out "Are you thinking about me? You should be." My head flies back against my chair. I'm so fucking worthless right now. Delete. I delete all of it. I think she's broken me. I sound like a major league pussy.

Weston: Dinner. Tonight. My place. 7pm.

Before I can stop myself, I hit send, and instantly want to take the message back. At least it's halfway demanding and not cringeworthy. This is stupid. She's one woman. I already fucked her, so why can't I move on?

I can see that she's read the message, yet there are no dots bouncing around. The dots always bounce immediately when I send someone a message. I don't know how to deal with rejection. I've always been the one not interested.

Why hasn't she responded yet? It's been two fucking minutes.

Growing more irritated with every passing second, I know I'm not being rational. Maybe she's at work. I toss my personal phone in the top drawer of my desk and bury myself in work.

Chapter Thirteen

BROOKE

This week has been insane. When I returned to work on Tuesday, I had twelve cases needing representation. I've been doing research and trying to pick those who need my services the most. The cases I don't take will get passed on to another lawyer like myself.

The sad part is some of these cases will never see a courtroom. Most settle when they can. I avoid taking on family court. It's mentally exhausting, and I become too invested emotionally with the kids. Some of them are bounced around from family member to family member but most end up wards of the state. It's a sad reality but it's the hard truth. I have more cases than I can count that come across my desk. Mothers who did time on drug charges and now want to gain custody of their kids back. Some of them do recover but more times than not they return to old habits. Rarely is there a good outcome or a happy ending. It's why I read and listen to audio books —to escape reality.

I stack four files to the side. They're in my *no way* pile.

As I go through another stack my phone lights with a text.

My heart jumps into my throat when I see his name.

Weston.

Weston: Dinner. Tonight. My place. 7pm.

All I can do is stare at the message for five minutes.

The man who doesn't do relationships.

It's been three days and I can still feel his touch.

Dinner seems too intimate. I know that sounds dumb when he's been inside me, but we agreed that it was a fling.

I eyeball the caseload waiting for me.

I type out four different responses, and quickly delete all of them. Nothing sounds good enough. My thighs squeeze together as I stare at the message from him.

Brooke: If you want to see me again we need to lay down some rules. Nothing personal. No dates. We meet at a hotel.

Send.

I stare at my phone waiting for a response as the dots move.

Weston: Presidential Suite. Four Seasons. 7:30 PM. Tomorrow.

This is it. I'm really agreeing to this. Another casual hook up. I feel so *Sex In The City*.

Weston: Can't wait to see you tomorrow night.

Brooke: The feeling is mutual.

Weston: What are you wearing?

The dots start to move then stop.

I wait for a response but don't get one. I start to type out a new message but a picture comes through.

Hot damn.

Brooke sent me a shot of her thigh. She's wearing a garter belt. Fuck me, I'd like to rip it off with my teeth.

Brooke: I showed you mine. Show me yours.

Weston: You didn't show me shit, tease.

Brooke: Don't keep me waiting or I might lose interest in playing.

Weston: Patience.

I hit the camera icon at the bottom. Before I do anything, I take the remote to my blinds from the top drawer of my desk and bring them down, allowing me some privacy.

Unzipping my pants first, I leave the button fastened to give her a taste of her own medicine. Two can most definitely play this game.

I take about five different pictures and decide on the best angle, maybe even do a little cropping. I hit send once I'm pleased with the shot.

Brooke: Tease.

Weston: Isn't that what you're doing? Don't give me that shit.

Brooke: If I were a cocktease I'd be sending you photos like this...

Attachment Loading...

An image pops up of her cleavage.

It's sexy as fuck, but I want more.

I want her down on her knees in front of me. Taking my cock in her mouth. Eyes watering, gagging on it.

I send her a shot of my pec to respond to hers. I caption it "tit for tit."

Brooke: Ha! Funny.

Weston: You'll see funny when I put you over my knee...

Brooke: Is that a threat or a promise? Because I have to tell you...thinking about you bending me over and spanking me...its hot.

Her confession has me growing hard and I can't stop myself from unbuttoning my pants.

Weston: It's* (sorry, couldn't help myself) And that can be arranged. See what you do to me.

Attachment Loading...

I send her a picture of my cock.

Brooke: You don't play fair. That photo has me touching myself and thinking about you.

Fuck, I bite the inside of my cheek.

Weston: Show me.

The dots start to move, and I wait to see if she's willing to go there for me or if she's all talk.

Weston: waiting...

Brooke: Patience.

Attachment Loading...

Fuck me, she went there, and I nearly blow a load on my hand. Two of her slender fingers stuffing that sweet cunt.

Weston: Where are you? I need to be inside you. Now.

I can't believe what's happening. I'm locked in my office sexting with Weston. I've never done anything like this before. He brings something out of me that's never surfaced. When he sends me a short video of him stroking his cock, I lick my lips, remembering how it felt taking him in my mouth.

In return, I send him a clip of my fingers sliding in and out of my pussy.

Weston: Where are you? I need to be inside you. Now.

Brooke: Patience.

Weston: Jesus, I can't stop watching that. I just came on my hand.

Brooke: I wish it was my mouth.

Weston: If you'd agreed to dinner tonight, we wouldn't have to wait...

Brooke: It's a tempting offer...but we have an agreement.

Weston: Care to renegotiate your terms?

Brooke. Now who sounds like a lawyer? I'll see you tomorrow.
xx

Weston doesn't message me back and I'm ready to get home.

As I leave the office my phone goes off. Part of me lights up and hope blooms in my chest at the idea that it's Weston.

I dig my phone out of my purse when I get in my car.

My hope fades. It's my mom. I never called her after my flight.

Mom: Haven't heard from you since last year. Wanted to make sure you haven't forgotten about us. You know…your parents?

I roll my eyes at her dramatics.

Instead of texting I call her like a good daughter would.

She picks up on the second ring. "So nice to finally hear from you."

"I know I should've called sooner. I've just been busy with work." I leave out the part about staying the night with Weston and all the orgasms.

"You work too hard, Pookie."

I groan. "I know."

"Good thing I'm in town to make sure you get out and live a little. Your father and I are staying at the Four Seasons. We have dinner reservations at six-thirty at Wynega's."

"Fine." I look down at my phone, It's already half past five. There's no way I can make it home to change and be on time for dinner. I was already regretting not taking Weston up on his invitation. Now, it's even worse. I could've said I had a date. That might be the one excuse Mom wouldn't question.

She's been after me to find a new man since I broke up with my ex.

She'd never understand the arrangement with Weston. She thinks a woman should be settled and having kids at twenty-five. I'm past my expiration date to find a suitable husband in her eyes. She's highly old fashioned when it comes to marriage. She'd probably have a heart attack if I told her I was fucking a guy and didn't even know his last name.

———

Wynega's is crowded and with good reason; they serve amazing food. It's one of the main reasons I didn't come up with an excuse not to do dinner with my parents. It may sound like I don't love them. I do. I love them more than life, but I can only handle them in small doses. My mom can be very, umm, overbearing. She's a helicopter parent and can't help it.

My parents are already seated at their table and Mom has taken the liberty of ordering for me.

"I got you a nice salad, but I told them to leave off the meat. You're looking a little thick around the hips. It's 'cause you take after me, and our family has always had dominating birthing hips." She winks and pats my hand.

I stand there and shake my head, then finally take a seat.

Dad frowns but doesn't say anything. He can never get a word in when the three of us are together.

"Have you met any nice men? I was telling your father he should set you up with one of the guys at the club. There's bound to be someone who'd want to date you. You're a catch."

"Actually, I met someone. We had a date on Sunday and we're doing dinner tomorrow. I was supposed to see him tonight, but I chose to spend time with you instead." It's not totally untrue.

"Well." She grins. "Why didn't you say so?"

I roll my eyes. Like she gives anyone a chance to speak.

"Is he a nice career man? Because your father has a lot of contacts."

I shake my head and down my wine. I'm going to need a miracle to survive this meal.

Our food arrives, and Mom finally stops talking to chew her food. Dad hasn't spoken one word. She means well, really, but tonight she's in rare form. It's been a non-stop onslaught since I sat down.

My phone vibrates from my purse, but I don't dare take the call or message at the table. Lord knows what my mother would have to say about my poor manners.

I excuse myself to the restroom praying she doesn't suggest we go together. When I get up from my seat and she doesn't budge I say a silent thank you.

Chapter Sixteen

WESTON

"Sir, I know you said not to disturb you, but Mr. Pike's wife is on the line for you. She said it was urgent."

"It always is." I sigh. "Put her through."

Straightening my tie, I wait for the transfer.

I hear her breathe into the phone speaker. "Mrs. Pike, to what do I owe the pleasure?"

"We need to talk. I have reservations at Wynega's. Seven tonight."

"You're in town?"

"I flew in this morning. I apologize for such short notice and would like to say I'd understand if you have other plans, but this meeting really needs to happen tonight."

I don't like people demanding things from me. She's lucky I wasn't meeting up with Brooke or I'd tell her to fuck off.

"I'll be there."

"Good. Thanks. This is important, Mr. Hunter."

The line goes dead, and I let out a frustrated growl. This meeting better not have anything to do with her hands and my ass or I'll assign them to Maxwell. I owe that fucker, anyway.

I'll admit, it's unusual for her to request a dinner meeting on short notice.

Gathering up my belongings, I meet Brodie at the elevator and we ride down together.

"Where are you off to?" I ask.

"Home. Think I'm still feeling my hangover from the weekend."

I laugh. He's always been the good one. Never been a heavy drinker. Always eager to beat me at everything but never succeeding.

"Amateur." I grin.

"Whatever. Did you fuck that hot piece of ass the other night?"

"Don't call her that."

He squints at me then waves his hand over my face. "Hello? Weston, bro, are you in there? Did aliens take over your body?" He chuckles.

"Smartass." I shake my head. "She's different."

He stares. "Kryptonite pussy. It's the only explanation for this."

"What?" My brother may be book smart but sometimes I swear he's an idiot. He says the weirdest shit.

"The one pussy that can bring you to your knees. It's from Superman. Jesus Christ."

I think about it for a second. Maybe he has a point. "Kryptonite pussy, huh?"

"Better get away now, before it destroys you."

———

I make it to Wynega's and arrive before Carol. I walk to the bar to enjoy a scotch while I wait. People-watching always fascinates me anyway. People are strange and stupid. That's when I see her. Brooke with a middle-aged couple. They must be her parents.

Pulling out my phone, I snicker. I can't resist the temptation to tease her.

Weston: Looks like you need some meat on that plate.

A moment later she gets up, walking in the direction of the bathrooms.

I finish my drink and place the rocks glass back on the bar.

Then, I stalk after my prey.

The bathroom door closes behind her and I wait a moment to see if anyone else comes out.

My phone vibrates in my pocket.

Brooke: Are you following me?

Weston: I'd call it fate, but you don't believe in that...

I don't wait for a response. I push the bathroom door open and find Brooke sitting on a padded bench that takes up the left wall.

She glances up and our eyes meet.

"Jesus Christ."

I don't allow her the opportunity to get another word out. I pull her up and into my body, claiming her mouth. After a few long seconds, our kiss breaks.

"I can't seem to stay away."

"I don't know what to say."

"Don't say anything. I'm meeting a client. Just wanted to kiss you."

I turn to leave and catch her touching her lips in the reflection from the mirror. I smirk to myself. Maybe I have kryptonite cock.

When I go back to the bar, the bartender informs me my table is ready and my companion has arrived.

I follow the Hostess to the table, greet Carol, and take my seat. Brooke is on the other side of the dining room, and I don't have a good view of her. It's probably for the best. I don't need any distractions right now. I don't have a good feeling about this meeting.

Carol's face is neutral. She's usually all smiles and acts like she walks on sunshine.

"You seem different."

"I've been reevaluating my life." She takes a sip of water and looks at her lap.

"How do I factor into this?"

"You represent my husband and his interests. It's important you have all the facts. He has a mistress. Not one of his usual flings. I think he may actually love this one. She's having his child. I kicked him out on his ass, and I need to think about what *I* want for a change."

Where the fuck is that server with my drink? I take a large drink of water and scan the room hoping someone will rescue me from this disaster.

"So, what do you want?"

"I want to ruin him."

"And you expect me to help you? You know he's my client. I shouldn't be discussing any of this with you."

"I'm hoping you'll represent me. I stand to gain everything. I emailed you a copy of our prenup, he knows what's at stake. I thought I could live with it but I can't."

This is a complication I wasn't expecting.

"Why come to me with this? There are others who would gladly take your case?"

She extends her hand across the table and squeezes mine. "I think it's pretty obvious. We could have everything we want and more."

I slide my hand away, not sure how to play this whole thing.

Technically, I represent his company, and if she's set to gain a controlling interest... Fuck, this got complicated, not to mention she looks like she wants to fuck me on the table right now. Regardless, I have to tread carefully. It's a huge account for my firm.

"I think you need some time to think. And you should know I can't be bought."

She laughs. "Please. You're the most bought and paid for man in this city. And if you can't handle it, I'll find someone who will."

"I guess I'll see you in court then."

Her red painted lips stretch into a broad and proud grin. "I knew you'd see things my way."

"You aren't understanding me. I'll see you in court when I represent your husband. I don't know what kind of game you're playing but I'm nobody's pawn. Good luck." I push my chair out and leave her sitting alone with her mouth wide open.

Fuck, that family. They need to get their shit together over there. Goddamn billionaires always need a babysitter.

As I walk to my car I see Brooke getting into hers. I start to approach her, but stop myself, or she really might think I'm a stalker. I need to quit while I am ahead.

Fucking Pike. His marriage is complicated. A marriage of convenience and money. I know what the prenuptial agreement states. I advised him on it. It might make me an asshole, but he's my client, and I have to do what best suits him. It's why he pays me so damn well.

When I get in my car I dial his private line on speaker phone.

"Don't tell me where you are or what you're doing. Just be at my office tomorrow morning. I had a conversation with your wife."

"Okay."

I end the call and drive to my building.

Chapter Seventeen

BROOKE

I f fate does keep bringing Weston and I together then fate is a sneaky bastard. I can't believe he came into the bathroom just to kiss me. He's confusing. He says one thing then does another. I never expected to hear from him. I thought he would be done after he got what he wanted. I have to admit, it's incredibly flattering being pursued.

I don't want to screw whatever this is up. We have chemistry, there's no doubting it, but I don't even know the guy. Sex is what I thought I wanted, but now I'm not so sure things will ever be casual between us.

I'm supposed to meet him at the Four Seasons. Only problem is, my parents are in town and that's where they're staying. I don't want them to see me sneak out of some guy's room after a booty call. Because that's exactly what this is. It isn't a date. I guess it's a date to have sex, which seems weird too. I've never planned sex before. I'm so new to all of this. I want to ask Misty for advice, but considering she's having her boss's baby, I hardly think she's the best source.

And he came inside me.

I shudder at what could already be happening in my body. Not to mention the fact that I liked it when he did. I liked it a lot.

I stand in my bedroom getting ready. I feel strong and sexy and seductive. I glance at my reflection in the mirror. I bought new lingerie when I was on my lunch break just for tonight. I hope Weston will like it. I hope it's not too much, or too forward.

I'm taking a leap and trying to do this without involving my heart.

With any luck, my parents will be in their room or out somewhere with friends. After my mom's behavior last night, I'm in no hurry to see her any time soon.

Slipping on my favorite little black dress, I grab my coat and step back into my heels.

I send a text to Weston to confirm the room number. I know I shouldn't be nervous. We've already done pretty much everything. I guess it's nerves, seeing as I'm going there with the sole purpose for him to put his cock inside me.

I mean, do I just knock on the door and start taking my clothes off once he invites me inside? Will he already be naked?

I'm overthinking this. It's what I do. And I'm the one who came up with these rules. What in the hell are we supposed to talk about? Will there even be any talking?

Brooke: On my way. What room is it?

Weston: I'll meet you in the bar.

My stomach twists with excitement and anxiety.

I need a shot to calm myself down, loosen me up.

———

The valet takes my car and I make a quick run to the restroom to do another once over with my makeup. I don't want to show up with lipstick on my teeth. That would be unfortunate.

I stare at myself in the mirror.

Okay, I can do this.

It's just sex with a man I've already slept with. No big deal.

I spot Weston at the bar the moment I walk in. He has his back to me, but I recognize his profile as he turns to order a drink.

I approach him slowly, enjoying seeing him when he doesn't know I'm watching. I saw him yesterday with his client. He didn't seem happy about the meeting. Today, he seems much more relaxed as he takes a swig from a rocks glass.

I slide onto the stool to his left and order a dirty martini, emphasis on the *dirty*.

"A drink that suits you." His eyes wander to mine and I light up with flames.

"Hi." I exhale the word as he takes my hand and brings it to his mouth, dropping a kiss on my knuckles.

"Hey." He offers me a sexy smirk. One that says I'm so going to do bad things to you. My body comes alive and screams *hell yes* and a warmth funnels straight down to my core.

I swirl the olive stick around in my glass before taking a sip.

Weston watches me closely as I pop one of the olives into my mouth. It might be the smoothest thing I've ever done in my life. Damn, I'm good. He appears to be enjoying it.

"Mmm." I stifle a moan. "So good."

"I know something better." His mouth seems to always find my ear.

"What's that?" For the first time I take him in. Head-to-toe in his suit. Not just any suit either. This one's been tailored to fit him like a glove. I wouldn't mind going to court as much if I had him to stare at all day.

He exhales his warm breath in my ear. "This pussy." His hand finds my inner thigh, and he lifts it so high his fingertips graze the edge of my entrance. "Riding my face." He smirks.

Goosebumps pebble down the backs of my arms, and despite the fact we're in public, I try to lower myself onto his hand.

He removes it before I can get the friction I need. I'm nothing but a hot mess. About to melt into a puddle on the floor. He grins at the way he affects me. "Upstairs. *Now*." He doesn't just say it in my ear. No, Weston growls the shit, and his voice is masculine as all hell and pure gravel.

I don't hesitate to slide off the stool. I swear he's conditioned me somehow, because I'm like Pavlov's Dog, responding to anything he does with complete obedience.

His hand goes to the small of my back as he guides me to the elevators.

"You look—fuck, just fuck."

My heart kicks into overdrive, thumping against my ribs. I make him speechless. There's something about knowing I have at least a little power over him, that keeps me walking into his arms no matter what.

"Brooke, sweetheart. Were you coming to see us? Is this the new boyfriend you told us about?"

I freeze.

Fuck. Fuck. Shitfuck.

My voice catches in my throat when I try to respond. I make some kind of sound that's best described as a jumbled gasp.

"You must be Brooke's parents. She's told me so much about you two. I'm Weston. Pleasure to meet you." He holds his hand out to my father and I try not to faint.

I told him nothing personal about me, other than I'm a lawyer, and now I'm introducing him to my folks.

"Will you be joining us for dinner? We only made reservations for two, but I'm sure they can scoot some tables together."

There is no way in hell I am subjecting Weston to a meal with her.

I clear my throat. "Actually, umm, we already ate."

Weston leans in my ear and whispers where they can't hear. "I haven't eaten—*yet*." He leans back up while I try not to wobble in my heels, on my legs that are now Jello. "Yeah, sorry about that. Maybe another time?"

"Yeah, some, uhh, other time."

"Sweetie, are you okay? You look a little flushed." Mom stares at me.

Weston grins. "It's okay. She'll be in good hands."

"Oh, all right. Call me later." Mom takes a step away. "Wow, he's so handsome." She gives me a thumbs up, and I think I might die.

Once the door closes Weston corners me against the wall. He's looking at me with those sexy dark eyes, and I might lose it. This has to be what going crazy feels like.

"You're hot when you're flustered." He sucks my bottom lip between his teeth, nipping at the skin. "So, who's this new guy you're seeing?"

"Don't tease me. You don't know my mom."

"First of all." He holds up a finger. "There will be more teasing than you or that sweet pussy can handle." He licks at my lips, getting me to part for him, then kisses me deep. When he breaks our embrace, he leans back with raised eyebrows. "You told your mom about me."

I'm going to bite that smirk off his face.

"She was pressuring me to meet someone my dad knows. I had to tell her something." I tug on his tie, wrapping it around my fist. I pull him closer, never wanting him that far away the rest of the night.

"You know what this means, right?"

The elevator stops and the doors open to our floor.

He sucks down my throat, not giving a shit who may be watching.

I gasp at his hot mouth on my neck. "It's going to cost me, isn't it?"

"You bet your sweet fucking ass it is." He nips at my ear. "Now, you owe me dinner and a movie."

"Against. Rules." I can't even form a whole sentence.

"Rules never stop me." He rakes his gaze up and down my body. "From getting what I want."

He leads me down the hallway, damn near at a power-walking pace. As soon as the door to the suite latches shut, Weston is on me.

I pull back. "What are we doing?"

Somehow, he spins me chest-first against the wall and yanks my dress up over my ass in one smooth motion. "I'm about to listen to you moan my name."

I push back against him, my mind not totally gone yet. "You know what I mean."

His hand wraps around my neck, and he kisses along my collar bone. "Brooke?"

"Yeah?"

"Shut up and let me eat this pussy." His palm smacks against my entrance.

I jolt forward.

Then he rips the expensive underwear right off me.

"Okay." I nod, surprised I got the word out.

"Better." He works me with his hand, massaging me, teasing my clit with his fingertips. "We need to get you out of this dress." He moves his hands to my back and tugs down the zipper as he walks me backwards toward the bed. "And on my face."

I've never been in the presidential suite before. It's incredibly beautiful and may be larger than my apartment.

The white bedspread is covered in red rose petals. Tealight candles are the only thing illuminating the room.

I spin around. "You did all this for me?"

"Stop talking." He presses a finger to my lips, and then falls onto his back in the middle of the bed. "Up here, now." He points to his mouth.

My skin grows warm and shocks of tingles bloom across my skin. I pull the dress up over my head once I've crawled onto the bed. His cock tents in his slacks when he sees the lingerie I bought for him.

"For me?" He looks me up and down.

I nod.

A devilish smile spreads across his face.

"I guess we're even." I glance around at the candles and roses.

"I guess so."

I get close, and he pulls me up to his face. I straddle his head, my knees on each side.

"Now fuck my face." He digs his fingers into my ass, pulling me into him as he lunges up with his mouth.

The second his tongue collides with my clit, my brain melts.

He owns me. And he knows it.

Chapter Eighteen

WESTON

For the past two weeks my nights have been spent making Brooke squirm beneath me. My days have been spent with Pike and handling his mess. The dumbass went against my advice. There's a clause in the prenuptial about affairs and children. If he did impregnate his mistress, he stands to lose everything. I've even got my brother and Maxwell poring over the paperwork to find any kind of loophole in their spare time. I don't trust anyone else with a case this huge.

So far it doesn't look good. Carol says she'll drop filing for divorce if he signs away his rights to the child and agrees never to see the other woman again. The whole thing is a clusterfuck.

I'm a shitty person on occasion, but there's absolutely nothing redeeming about some of these clients. It's bad enough to make you want to strangle them.

My advice to him is to tell Carol what she wants to hear and find something or someone to occupy her attention. If they were actually in love with each other my advice would be different, maybe counseling. Carol doesn't love him. She refused to give him an heir. It's all a power play, and now kids are involved. I'm not sure what she thought would happen when she refused to sleep with her husband. He was bound to go elsewhere. I don't know why he'd jeopardize his empire by coming inside his mistresses. I'm sitting down with them and her lawyer today.

I'd rather not deal with Carol at all after her pathetic attempt to get me to what? Run away with her?

Fuck my life.

They arrive before Carol's lawyer.

"Please have a seat. If you'd like a drink, my assistant can get you something." The new assistant has only been with me for two days. Hopefully, this one lasts longer than a week.

Pike holds his hand up and makes a no thanks face.

"Is your attorney on the way?"

"No. I changed my mind. I want his little slut to give me the baby when it's born. If she does that, I won't pursue the divorce."

I roll my eyes with a loud sigh. "I don't handle family law. If you'd like me to refer you to someone—"

"No. No." Carol cuts me off while Pike sits with his tail between his legs. "You'll represent us."

"If I refuse?"

"You don't want to make an enemy out of me. You should know this." She glances out toward the lobby. "That a new assistant? You seem to go through those fast. Probably a few that have a good reason for leaving."

This fucking bitch.

I hold up a finger—since her husband doesn't seem to have a set of balls attached to his body—and grin. "Don't threaten me. It won't end well for you."

She sneers and pushes back her chair. "I'll leave you two to discuss details."

Pike rolls his eyes once she's gone. "I'll take a whiskey."

I call Melody on the intercom and have her bring one in.

He flashes her his snake charmer's smile. "I know how it sounds but hear me out. We just need to pacify her. Have a courier deliver the proposal to Misty. I'll get Misty to sign it. By the time the baby is here I'll have found a way to be rid of Carol."

"What? There's no way Misty will go for that. You're talking about a child." Jesus, I've done some shitty things, but this will take the cake.

"No, she doesn't know." He shakes his head. "I'll get her to do it, trust me. It'll all be fine."

"You might lose her, just mentioning this. It's crazy."

"I'll take the risk."

I just want him out of my goddamn office. "I'll draw up the paperwork. It's going to be *very* fucking expensive."

"I'm good for it." He raises his glass to me then knocks back his drink.

Once he leaves I collapse in my chair and rub my temples. Carol's perfume gave me a headache. The only good part of my days is spending evenings with Brooke.

I can't wait to get between her thighs again and hide from the world.

I'm tempted to text her but if I want to pacify my clients I'd better get busy drafting the proposal.

This bullshit is a perfect reminder of why I steer clear of relationships. When feelings are involved, people get hurt. And it's even worse for the innocent parties.

I'm not a man that feels much, but how people can treat children as leverage just floors me sometimes. I have zero hope in humanity.

———

I finish drafting the proposal and have it delivered to Pike. The final draft will be more in-depth and formal, but I hope he's pleased with what I wrote up for him. It's basically a bunch of legal bullshit that sounds fancy and means absolutely nothing. Usually, I would have an associate draft the thing and I'd just review it, but I can't have them writing up shit like this. There's one other problem too. If Carol decides to have one of her attorneys go over it then we may be in trouble.

I don't take comfort in hurting someone on purpose or trying to separate a mother from her child. Even if Pike has good intentions, I'm afraid this will backfire in his face. I'll be stuck cleaning up the mess.

I'm going to bill him for every goddamn second I even think about this, and the therapy that might come after.

By the end of the day it's late and for the first time in my life, I'm too tired for sex. I should text Brooke and tell her tonight is off, but I still want to see her. She's the one bright spot in my life.

When I get to the room she's already there, sitting at the counter eating fruit. After a week together, I was able to get her to at least have room service dinner with me. We both have to eat so why not do it together?

Even though she tries to avoid personal conversations, I get a few things out of her. I know she loves audiobooks and has a cat named Casper who hates when she comes to the hotel. It means she isn't home taking care of him. She's like his human slave. I've received a few pictures of her curled up on the couch with him.

I've always been more of a dog guy but don't have time to care for one. They need too much attention, like children. Which is why I don't have them, like a responsible human being.

When I approach Brooke at the dining table she pops a grape into my mouth.

I bend down and lick her finger. I thought I was too tired for sex, but now that I watch her eating fruit and looking all hot as fuck, my dick has other ideas.

"You look tense."

I scrub the back of my neck. "Yeah. Long day."

Her eyes narrow and the corners of her mouth curl up. "How about a massage?"

"Fucking perfect."

She nods. "Okay."

"One condition."

"And that is?"

"You have to be naked."

Yeah, she's getting fucked and I'm getting a massage. Win win.

Chapter Nineteen

BROOKE

It's Friday night. I should be letting Weston spank me and do dirty things right now, and instead I wait for Misty to come over. She had a fight with Pike and asked if she could crash with me for the night. I don't know what's happening, but I wasn't about to turn her away.

This is exactly what I was afraid would happen. Pike would fuck up and she'd end things with him or he'd end things with her. Then she'd be stuck up shit creek without a paddle.

I'd never turn her away, but my apartment has one bedroom and it's my sanctuary to escape real life and problems. Though lately, it seems like I never sleep here anymore. I practically live at the Four Seasons now.

Maybe I'm jumping to conclusions about Misty and Pike and it's nothing.

When I open the door, her quaking voice leads me to believe otherwise. She stands there with a tear-streaked face and trembling lips—bag in hand.

"Come here." I hold my arms out and embrace her with a bear hug as she sobs. The door shuts behind her and I lead her over to the couch.

"Here, sit down."

Her breathing speeds up, almost to the point she's hyperventilating.

I worry she might be having a panic attack, and that can't be good for the baby.

"Breathe, Misty. Just breathe. Come on, sweetie."

After a few moments, she seems to calm down and I hand her a box of tissues.

"What happened?"

She sniffles and rolls her eyes. "Go ahead and say it. I know you're dying to. You warned me. You told me. You could see it, but I was a blind idiot."

"Hey." I take her by the arm, gently. "I don't want to see you hurt. I'm not going to say anything. I love you. If you aren't ready to talk about it, that's fine. But holding it in probably isn't good for the baby. Right?"

"You're right. It's over. Pike—h-he fired me, and I was served with this." She pulls out a large envelope. The return address says it's from the Hunter Group. I've heard of them. It's four men and the rumor is they're ruthless attorneys. I don't have any experience with them, but this can't be good.

"What is it?"

"Apparently, Pike is staying with his wife and they want to pay me off and take my baby."

"What? No. No." I grab her by the arms. "I will *never* let that happen. I don't care how much money they have. Misty, you have me. We'll get through this."

I go into the kitchen to get her something to drink and I start reading over the document.

It's a bunch of legal language that doesn't mean anything. Whoever drafted this made it a fancy but empty-worded proposal.

This is garbage. Junk.

I get to the end of the papers and see a familiar name.

Weston Hunter.

I drop the documents on the counter and back away. It can't be the same guy. Weston is a common name.

He wouldn't be involved in something like this. He's an asshole, but I can tell he has a soft side too. He's not an animal.

I know he loves listening to the blues. He likes mushrooms and double cheese on his pizza. He has a tattoo of praying hands on his left pec with his younger sister's name in cursive font underneath it. She died when he was seventeen of a rare form of brain cancer. She was six years old. He has a soft spot for kids, whether he admits it or not. I know all these things about him and yet I don't know his last name or where he works.

I should do the adult thing and ask.

I give Misty a glass of water and pull out my laptop.

"Find us a movie. A horror flick where everyone dies."

She laughs. "Its fine. I'll be okay—eventually. Let's watch Pretty in Pink and I can bawl my eyes out."

I nod in agreement. I always wanted Ducky to get the girl, but Andrew McCarthy was hot.

I type 'The Hunter Group Dallas' into the search bar and wait for the results to populate.

There he is.

Weston.

I glance over at Misty and look away super-fast. A knot tightens in my stomach. How can he be a part of this?

I can't date or sleep with a man or whatever we're doing. Not one who would do something like this.

I can't stop myself from looking at his social media. There are so many women on his arm. He wasn't kidding about getting around.

My phone vibrates on the coffee table and my gut tells me it's him. I don't want to look. I don't want to be tempted to text him back. Because if I do, he'll say something charming and convince me to come to him. Lawyers are the best excuse makers in the world.

Twenty minutes go by and Misty falls asleep. The movie is failing to hold my attention.

My phone has gone off three times now.

Giving in to temptation, I snatch it from the table and unlock the screen.

Weston: On your way? I ordered Thai.

Weston: If you don't want Thai we can order something differ-ent. Your choice.

Weston: You standing me up? Bold play. It's gonna cost you.

I want to respond but right now I don't know what to say.

We'll see who it costs.

Chapter Twenty

WESTON

B rooke completely ghosted me, and I can't figure out why. Maybe her phone died and she couldn't text me or she was working late. She *is* a workaholic. Or maybe there was an emergency.

I didn't know if anything happened to her. She could've been in a car wreck. So many terrible possibilities run through my mind. What if she's in the hospital? I have no way of knowing. The realization that I care about her more than I've ever cared about anyone slams into me like a wall of bricks.

I've never wanted a relationship, but I'm enjoying what we have going on. I thought I could maybe try for her.

I finally got tired of waiting on her and asked my driver to scope out her building. He said he saw her and a friend sitting on her balcony. I can't stop picturing her in her sexy lingerie giving me a massage, taking me in her mouth, bending her over the counter and fucking her senseless till her body was putty in my hands.

I haven't decided what to do. It won't end like this. It might serve me right for all the broken hearts I've left scattered along the way. Maybe this is payback for all the women I've kicked out as soon as I was done with them. The one woman I want doesn't want me. How fitting is that?

Maybe her friend was just having a bad day and she had to comfort her. Chicks do that kind of stuff, right? It's like meeting a buddy at happy hour to bitch about nagging girlfriends or wives or something? How am I supposed to know? But, why wouldn't she call and cancel? That's what adults do.

My assistant buzzes me over the intercom. "Mr. Hunter, umm, sir? There's a Brooke Murphy to see you. She doesn't have an appointment."

Maybe she's here to explain. My heart comes alive. I'll definitely be using this to my advantage later. "Send her in." I straighten up my suit using my reflection in the window.

I stand by my desk, watching her walk down the hall through the glass walls. She looks fucking sexy dressed up in her attorney outfit.

Her hair is pulled back from her face and she struts through my door in a form-fitting charcoal skirt and white top that hugs her tits just right.

I lean against the edge of my desk and fold my arms over my chest to stop myself from kissing her. Is she here on business? Maybe we should role play this some time, because I like what I see. I flash her a fake glare. "Well, this is a surprise. Can I get you a coffee or something?"

She matches my glare right back, and her teeth grind together. "I'm fine."

Interesting. She looks legitimately pissed off. What the hell did I do? "Seems like you're upset. Are you here on actual business?" I quirk an eyebrow up at her.

One hand moves to her hip and she taps one of her feet. "Yep."

"Not sure what I've done. You're going to have to enlighten me."

She tosses the manila folder full of the Pike proposal that I drafted right at my feet.

You've got to be fucking kidding me.

"Wanna explain that shit?" Her eyes dart to the folder and back up at me.

My jaw ticks as the worst thought possible hits me. "Please don't tell me your name is actually Misty. I might need to take a shower—in battery acid." A shudder rips up my spine at the thought of Brooke banging Pike.

Her face tightens, and then grows hot like an ember in a fire. "You." She points a finger like she's still searching for words. "You just keep digging your hole even deeper, you dumb fuck. Do I look pregnant to you?" She balls her hands into fists.

For whatever reason, my eyes immediately dart down to her waist before I can stop them.

"Don't you dare fucking answer that question."

She looks like she wants to put my nuts in a vise and crush them.

I take a step back, and for some reason, my cock gets hard seeing her like this. "I need some fucking information because I don't know what's going on here. Can you please help me understand?"

"Misty's my best friend."

Oh fuck.

"She was at my apartment bawling her eyes out all weekend. Understand now?"

My jaw tensed. "Did you read the proposal?"

She shoves a finger in my face. "Don't talk to me like I'm stupid."

"No, I mean read the proposal. Like read between the fucking lines." My eyes widen.

"Don't worry, *Mr. Hunter.*"

God, my cock aches when she says my name all pissed off like that. For the first time in my life, I want him to go away and leave me alone.

"I'll be representing her." She crosses her arms and it pushes her tits up high and tight against her blouse.

I turn away and try to think about anything but spanking her for talking to me this way. "Fuck, fuck." I mumble the words where I think she can't hear.

"Something in your throat?"

Jesus, she's ruthless. I might be falling for her. "Can we discuss this like adults if you're going to represent her?"

"Are you suggesting that I'm behaving like a child, Mr. Hunter?"

Goddamn it!

I've had about enough of this. I whip around to face her and try to look through her like I do every other attorney that steps up to me like this. "If you're going to come into my office." I take a step forward and she backs up a step. "You'll treat me with respect, or you'll get the fuck out."

I watch her heartbeat speed up on her neck. She's aroused. I can practically smell her wet pussy under that skirt.

"You have to earn my respect."

"It goes both ways. So if you want to talk shop, sit down and we can discuss this without you jumping to conclusions and acting like an asshole in here."

She doesn't admit to doing any of that, but slowly takes a seat in one of the chairs in front of my desk. She waves me forward with a flippant hand and crosses her legs. "Proceed, counselor."

I tell her about Pike's plan. I shouldn't, but I'm at the point where

I don't even give a fuck if I do something to get me disbarred. I have enough money to last ten lifetimes and I'm sick of all this shit.

"You remember Maxwell? He's got a PI investigating Carol. If we somehow prove she cheated first, then the clause about kids won't matter. Right now, the best thing for Misty to do is lay low. Pike will make sure she is cared for." I lock eyes with her. "Is this why you ghosted on me?"

She looks away as I lower the blinds to my office. "Yes."

"You know what I think?"

"What's that?"

"I think you're too close to this and you need to take a deep breath. Misty and Pike are adults. They can figure their own shit out. They made their bed and now they need to lie in it. And I have to do what my client wants. So do you. Remember?"

"He's a piece of shit. How do you work for a man like that?"

"It's business. My job. I feel bad for the kid. I really do. But you can grow up worse ways than having a billionaire for a parent."

"Is that what you tell yourself to sleep at night? Rationalize this huge office building and a penthouse? It's my job too, but I don't represent assholes like that. We're allowed to turn down cases. You learned that at—" She stares off at my wall, and then down at the ground and mumbles, "umm, Princeton. Right?"

"Yeah, you don't own a firm. I have other people to consider besides myself. And it doesn't change the fact that you're emotional. Misty is your friend. You're mad at the situation. Not at me. Be mad at Pike. He could throw everything away and run off with your friend if he wanted. They're grownups."

"He made his choice."

"Yeah, I had no say in it. You think I want your friend to hurt?"

She shakes her head, staring off at the wall.

"Still not a believer of fate?" I crouch in front of her and run my fingers up her thigh.

She tenses under my tender touch.

"I believe in choices and consequences. You know that."

"Then why does the world keep shoving us together every chance it gets?" I kiss her hand. "I think we could have something if you'd give us a chance."

"I should go." She tries to push me away, but I don't budge.

She's too worked up. I need to help her out with that. Show her what a true humanitarian I really am. I need to remind her how good we can be together.

Pressing my lips to hers, I lick the seam of her mouth, begging for entrance.

"We both know what you want right now." I press my cock up against her.

Finally, she kisses me back. Her tongue sweeps across mine. She tastes like—home. I could kiss her forever and never want to let her go.

I back her up to the window, not giving her a chance to break away from me, and I lower the blinds. One by one, I walk her around the room, until it's just us and the door is locked.

My hands move to her blouse. It's in the way and it shouldn't be. I grab her firm tits, growling when her bra is in the way. I yank it down to her stomach, and take both nipples between my fingers and squeeze, hard.

"Holy shit." She pants like she just ran a marathon. "Weston." She breathes out my name. "We're in your office."

"No one can see us." I flip her around and bend her over my desk. "You know better than to come into my work." I pull my tie off with a swipe of my hand and tie her hands up behind her back with it. "Disrespect me." I yank her skirt up over her ass.

My cock grows harder, thinking about how sweet my handprints will look on it.

"Turning me on. Teasing me. Being a naughty little bitch, back-talking me."

"Oh my God." Her cheek rests flat on my desk, and I walk around to her side.

My cock juts out in my pants, and she licks her lips at the sight of it inches from her face.

"You want to suck that dick right now, don't you?"

She shakes her head in defiance.

"I know what you want, Brooke. I know you. And you're going to sit there, while I turn this ass pink."

"Jesus." Her breaths are still labored while she stares right at my dick.

"If you behave. Maybe I'll put it in your mouth."

"You're such an arrogant prick. You think everyone wants you."

Fuck, I want to give her a gold medal for turning me on. So fucking sassy.

I lean down to her ear and snake my hand up the back of her thigh, all the way to her ass. "Now, tell me the truth. You want me to fuck you right now, don't you?"

She shakes her head, but with a hint of a smile on her face. "No."

I shift over behind her and go to my knees, then exhale all the way up the back of her legs. When I reach her pussy, I grip her thighs in my palms and spread her out with my thumbs. Then I sniff the air right next to her hot little cunt. "The court determines that's a lie."

"Holy shit."

I shift her panties to the side and stand up straight. Fuck getting my cock sucked, this needy cunt is like a magnet, pulling me toward it. I unzip and don't even bother pulling my pants down.

I smack one of my palms down on her bare ass and the sound echoes through my office.

Brooke jolts for a second, her whole body stiff, then relaxes into it and lets out a sigh of approval.

"That's for calling me a heartless asshole."

"I didn't—"

Crack!

"That's for backtalking me just now." I smile at my handprint on her ass, and then groan at how bad it makes my cock ache.

"Is that all you've got, *Mr. Hunter*?"

I shake my head and trace the outline of her pussy with the head of my dick.

She squirms a little, then tries to push her ass back onto it.

Crack!

"What was that one for, sir?"

"Because I wanted to." I slam into her from behind, and I have to imagine it's what shooting up heroin or morphine feels like.

Instantaneous euphoria rushing through my veins.

When she squeezes around me I forget where I'm at and what I'm doing for a moment. All I can do is stand there and grunt.

"Fuck me hard."

I ball her hair into my fist, and her back arches, giving me deeper access. "You want it rough? Want me to take my day out on you?"

"Mmhmm."

I start a steady pace, pumping into her from behind while light moans roll off her tongue.

"That can be arranged."

"Arrange it then, pussy."

I smack her ass again, and ignore her little attempt at insulting me. "Fuck, I missed this sweet cunt."

"Is that all you missed?"

My hand slides from her hair to her shoulder, and I grip her around her collar bone. "No."

She bucks her hips back into me, taking it just as hard as I give it.

I need to come inside her. I need to mark her. Own her. Show her she's mine, and nothing will ever change that.

I've met my match.

She's my one.

Before long, I'm hammering into her so fast and hard I'm sure the entire office has heard what's going on. I don't give one fuck. I'm in love with her, and I don't give a shit. She clamps down on me with her second orgasm in as much as ten minutes, and I blow my hot load all inside her pussy, like I always do. I have every time I've been with her, and I don't plan to stop.

I want it all. I don't want anything between us.

She's real. The most real thing in my world, and I'm not giving that up for anyone or anything.

After I collapse into her back and push some sweaty strands of hair from her face, she turns to me.

"We're out of control."

I smile. "Yeah, we definitely are. But that's how I like us."

She glances away and blushes. "What are we going to do about Misty and Pike? I can't have her on my couch forever."

"Let her have your bed. You can sleep in mine." I smirk.

"Don't you think that's a bit fast?"

"We practically live together at the hotel anyway. Now, we'll be in my bed where we belong. I don't know what we're doing. I'm not making any promises. I just know this thing with us—it feels right."

"I don't want any promises. But okay. If you're willing to try, so am I."

"That's all I want."

I kiss her forehead and untie her, then pull her into a hug.

When we walk out of my office the whole damn floor erupts in applause. My brother is the damn ring leader.

I grin and shake my head at him.

Motherfucker.

Brooke blushes but I tilt her chin up and kiss her again in front of everyone. They all need to get used to it, because she's not going anywhere.

Chapter Twenty-One

FIVE MONTHS LATER

Weston

"Y ou sure everything's okay?"

Brooke's on the other end of the phone. "We're fine. Misty doesn't want you to tell Pike. It's a false alarm."

"You sure? It's his baby."

"Stop looking for excuses to bail on the bachelor party. Go have fun. I trust you. It's him I worry about."

"Yeah, I'll keep his ass in line."

"You better or I'll fuck you up."

"Sounds kinky. Tell me more about how you want to fuck me." I chuckle into the phone.

"I'll see you when you get in. Have fun."

"I love you, fiancée."

"Stop saying that. You sound like a dork."

"I don't give a fuck how I sound, to anyone." I can practically feel her smiling on the other end of the call.

"I know you don't. And it's why I love you too."

I end the call and get back to the party. Misty was having false labor pains.

When I first met Brooke, if someone told me that I was going to propose to her within three months, I would have laughed in their face. I may have actually died from laughter. Straight up dead.

Now, though—fucking fate.

I glare over at Pike's ridiculous ass. He's keeping his hands to himself. I don't know if it's because he's being good, or if he knows I'll break his face if he brings more trouble into my house.

I'd do anything in the world to make Brooke happy. Anything. Including sharing a bachelor party with fucking Pike.

Carol gave him the divorce and settled for a percentage of his holdings, the shares that originally belonged to her father. I'd say it was a fair trade. He gets to be with Misty and they'll raise their son together. I'd call that a win.

Now, if only I could get my brother in line. When I return to the living room of the penthouse suite, I see Brodie with a stripper on each arm, heading upstairs for the bedroom.

Fuck. This has trouble written all over it.

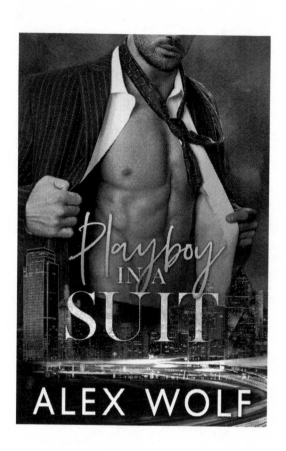

Playboy
IN A
SUIT

ALEX WOLF

I'm a playboy in a suit.

I like to do two things—whatever I want and dominate in the courtroom.

My brother and I run one of the most powerful law firms in Dallas. I have a reputation.

Weston was the same, until Brooke came along and tamed him. That leaves me.

One of us has to take care of all the smoking hot women in the city. I knew better than to let my guard down at his bachelor party with all the booze floating around.

Apparently, I hooked up with the hottest stripper there. She was meant for my brother, but I kept her for myself.

We were so wasted I can't remember anything about her.

When a dancer named April shows up at my firm a few months later wanting to sue her boss, one of my biggest clients, there's a conflict of interest.

She looks familiar.

A lump forms in my throat when I notice a baby bump.

I have a sinking feeling she's the one I hooked up with, and that baby might be mine.

No matter how hard I fight it, I know one thing—I want her, and the baby too.

She can fight it all she wants, but I'll get her. I always get what I want. And I take care of what's mine.

Because I'm Brodie Hunter, Attorney at Law.

Chapter One

APRIL

"Have you seen my gold hoop earrings?"

Jenny is always borrowing my stuff. I wouldn't mind if she'd remember to return what she took once in a while.

I finish applying my lipstick while I wait for her to make an appearance.

I grow impatient, combing through my jewelry case again to see if I overlooked them. *I'm going to be late.* I took on a private party to earn some extra cash but if I'm not on time I can lose out on some good tips.

"Sorry." She sucks in a breath through her teeth making some weird whoosh noise. Her fingers brush her hair behind her ears as she pokes her head through my bedroom doorway, revealing my earrings.

Rolling my eyes, I hold my palm out. "I'll probably be out late tonight."

"Well, be safe and all that." She smirks, dropping the hoops into my awaiting palm.

"Always." I grab a makeup wipe and clean off the ends before pushing them through my ears.

Picking my bag off the bed, I close my door behind me, half tempted to lock it so that nothing else of mine crawls off and disappears while I work. I adore my roommate, but she treats my closet like a five-finger discount store. I mean, I can't blame her. I *do* have impeccable taste when it comes to fashion.

On my way out the door, Jenny stops me.

"Michael's coming over, and I think it might be the night." Her brows waggle.

I laugh. "Use protection."

"Yes, Mother." Moving her hand to the top of her head she salutes as I shut the door behind me.

She's been seeing this guy, Michael, from her class for a month now, and they've yet to sleep together. I'm all for taking it slow but I'm pretty sure he's gay. The guy dresses too nice and his brows are sculpted better than mine. I hate to see Jenny hurt but I'd bet that she'll be crying into her Ben & Jerrys later when she makes a move and he gives her the just friends talk.

When I arrive at the club, Sheer Fantasy, the girls are already getting in the van. Shit. I'll have to change on the way.

Five of us were hired for a bachelor party at some swanky building downtown, which means the money will be damn good. It's the only reason I do private parties outside of the club where I dance. I park my car and grab my stuff as I rush for the van. Ben, our driver and security for the night laughs as I breathlessly climb in the back dragging my clothes with me.

"Don't start." I wag my finger at him with an airy laugh.

He shakes his head and starts the vehicle while I do my best to change clothes as he swerves in and out of traffic. He steals glances as I change, but I don't mind. It isn't anything he hasn't seen before. He's always a gentleman. Walks me to my car at night. Some of the customers can become infatuated and want more. Their lens between reality and fantasy blurs on occasion. One guy bought me an engagement ring without ever having a conversation. He's since been barred from frequenting the club, for my safety.

"I love this." Crystal runs her fingers over the sequins on my cop costume. "Did you make it?"

"Yeah." I grin like an idiot as I hook the halter-style straps around my neck. I love making new outfits and costumes to wear to the club. When you dance four days a week, building a wardrobe can get expensive. Just because I take the clothes off doesn't mean I don't like a variety and to look good.

"Rod should hire you to make our stuff. You do great work."

Stacie sneers at Crystal's compliment. She's a jealous cunt who doesn't like me because I'm a headliner and bring in a lot of customers. Heavy tippers. It's not my fault they don't like her flat, dimpled ass. That's not me being a catty bitch, it's the truth. She doesn't have the numbers to back up her attitude and she doesn't take care of her body. Rod's always threatening to fire her for drinking on the job, but he never goes through with it because they're sleeping together.

I work out three days a week and take a pole dancing class at a local studio. I work hard to maintain my body and to earn paper.

What I really want is to open my own boutique someday, selling my own jewelry and costumes. It's a pipe dream but it's pretty much all I've got.

I'm not naïve enough to think I can strip forever.

By the time I'm ready, Ben is parking in the private underground garage of the building.

We all get out and he punches in the security code for the private elevator. As I step inside he whistles, thoroughly checking me out. Maybe I'll give him a private dance one day.

When the elevator doors open, a grin spreads across my face. Judging by the penthouse we're walking into, I'm about to get paid. The entryway is nicer than my apartment.

Chapter Two

BRODIE

I stand at the open bar. It's my brother and his client, Pike's, joint bachelor party. I still can't believe my older brother is getting married. He was a sworn bachelor until he met his fiancée, Brooke, whom I suspect he's on the phone with now. I saw him sneak off a few minutes ago.

I'm happy for him, but I'm here for the booze and strippers. The strippers are my treat. I hired a few girls from the club of one of my clients. He's a friend from college. Rod was always a dick, but he pays me to handle his business, not care about his lacking personality.

I hear a few cheers as some busty blonde steps into the middle of the living room wearing a smile and the skimpiest police uniform I've ever seen. It fits her like a second skin and compliments her golden hair and deep tan. The boy shorts she's wearing show off her curves and an ass that screams for me to spank it.

"Sorry to bust up the party, boys, but we've had several loud-noise complaints." She taps the fake club against the palm of her hand. I step closer to the center of the room—where all the action is —closer to her. "You've got the right to remain silent but I kinda wanna hear you beg."

Her pearly whites graze her bottom lip and my cock stirs, jumping to life at thoughts of her doing just that—trying to make me beg.

Fuck, she's sassy and gorgeous. Her long legs look like they could wrap around me three or four times.

The redhead standing next to her isn't so bad either. I've got to hand it to Rod, he knows how to pick them. I regret not accepting his invitation to visit the club and receive the preferential treatment. He has a 'don't ask don't tell' policy when it comes to the girls taking money under the table for more than a lap dance.

"Where's Mr. Hunter?" She stares around the room.

I know she means my brother, but I can't stop myself from stepping forward and saying, "That'd be me, sweetheart."

"I've got it under strict authority to take you upstairs for interrogation."

"You gonna cuff me too?" I wink and hold out my wrists.

"That depends on how bad you've been." Her hips sway as she steps toward me and smacks my ass with her club. The redhead joins her, each of them taking an arm. I grab a bottle of liquor as I lead them to the stairs as hoots and whistles sound in the room below. Glancing over the balcony I see Pike sitting in a chair straddled by a woman with a whip.

My brother stares up at me, shaking his head, and I shrug before taking the girls into one of the guestrooms for a little fun.

We share the bottle of liquor, passing it back and forth between the three of us. It's strong. I already feel buzzed.

"Sit down." The busty blonde pokes me in the chest with her black baton.

I sink down on the edge of the bed as her friend slinks across, coming up behind me. She pulls my jacket off. Her fingers go to my tie, loosening it. "Are you a stuck-up suit?" Her soft voice whispers in my ear. "Or are you a bad boy who needs punished?"

I start to answer when the blonde cuts me off. Her long red nails grab my mouth. "No more talking." She pulls a phone from her back pocket and turns on some music.

Her girlfriend rubs her hands over my chest and breathes heavily in my ear. Blondie's got her back to me and her hips start to move, nearly hypnotizing me. Chick has an ass from heaven.

She moves closer and closer to my lap, and I want to pull her down on me. Her ass is so damn tempting. I'd like to sink balls-deep inside her.

Before I can act she turns around to face me.

Her full red lips lift into a sexy smirk as she continues to dance.

Her fingers tease at the cleavage of her top, promising to reveal more skin. I can't wait to see what she's hiding under her skimpy uniform.

Sensual and seductive, her dance continues.

Damn, I love the way she moves.

Her body grooves in time with the beat of the music. My eyes follow every thrust of her hips as her tits bounce in my face.

Spinning around she grinds her ass over my crotch, and I can't help but smack it. Tossing me a cheeky grin over her shoulder she drops down, grinding her firm cheeks over my growing cock. Up and down and side to side—she's driving me wild.

The attractive redhead works on unbuttoning my shirt, wasting no time getting down and dirty. Just how I like it.

"Do you have any party favors?" Her tongue traces the shell of my ear.

"Sorry, sweetheart. Try downstairs." Cocaine has never been my thing. I prefer alcohol or a fat joint on special occasions.

"Bummer." She pouts and leaves the room.

Blondie shrugs and begins her strip tease.

The more skin she reveals the harder I get.

Her soft fingers brush along my arm, igniting a fire in me that has my cock ready to burst from the seams of my pants.

I'm going out of my mind, I want her so bad.

I need to taste those tempting lips.

There's nothing stopping me but the small voice in the back of my head telling me I don't know this chick. But as she grinds down I find I'm unable to resist. I'm a fucking man after all.

Chapter Three

APRIL

The man I'm giving a private dance is hot as fuck in that tortured, cocky asshole kind of way. Medium brown hair that has that tousled look. Deep green eyes and a smile as sweet as apple pie yet deviously evil. I've danced for some attractive men before, but this one, I wouldn't mind taking home. Too bad this is a bachelor party, and he's the groom. I'd do him in a New York minute.

Watching him get worked up is such a turn on. His hands keep finding excuses to touch my nearly naked body. I'm down to my thong and his mouth is extremely close to my breasts.

With every stroke of his heated fingers on my hips, he brings me closer to his erection. I'm straddling his lap, practically dry-humping him. To say my pussy is wet would be an understatement. I've never been so turned on by a client. Maybe it's drinking the liquor he offered me too fast. Maybe it has gone straight to my pussy because I seem to be like a man thinking only with his dick.

A lot of the men we dance for are usually older. This guy seems to be early thirties. Probably three of four years older than me.

The tip of his cock rubs against my pussy and dear lord he's thick.

His mouth caps over my nipple and what little self-control I'd preserved goes sailing through the air like a deflated balloon. Flicking his tongue over the heated skin, he's relentless in his pursuit.

Breathless, I meet his hungry gaze and all thoughts of this being wrong leave me.

We're two consenting adults. What's one night in the grand scheme of things?

"Fuck, you're hot." He growls the words before paying attention to my other breast.

My fingers comb through his soft hair. "Not so bad yourself."

His fingers make work of the strings on my bottoms.

With two swift movements he tosses them to the floor. My bare pussy grinds up against him.

His thumb rubs over my clit, and I throw my head back, loving the sensation. I've always been a wild one, but this is new for even me—making out with a client.

I've always played it safe. I never get involved with men from the club. I've had several older men offer to be my sugar daddy, but that isn't me.

Running my fingers over his chest, I explore the contours of his muscles. He's ripped and defined in that lean kind of way.

"This is happening." He claims my mouth.

Our tongues meet in a burst of passion filled with pure carnal lust. He deepens the kiss as he maneuvers us farther up on the bed.

My hands seem to move of their own accord to rid him of his shirt and undo his zipper, freeing his hard cock. I've never thought dicks were fun to look at but his, it's fucking gorgeous. I lick my lips wanting nothing more than to taste him. I'm eager to see if I can take all of him.

He smacks my ass harder than expected. "Fuck." His fingers dig into me as he groans into my mouth. His fingers fill me to the brim.

My pussy greedily clenches wishing it were his fat cock in me instead.

"God, take what you want." I gasp the words, needing him to fill me. Whether it be my mouth or my pussy, I want him.

A guttural *fuck* rips from his throat. He leans his forehead against mine, never stopping his fingers that now piston in and out of my tight center.

I'm panting into his mouth as he continues to work my body.

Gripping his shaft, I jerk and rub my fingers up and down, never missing a beat.

We're nothing but a flurry of fingers and mouths as we taste and tease one another. My skin is fevered with pure desire. This man is driving me crazy with lust.

I moan into his mouth again as his tongue seeks out mine, reuniting as if they're old friends. Sweeping in sync against one another in perfect harmony. God I'm so hot for him.

I angle myself so that I can take him in my mouth. His cock is so thick and long, I can hardly wrap my lips around it. His free hand fists my hair pushing my head down until he hits the back of my throat. He's so commanding and controlling, and something in me surrenders to it. It's not something I'm used to. Tears spring from the corners of my eyes but I fight through the burn of my lips stretching to take him in all the way.

I can hardly breathe as I work his cock with my tongue and lips, bringing him pleasure as he growls and thrusts his hips up to fuck my mouth. Precum beads at the head of his cock and I savor the taste as it spurts onto my tongue. It's a salty, earthy taste that I can't describe except to say I like it.

Pulling my head back, he slips from my mouth. "I'm not ready to come yet, sweetheart. Not until I've been balls-deep in that cunt."

His dirty talk would be a turn off coming from anyone else, but this guy just has this sexiness and confidence that has me completely captivated.

"Aren't you getting married?"

"That's my brother."

I pant as his fingers continue to bring me close to orgasming. "Fuck it then."

"That's what I plan on doing." He whispers the words against my mouth and replaces his fingers with the head of his cock.

Forcefully, he slams into me and I cry out in a wave of pleasure and pain. He already had me stretched from finger-fucking me but not nearly enough for the size of him. I ache between my thighs in the most delicious of ways.

Over and over his body slaps against mine as he pounds into me.

"So tight."

Pound.

Thrust.

"So hot and wet for me."

Laughter bubbles in my throat but quickly dies down when his darkened eyes meet mine. He's looking at me like a man possessed, with nothing on his mind but dominating my body. Bending me into every position, he takes me hard, without mercy, pulling my orgasm from me precisely like a skilled surgeon.

His smooth body weighs me down as he comes at me from

behind. One hand teases my clit while the other fists my hair. He bites down on my shoulder as he pistons in and out. All I can hear are wet smacking sounds of flesh on flesh echoing through the room.

I can barely catch my breath as he brings my head back and captures my swollen lips with his eager mouth. His tongue dominates mine in the most delicious fashion.

Chapter Four

BRODIE

The way her tight cunt squeezes around my cock is incredible. She fits me perfectly, like a glove. I've never wanted a woman so much in my life. I don't know what it is about her, but she must have a fucking kryptonite pussy because the moment I saw her I wanted her.

Maybe someone drugged that liquor bottle because every sense is heightened, and euphoria rips through my veins.

I'm on the brink of exhaustion, but the drive to feel her come all over my cock urges me on. I want her greedy, hot pussy milking my cock of every last drop when I shoot my load in her and claim what's mine.

I flip her over and hold her hips in place as she rides me. Right when she gets into a rhythm, I thrust up as hard as I can. Her eyes go back in her head as she clenches around me. The feel of her arousal spilling down the sides of my legs does something to me. My balls tighten and lift. I hold it back with everything I have. Finally, my cock kicks hard, and I blow right up in her tight hole, filling her completely.

Her gorgeous eyes flutter open as she collapses on my chest.

I trace a finger along the soft curves of her back. "That was—"

"Wrong." She lifts up, and a look of horror washes across her face. "I have to go. Oh my god I can't believe I fucked you."

"You know it was good." I quirk my brow at her, leaning up on my elbow as she struggles to get dressed.

"Yeah, it was—fuck." She scrambles for part of her outfit. "I don't normally do this." She waves a hand between us.

"Do what? Fuck a stranger like a champ?"

"Sleep around on the job. And I wouldn't call it the best of my life." She smirks.

It's all for show.

"Please. Your pussy is begging for more already." I stroke my dick, and her mouth practically waters.

She shakes her head and looks away. "I need to go." Her voice cracks and I know I almost have her where I want her.

"You need to come sit on my face." I grin when she looks over, drops her clothes, and slinks back onto the bed.

I never lose. In the bedroom or the courtroom. I know how to run shit. Bringing this woman to the best orgasm of her life will be no different.

Laying her back on the bed, I spread her legs wide. It makes me so fucking hard when I watch my come spill out of her cunt. I massage it into her skin and flick her clit with my tongue as she spreads her pussy lips for me.

In one long lick, I sweep my tongue from her ass to her clit. It's probably not the smartest thing I've ever done in my life, fucking a random stripper who was meant for my brother at his bachelor party. Right now, though, I'm too caught up in the moment. Too tangled up in her to care.

I slide a finger in, hitting her spot just right as my tongue strokes across her.

Her hips arch up off the bed and I increase the tempo.

The last thing I remember is her fingers in my hair and her baited breaths as her orgasm rolls through her body.

———

My head pounds when I come to the next day. I don't recognize my surroundings and stumble from the bed in search of a bathroom. I'm about to race like a pisshorse. Yeah, I say it backward because I find it funny.

I fumble with the light switch, falling into the open doorway of the private bathroom.

Slapping some water on my cheeks, I try to remember where the hell I am and what I did last night to have my tongue so damn sore. I uncap the toothpaste and squirt some on my finger and rub it across my teeth. My tongue feels dry as sandpaper.

Catching a glimpse of my disheveled appearance in the mirror, I do a double take at the lipstick marks on my throat.

When I walk back into the bedroom, the only trace of another person is some dark sparkly sequences on the white rug.

What did I drink last night? Everything is a blur.

Downstairs in the kitchen I run into Pike.

The night before rushes back to me in a blurry haze. Strippers and liquor.

"Wondered what happened to you." He eyes me over the top of his newspaper.

"I think someone drugged me."

"Hah. Lot of drugs floating around last night. Not entirely out of the realm of possibility." He snickers into his coffee.

"It's not funny, dick."

"Relax. You didn't die."

My skin blazes where the lipstick-stained bruise covers my neck. "At least tell me she was hot."

He nods. "People weren't too happy about you stealing their entertainment."

I nod and slowly pour myself a cup of coffee. I feel fucked ten ways to Sunday. I don't even know what day it is right now.

Chapter Five

APRIL

I massage my temples. It feels like someone's jamming a knife into my brain. I don't know what came over me last night. It was completely out of character for me. I don't shit where I eat. Meaning I don't get involved with men I take my clothes off for. Sure, they're paying, but only to see the goods, not taste and touch them.

My thighs squeeze together as I remember blurred details of the night before.

I don't even know the guy's full name and I let him come in me like it was no big deal.

I had to have been drugged. There's no other explanation for it. I mean, I think he was hot. What I can remember of him was anyway, but I don't fuck around like that.

I enjoy being a single girl in the city.

I hear Jenny and Michael giggling from her bedroom, and every sound they make amplifies in my head. The Aspirin I took isn't helping. It's making me nauseous.

I think about taking more meds, but I feel dizzy and find myself retching in the trashcan next to my bed.

I'm never drinking again. It was embarrassing enough that Ben had to come find me when it was time to leave the party. A party I barely remember. I know I'm not the first to let things go too far, but it sucks that he saw me like that. I kind of liked him. I didn't want to date him or anything because we work together, but I always thought maybe if I saved up enough to get out of the stripping game I'd want to give him my number.

That likely won't happen now. He probably thinks I'm a dirty whore. I feel like one right now. Driving home even seems to have slipped my mind.

How could I be so irresponsible?

The following day when I go into work, Rod asks to see me in his office.

"Must have put on quite a performance the other night. My friend tipped you extremely well, and he wants to see you again."

I freeze in place.

"You okay?"

"Just tired."

"When can I set this up?"

"I'm not a hooker. I don't think it's a good idea. You know how clingy and weird some of the customers get."

"If that's what you want." He stares out the window. "The guy's loaded."

"Not interested. Maybe Julia."

"He requested you."

I give him a tense smile as he hands me an envelope stuffed with money. "Earnings from the party."

My mouth drops then snaps shut as I take in the amount of hundred dollar bills. There's got to be over five thousand dollars.

For a brief moment, the temptation of saving up for my business almost swallows me whole, but I swore I'd never fuck for money, and I'm not about to start now. I may be a stripper, but I have integrity. Even if it was absent for one night.

Chapter Six

TWO MONTHS LATER

"You sure you don't want me to take you to a doctor? This is the third morning you've been puking everywhere."

"I'm fine." *I'm not fine.*

Jenny waits patiently on the other side of the door for the shower. "Okay."

Her voice trails off. I wish she'd leave me alone to die. I feel awful. My sense of smell and my taste buds are off. I'm probably coming down with a virus again. One of the girls at work was sick with it last week. Said her kids brought it home from school.

My insides finally stop gurgling and I move to the sink to wash my face. When I go to grab a washcloth, my untouched box of tampons catches my eye.

Attempting to count back in my head, I can't remember my last period. I haven't had sex since—

No.

Please no.

I clap a hand over my mouth and tears well up in the corners of my eyes.

I can't even think the word as my chest threatens to break out in hives.

I'm going to be sick all over again.

This can't be happening.

It has to be a virus.

Opening the medicine cabinet, I look to see if I have any antibiotics from the last time I was sick a few months ago.

No dice.

I just need to suck it up and go to the doctor. They'll write me a prescription and I'll be good as new.

I stare at my reflection in the mirror and stare at the dark circles under my eyes. Guess I'm not sleeping well either.

I hate to miss a night of work, but I need to take a day off. Whatever this is, it's kicking my ass.

———

I not-so-patiently wait for the doctor to see me. The nurse insisted I do a pregnancy test even though I assured her it isn't possible. I'm on birth control and I'm not sexually active. It's dumb. I can't be pregnant, but when the doc comes into the exam room grinning like a fool, I know something is up. You don't smile like that when you're about tell someone they need antibiotics and chicken broth.

He hands me a sucker and a bunch of pamphlets that I can't bring myself to look at. I don't need to look to know what they are.

My heart surges up into my throat.

I'm pregnant by a man I don't even know. A man I had sex with one time at a fucking bachelor party. How's that for how I met your father?

Nope. I can't do this.

The walls threaten to close in around me.

"This isn't possible. I-I'm on the pill."

"I took a look at your chart. You were on some antibiotics that could have interfered with your birth control, making it less effective. It happens more often than you'd think."

I wish the floor would open up and swallow me whole.

I can't have a baby with a stranger.

I don't even know his name.

Shame washes over me as I try to fight through the tears falling steady as rain down my cheeks.

Chapter Seven

BRODIE

Two months later

"Mr. Hunter? Your next appointment is here. She's waiting in your office."

"Thanks." I straighten my tie and walk in to see a gorgeous woman waiting for me.

Our eyes meet across the desk as I hold out my hand to her. I could swear I've met her before. Surely, I'd remember someone so gorgeous.

"Brodie Hunter. What can I do for you?" I glance down at my appointment book.

"April." She stares down at the table. "I spoke to your secretary, but I don't think she understood why I wanted to meet with you."

"You're a former employee of Sheer Fantasy? That correct?"

"Yeah." She tries to force a smile.

Reading people is what I do, and something slams into the pit of my stomach.

I can't stop staring at her. I cant my head slightly to the side and take her in. "I'm not sure what I can do for you, but have we met before? I get this feeling like I know you."

Her fake smile falters and she hesitates to answer. "I, umm, I don't know. It could be possible. You ever go to the club? I was the spotlight dancer."

I don't remember ever going into that shithole. "No." I tap my chin and look around to make sure nobody is watching us. "Maybe at a party or something? My brother had a bachelor party a while back and there were, umm, performers."

Her face flushes and her chest grows red.

"You don't look so great. Can I get you a water or something?"

Her slender hand goes to her throat. "Water would be good." Her voice cracks when she speaks.

What the fuck is going on here?

"No problem." I go over to the minifridge and take out two bottles, handing one to her.

"Thanks." She fumbles with the lid, refusing to look up at me. "About the, umm, party?"

I stare off at the wall and shake my head. "Did something happen? How can I help you?"

"I want to sue Rod and his company for wrongful termination and for stuff they stole from me and refused to return."

I take a step back and hold up my hands. "Look, I represent Rod and his business interests. You'd want to find a different lawyer. It'd be a conflict of interest for me."

"I'm not really in the financial position to be paying legal fees now that I no longer have employment. Don't you represent his employees too?"

Twisting the cap off my water I take a drink. "You're not really an employee any longer, right? Why'd he fire you?" I shouldn't even be discussing this, but it's more entertaining than the rest of my day.

"He said I was too fat and unattractive to work for him."

My brows knit together. "He said what? You're gorgeous." *Well, there goes being appropriate.* I straighten up. "Any witnesses willing to back up your story?"

"Yeah." Her chair moves back, and I catch sight of her stomach. It looks like a pregnancy bump.

I fight the urge to cough and take another drink of my water too fast. It goes down the wrong pipe and I start choking. "Sorry. Shit. Excuse me."

Personally, I can see where Rod's coming from, making her take off work until after she's had the baby. It's an asshole move for sure, but, not many men are willing to pay to see a pregnant woman get naked. It ruins the fantasy. "So, you're pregnant?" I make an uncomfortable face and hook my finger on the collar of my shirt in an attempt to get some air flowing.

I'm starting to sweat. This isn't the shit I signed up for. Saying the 'p word' can be fatal if you mention it to a woman and you're wrong. I need to know the facts, though.

Actually, I don't. I should send her ass right out of my office. But, something about her... I just can't put a finger on it. I want to help her for some reason I can't explain. My brother and I pride ourselves on being assholes who love three things—power, pussy, and money.

"Correct. I'm pregnant. Not handicapped. I can still dance, and he owes me for the costumes his skanky girlfriend stole from my locker. I designed them myself. He refused to let me on the property to get my things. The only thing he gave me back was some glitter. Those costumes were invaluable to me. I'm out of work and unable to pay my bills. I have a month left if I'm lucky before my bank account is drained, and I have a kid on the way."

"It is totally none of my business, but what about the father? Is he able to help?"

She shakes her head and looks at the floor.

Why am I still entertaining this episode of Jerry Springer in my office? Maybe I'm going soft.

"Tell you what I can do. Rod's a client and a friend. I'll talk to him for you. Maybe I can get him to give your stuff back and find you some work. You'll have to meet him halfway. I doubt he's going to let you dance. I'm sure it's going to be a pay cut, but it's better than nothing until you figure out what you want to do. If you'll leave your contact information, I'll give you a call when I have news."

There's a hint of a smile on her face, and somehow it makes me feel that warm fuzzy shit in my stomach that makes me think I just sprouted a vagina.

She walks toward the door. "Thank you, Mr. Hunter."

"Just call me Brodie. I'll be in touch."

Great. Now I get to do some bullshit that's going to take my time and effort. And why? Why am I helping this woman? I deserve a humanitarian award. I'm definitely not saying shit to my brother about it.

———

"Business or pleasure?" Rod walks over to the bar and head nods for me to join him.

"I wish it was pleasure." I accept a rocks glass of whiskey.

It's the middle of the day and the girls on the stage aren't anything to write home about.

I look around the club and have to say Rod has done well for himself. For a strip club, the place is pretty classy. High-end bar and a full house. Mainly middle-aged lonely bastards but they spend money.

I quirk an eyebrow up at him. "One of your former employees stopped by my office this morning. Said you fired her for being pregnant."

"I'm running a business not a charity. Men come here for a fantasy. If they want to see their pregnant girlfriend, they can stay home." He grins.

"Said your girlfriend stole her costumes."

"Fine, I'll get her shit back and find something for her to do if she wants. She's still hot, but I can't let her dance. She can take the stage once she pops the kid out—if she keeps her, umm, form. She was my headliner. But the weight started coming on, and I lost a few customers. It's the nature of the business. Surprised you didn't recognize her."

"What?"

"She's that piece of ass you were chasing at your brother's party. I'd still fuck her, but the customers want big tits and a tight ass. Not a baby bump in their face. Well, ninety-nine percent of them anyway."

My stomach twists into knots, remembering her face when I asked her about the bachelor party and the father of her child.

"So, is the bitch gonna sue me?"

My jaw ticks. Part of me rages when he says he'd still fuck her. I have no claim on her, but I have a sinking feeling that baby in her belly could be mine. I knew she looked fucking familiar. Fucking Pike and all the goddamn drugs at his party.

"No." I shake my head. "I told her I'd talk to you. I'm going to level with you. She *could* sue and probably win with a halfway decent asshole for an attorney. You don't want a bunch of feminists going after you in the media. It could turn into a real shit show, fast. My sister-in-law would eat you alive in the courtroom on this. My advice, pay her a month's salary and return the clothes or buy them from her. Maybe even give her some kind of work to keep her busy."

Rod rubs his chin and downs the rest of his drink. "I'll cut her a check. You can deliver it to her. Just make sure she signs that she won't come after me."

"Done." I let out a sigh of relief. One problem down. "You happen to know how far along she is?"

"Why?" He chuckles.

I shrug. "Just curious."

"I don't know, man, maybe four or five months."

I nod as I try to do the math in my head.

Rod writes a check, and I have another drink contemplating my next move.

Did she know who I was when she came into my office? Is that why she was being so weird?

My stomach churns as I take the check, tucking it in my inner jacket pocket.

Stopping off at the drugstore, I buy some antacids. My chest is tight. Feels like I'm having a goddamn heart attack.

Cold sweat drips down my back as I make my way back to my office.

My brother calls out to me from across the hall.

"You okay? Don't look so hot."

"Actually, you got a minute?"

"The fuck did you do now?" He smirks.

"Don't be an asshole."

"Impossible. Close the door."

I do as he says and collapse on the couch.

"Who is she?"

"What?"

"The look on your face says one thing. You had a bout with kryptonite pussy."

I glare over at him and flip him the bird. "Don't use my own shit on me."

He smiles his pecker off.

I shake my head and stare up at the ceiling. "I think I knocked her up."

Weston goes into a coughing fit. I expected him to be pissed, but it looks like he's laughing.

Motherfucker.

He finally stops and tries to maintain his composure. "So, who's the lucky lady to birth the next Hunter heir?"

I groan, not wanting to answer, but I need his advice. "Remember that stripper from your party."

He's shaking, and his face is beet red, trying to hold back the laughter.

I start to get up. "Fuck this."

"Sit down. Don't be a bitch. You'd be doing the exact same thing to me right now. I only get one shot at this. Gotta make it count."

"Like I don't have enough fucking problems right now." I drop down on the couch and hold my face between my palms.

"So, it's that hot piece of ass you couldn't remember fucking? The one who turned down your offer to see her again? Who was actually meant to entertain me, and you snaked your way in?"

"I see what you did there."

"Thanks. I was pretty proud of it."

I explain to him about her coming in, and that I think maybe she was drugged that night too. We were drinking out of the same bottle.

"Damn."

I kick my feet up on his expensive ass pillows Brooke got him.

"My advice. Invite her to dinner to deliver the check and talk to her. She may be just as freaked as you are. Chances are the kid isn't even yours. But if it is, you need to man the fuck up and do the right thing. We aren't bitches in this family. And we take care of our own. If that's your kid, then it's my niece or nephew and a future heir to this company."

I know he's right but saying and doing are two different things.

Chapter Eight

APRIL

"**D**inner? Umm—" Cupping my growing belly, I feel conflicted. I'm a hundred percent certain he's the father of my child. I hadn't been with anyone else. His statement about trying to find the girl from the party makes me wonder if he recognized me too.

I've been contemplating what to say to him since I saw him in his office. The minute I laid eyes on him something in me just knew. It was his eyes that gave him away. The night we shared, though blurry, still made an impression. My body ached for days after we were together. An ache that said he owned my body that night. And in a way I guess he still does. I'm carrying his child.

"Miss King. You still there?"

I blink my eyes, breaking from my thoughts. "Sorry. Dinner. Sure." I can only utter one-word sentences like an idiot.

"You like steak?"

My belly growls at the thought of a big juicy steak. "Steak? Yeah. Sounds great."

"Perfect. Can you meet me there or do I need to send a car for you?"

"I can drive. Just text me where and the time."

"Great. See you soon."

"Yeah." The line goes dead, and I feel ready to vomit. I thought I was over the whole morning sickness crap.

Oh god! What am I going to wear? I'm fat. Well, I'm pregnant but I feel like a whale.

Going over to my closet, I yell for Jenny.

Her head pokes around my bedroom doorway. "What's up?"

"I need you to help me find something to wear that doesn't make me look like Violet when she turns into a blueberry in Willy Wonka."

Jenny rolls her eyes. "You aren't big. You just have a baby in your belly." She grins and puts her hands on my stomach. "Ain't that right, peanut?"

"If this baby comes out thinking its name is peanut, you're paying for his therapy."

Her brows quirk up. "Did you find out the sex?"

I shake my head. "No, I just—I feel like it will be a boy. I want a boy. Girls are drama."

Jenny laughs and rifles through my clothes. "You could probably make some badass maternity clothes. You have the talent and the skills."

"There's an idea. Maybe I can sell them to cover my half of the rent." I frown, and Jenny grabs my hands.

"Things will turn around. You'll find another job. If worst comes to worst, I'll ask my dad for a loan."

"Not gonna happen. You've already done too much."

"You're my best friend. It's what friends do. We look out for each other."

"I'm not your responsibility. I got myself into this situation. It's just no one wants to hire a pregnant stripper. Doesn't exactly look great on a resume."

"Everything's gonna be fine. Don't stress. It's not good for the baby. And wear this. Red looks great on you." She smiles and pulls a red tunic off a hanger with black leggings. "What's the occasion anyway? Who are you meeting with that has you worried about what you're going to wear?"

I should probably tell her about Brodie Hunter, but I don't want to say anything until I'm sure.

"The lawyer I went to see about suing Rod for wrongful termination."

"Is this a date?" Her brows wiggle.

I shove at her playfully, moving her out the door so I can change. "No. It's about my case."

"Right." She draws out the syllable. "That's why you have that dreamy look in your eyes."

"Don't."

"April has a crush." She singsongs her words like a twelve year old as she goes back down the hall.

April doesn't have a crush. April has a big fucking dilemma.

How the hell am I going to tell this guy, *"hey by the way you don't remember me, but we fucked, and your baby is growing inside me"*? That's not going to send him running for the hills.

I finish getting ready and decide to just get the shit over with.

The text he sent said Hidalgos' at seven. I've never eaten there but I've heard it's amazing. I hope I'm not underdressed. With my expanding waistline I don't have as many clothes these days. I had to use my savings to pay for my prenatal appointments.

Checking my makeup in the visor mirror, I make sure I look presentable. Running my fingers through my long blonde hair, I smile at my reflection and give myself a mental pep talk.

I'm a rock star.

I can do this.

Fuck.

I don't want to go in there, but a tiny flutter in my stomach reminds me that this isn't about me. I have a life growing inside me who is depending on me to make the right choices.

I feel like I don't belong the moment I enter the restaurant. I'm definitely underdressed. I don't fit in. The hostess makes it apparent as she sneers at me when I approach her podium.

"Hi, umm, Hunter party of two." I hold up two fingers like a dummy.

"This way, please. He's waiting at the bar until your table is ready."

I follow her, feeling eyes on me and my stomach as I make my way through the crowded bar.

Brodie immediately stands when he sees me walking over.

All the air sucks from my lungs with each of his steps toward me. "You came."

I bob my head up and down, unsure of what to say.

"Something to drink?"

"That'd be great."

His hand moves to the small of my back. It feels too intimate for this to be strictly business. The gesture should make me nervous, but in a way, it soothes me—his touch. His hand fits perfectly, inches above my ass.

"Are the stools okay?"

Brodie's going out of his way to make sure I'm comfortable. He's sweet. Gentle.

The bartender eyes my stomach and gives me a questioning look.

"Water with lemon, please."

The man shoots me a bashful smile, probably hoping he hasn't screwed himself out of a tip.

"I spoke with Rod. He has an offer. If you agree to the amount, I'll have you sign a document and hand over the check."

"Okay." Sipping my water, I wait for him to elaborate.

"I have a check for ten thousand at my office. If you'd like we can go there after dinner."

"I can't help but feel like there's a catch."

"There are a few minor details, but we can discuss those later. Right now, I want to get to know you."

Before I can muster a response, the hostess is back to inform us our table is ready.

Chapter Nine

BRODIE

I can't keep my eyes off April. She's beautiful. Maybe it's the fact that she might be carrying my kid, but she has this light about her. She fucking glows. I'm not the only one who sees how gorgeous she is. All the men, and some women, in the restaurant stare at her, envious. They think we're a couple, but that couldn't be further from the truth. We're two strangers who fucked. For now.

There's more to the deal I'm writing up for her, but the terms aren't Rod's. They're mine. If she's having my baby we have a lot to discuss and work out. This is a delicate situation. I hope the arrangement I seek will be agreeable for her.

The black pants she's got on are hugging her ass and it has my mind straight in the gutter imagining being behind her. An image of the party flashes through my mind. My fist in her hair. My mouth on hers as I took her from behind. *Fuck*, she is the one.

Our table is in a more secluded corner in the back. I wanted privacy but also wanted her to feel at ease by being out in public with me in case she's nervous.

Why hasn't she sought me out about the baby?

I don't know anything about her but that's the point of this dinner. I asked her here tonight to get to know her on a more personal level.

My head is ten kinds of fucked up right now.

Once we're seated and have placed our orders, silence stretches between us. Neither of us seems to know where to start.

"Do you know the sex of the baby yet?"

"No, but soon. I think I'm having a boy. The doctor hasn't confirmed it. It's just a hunch."

A few months ago, the thought of a son would have scared me shitless, but right now, looking at this woman before me, the idea is strangely exciting.

I'm still nervous about the idea of being responsible for another person. Fuck, I have a lot of freedom right now, only worrying about myself. But then, Weston settled down and got married. He'll be having children soon, and I want our kids to grow up together and be close in age.

The timing may not be perfect, but I feel like maybe it's happening for a reason. I don't know what that reason is yet, but I'm going to enjoy getting to know April whether she wants me in the picture or not.

She needs me even if she's too proud to admit it. I've spent the past few days poring over it all, trying to remember that night. The only thing clear to me is that I blew inside of her without a condom. I've done dumber things, but not many.

The waiter comes out with the first course, and we eat in a comfortable silence until she asks how I know Rod. I explain that we went to college together and she laughs when I tell her I think he's a dick.

Fashion and jewelry design are her passion. The bracelet on her left arm is one of her creations.

"Seem to have quite a talent. I don't know shit about jewelry, but it looks nice."

"That's what I was saving for. I wanted to open my own boutique, but life happened, and I needed money to cover my medical bills."

Guilt pangs in my chest that she's been doing this alone.

Our meal ends, and we still haven't tackled the elephant in the room.

"Are you ready to get out of here? I can drive us to my office and bring you back to your car after. We can discuss the details there, so you can see it all in fine print."

"You don't have to go to so much trouble. I can meet you there."

"Whatever you're comfortable with."

I pay the bill and escort her to her car, trying to resist the urge to kiss her. It seems crazy and wild but she's the sexiest pregnant woman I've ever seen. Something keeps pulling me to her. I'm definitely attracted to her the same way I was that night. I want to know all there is to know about her. Where's she from? Does she have siblings? Is she single?

"See you in a few. Drive safe."

A quick wave of her hand and she starts her car up as I close the door for her. I watch her pull out then get into my own ride and head back to the office.

It's after hours and the place is empty, just as I'd hoped. I'm sure what I'm about to propose may very well piss her off.

The idea I have is a crazy one, but I've thought on it, and it's what I want.

I unlock the door and quickly reset the security system once April walks in.

Neither of us say anything as we ride in the elevator to my office but the tension between us could be cut with a knife and our eyes lock briefly. My lips curve into a smirk knowing I have an effect on her.

Chapter Ten

APRIL

W hen we step into the elevator, his scent envelopes me, and a wave of images nearly knocks me off my feet. His eyes lock on mine, and it's like opening up a locked chest. Memories of the night we spent together hit me hard. The desire, the passion—feeling him inside me. I'd never felt more wanted. More Alive.

Standing inches apart, I'm so tempted to lean into him and let nature take its course. Some things you can't fight. Like fate. You can't fight fate. Fate will always find a way.

His intense gaze pierces me. It shoots straight to my heart and down to my pussy. He looks like he feels it too. This magnetism drawing us closer.

He steps forward and I meet him, taking a step of my own. This is crazy. Insane even, but I can't deny the attraction that exists between us.

His fingers brush across my cheek. "I know you don't know me, but something's happening here."

Closing the gap between us, I part my lips in anticipation.

Quickly, his tongue darts out and runs over his lips.

Kiss me, I shout in my head.

Right when his lips hover over mine, the elevator dings open, breaking the spell.

He clears his throat, and I close my eyes briefly. When I open them, a man is waiting for us to exit the elevator.

"What are you doing here so late?"

The man's eyes widen, and an evil grin spreads across his face. "And who's this?" His eyes move to my stomach and back to his friend as his smile widens.

"Client. Contract to go over."

"I see. Well, got what I came for." He holds up a briefcase and we step around him.

He steps into the elevator. "See ya tomorrow, big guy." He winks.

"Fucking Weston and his big mouth." Brodie mutters the words to himself.

"What?"

Squinting, he pinches the bridge of his nose. "Nothing."

I follow him down the hall sensing a change in him. His shoulders hunch forward and he rolls his neck, rubbing it, as though he's now tense.

The moment that transpired between us is long gone.

"Have a seat." He extends his hand toward an intimate seating area to the side that overlooks the city.

"Quite a view." I remain standing, enjoying the picturesque night-time Dallas skyline.

Instead of taking his seat, he walks over and stands next to me.

"It's nice." His jaw ticks as he speaks.

"I bet you feel on top of the world. Up here looking down..." I press my palms on the glass and look below at the city lights wondering what to say next.

"We both know we have something else to discuss."

I gulp and my breath hitches. He knows, or at least suspects.

"Yeah. You wanna start, or should I?"

He sighs. "Let's sit."

"Okay." I follow him back to the chairs.

He takes one and I take the other.

Brodie turns to me, our knees touching as he takes my hands. Electricity sparks between us and his eyes shine, telling me he feels it too. We share an undeniable attraction.

He stares at me long and hard. "Is it mine?"

Tears burn in the corners of my eyes and I don't know why. It's a simple question with an easy answer. *Hormones*. It has to be the pregnancy hormones making me so weepy. Emotions are a bitch, and everything about this amplifies times a thousand.

I suck in a breath and close my eyes trying to fight the tears. "Yeah." I whisper the word. "It's yours. I know you don't know me or if I am telling the truth. But I wouldn't lie about this."

"I believe you. I think someone put drugs in the bottle we shared. Everything's a blur."

I wipe my eyes. "Makes sense. A lot about that night was a fog until I walked into your office a few days ago."

"Is that why you hadn't told me?"

"It's a little embarrassing not remembering who you slept with. Can't exactly go door to door."

Tenderly, he tilts my chin up, forcing me to meet the seriousness of his gaze. "You aren't in this alone. Not anymore. That's what I want to talk to you about. Rod wrote you a shit check, he's a dick, but I want to make you an offer."

"What?" I ask, confused by his words. "An offer. For what?"

"I've thought long and hard about what I'd say to you. I don't want you to take this the wrong way. I know you probably weren't planning on getting pregnant by a random stranger at a party."

"It was some antibiotics I'd taken. They counteracted against my birth control. Lucky us." I laugh bitterly and wipe my eyes. I love the baby growing inside me, but I wasn't prepared for this. I wasn't prepared to care for Brodie in a way I'm not sure I understand, but hearing him say he wants to be a part of this journey with me—it means a lot.

Growing up in foster care I always felt alone. Like I didn't have anyone else in the world who gave a damn about me. I was just another kid in the system being shuffled from home to home. Jenny and I only met because I'd posted an ad looking for a roommate when my loser boyfriend at the time cut and run, sticking me with all the bills.

She wanted to get out from under her daddy's thumb. She wanted freedom from her family. She comes from a very religious upbringing. If they knew I was a stripper, they'd cut her off or force her to move back home.

"What's done is done. Here we are. You said you were low on money. I want you to know that I'll step up and do what's right. If you marry me, I can get you and the baby on my insurance. It'd be a marriage on paper. I'm not asking out of love, but convenience. I want you to live with me. I'll take care of you and the baby. I'll even look into setting you up with your boutique store."

My smile falters. I wasn't expecting those words to come from him. I don't know what I thought he'd say, but he wants to set me up just like a sugar daddy would. I frown as I stare up at his piercing eyes. "You can't *buy* me."

"Look, I don't mean for it to come off cold like that. Like I'm buying you. But that baby is part of me. I want to be in my child's life. You said yourself you aren't in a financial situation that leaves you with a lot of options. Let me take that burden away. Marry me and move into my apartment. You'll have a great life. Who knows, somewhere along the way we might actually like each other. I'd like to be your friend."

I get where he's coming from but shake my head at the same time. I guess there's still a part of me wishing for a fairytale. For a man who loves me without a doubt. "It sounds great and everything. But what happens if you meet someone else? Someone you want to marry and have a real family with?"

"You're not even going to consider this? I'm offering you everything."

"But not your heart. I want to marry someone for love not money."

"Okay. So don't marry me. Just move in with me. I want us to do this together. I don't want to miss out on anything. I want us to have a partnership. Agree to move in with me and I'll invest in your business."

"What if I'm terrible at what I do. Why would you risk it?"

"Everyone deserves someone who believes in them. You don't have anyone in your corner. Let me be that for you. Do it for our baby. You know our child deserves the best life we can give him or her."

Indecision weighs on me. It's all too much at once. "I have a roommate who depends on me. I can't just up and leave her."

"You don't have to decide right now. Take a few days or a week." He takes my hands in his. "I'm making you a great offer. I have the means to support you and the baby. I take care of what's mine."

"I'm not yours." I shake my head. Yet, at the same time I war with myself. I can't pass this up. I have to put my own shit aside and do what's right for the baby. He or she is all that matters. That's what happens when you're going to be a parent. I look up at his pleading eyes. "Where do I sign?"

Chapter Eleven

BRODIE

E verything is happening fast. My brother thinks I'm crazy. So do Jaxson and Maxwell. Maybe I am but they didn't knock up a stripper. It's easy to coach from the sidelines.

I gave April a week to get her affairs sorted. Today is the day. Move in day.

I've been in court all afternoon and been unable to supervise what's happening at my place. I've never lived with a woman other than my mother, so I have no fucking clue what I'm getting myself into, but I meant what I said. I *will* take care of April. I have to. It's the one constant in my life that I know to be true.

Jaxson has been riding my ass because I didn't ask for a paternity test. I don't know how I know but I feel it in my gut that this baby is mine.

I should be terrified but the idea of having a sexy woman like April waiting for me at home with my kid on her hip at the end of the day excites me. I can't help how I feel. I never in a million years thought I'd want something like that, but now that it's happening—I can't deny the allure.

It's like I just aged ten years in a matter of days.

The first thing I did when she signed the agreement was set her up with a doctor that Maxwell represents. He's the best gyno-whatever in Dallas. And I only want the best for the mother of my child. They'll have nothing less.

Weston and Brooke are coming over for dinner to help ease some of the awkward tension between April and me. They need to get to know her too. She's going to be in my life for the next eighteen years at least. I didn't ask her to move in with me lightly. I know I'm taking a chance that we won't be compatible, but I'm hoping we can be friends and raise this child in a happy and loving home. April doesn't know it, but I had a detective I know look into her. It was one of the first things I did after the shock of her being pregnant wore off.

I don't do anything without all the facts. That's how you get fucked. It's a life lesson I learned early.

She grew up in foster care and was lost between the cracks of the system. Her father died in prison. He was incarcerated on drug-related charges. Her mother was a teen mom and unable to care for her. She still lives here in Dallas. I don't know if April has contact with her, but it doesn't appear that she does.

When I open the door, she's settled on the couch reading a pregnancy book. The sight makes me smile because I had them delivered this morning and I wasn't sure how the gesture would be received. Truth be told, I ordered them for me. I want to know everything there is to know about being a dad. I refuse to be a shitbag father. I don't do anything halfway. Don't give a fuck if I have to dress up like Iron Man or have tea parties. It'll happen. My kid will *always* smile.

April's blonde hair is in a braid that lays to the right side of her shoulder and I have the desire to undo it and run my fingers through the silky strands.

She's gorgeous and I'd be a liar if I said I don't find her attractive. I know we're compatible between the sheets, but personality wise I don't know. She's pretty damn stubborn. Doesn't seem to like being told what to do. I don't much like explaining myself about anything.

We'll just have to get to know each other and see where things lead.

"Hey." A big yawn escapes her throat as she closes the book and smiles over the back of the couch at me.

"Settling in okay?" I set my briefcase down and loosen my tie.

"I am. But seriously, you shouldn't go to so much trouble for me. I can cook my own meals." Her eyes shift in the direction of the kitchen where Klaire, my housekeeper and personal chef currently makes dinner.

"My brother and his wife are coming down for dinner." I take off my jacket.

"Down?"

"They live a floor above us. Jaxson, the guy from the office the other night is two floors below us and Maxwell has a floor as well. We own the building together."

"You own the building?"

"Yeah." I grin. "I told you, I can take care of you." Going over to the couch, I kneel next to her and place my hands on the bump. "How's daddy's princess today?"

April smacks my hand. "It's a boy."

"Well we'll know for sure next week, won't we? I got you an appointment with Doctor Reynolds."

"I have a doctor already."

"My guy is better."

She rolls her eyes, and I have a sudden urge to bend her over my knee and spank that ass of hers.

"I'm going to take a quick shower. You need anything? Room okay?"

"I'm fine. Klaire has asked me a thousand times if I need anything."

"It's her job to make sure you're okay when I'm not here."

She sighs. "I'm just not used to all this—the housekeeper, luxury apartment. A private driver. It—it's not me."

"You'll get used to it."

She grumbles something under her breath. It's like a sexy purr and makes my cock hard as fuck.

I stalk off to the shower to tend to the growing issue in my pants. If I get my way, April will be taking care of it...sooner rather than later.

Chapter Twelve
APRIL

"How'd you two crazy kids meet?" Brooke glances at me.

Brodie coughs and glares at his brother Weston. He's definitely the more athletic of the two brothers, but Brodie is more handsome.

"At a party. I took one look at him and I was smitten." It isn't a complete lie.

"I'm surprised Brodie hasn't brought you around before now."

"I like to keep her to myself." He shoots me a smile, and his brother shakes his head. He obviously knows how we met. It's nice that he's letting us have our little fake story. Not that I really care if Brooke knows the truth, but it's nice that she doesn't stare at me like some whore stripper looking for a handout.

"Is anyone planning a baby shower?"

Her question catches me off guard. Jenny is really my only friend and I had to leave her with the apartment, even though she told me not to worry about it. Michael agreed to move in with her. I don't know if she's really the type to throw a baby shower, though.

"Not that I know of. I can ask my friend Jenny. I honestly don't think I need one at the rate Brodie is moving. He'll have his or her wardrobe bought up until they graduate."

Weston laughs, and Brodie narrows his eyes on me.

"Don't give him shit." She turns to Brodie. "I think it's sweet that you want your baby to have the best of everything." Brooke stares at her husband. "I'm sure you'll be the same way when we start our family."

His face pales and Brodie grins at him.

"Yeah, brother. When you gonna get started on a family? Better get busy. I want our kids to grow up together."

"We haven't discussed it, but I'd like to have my wife to myself for a few more years." Weston brings her hand to his mouth and kisses her knuckles. The man obviously adores his wife.

"Want to enjoy your freedom." Brodie mutters his response and chuckles at the same time.

A knock sounds at the door and Weston gives Brodie a devilish grin.

Brodie excuses himself and opens the door to two dudes. One of which I saw at the office. Jaxson, I believe.

"Aren't you going to invite us in so we can congratulate you and the lady we all know nothing about?" They both walk past Brodie.

Weston grins his ass off.

Brodie comes to stand behind my chair, placing a comforting hand on either of my shoulders.

"Maxwell, Jaxson, meet April. There, you've met. Now get out."

"Ouch." Maxwell ignores him and holds a hand out to me.

"Isn't she the client you had with you at the office last week?" Jaxson grabs a beer from the refrigerator like he owns the place and walks back over.

What am I getting myself into?

"Hey, I remember you. Weren't you at—" Before he can say more, Weston smacks him in the gut.

Brooke tosses her napkin down on the table. "Okay, what's going on?" She gives Weston a side eye that says he'll be in trouble if he doesn't tell the truth. As far as I'm aware, he did nothing wrong, but then again, I don't remember a whole lot about that night other than I conceived a child.

"April's an exotic dancer. I hired her for Weston but when I saw her I took her for myself. One thing led to another and now here we are. Happy now, assholes? You all have the full story."

I want to crawl into a room somewhere and die.

Brooke looks across at me and then back at them. "Why was that a secret? You think I'd be mad that there were strippers at a bachelor party? Jesus."

Weston shrugs and Maxwell and Jaxson look embarrassed. I think they all like to give each other shit, but this time maybe they went too far.

"Well this was fun, but I'm calling it a night." Brooke leans over the table and stares at me.

She looks kind of evil and I don't think I want on her bad side.

"Don't take any shit from these *boys*." She glares back at all of them. "We'll do lunch soon. I'm throwing you the best baby shower Dallas has ever seen. It was nice to meet you." She stands up and points a finger at the rest of them. "Do whatever you want at the office, but stop being dicks or I'll chop them off. Understood?"

"Yes, ma'am," they all say in unison.

"What I thought." She stalks out of the room with Weston following behind.

I try to hide my smile, but it's impossible. I like her.

———

Lying in a bed across the hall from Brodie's room, I feel a bit like Julia Roberts in *Pretty Woman*.

Maybe it won't be so bad after all. Brooke seemed awesome. She didn't seem to judge me at all. That's the thing. None of them really seemed to judge me, other than the guys giving each other shit, which is normal for guys I guess. I wonder if Brodie is embarrassed by it. He seemed hesitant to tell Brooke. Maybe he thought I'd be uncomfortable with her knowing?

I'm so out of my element. I grew up in bad neighborhoods, and now I'm in a penthouse apartment that probably cost more than I could make in five lifetimes.

I don't want to mooch off Brodie and hope he meant it when he said he wants to invest in my business and be partners.

Brodie is complex and confusing. One minute he talks about wanting to be my friend, and the next he looks at me as though he wants to devour me.

Attraction and chemistry is there. I can see it in his eyes when we talk. He stares at my lips. Most men go straight to my tits or my ass but not him. I'm still coming to terms with the fact that I agreed to this insane arrangement.

Am I supposed to live with him for the next eighteen years? Or eventually, once the baby comes and I'm back on my feet, will he let our child and me move into a home of my choosing? I don't want to spend my life chained to a man who won't love me. Sure, being taken care of sounds nice but I've only been here for a few days and I'm already lonely even though he's across the hall.

Jenny drove me crazy at times, but I miss her. I'm so used to sharing my day with her.

Picking my cell phone up from the nightstand, I snap a picture of my new bedroom.

April: Can you believe this room?

Jenny: No wonder you moved out! Did you decorate or was it already like that?

April: Brodie asked me my favorite stuff a few days ago and today it was like this. I'm seriously crushing on him. I don't know what to do. He says he wants to get to know me and be my friend, but when he looks at me I swear he wants more.

Jenny: Well you have eighteen years to make him fall in love with you.

April: HA! Funny.

Jenny: Just saying ;)

April: You suck.

Jenny: Michael says I'm good at sucking :p

April: TMI – BTW have you told your folks he's moving in?

Jenny: Pfft no. You know how crazy they are.

April: True... I'll talk to you later...Brodie just knocked on my door...

Jenny: Don't leave me hanging too long. I'll come see you soon. Promise. I need to see your sugar daddy lifestyle in person.

Ugh! I do *not* have a sugar daddy. I shake my head and pad across the floor to the door.

Chapter Thirteen

BRODIE

"Need anything?"

April's gaze falls to my abs and down to my workout shorts. Maybe I can channel that physical attraction into something more. We're having a baby. I'd like us to have a real relationship. One our child can look up to. I don't want the night we made our child to be nothing but a meaningless fuck.

It's time I punch my bachelor card for good and think about settling down. A child is a lifetime of responsibility. I don't take it lightly. Only, I don't know what April wants. The easy thing would be to ask her, but I don't want her to feel obligated to be with me because of the kid, and I don't want her thinking that's the only reason I am wanting to try. My feelings for her are genuine. I've never felt this way around a woman.

I know I need to take my time and let things progress naturally. I need to woo her. Win her over. Show her that even though we only have a physical attraction right now, there can be so much more between us.

Running a towel over my sweaty head, I wait for her to reply. Her cheeks flush and she shakes her head ever so slightly.

"No, I'm good."

"Klaire will have breakfast ready in about ten minutes. I have a meeting, but after that I'll be free for the weekend. Thought maybe I could take you around and show you some buildings I have in mind for your boutique."

"Seriously?" Her whole face warms and she smiles.

Fuck, I could watch her smile like that every day. I'd spend the rest of my life trying to recreate that look on her face.

Her arms hook around my neck with gratitude and excitement. Soft and warm, her baby bump presses into my stomach. Releasing the towel I was using to dry my hair from my grip, I embrace her, holding her against me and breathing her in.

She pulls away, and I immediately feel cold all over. "Sorry. I, umm, got caught up in the moment for a sec. Are we really going to look for a place?"

I nod. "Uhh, yeah. I don't say shit I don't mean. I told you I believe in you. That smile looks good on you. Let's see if we can keep it there." I touch her nose lightly with the tip of my finger.

"This is all happening so fast."

I place a palm on each of her cheeks. "I *will* keep my word. Always. If I promise you something, I will deliver."

Her eyes close briefly. "Thank you. Just—" She sighs. "Thank you."

"Don't mention it. Have to find a building we like." I probably look like an idiot falling all over myself in front of her, but I don't give a shit. It's hard not to take her in my arms and kiss her breathless and senseless. She looks so damn sexy in her little booty-hugging shorts and tank top. The edge of her shirt is riding over her baby bump and I want to go down to my knees and kiss her navel, but I don't want to freak her out. "Anyway, be ready around one."

"Okay." She grins eagerly, and I head across the hallway to get dressed.

———

April and I spent the weekend touring several possible locations for her boutique but none of them felt right. Her determination and confidence in what she wants is a huge turn on. The woman is driven and wants to work. Weston was afraid that this arrangement would have her bleeding me dry. I felt it in my gut that it wouldn't be the case with her. It's nice to know I can read a situation better than him. She's special, and not because she has kryptonite pussy.

The location needs to be perfect. An area upstairs large enough for her to do her designs and house a nursery for our child. I told her we could hire a nanny, but she rejected the idea quickly, stating she wants to be the one raising her baby. I have a feeling she may change her mind when she tries to juggle a new business and a newborn. Ambitious is an understatement with her.

I keep the thought to myself. Her hormones have her emotions running high. I wouldn't say I walk on eggshells around her, but I choose my words and battles wisely.

Today is the day we find out the sex of our baby. I reworked my schedule to take the day off. I want to be with her every step of the way.

Stunning. Simply stunning is how I would describe the way she looks right now laying on the exam table with her dress rolled up over her bump. The technician is squirting some jelly on her stomach. Her blonde hair is fanned out around her head as she looks over at me wearing an anxious smile.

Reaching over, I take her hand in mine. I want her to know she has my support one hundred percent. Giving me a gentle squeeze back, I know she appreciates the gesture. A whooshing noise sounds, and the technician explains that that amazing thumping sound is our baby's heartbeat. It's so fast.

I've never been emotional in my life, but hearing that sound—it's like everything hits me at once. I'm completely overwhelmed with something I can't even describe. The tiny life we created together comes into focus on the screen and a tear trickles down my face. Chills buzz up and down my arms as I watch the screen.

"He looks like he's talking on the phone." April laughs.

"Do you want to know the sex?" The woman turns to us.

April bites her bottom lip and looks over at me. We'd talked about possibly waiting until birth on the way over here, but I have to know. The anticipation is about to do me in.

"Yes." I answer for both of us before April can respond.

The lady smiles and moves the wand around. "Congratulations. It's a boy."

April smirks at me. "Told you so."

"Yeah, yeah."

I'm having a son.

I'm having a son!

April's eyes linger on mine. I swallow as her warmth penetrates my hard walls. God, I want to kiss her and almost do, but then the technician hands me the printout of the pictures, interrupting the moment. I settle for bringing her hand to my lips, brushing them lightly over her palm.

April gives me a quizzical but happy look.

Chapter Fourteen

APRIL

My appointment with the new doctor went well. To celebrate finding out the sex of our baby, Brodie insisted on treating me to ice cream and a shopping trip to an upscale baby boutique.

I can't deny how adorable he is. He tries to buy the whole damn store. Insists we need everything and that he's going to have the immaculate apartment cleaned and sterilized from top to bottom.

I don't know why, but something feels like it's all too good to be true.

We're having a great time. It almost feels like we're a real couple. He's been sweet and affectionate. When we walk down the street he holds my hand wearing a goofy grin and stands between me and the street. I know he said he wanted a girl but the way his eyes lit up when the ultrasound technician told us we were having a boy, I know he is overjoyed at the prospect of a son to spoil. He's already talking about hunting trips and going fishing. He said something about wrestling. I guess he and his brother were both on the team in high school. They are definitely built like they were athletes.

As we come out of the baby boutique, a woman runs up to Brodie, squealing. Her arms fling around his neck and his eyes dance with shock and excitement. "Lisa. Wow. Long time no see."

"I just moved back last week. How are you? God, I've missed you." She pulls back to gaze into his eyes.

I know we're not together, but something inside me gets territorial. Maybe it's the hormones but I want to claw her eyes out for hugging him. Fuck, I'm a mess.

As they gush over one another, I feel completely forgotten and like a third wheel. I shouldn't be jealous but I am. The way they stand so close and pet each other like lovers would turns my stomach, and I feel the ice cream I had earlier creeping up my throat.

Brodie's driver is parked a few spaces down. Instead of standing there being awkward or making a scene, I quietly start for the car. That woman is classy and beautiful in a way I'll never be. Her outfit probably cost more than my whole wardrobe. Why did I think I stood a chance at making this into something real? He belongs with a woman like that. Not a one-night stand that anchored him with a baby.

"April?" Brodie hollers at me and I hesitate to turn around. I put on my best and bravest smile, hiding my unshed tears.

"I was just going to go to the car and give you some privacy."

The woman, Lisa, looks me over and her eyes immediately narrow on my bump that is growing larger by the day.

"Don't be crazy. I want Lisa to meet you." He stares at me like I've grown a second head.

I shuffle over to the pair of them.

"It's a pleasure to meet you." Her hand goes to my stomach and I flinch, not wanting her to touch me. Why do strangers think it's okay to grope a pregnant woman's belly?

"Sorry. Where are my manners? Are you two…?" Her eyes widen as she glances between us.

Brodie surprises me, securing an arm around my waist. "Lisa, this is April, the mother of my son." He beams with pride, but I notice he was careful not to put a label on me outside of mother of his baby. I can't blame him. I don't know why I'm being so weird about this. I never stopped to even wonder if he had someone. I mean, a man like him must have had a ton of relationships. Maybe Lisa is an ex.

"Congratulations." Her smile is as fake as her boobs.

"We should do lunch. I'd love to pick your brain about the business we're starting. Does your brother still have his real-estate company?" Brodie carries on with the conversation, totally oblivious to everything happening.

"Yeah." Her eyes dazzle at the invitation back into his life. Now she has a reason to contact him.

"Great. Call my office this week and we'll do lunch. I'm eager to start this project."

"Sounds great."

They exchange goodbyes and I follow Brodie to the car.

He wants to see her again. If he didn't he would have asked her to pass along his request.

I feel stupid because today I had let my guard down and thought that maybe we were starting to open up to each other.

"You want to catch a movie or something?"

I get in the car next to him. "Some other time. I'm tired. I think I need to lie down."

Thoughts of Brodie and her having lunch forces scenarios into my head that have me balling my hands into fists. Like I've lost something somehow, but I never really had him to start with.

His hand goes to my knee and gives me a gentle squeeze. "You okay?" His eyes show concern, but I'm pretty sure it's only because I have his son inside me.

"I'll be fine. You should probably call your friend and ask her to dinner or something. Get an early start on your project."

"You think so? You don't want to come?"

God, he's clueless. "No. You go. I'll probably take a bath and sleep all evening."

I don't even finish my sentence before he has his phone to his ear inviting her to the restaurant he took me to. In the end, they agree to meet in the bar of her hotel. Perfect. Fitting. They can have drinks before they fuck.

God, I hate myself right now. I'm being irrational, but I can't stop myself. Maybe it's jealousy or me being an idiot. Possibly both, but when I get back to the apartment I text Ben and ask him if he wants to meet up.

I haven't talked to Lisa in a year or more. She'd moved to New York to intern for some designer. I didn't want to get April's hopes up, but she'd be a perfect asset to our business. Or at least she'd be handy as a consultant. Lisa knows the ins and outs of fashion. I think April and her would make a great team, possibly partners. April said it was her dream to have a boutique and I want to make that happen for her. I don't know a damn thing about fashion or running a designer-operated store.

Lisa and I used to be fuck buddies, but that was a long time ago. We both moved on with our lives. I hope she doesn't get the wrong impression about why I asked her to dinner so quickly.

I wish April felt up to coming along. I don't want to make choices that she won't be happy with. All of this—everything I'm doing is for her, to give her some security and to show her I'm serious about us raising this baby together.

But, at the end of the day, I want April.

She's beautiful and sweet. Down to earth. Just a good person. I know she probably thinks I want to meet up with Lisa to fuck her and she's willing to set aside her pride or whatever feelings she may be having. I probably should have told her that it was simply business, but it does make me hard to see her squirming with some jealousy. It shows me that she does feel something for me.

I haven't left all my devious ways behind.

Knocking on her bedroom door before I go, I don't get a response.

Maybe she's asleep, but I can't leave without making sure she's fine. She did say she wasn't feeling so hot. Maybe I should cancel.

Cracking her door open, the light in the bedroom is off but light spills out from her private bathroom. The door is ajar, and I know it's an invasion of her privacy, but I want to make sure she doesn't need something before I head out.

Tapping my fist on the door, it gives and fully opens. "April, you decent?"

"I'm in the bath tub. You can come in."

When I walk inside the room, I'm not prepared for the sight before me. April is in the tub. Her hair is pulled up on her head in a messy bun. One leg is propped up on the side as she glides a razor over her tan skin.

Fuck me. My cock wants to explode at the sight in front of me. Everything in me screams to claim her. To lift her up from the tub and take her to bed. Lay her out and eat her pussy until she can't see straight. I need her coming on my face. I want to hear her cry out as she unravels from my touch.

"Are you heading out?"

"Yeah. I wanted to make sure you were okay and see if you need anything before I go."

"I'm fine. You don't have to wait on me hand and foot. I've got Klaire here, and I can drive and manage things on my own."

Damn. I'm smothering her. April is used to being on her own. She's probably uncomfortable with all the attention I keep laying on her. Hell, I practically offer to wipe her ass, but I just want things to go well. I want to make sure her pregnancy is a happy and healthy one.

"Right, well you have my number. I'm not sure what time I'll get in."

"It's fine. Go have fun and catch up with your friend. Go do what *single* men do."

I don't miss the dark look in her eyes when she says single. Is she telling me I have her permission to fuck Lisa? I don't need it. It makes my blood boil nonetheless. Not because she thinks she needs to give me her blessing to go out and fuck someone, because if I want to go and fuck one or ten women I will, but I wish she'd tell me if she has feelings for me. I wish she'd open up and be honest if she doesn't want me to go out to dinner with another woman.

Stealing a glance at my watch, I see I should've been out the door ten minutes ago. "Right. I gotta go. If you're still up when I get in, we should talk."

"Okay. Sure. Have a nice time." She shifts in the tub to rinse her leg off and her belly and tits pop up out of the water. Fuck. I never knew the sight of a naked pregnant woman could do it for me like this.

Leaving the room in a hurry is all I can do to keep from jerking her up, bending her over the sink, and fucking her brains out.

————

When I get to dinner Lisa is already seated and having a glass of wine.

"Sorry, traffic." It's a lie, but I don't give a shit.

"No worries, I haven't been waiting long. Though I must confess, I can't believe you wanted to meet up so soon. Is playing house not all it's cracked up to be?" She grins over the brim of her glass, taunting me as her long lashes flutter.

I cock my head to the side. "It's great actually. I asked you here on business. On the street earlier, I didn't really explain why I wanted to grab lunch. I have a proposition for you."

"Don't tell me you want me to be your mistress. We had a good run but that was before I met Karma."

I blink. "Karma?"

"My girlfriend. The super model."

"I have no idea who that is but congratulations."

"Thank you. I'm happy for you. Have to admit though. It was a shock to see you with a woman on your arm and starting a family."

"Shock to me too, but a welcomed one. Anyway, the whole point to this meeting is April designs her own costumes and jewelry and wants to open a boutique. I thought maybe your brother would know a good listing. All the places we've seen are shit." I pause, meeting her gaze. "You have experience in fashion. I'd like to bring you in to work with April on this. I can't dedicate the time it needs. I have my own workload to handle at the firm."

"I'm intrigued. I'd need to see her work, but it's tempting. I do miss being in Dallas. Does she have a portfolio?"

"I'm not sure. I haven't told her about your part in this yet."

Her brows pique. "Why not?"

"Because I'm an asshole and like making her jealous. Our arrangement is unique."

"How so? You aren't together?"

I shake my head and take a drink of my whiskey. "Nah, it's a highly complicated situation. We're living together, but I'm working on it."

"Some unwarranted advice. Don't screw around with her emotions. Be honest about what you want. You know men say women are confusing but all it takes is some communication. Go home and talk to her and see if she is cool with me coming on as a partner. I'd like to sit down with her and see if we can reach an agreement, but she has to actually like me, or it'll never work."

"I'll be in touch." I finish off my drink, eager to get home to April and give her the good news. When I get in she isn't anywhere to be found. Klaire says she left, all dressed up to meet a friend. A guy named Ben.

What the fucking fuck?

The first thought through my mind is running my goddamn fist through Ben's face. I don't know what's coming over me. I want to say it's because she's pregnant with my son, but it's more than that. A possessive rage comes over me like I've never felt before. Where the fuck did she go? She's not a prisoner, but Jesus. Smiling in the tub. Shaving her legs for another man with my child inside of her. Fucking ridiculous. I told her where I was going.

"Did she take the car?"

"No, sir. I believe she was driving herself."

Fuck. If she had my driver take her I could find out where she is and force her home where she belongs…under me. I have no choice but to wait it out. The thought of her with Ben has me pacing around the apartment.

Klaire makes herself scarce. I have a feeling I made her uncomfortable.

I have no idea what I'm doing but if Brodie can go out, why can't I? Being pregnant doesn't mean my life is over and that I can't date. I'm a sexy, single woman. Maybe not as sexy as I once was by the way Brodie ran out of the bathroom at seeing me naked, but Ben always did flirt with me.

When I asked him out, he was more than eager to meet up.

I let Klaire know that I'm meeting up with my friend Ben, in case Brodie magically comes home and wonders where I am. Judging by the hungry way Lisa was looking at him in the street earlier, I doubt he'll ever even know I'm gone. Would he even care that I am out with another man?

I arrive at the bakery and coffee house at the same time as Ben. I can't have alcohol, but a tea and muffin can't hurt.

When Ben's eyes land on me, he takes in my stomach and smiles. Immediately he draws me into his large arms, crushing me with a bear hug. "Damn, girl. Look at you all sexy, rocking motherhood like nobody's business. I don't give a damn what Rod said, I'd pay to watch you dance any day.

"Thanks." I laugh as he releases me. His cologne smells nice, but nothing in comparison to Brodie's.

"I'm glad you called. I've missed seeing your smiling face and that fine ass. You know I quit the club after Rod fired you. That shit wasn't right."

"You didn't need to do that. I'm fine. Things have worked out relatively well."

"Don't mention it. I got me a job working out in the oil fields. You just happened to catch me on my off weekend. Don't get many of them but the pay is damn good."

We make our way inside to place our orders and grab a table. My phone goes off a few times, but I ignore it to give Ben my full attention.

"So, what made you call me?"

"I don't know. Guess I was thinking about you." I pick at my muffin, unsure of what to say. Now that he's here I can't stop thinking about Brodie and imagining him fucking that bitch.

Before I found out I was pregnant, I was attracted to Ben, but now no one compares to Brodie. I'm afraid he's ruined me. I came here expecting fireworks. The big ones that bang, but all I'm getting is cheap sparklers and snap and pops.

"It's good to see you. Gotta be honest with you though. I'm not really into the seeing some other dude's baby mama drama. I like you. Always have. I think you're a beautiful woman, but I want to make my intentions clear. Once you have the baby if you're still single, hit me up."

I appreciate his honesty, and we spend the rest of our time catching up. He fills me in on some of the drama from the club right up until he quit. Rod caught Stacie fucking two dudes in one of the VIP rooms and lost his shit and finally got rid of her. I'm not surprised she was doing two guys at once. Only surprised Rod kicked her to the curb.

Ben kisses my cheek when he walks me to the car. I feel nothing. No boom. Not even a tingle. He's cute, but I know I won't be calling him again anytime soon. He doesn't compare to Brodie, and I'm afraid no one ever will.

When I get back home he's at the bar pouring a drink. He doesn't seem happy. Maybe his reunion with Lisa didn't go as expected.

As I put my purse on the counter he stalks toward me with a dark look in his eyes that I don't like.

"Where have you been? I called you several times."

"Was out with a friend. Not that it's your business." I give him a confused look. Nowhere in our agreement did it say I have to answer to him or explain my comings and goings. I don't answer to Brodie. I'm my own person.

"Ben, right?"

"Klaire told you."

"She did. Is he a friend, or someone you're seeing?"

I don't appreciate his tone.

"Does it matter?" I scoff and stare out one of his giant windows. "You were out with Lisa."

He shrinks back as though I slapped him. "I was meeting with Lisa because she works in the fashion industry. I wanted to hire her to be a consultant for you to handle the parts of the business I don't understand or that we can't take care of ourselves. I was seeing her for you. I wanted it to be a surprise. She's interested in being a partner if she likes your portfolio."

My stomach drops. I feel like an asshole.

"So, you weren't meeting her because you wanted to fuck her?"

With a heavy sigh he steps into me, backing me against the wall. "I won't lie to you. Lisa and I briefly dated, years ago. She's an old friend, but no, I didn't go to her tonight because I wanted to fuck her. Did you go see Ben to fuck him?"

There's no space between his face and mine. Our mouths are so close I can feel and taste every breath he takes.

"Yes." I whisper the word.

"And did you? Did you fuck him?" He growls his questions in my ear.

I shake my head ever so lightly from side to side.

"Good." He shifts around so that his face is right in front of mine. "Because no dick but mine will go inside you while my child is in there. You want fucked—" His hand moves between us and up my dress. Grabbing my pussy, he grits in my ear in a low and dangerous voice. "You come to me to get fucked. You want to get off, I'll make it happen. No one else. Understand? No one will fuck you but me. No one will taste your cunt but me. No one will spread these fucking thighs and make you come but me."

A whimper leaves my throat and his mouth is on mine.

April pants against my mouth, breathless as I continue to rub my fingers over her panties. She's fucking soaked. Fuck taking shit slow and getting to know her better. I want her, and I'll have her. I'm a Hunter. I never lose. I take what I want. I'll have her in my bed. April is mine. No one else touches what's mine. Her pussy belongs to me. Her body is meant to be taken by me.

Plunging my tongue deep in her mouth, I take everything from her, swallow every goddamn sound she makes. She'll submit and give in. I'm not taking no for an answer. She wants me. Her body squirms against my hand seeking pleasure. Only pleasure I can give her.

"Fuck, you're so wet."

"And you're so hard." She palms my cock over my pants.

"I'm done waiting. Tried it. Doesn't work for me. I want you. You're mine. I'm taking this pussy tonight." Sliding her panties to the side, I insert a finger, then two. I pump them in and out, twisting and finger-fucking her slick heat.

Her soft moans grow louder with every thrust of my fingers working her greedy cunt. It squeezes around me.

"Naughty little bitch. Trying to make me jealous." I palm one of her tits and squeeze her nipple between my thumb and forefinger. "Like anyone else knows what you want." I shove my fingers in farther and curl them up to hit her spot.

"Oh my God." She coos against my neck.

Damn, she feels amazing. Primed. Tight and ready to be fucked.

When I pull my fingers out of her, she gasps. Her hips buck toward my hand, searching for something to keep her filled. "Don't stop. Please."

Sweeping her up in my arms, I move for the stairs that lead to our bedrooms.

Taking her into my room, I drop her on my bed.

I have to control myself from getting too rough. I don't want to do anything to hurt her or the baby. I won't risk their wellbeing. But fuck me, I need to be inside her soon.

I take my time undressing her. Paying attention to every curve of her body, worshiping her skin with my mouth.

Her legs slide up and down the sheets as I pepper small featherlight kisses over her growing stomach. Some stretchmarks have formed on her skin, little pink marks that turn me on, knowing they're there because her body is making room for our son.

He may not have been conceived in love, but I'll show April I can love her. I can make her life a good one. I want to give her the world.

Her fingers thread through my hair, stroking softly as I spread her legs apart and inhale her scent.

She smells intoxicating. Delving my tongue over her sensitive skin, I taste and tease her tight bundle of nerves. Fucking heaven in my mouth, licking her sweet essence.

Her hips arch, begging me for more as I take my time, licking her slowly, parting her pussy lips wide, so I can stare at what belongs to me. I pinch her clit between my fingers. "This is for my pleasure." I lick her once from front to back. "No one else will ever taste your sweet cunt." I flick my tongue, teasing at her sweet heat. Her thighs squeeze around my face, but I force them back open. My fingers go to work in her while my tongue strokes her clit. "No one will ever know how good and tight you feel, but me."

"Oh, Brodie, yes. Fuck." I look up at her as she gasps for air. Her teeth graze over her bottom lip as she trembles under my touch. Keeping my fingers inside her, I glide up her body, until I reach her tits. Taking a nipple in my mouth, I suck on it tenderly, being gentle and careful not to put my weight on her stomach.

"Tell me you're mine." I breathe against her mouth. "Tell me you'll always belong to me."

"I'm yours."

I replace my fingers with my cock, easing into her slowly.

"Oh my God." She cries out in pleasure, as I sink deeper inside.

My legs wrap around Brodie's waist as he thrusts into me. My heels dig into the top of his ass as he picks up his pace. My body is his for the taking. I know without a doubt that what he says is true. I belong to him. My body is his to please. Even when he makes love to me he's fucking powerful. He can call it fucking all he wants but I can feel the emotions pouring out of him. I can see love behind his eyes.

This man feels for me. He cares more than he wants to admit. That doesn't matter though because when he kisses me, I feel adored. Worshipped even, as he works his cock in and out of me. His eyes have been on mine the entire time, watching every emotion that rips through me. He sees every ounce of pleasure that washes through me as he takes what he wants and gives me so much in return.

Rolling to the side, he orders me to ride him.

Sinking down on him, a shudder rushes through me. Our bodies fit perfectly together, and he doesn't make me feel unattractive. In fact, just the opposite. He makes me feel like the most desired pregnant woman in existence as he goes the extra mile to make sure I get off.

"Christ, look at you." His fingers reach up to brush my hair out of my face. "You're beautiful. Let me watch you come." His thumb goes in my mouth and I suck the salty skin as he thrusts up into me, pushing deep in my walls, hitting my sweet spot. My orgasm pulses and I shatter into a million pieces of pure bliss.

Raising up to kiss me, he growls and tugs on my hair, biting my bottom lip as he finds his own welcomed release. His cock twitches and he grunts my name over and over. He fills me up with his arms wrapped tight around me, not daring to let anything break our connection.

My body goes limp, and I collapse on the bed next to him, unable to move.

I let out a long yawn, totally spent. "Do you mind if I sleep here tonight? I don't think I can move unless you carry me."

"Look at me."

I open my eyes, trying to fight the weight of sleep pressing down on me.

"You'll never sleep anywhere else. I want nothing more than to fall asleep next to you every night and wake up to you every morning."

"Do you really mean that?"

He cups my face in his palm. "I wouldn't lie to you. If I didn't want you here, you wouldn't be. I could have put you up in one of the empty apartments downstairs. I want you here. I want us to be together and make this work. One day I want my ring on your finger and to put more babies in you, but we have to get this one here first." He smiles and kisses me softly as sleep claims me, leaving me unable to argue with him.

_

The last two months has felt like living in a dream. True to his words, Brodie has kept me in his bed. Even going as far as moving my stuff into his room. It feels surreal to be getting my happily ever after. After years of not having a family, the Hunters have welcomed me with open arms. Brodie finally told his parents about me, leaving out the detail of me being a stripper.

I've been meeting with Lisa daily for the past month to get our business started. Things don't happen overnight, but we're working our way towards a grand opening now that her brother has secured the perfect location. I have to admit, I misjudged her. She's snarky and funny to be around. Her girlfriend is going to do some promotional shots for us for advertising.

I can't believe she's dating Karma. The woman is super famous. I couldn't believe Brodie didn't know who she was. My man spends too much time in the courtroom but I'm breaking him in slowly and making him watch reality TV with me.

Brooke has gotten in touch with Jenny, and the two of them have been planning my baby shower. I'm sure whatever they come up with will be amazing, but I hate how secretive they've been about the whole thing.

The only involvement I've had is getting to go with them to taste the cake samples. The look on Brooke's face when I told her to just get something from the grocery store was priceless. I thought her head was going to explode. Not because she's a snob or anything, but she's gone out of her way to make this special.

When she found out I didn't have any family of my own I thought she was going to cry. She told me that I have a family now. That her and Weston and Maxwell and Jaxson come with the territory.

I still think they're dicks, but they're growing on me.

Even though Brodie and I didn't have the best start, I do believe without a doubt that he is the man for me. The only man.

Every day we learn something new about each other, and it's exciting.

I just got home from going over the renovation plans on the building Lisa and Brodie acquired for our company, Sassy Girl Designs. We haven't agreed on a name for the boutique yet. Nothing seems to have that wow factor.

I'm lying on the couch eating the sandwich and pickles Klaire made me when Brodie gets in. He's been working overtime, trying to lighten his case load for when the baby comes.

Coming over to the couch, he goes down on his knees looking so damn sexy in his suit. It's tailored to fit his body like a glove. He's every woman's fantasy.

Grabbing his tie, I pull him closer to me. "Hey."

"Hey yourself." He gives me a quick peck on the lips. "Ugh, pickles."

"Our growing boy likes them."

As if he's listening to our conversation my belly moves, sending my plate to the floor.

"Easy, slugger." Brodie puts a hand on my stomach. His hand is always there, anytime he's in the room with me.

Chapter Nineteen

BRODIE

I never imagined having a one-night stand would change my life in the most unimaginable and greatest of ways. I can't imagine my life without April in it. She's my world. My reason to get up every morning. The woman has given me purpose. Every day with her is better than the last.

I'm always eager to come home to her. Before, I couldn't imagine coming home every night to one woman, but April keeps me on my toes. I never know what the hell I will walk into. She's made herself at home now in my apartment. Her love of design has spilled over into every room.

It started when Lisa offered to help her with the nursery.

Once they had painted clouds and animals on the walls, they moved on to redoing the spare bedroom, and now mine.

I like Lisa, but she's eating up every minute of my woman's time these days. The renovations on their store are almost complete and they have a warehouse of goods ready to stock the racks and shelves.

The two of them do make a great team. A great team who loves to spend my money. I have no doubt that their business will take off. Karma has several of her friends from New York flying in for the grand opening. If this store does well, there's talk of them opening a second location in New York.

I warned Lisa that she isn't sending April to New York if that comes to fruition. I don't need her cutting in on my time any more than she already does. She'll have to handle that shit.

When I walk in the door I expect to see my woman lounging with her feet up, but instead, she's standing in the kitchen, hunched over the counter with Klaire and Brooke rubbing her lower back.

"Is she okay? What's going on?" Worry etches over my face. Our due date is still two weeks away.

"Just some contractions. We've already called the doctor. Could be false labor, so we're monitoring her."

My heart jumps to my throat. *I could be a father soon.*

I go over and see if there's anything I can do but they all shoo me away, telling me to make sure the hospital bag is by the door and ready to go in case we end up taking her in.

Eventually, Weston comes to my apartment when he doesn't find Brooke upstairs waiting for him. He calls me pussy whipped, but he's just as bad as me. It's the kryptonite pussy. I don't even look at other women these days. None of them hold a candle to April, the soon-to-be mother of my child. I've fallen in love with her.

I haven't told her those three little words that keep getting caught in my throat. The timing never seems right, and I can't seem to get her alone for long these days. Everyone loves her and always wants to be around her. I'm glad they all adore her, but I'm ready to have her to myself again.

I don't know if that day will ever come now because Brooke yells for me to call for the car. *It's really happening. I'm going to be a dad.*

Holy fucking shitcake.

Our party makes it to the hospital and only myself and Brooke are allowed in with her. Weston doesn't seem to mind. I wouldn't either. The whole birthing scene isn't really his thing. Brooke's bursting to have a baby now. She's got the fever now that she's been spending so much time with April. It makes me grin, knowing I can give Weston a bunch of shit about it.

April's contractions are coming minutes apart and there isn't time to give her an epidural.

She squeezes my hand so goddamn tight I may leave with broken fingers.

Brooke is being her cheerleader, wiping her brow and feeding her ice chips as needed. All I can do is stand here in a stupor as the shock that I'm about to meet my child settles in.

As I stare at April, laying there in so much pain but determined to be brave, the love I feel for her hits me square in the chest.

Everything is happening so fast.

The doctor tells her to push but something is wrong, and the baby isn't moving like they'd hope. Fear grips me tight as the doctor barks orders and Brooke is ordered from the room.

They need to take April back for an emergency C-section. The cord is wrapped around the baby's neck and they have to move now.

April squeezes my hand. Her grip is weaker than before. Leaning down to her I brush my lips over hers, hoping she feels the love I have for her.

A nurse escorts me to a surgical prep room where I scrub down and wait to go into the room with April to witness the birth of my child. I'm terrified and nervous.

They keep saying everything is okay, but the way they're scrambling around. Fucking hell. What if I lose one of them, or both of them? I have to be strong. It's my job. I'm the goddamn leader of our family.

I shake my head to rid myself of any insecurity. April needs to know that I'm a man who will be there no matter what. I have to be an oak.

When I get into the room April is on a table with a curtain separating her chest and stomach.

I'm positioned behind the top of her head, where I'm able to talk to her and hold her hand.

She grits her teeth and smiles at me just as beautiful as ever but even more so now. Seeing what she's going through to bring my son into this world has guilt slamming into me. Making me feel like an utter tool for not telling her that I love her. There are no perfect moments. There is no such thing as perfect timing, there's only life and the moments we live in as we experience them. My timing may be terrible, but we aren't about perfect timing. The way we met can testify to that.

Looking into her eyes as she stares at me full of hope and determination I tell her what I have been too scared to admit. Because saying the words aloud makes them real. They aren't words I say lightly.

"Brodie, I'm scared."

I take her hand and lean down to her ear. "Listen to me. You're a warrior. A goddess. You are strong and you're a mother. We can do this together. I've got your back. There's nothing to be afraid of, because I will never let anything happen to you. I love you. And as soon as I get you two home, I'm marrying you."

Tears stream down her face. Before she can say anything the sound of our son crying fills the air. Happy tears fill my eyes the second I lay eyes on him. He's the most beautiful thing I've ever seen.

Once he's been weighed and taken care of, I don't leave his side while they take April back to sew her up. My eyes don't leave his body. Not for a second. He's my responsibility. Everyone stares at us through the glass. I give everybody a thumbs up.

Finally, they take us to a room and everyone spills in. It's fine for now. They all want to see my boy. But once April is here, I'm chasing them all away. He needs alone time with his mom.

Maxwell sits with Weston and Brooke along with Jenny. My brother's face lights up when he sees his nephew up close for the first time. I knew he was a softy for kids. Just doesn't know it yet. I can tell he wants to hold him, but nobody is touching him until April has held him.

Jaxson comes rushing down the hall with some woman following closely behind him. "Who's that?" Brooke questions Weston.

Weston turns to her and smirks. "His client."

I don't even want to know. The nurse comes in and takes my boy to test his hearing and do some other things. She has to practically pry him out of my arms.

———

A little while later they bring Charlie back and roll April into the room. I shoo everyone away, promising them they can come back in a bit.

I watch her as she sleeps.

A short while later she wakes up asking to see Charlie.

Charlie. My son.

We decided to name him after my father.

"Was I dreaming, or did you ask me to marry you as our son was being born?" She smiles lazily at me, and she's still the most beautiful woman I've ever seen.

"Not a dream." I take her hand in mine while she clutches our naked son to her bare chest. "I promise to always love and cherish you. So, I will ask you again. Will you marry me?"

"Come here." She uses all her strength to pull me closer.

I lean down with her hand in mine against her heart, our son on the other side of her chest.

She smiles. "Yes, I will marry you."

Player
IN A
SUIT

ALEX WOLF

I'm a player in a suit.

I was a good man once.

Had a woman I loved. We were supposed to run away together. She didn't show. Never saw her again.

Lesson learned.

My family worked for her father on their ranch.

When she stood me up I made a vow to conquer the world, come back, and buy their piece of sh*t property and sell it off for parts.

She turned me into the man I am today.

I loved her with all my heart. She ripped it out of my chest and stomped on it.

Now, I'm a partner at a powerhouse law firm in Dallas. I don't even think of her. I'm done with women. They're nothing but sexual transactions in the bedroom. I get off and move on.

Imagine my surprise when Jenna Jacobi strolls into my law firm and asks me to handle her divorce.

I should turn her away or pawn her off on some junior attorney. I was done with her a long time ago.

But something deep down inside of me filters back to the surface. No matter how hard I fight it, she still gets to me. We were meant to be together forever.

I can't let her hurt me again. Idiots repeat history. I'm a different man now. A cold bastard. I can't be reformed.

I'm Jaxson Parker, Attorney at Law.

Chapter One

JAXSON

J enna Jacobi is my life.

I grin while I wait for her to show up.

Never thought we'd go from two kids that hated each other to where we are now. When we were younger we fought non-stop. Constant bickering.

Jenna's family has money. More money than I'll probably ever see.

None of that matters now, though. We grew closer in our teen years.

We love each other. You can't put a price tag on something like that.

Staring at the letter on the counter, I can't wait to give her the news. We finally have our ticket out of this shithole. Away from her asshole father who thinks I'll never be good enough for her.

I haven't even told my dad yet. He's still out in the field repairing fences. He works his ass off to put food on the table and keep a roof over our heads. I'm not sure how he'll take the news.

I hate how hard he works for basically nothing.

He does whatever Carver Jacobi wants and that prick acts like we aren't good enough to look in their direction.

Dad thinks I'm going to follow his footsteps and work at the Jacobi ranch, but I've been busting my ass studying, making good grades. I applied for every scholarship I could, and it just paid off.

I have a full ride to Duke. I have bigger dreams outside of this farm.

I want to take Jenna with me and prove to her old man we don't need his money. We can both get jobs and if we get married we can live in family housing.

Grabbing the letter, I fold it in half and shove it in the back pocket of my jeans.

When I get to the barn, Jenna's waiting for me up in the hayloft.

We sneak up here all the time. It's *our* place.

Our first kiss was in this barn as well as our first time. It's like the world doesn't exist when I'm up here with her.

I never thought I'd find myself in love with snotty little Jenna Jacobi but she's my entire world.

When I climb up the ladder, I find her curled up with a book. She's so damn beautiful she takes my breath away.

Long sun-kissed hair that hangs over her shoulders. Toffee eyes that melt me with one look. There's a dust of freckles over the bridge of her nose and a smile that just screams—hope. Any time I look at her I know we'll be okay.

"Hey." Her word comes out on a soft breath.

"Hey." I pull her into me and claim her delicious cherry lips.

One kiss turns into a heavy make-out session. I find myself pushing her down on the blanket spread across the hay and moving the straps of her dress down, so I can kiss her freckled shoulders.

"God, I love you." I trail my lips up and down her throat.

"I love you too, always."

"You'll always be mine. No matter what." Pushing her dress up her hips, I work her panties off, eager to be inside her. When I'm with Jenna I truly feel at home. Like I matter to someone.

To Jenna's dad I'm a loser with no future. The son of a broken man with nothing to offer the world.

But Jenna sees me.

She believes in me and I believe in us.

Chapter Two

JENNA

Tonight's the night. Jaxson and I will finally leave this town behind to start our forever.

I've had my bag packed for weeks. He got his scholarship and has an apartment lined up for us to live with three other people. I'm terrified of what my father will do when he finds me gone, but I love Jaxson and want nothing more than to be with him. I've loved him since I was a little girl when he'd pick on me and put dirt in my hair.

I'm supposed to meet him at the barn then we're walking to town to catch the first bus out in the morning.

At dinner I can't stop fidgeting. My knee bounces up and down uncontrollably. My stomach's been in knots for weeks. I've been afraid my dad will know something is up. Mom keeps asking me if I have ants in my pants. I lie and tell her I'm nervous because I haven't heard from any of the schools I applied to. Dad shoots me a weird look, like he knows something I don't. The way he grins makes me want to vomit. It'll be hard leaving my family behind. I love them, but Jaxson is my life. I can't live without him.

I ask to be excused and start pacing the second I walk into my room, waiting for the right time to slip out of the house. Every night after dinner Dad goes into his study to have a drink.

It isn't long after that he goes to bed. That's when I'll make my escape.

Taking a look around my room I wonder if this is the last time I'll see it. Dad will probably cut me off when he finds out what I'm doing.

I don't need his money though. I wish he'd give Jaxson and me his blessing.

I don't know why he hates him so much. He hates Jax's father too, even though he has them living in a guesthouse on the far end of the ranch.

I look at the clock. Dad should be in bed by now.

An unexpected knock sounds at my door.

It's my mom, and her face is pale. I've never seen her look so —frightened.

"What's wrong?"

"Your father wants you in the study."

My stomach drops.

He knows.

I'll play dumb, and when he's satisfied I'll make a run for it.

When I walk into the study there are three men I've never seen before.

Dad sits behind his desk smiling.

"Daddy?"

He looks up at me like he's won. In his own way, I know he loves me. But he loves business more than anything, even my mother. It's something everyone knows but never says.

"Princess, I have someone I'd like you to meet."

"Umm, okay." The men eye me up and down like I'm cattle at an auction.

The youngest of the three has a devilish grin spread across his face.

I want to turn and run. Bolt straight into Jaxson's arms.

He's probably wondering where I am by now.

"This is Mr. Reyes, his son Leonard, and one of their associates." Dad nods at them.

My body tenses. Something seems very wrong about these men. "What's going on?"

"Sweetheart, you and Leonard are going to be married. It's been arranged."

My world flips upside down, and a cold sweat breaks out along my hairline. "What?"

Leonard steps forward. "I know you don't know me. But, you'll learn to love me. I promise." He winks.

My stomach curdles, and I fear I might lose my dinner. What is this? The nineteenth century? This can't be happening.

I pull my hand behind my back and shake my head. "I won't marry you."

"It's for the best, sweetheart. We'll merge the two ranches."

I shake my head, tears stinging the corners of my eyes. "So, it's about business? I'm a business transaction?"

Dad stands up and scowls. "Did you think I'd just let you run off with that derelict piece of shit?"

I look away at the wall and wipe the tears from my eyes. This can't be happening.

"You think I didn't know." He walks over and looms above me. "Did you think I didn't know?" He scoffs. "You're marrying Leonard. This *is* happening."

"I won't do it."

He grins as Mom shakes behind him. Why won't she stand up for me? It's my life, not theirs.

"Oh, yes you will."

"You can't do anything to me. You don't own me."

Dad glances to Mr. Reyes and back at me. "No, I can't. But I can throw your little boyfriend's family out on the street. And I can make sure they never work in this town again."

Horror floods my body. I can't move. It's like I'm paralyzed, stuck in a nightmare where I can't scream or run.

"That's what I thought."

Leonard walks over and leans in next to my ear. "Like I said, you'll learn to love me."

"Is there a problem?" Mr. Reyes glances at Dad then over to me.

I have to go through with this. I love Jaxson too much. His family will be homeless and out of work if I don't.

I glance around at all of them, then stare at the floor. "Okay. You win."

Dad smiles. "That's my good girl."

Chapter Three

JAXSON

13 Years Later

"That's it, sweetheart." I grip Sonya's hair as she deepthroats my cock.

My fingers tug on her wispy dark strands, pulling her head farther down as I hold back the load building in my balls.

She looks up at me as tears form in the corners of her eyes. Her thin lips stretch around me as I record her with my phone.

"Beautiful." I growl the word, watching as I slide in and out of her mouth with ease. Her tongue moves up and down my shaft as her fingers stroke my taint.

She's dirty, and I like that about her.

I'm close but not fully there yet.

Sonya's perfect melon-sized tits sit on full display in a sexy red lace bra. She's fucking gorgeous. A pinup model who poses for tattoo magazines and calendars. Any man would love to have her, but she has one purpose for me—a hot, wet place to get off.

There's an understanding between us. When she comes to town we meet up at a hotel for drinks then I take her to a room and fuck her brains out.

It's been our thing for three months now, but she seems to be growing restless. Sonya wants more. I understand that she craves companionship but I'm not the man to provide it.

I'm not interested in anything other than meaningless fucking.

Pulling out of her mouth, I bring her up from the floor and order her to bend over the couch of the hotel suite I paid for. We won't be sleeping here.

I plow into Sonya from behind and fuck an orgasm out of her. It's not *all* about me. We both have needs, and I want hers to be met as well.

Later when we're finished, I'll use the shower and leave. Sonya can stay if she likes but I never stick around. There's no cuddling. No whispering of sweet nothings. Just a mutual exchange.

Sonya loves rough, dirty talk and I'm cast perfectly in that role.

I tease my cock around her entrance before ramming it deep. "Such a dirty little slut. That's how you like it, huh?"

"Mmhmm."

I pull out to the tip and drive back in. "Look at this sweet fucking ass." I smack her left cheek hard enough to leave a handprint and yank on her hair.

She practically salivates while she screams my name for more.

The only sounds in the room are wet bodies slapping together and the moans that leave her throat.

Then, she ruins it.

"Jaxson…"

"Yeah, say my name when you take that dick, you dirty little bitch." I ram into her once more as she clamps down on me.

Her whole body shakes as she rides out the orgasm. I'm so fucking close my balls ache with delight.

"Jaxson." She breathes out the word.

"Yeah?"

So.

Close.

"I love you."

I stop moving.

Time stands still.

My cock practically shrivels and wilts away and I know a raging set of blue balls awaits in my near future.

My eyes widen as she glances back at me, still panting. "What did you just say?" She might as well have said she was pregnant or had syphilis.

What the fuck is happening right now?

Her eyes stay locked on mine over her shoulder. "I love you."

I lean back and sit on my heels, still wondering if I heard her correctly.

Fuck. Fuck. Fuck.

Here's the thing. Any other woman I'd have been out the door already. But, Sonya seems nice. I'm an asshole, but the last thing I need is her bashing my windshield in with a baseball bat or showing up in tears at my office. I don't know her well enough to know if she's a little higher on the crazy scale than she seems.

"Umm…"

"Umm?" Her face turns that fiery red that has me wanting to sprint from the room. She doesn't seem like the kind who's ten shades of crazy, but I don't want to risk it.

"Look. You caught me off guard a little."

How can I play this? I need to let her down easy. I could tell her to fuck off, but that invites conflict, and conflict breeds catastrophe.

"You're nice, and I, umm, care about you and stuff…" Christ, I can't even look at her when I say it. It sucks, but that wasn't the arrangement. She knows better than to pull this shit. I have to just rip the Band-Aid off. "So, this was great, but I think it's best we don't see each other anymore."

"What?"

"It's just chemicals firing. We have to be reasonable about this. You don't know me well enough to love me."

"That's not true." She sits up and slumps into the couch as I move to pull up my pants.

I let out a heavy sigh. "I don't do relationships. It's not personal. And no, you don't know anything about me other than that I like to come here when you're in town to fuck. You know I drink bourbon. That's really about it."

Her bottom lip trembles and I hope to fuck she doesn't start crying. I don't do tears either. Well, except for earlier, when she was sucking my dick. That's different, though.

"You're an asshole." Her hazel eyes turn a dark shade I haven't seen before.

"Not denying that." I grab my jacket from a nearby chair. "Listen, we had fun. I'm sure you'll meet the right person who will love you back. I'm doing you a favor here."

"Fuck you!"

I'll be damned if she doesn't hurl an empty rocks glass at me and it shatters across the wall.

Fuck this. I tried to be nice about it.

"You already fucked me, sweetheart." I smirk and walk out the door.

I don't do feelings. I do the fucking.

She really is better off.

Chapter Four

JENNA

Wiping my mouth, I look down at my hand where blood streaks my pale skin.

Leonard, my husband, glares. "Where's the money?" He gets nose-to-nose with me again.

I laugh in his face knowing it will earn me another blow. "Get one of your whores to pawn the jewelry you bought them. I don't have anything."

Grabbing a fist full of my hair, he yanks me closer. The stinging pain isn't anything I haven't felt before. He's dished out far worse in the past.

I grin. "Gonna hit me again?"

His eyes seer into mine but his voice is calm and collected. "I want my fucking money."

"What makes you think my father's money belongs to you?"

His fist goes back and he takes a huge swing. I jerk out of the way and duck as his hand smashes the wall. There's a puff of drywall and some of the sheetrock crumbles onto the floor.

I don't wait for him to react. I take off running out the back door and through the fields. The whole time I sprint I pray he won't catch up to me.

I never wanted things to be this way. When Dad told me I had to marry Leonard or he'd toss Jaxson's family out on the street, I did what I had to do even though it crushed my spirit.

I still love Jax. He's my soulmate. I'd do anything for him.

Leonard slings open the glass back door on the patio and it shatters all over the concrete. "I'll find you, bitch." He snickers and turns around. "I always do."

I hear him go back inside, but I don't dare look back. One of these days he's going to kill me. I just know it.

Part of me is glad my Dad passed away and can't see the hand he dealt me. Mom would be so ashamed. She's probably turning over in her grave. She raised me to be a lady, but she didn't raise me to be an idiot. The fear of death is the only thing that's kept me in this marriage after they died.

The truth is, Leonard scares me, and I know he'll find me. I've learned to live with it. Always in survival mode.

Stopping at a tree to catch my breath, I lean my arm on the bark.

I've been running for ages it feels. Sweat drips down my back as the sun begins to set.

One night is usually what it takes when he does this. When I go back, he'll apologize and say that he loves me. Things will be fine for a while, and it'll happen again. It's a vicious cycle.

I can't look at myself in the mirror. I know I actually am an idiot. It's all I've known the last thirteen years.

The bottoms of my feet crack and bleed but there's no way in hell I'm going back tonight.

Hopefully Leonard stumbled to bed and passed out in a drunken stupor. With any luck I can sneak back into the house tomorrow once he's left for his trip. He can find his own means to pay off his debt this time.

I stand there, shaking, panting uncontrollably.

This has to end. I can't do it anymore.

I've told myself that before, but this time I mean it. I am done. If he kills me, he kills me. He can have the ranch. He can have all the money.

I'm done.

A name pops out on my schedule in big bold letters. A name I hoped I'd never see or hear again.

Jenna fucking Jacobi.

The one and only.

The bitch that broke my heart and turned me into a monster.

I wasn't always an asshole. I cared about people other than myself. It's hard to even imagine it now. Goddamn, I was a fucking pussy. A little boy with a crush who didn't understand how shitty the world could be.

She changed all of that for me. Taught me that lesson in a hurry. And now, I run shit. Nobody will ever hurt me again.

What the fuck is she doing on my planner?

No fucking way am I doing this. Nope.

I take a deep breath.

I don't want to see her, yet at the same time, I'm curious.

My notes say she's here for a divorce consultation. Maybe I can rub it in. Let her know what she's missed out on. Give her a glimpse of the powerful asshole she created.

Bet she's popped out a few kids for her cattle rancher husband. Probably fattened her up. Bet her husband's trading her in for a younger, hotter model.

Even as I think horrible things about Jenna, I can't help but notice something I haven't felt in a long time. Anxiety digs into the pit of my stomach, just at the thought of her. I don't get nervous, ever. Not my style. Yet, it's like I've shoved something deep down inside for a long time and never dealt with it, never let it out of its cage. It's bubbling toward the surface.

And I plan on doing what every other man on the planet does. Shoving it down farther, burying that fucking weakness. There's no place in my world for it. Maybe I could've been a nice guy. I would've been, for her.

Now, I've evolved and moved on from that farm boy she knew. The one who wasn't good enough or rich enough for her family. She's going to know she fucked up when she takes one look at me. Choosing that piece of shit. Not showing up.

I hope she feels every knife in her stomach that I felt when I stood there that night, alone. I hope she cries every fucking tear I cried, leaving without her. I hope she fills buckets with those tears.

My days working on their ranch are long gone and I have more money than their shit family could dream of. I told myself one day I'd come back and buy that filthy-ass ranch and raze the whole fucking thing. Develop a subdivision on top of it, or strip malls. Everything her father hated about society.

I guess over the years I forgot my plans of revenge. I moved past it. I was better than them. Better than the entire Jacobi clan. I've been over Jenna for years. Haven't even thought about her until this moment.

Biting the cap of my pen, I debate whether I should refer her to Maxwell.

I'm too close to this.

It's bad form to mix personal with business.

The dam has broken, and memory after memory floods into my mind. Visons of rolling around with Jenna in the barn play on a loop. She was so damn beautiful.

Then it happens.

I catch a glimpse of her through the glass walls encasing my office.

Her strawberry blonde hair bounces against her back in long curls. I remember all too easily how it felt when I would thread my fingers through the strands, just completely lost in her. I can smell her just by looking at her. How is that even possible?

I couldn't breathe without her. She was life.

She destroyed me.

I've never loved another woman. Not even close.

I fuck to get it out of my system and I go back to work. I wouldn't say I'm a manwhore. Just a pragmatist. I have arrangements. No feelings. No dates. It's biological and efficient.

Hearts and flowers? Naw. Dating and emotions? Naw.

That part of me is long gone.

I'm a cold, objective courtroom killer.

My secretary buzzes me and I exhale heavily through my nose, making sure the figurative walls are up and locked in position. The only woman I've ever loved is in my sights, and I'll be goddamned if she thinks she's going to blow up my world again.

Her eyes meet mine through the glass and she smiles. It's an invigorating carefree smile. Happiness seems effortless with her.

Never again.

I'll make it through this appointment. Collect my retainer and put one of the junior partners on her case. I'll never have to see her again. Only her money. Just like that.

Should be easy enough.

"Show her in." I growl the words into the phone.

"Right away." Brittany's inflection tells me she picked up on my tone. She's adept at reading my moods. Let's just say if I'm not happy, no one's happy.

I like things the way I like them. I have a low tolerance for bullshit. It's called being professional. If people do what they're supposed to do, we have no problems.

The first thing I notice is Jenna's figure. Those hourglass hips strut into my office looking every bit like the snotty spoiled bitch she's always been. I couldn't see it then, but I do now.

Under that fake tan, plump lips, and luscious tits, is a woman who can't think for herself. She does whatever Daddy tells her to. I bet it's the reason she's getting divorced. Daddy probably snapped his fingers and she jumped to attention.

There's only one question that I want an answer to at the moment.

Why'd she seek *me* out?

"Have a seat. Mrs. Jacobi is it?"

A frown crosses her face and I smirk on the inside. "Jaxson?"

"It's Mr. Parker."

"Oh, umm. Do you know who I am?"

"My one o'clock." I really do have this 'being a prick' game down to a science.

"It's me—Jenna. Why are you being so..." Her head tilts to the side as she stares. "Quit playing games. You were my first boyfriend."

"We can skip the trip down memory lane. I vaguely remember you strutting on your dad's ranch in short shorts and expensive boots. I see here you want to file for divorce. I'm going to need a list of your holdings and assets both single and joint. If there's a prenup I'll need a copy of that as well. What are your grounds for divorce? Infidelity?" When I look up her mouth is agape and her eyes are wide.

It almost looks like she's holding back tears.

Maybe it was harsh, but fuck it. Like it's not harsh what she did? Life's rough, sweetheart. This is a tickle compared to the way she fucking broke me. No phone calls. No goddamn email. Nothing.

Piss on her.

"This was a mistake," she whispers.

Linking my fingers behind my head I lean back in my chair. "Just trying to do my job in a professional manner. You're the one trying to make it personal. I don't do personal. Haven't in thirteen years." I look right at her puffy eyes. "If that's a problem I can suggest one of my colleagues to handle your needs."

"I-I came here because I thought you'd be a friend and make sure I'm taken care of. I just—wanted someone I can trust."

"What?" I scoff. I shouldn't take the bait, but I just can't help myself. "What makes you think I give a shit if you keep your pampered lifestyle? Why would you trust me? You're nothing to me."

She clamps a palm over her mouth, and here come the fucking waterworks. "How can you say that? You were..." She trails off.

My jaw ticks. I'm bored with this already. It's not as satisfying as I imagined. "Let's focus on your case."

She nods against the hand still pressed over her mouth and grabs her purse. "Right... Everything you need is in here." She holds out a flash drive.

"I'll go over it and get papers drawn up." I take the information from her slender hand. Her fingers brush over my palm and I remember her touch like it was yesterday. Fuck. I should send her away. Give the case to Maxwell.

I need to get far away from her. The one big problem is, I don't know if I want to.

Chapter Six

JENNA

I can't believe it's finally happening. I'm finally going to be free.

One day of freedom without Leonard is better than fifty with him in my life.

He really pulled the wool over my father's eyes. Despite the horrible thing my father made me do, I truly believe he thought he was securing my future. Not that I'm so naïve to think it wasn't about him too.

His business and legacy always took precedence, but I think he was still just trying to look out for me.

He barely knew Leonard. But he knew he was the son of a wealthy casino owner from Las Vegas. Leonard and his father were buying up and consolidating the ranches nearby, and they would've eventually taken over ours too. This way, Dad got our family name on everything as partners. Dad got to run our ranch as long as he wanted.

Once Dad passed away, Leonard drove the business into the ground. Sold off a lot of the land. He wasn't a brilliant businessman. I think Leonard's dad sent him to Texas to get him out of his hair, so he wouldn't screw up the casinos. That's where their real money came from. Since Dad died, Leonard has practically liquidated and lost every asset we own.

When Jaxson asks for financial statements I want to laugh. It's not funny, but at the same time it is in some morbid way. I have nothing. The girl who always had it all is left with nothing but my family name. I have some land and the family home that's fallen into disrepair. I'll be lucky to sell it for half of what it's worth. If I even get to keep it.

Leonard has no idea I'm even filing. He's in Vegas with his newest whore, I'm sure. The only good thing I've done in my life is not giving that man a child. That would've required us sleeping together.

I'd rather be celibate for life than to touch Leonard. I think that's one of the things that made him beat me up so much, but I didn't care. I never slept with him, not once. Jax is the only man I've ever been with. Leonard makes me sick. The thought of even hugging him is repulsive.

He's an alcoholic who'd rather smack me around than show me any affection. He wants the last remaining bit of my father's estate. He won't get the family home. I'll kill him before he touches the house I grew up in. If Jaxson won't help me I'll find someone who will.

Jaxson is even more handsome than I remembered. Dark brown hair and the deepest gray eyes that look like raging thunderstorms. Eyes I used to love getting lost in. He was my first everything. The farmhand's son who helped out on our ranch. They lived in one of the tenant houses. We sold it off a few years ago, when my father suffered his first stroke. It nearly killed me when we let it go. It was all I had left of Jax.

And now, Jax hates me. Of course he does. Why wouldn't he? I'm surprised he's taking the case at all. It was a hail mary coming here.

"I'll go over it and get papers drawn up."

I hand Jax the drive with everything on it. The feel of his hand is the exact way I remember it. I'm not sure why I'm so surprised that he's being so cold. He never got an explanation of why I left him there.

I guess I always thought if he knew the truth, he'd overreact. He would've fought for me, and he would've gotten hurt. The Reyes family is not a family anyone should mess with. And we were just kids. Jax would've gotten himself killed trying to defend me.

"Did you try marriage counseling?"

"What?" His question catches me off guard.

"You never gave me a reason for divorce. When it goes to court they'll want to know why."

"No, we didn't do the whole counseling thing. He's in Las Vegas with his latest mistress. Leonard keeps an apartment there. We were never in love."

"Children?"

"No."

"Good, that should speed things up a little. When was the last time your property was assessed?"

I shake my head. "I don't know, a few years ago, maybe."

"With the amount of property you have, an expert may be required. That could take time."

"How much time?"

"Months. Years. It all depends." He shrugs.

"I need this over. Is there a way to expedite the process?"

The corners of his mouth turn up into a grin. "I might know someone who could do a favor. If I felt like calling it in."

"Jaxson, please. You don't understand. I can't spend another day married to that bastard."

I'm ready to go down on my knees and beg him to put an end to my suffering. "I'll do anything. Seriously, please."

"You know?" Jaxson stands and walks over to a window, refusing to look at me. "I used to imagine this day. All the time."

"Jax…"

"Let me finish." He whips around, his eyes cold and dark.

I've never seen that look before. I can't help but think I'm responsible for the man he's become.

"I don't like seeing you like this, Jenna. I thought I would. But it's just humiliating. You all—desperate." He takes a few steps and stops right in front of me, his eyes glaring down at me. "You chose this. Do you know how long I waited for you?"

Tears stream down my face at the thought of him standing there, wondering where I was. He had to have felt so alone. He must've been so hurt.

He snickers to himself and looks back out the window, but his hands ball into fists at his sides. "Kept telling myself you'd show. Told myself you were running late. That you were waiting for the right time to sneak out. That there was no way you'd backed out."

He has no idea how I wished every single day since then that I'd ran far away with him and never looked back. I just didn't really have a choice.

"Jaxson, I…" How do I tell him the truth? That I was a pawn in a sick and twisted game. I was a business transaction. I'm so ashamed.

I don't know what I expected coming here. I had this weird idea that maybe he'd found some way to forgive me.

"It's okay. We were kids. You don't owe me an explanation. I'll go over this and call you if I have any questions."

"I want to tell you what happened—"

He cuts me off. "I have an appointment."

I stand up.

Jaxson follows me to the door. I forgot how tall he is. His hand touches my hair, tugging one of the curls.

I stare up at him, trying to hide the fact that I'm still in love with him. I never stopped loving him. "It was nice to see you. You've changed." I offer him a faint smile, touching my fingers to his cheek, wishing things could've gone differently all those years ago.

Leaning into my palm, he presses his cheek against my warm skin. So many feelings and memories come rushing back to the surface.

"I want to hate you. I don't know if it's possible."

He has no idea how much guilt and shame I live with daily.

I stare up at him feeling a lifetime of regret. His eyes meet mine and I see the boy I fell in love with. His chin dips down. Then those lips I've dreamed of so many times come down on mine. Pure. Soft. True.

My mouth moves against his as though we haven't spent thirteen years apart.

His large fingers bite into my hips and I run my hands through his hair just like old times. His tongue presses against the seam of my lips and I open to him completely. His kiss still makes me weak in the knees. I've missed the touch and taste of him, but this is wrong. I'm still married to that bastard. Maybe I'm a horrible person but wedding ring on my hand or not, I'm only married on paper, not in my heart. My heart has always been with Jaxson.

He pulls away much too soon with a dark look in his eyes. "This won't happen again."

"You still feel something for me." I challenge him to tell me differently.

"You're a client. Nothing else." He adjusts himself and steps away, my body instantly missing his touch.

I can't do anything but stare at him wishing I knew what he was thinking. God, he looks good in his suit. It fits him perfectly.

I don't know what to expect now.

But Jesus, that kiss. I miss him so much.

Chapter Seven

JAXSON

F uck me. I wasn't expecting for things to go that far. I can still taste her on my lips hours later as I meet up with Maxwell at the bar. It's not far from the office and it's a nice place to unwind. We hang out here a few times a week. Brodie and Weston used to join us, until they became pussy whipped. Kryptonite pussy. Jenna's the only one who has it, and that ship has sailed.

Brodie won't admit it, but he's falling hard for the sexy stripper he knocked up. He'll be married before he knows it.

"So how long until I'm in here by myself every week?" Maxwell grins.

"What?"

"Heard you were making out with a client earlier." The cocky bastard smirks at me.

"Were you wearing a raincoat rubbing one out in the corner or what?"

"Pffttt. Please. Girls were giggling about it in the break room."

"You heard wrong." I knock back my drink trying to get the image of Jenna out of my mind. I'm not going there. Too much bad history and shit I don't want to think about.

"Who was she?"

"No one special. Old acquaintance."

"Right. She need a job?"

My brow lifts. "You burn through another assistant?"

He shrugs and runs his fingers through his hair. "You know me."

"What's wrong with this one?"

"Shit at making coffee and fucked up my schedule. Booked an appointment pro bono for a murder defendant. One of those 'I didn't do it even though all evidence points otherwise' fuckers who can't pay. I'm not a charity worker and I'm too lazy for that shit."

I chuckle and a brilliant idea pops in my head. "I know a hard worker and you'd never dream of touching her or I'd kick the shit out of you."

"Who?"

"My sister."

He sighs. "You're kidding, right?"

"No. She called yesterday. Looking for a new job. The company she works for is on a downward spiral. Owner's filing bankruptcy and closing up shop."

"Let me get this straight. You want your sister. To work. For *me*."

I shrug. "Why not?"

"All right. Send her resume over. If she's qualified, I'll set up an interview."

I stare at him like he's an alien. "I put her through college. She's more than qualified to make your fucking coffee."

He shakes his head. "Jesus. Some acquaintance."

"Huh?"

"That chick from earlier has you all worked up."

I don't answer. That flash drive she handed me earlier damn near burns a hole in my pocket. I haven't taken a look at it yet.

Thinking about it sends anxiety coursing through my blood. You can tell a lot about someone by their bank accounts and personal files. I might not like what I find. In fact, I know I won't.

They're old wounds that should stay in the past.

"Want another drink?"

"Naw. I'm good."

"You sure?" He looks past me. "Two targets just walked in. I feel generous enough to share." His mouth twists into a smile.

"They're all yours." I should join him and the two hot blondes he'll most likely fuck later, but I have too much shit on my mind.

Jenna fucking Jacobi.

I smack Maxwell on the shoulder. "Don't end up with bugs on your dick." I flash him a grin.

"Eat my ass."

I laugh and leave him to it. "Later."

"Later, bro."

———

When I get home my sister, Claire, waits by the door. Tears stream down her cheeks.

Jesus, how many emotional women can I deal with in one day? I stare up toward the ceiling and shake my head at God. It's like he's torturing me.

"What's wrong?" I unlock the door.

She's always been sensitive. Our father coddled her too much because she was the baby and the only girl in our family. Our mother passed away during childbirth with her.

Dad was never the same afterward. Treated her like she was made of glass.

"Brian broke up with me." She hiccups on a sob and follows me into my apartment.

"That guy was a fuckbag. He did you a favor." I sigh as soon as I say it. I should be more understanding, but for fuck's sake. I can't handle this shit right now. Part of me wants to go beat the shit out of Brian's bitch ass. I don't know if it's because him breaking up with Claire has created an inconvenience for me, or because he's broken Claire's heart. Probably a combination.

"I loved him. I really thought he was the one."

I stand there and stare, shaking my head at her for a second. Finally, I sigh and muss up her hair like when we were kids. "He didn't want commitment. He wanted what he couldn't have. You were a challenge. He wanted in your pants. He either got what he wanted or gave up and got it elsewhere." Someone has to be honest with her. "Listen to me. Men are pieces of shit. All of us. Even me."

Growing up, I practically raised Claire. Dad wasn't around much. He was too busy working and he couldn't afford daycare or to hire a sitter. Our older brother was out the door the moment he turned sixteen. He was heavily into drugs and last I heard he was living in a halfway house in California. I tried to help him get his life together, but he didn't want it. He wasn't ready to help himself.

Whenever Claire needs anything she counts on me. Hell, maybe I'm as bad as our dad.

When I went off to college I felt guilty for leaving her behind, but I worked my ass off and sent home what money I could.

We're definitely close.

She looks like she wants to die. I don't usually deal with these *things*. Maybe if I change the subject…

"May have a job lined up for you. Maxwell needs an assistant."

Her eyes brighten, and she sniffles, rubbing her nose with a tissue. "Really?"

"Just talked to him about it. Dust off your resume and get it to him tomorrow. The benefits are great, and you could probably move up quick at the firm."

"You know I don't want to be a lawyer. I hate the whole corporate scene. I love to write."

I try not to roll my eyes. Claire has been writing her epic novel since she was fifteen. She refuses to let anyone read it until it's perfect. I tried to get her to send it to one of my contacts in New York from my college days, but she refused and said she wants to make it on her own. I don't know a lot about the publishing business, but I know few people succeed at it. It has to be hard to get your foot in the door. Why would someone turn down a guaranteed meeting with a fucking agent?

People baffle me. Even my sister.

She'll change her mind once she gets tired of Maxwell bossing her around.

I take one look at her and I just can't be a prick to two people I actually care about in one day. It's exhausting, mentally and emotionally. "Call in some takeout."

"Chinese?"

"Whatever you want." I loosen my tie and head to my room to change out of my suit.

Claire smiles. Good enough for me. Maybe she'll help take my mind off that fucking kiss earlier.

I doubt I'll be able to eat. Maxwell was right. Jenna has me in fucking knots. That goddamn kiss. I had no intention of doing it but when she was staring up at me all helpless, it was like I was transported back in time and we were two stupid kids in love again.

I'd never admit that to anyone in my life.

I pull out Jenna's flash drive and plug it into my laptop, then join Claire on the couch for some ridiculous reality show.

"I ordered pizza. Got your favorite. Ham and pineapple. It's disgusting."

"Better than that shit you eat with barbecue sauce."

"Whatever. We're in Texas. It's like a sin not to love barbecue on everything." She grins.

I grab the remote and turn the TV to an MMA fight.

"So barbaric." She scrunches her nose and sighs.

"That's nothing compared to what I'll do to Brian if you end up crying by my door again." He wouldn't be the first asshole I fucked up for hurting her.

"Seriously, I'll be fine. It just sucks."

A while later a knock sounds at my door. Must be our food.

I look through the peephole. Maxwell's holding a pizza box.

I open the door and he just walks on in. "Got the wrong apartment. Would've kept it if it didn't have that shitty pineapple on it. You need help for eating that shit. You owe me thirty bucks." He smacks me in the gut after setting the pizza box on my kitchen counter. His head whips over to the couch. "Oh, hey, Claire, didn't see you."

"Hey." She offers him a soft smile, waving as she hangs over the back of the couch staring at us.

"Be at my office next Monday if you want a job."

Her face lights up. "Great! Thanks."

"Thanks, man." I give him a head nod and hand him thirty bucks.

"No problem." He pops the top of the box open and steals a slice. "Now, if you'll excuse me." He leans next to my ear. "I have two blondes that need some dick."

I shake my head and grin as he walks out the door. "Later, bro."

Claire and I fill our plates with pizza and plop down on the couch.

Jenna's still running through my mind. I don't even touch my food. Probably look like a damn zombie.

"You okay?"

"Do you believe in ghosts?"

"I don't know. Never really thought about it, why?" She takes a bite of barbecue bullshit.

"I saw one today."

Her nose scrunches up and she laughs. "What?"

"I saw Jenna."

Claire's jaw drops.

"Had the same reaction."

"Did you talk to her?"

"I don't want to talk about it yet."

"Seriously? You can't drop a J-bomb on me and not say anything else."

"I can't say anything. She's a client."

"Oh."

It's one of the perks of being a lawyer. Even when it's not true, if I don't want to talk about something I bust out attorney client privilege. People always buy it.

"Yeah." I sigh and take a drink of my beer.

At least I have pizza and beer. It's the one constant in my life that never gets shitty. Pizza and beer.

Chapter Eight

JENNA

I can't believe Jaxson kissed me. I can't stop thinking about him and his tempting lips. I know he's right. It shouldn't have happened, but I'd be a liar if I said I didn't want him. He's all I've ever wanted.

When I left him waiting, I thought I'd lost him forever. But what if I haven't?

That kiss spoke to me in so many ways.

I mean, it was definitely hot. But, it was possessive too. It also showed Jaxson still wants me, or at least feels something.

I didn't see a wedding ring on his finger. He could still have someone. But why would he kiss me that way?

Maybe it's just silly thoughts of a fairytale ending after all. Does anyone ever stop wanting that? I have no idea who he's become. What kind of man he is now. But people don't change. He has to still be that sweet boy I fell in love with so many years ago, the kind soul I never stopped loving.

The house is empty when I arrive. For some reason I feel lighter. Free from the chains for now.

For the first time in as long as I can remember I stare at my reflection in the mirror and don't hate what I see. I feel something I haven't felt in a long, long time—hope. Maybe I can get back parts of me I thought were lost forever.

I go to the bar and pour myself a drink.

I need a fresh start.

A mulligan.

The first thing I do is take off my wedding ring. My hand feels strange without it. It was my grandmother's ring, and I should've never worn it to begin with. Not for Leonard.

I walk to the bedroom and yank Leonard's clothes off the hangers. The rage builds as I stare at all the expensive suits paid for with my family's money. I want to hurt Leonard like he's hurt me.

Burning his shit won't do anything but piss him off but it'll make me feel a hell of a lot better.

He's usually gone for two weeks or more at a time when he goes to Vegas.

When he comes back his shit will be nothing but ashes as he's served with divorce papers.

I'm not brave enough to watch it in person, so I'm having security cameras installed with the little money I do have tucked away on the side. I want to make sure I have evidence of him receiving the documents.

God knows he'll make everything as difficult as possible.

If he knew about my rainy-day account, he'd have drained it years ago. I've been siphoning here and there for years and figured anything extra I'd use to revive a charity my mother had started.

I stare around at the house, knowing that not many people are aware of what really happened behind these walls. Dad told everyone she died in her sleep from a heart condition that had gone undetected, but truth is she took her own life. She took a bottle of sleeping pills. Couldn't bear the thought of all the things they'd done. I don't know if it was because of the deal Dad made for me, but I think it might've played a role.

I was staying at the house while Leonard was in Vegas. She told me goodnight like she did every night.

Kissed my father's cheek and went upstairs. She dressed in her favorite nightgown.

She was already dead by the time Dad went to bed. He slept next to her all night long. Was too drunk to notice.

It wasn't until this that something happened—it wasn't until he woke up next to her and she hadn't moved, that it really sunk in.It was the only time in her life that she didn't wake up and cook breakfast for everyone.

I fell into the same pattern. Doing the same things. Cooking for Leonard every morning. I became the docile wife that stood by, afraid to do anything.

I take another drink straight from the bottle as I think about all the horrible things I've endured.

The pain sears through my heart like a hot knife.

I'm angry but not bitter. Seeing Jaxson today and feeling his lips —lips I never thought I'd taste again—I have hope.

I deserve better.

I deserve Jaxson. I know I do. He needs to know the truth. But how do I tell him?

As I carry Leonard's belongings to the firepit out back, I feel rejuvenated. Every step is like reclaiming my life.

Dousing his stuff in lighter fluid, I smile to myself, wishing I'd have been strong enough to do this years ago. I should have run away. What would have been? I'll always live with that regret.

I walk back in the house and look for anything I can burn. Anything that links me to Leonard—I want it gone. My wedding dress comes to mind. As I rifle through the attic I find a box I haven't come across in years. My memory box full of letters and keepsakes from Jaxson.

I hold his class ring in my palm. It still has the embroidery thread wrapped around the band so it would fit on my finger.

The day he gave it to me he promised one day he'd replace it with an engagement ring. He said it was his promise to me. If only I'd given him an opportunity to keep that promise—I wouldn't be where I am now.

So many nights I spent thinking about the life we would've had.

Jaxson would've worked his way through college and I'd have gone to vet school. Tears roll down my cheeks thinking about the kids we'd have running around. I could've been so happy. He wouldn't be so cold. We could've had such an amazing life.

Things weren't supposed to be like this. I guess life has a way of being cruel. The world can be a very cold place.

I want to go back and do it all over again.

Slipping his ring on my finger another tear drips onto the plywood floor.

The look he had on his face when he first saw me today was like plunging a dagger into my chest. Part of him hates me, and I don't blame him. Even if he never gives me another chance, I owe him the truth. He needs to know I did it for him and his family.

I love him.

Rubbing my finger over the stone of his ring I know I always will.

I'll never stop.

How could I?

He was meant to be mine.

We were made for each other.

I smell the blaze from the backyard as I make my way back down the stairs. I wonder if this place can ever feel like home again.

I don't think it will. Maybe I should burn the house to the ground. Without this house I have nothing left for Leonard to take. Nothing worth fighting me for in the divorce.

He's taken everything already.

I drag my wedding gown and memento box into the backyard. The train of the dress rakes through the dirt and I want to stomp on it.

The fire burns hot on my face and I want the house gone. Want nothing to do with all of this.

A candle too close to the curtains upstairs would be enough to get the fire started...

Chapter Nine

JAXSON

I haven't slept for shit after looking at the flash drive. She documented everything. The bruises on her skin had me balling my hands into fists. I was such a bastard to her at the office. It was shitty of her to leave me, but I never wished that kind of pain on her. Sure, I wanted her to hurt the way I did but what that bastard did to her—I want to kill him.

I've never been an angry person. I'm always the calm and collected one who thinks rationally.

But, a rage I've never felt before courses through my veins and I don't know what to do about it. There's nothing I can do but try to burn it off in my home gym. I run five miles on the treadmill, practically sprinting the whole time, and I still can't get the pictures out of my head. I almost wish she hadn't shown them to me. There's no way I'll ever trust her again, but I'll still keep her safe. Get her away from that piece of shit.

She said he was in Vegas but what if he comes home early? What will he do once he finds out she's filed for divorce?

It's a crazy idea, but I want to bring her to my building.

He can't get in without a code and we have great security. She'll be safe here.

I don't owe her anything. I know that, but I can't look the other way. I can't walk away when she needs me. She may have left me hanging, but that's not my style. I still care about her as a person.

She sought me out for a reason. Maybe it was a last-effort cry for help. I'm a damn good attorney. I can get this fixed for her.

I can still guard her heart even though she didn't guard mine.

I want to laugh when I see all that her father had left. He lost everything because he was an idiot. It should make me happy, but it doesn't. I can't revel in it because it's Jenna's livelihood.

I haven't looked at her husband much yet, but I bet the fucker's dirty. Something doesn't sit right about the whole thing. The date of her marriage puts it a short amount of time after I left. There's no way Jenna could've hidden another relationship. People surprise you, but there's just no way—something happened.

I know Jenna loved me. I was too proud to look back, but I can't help but think about what would've happened if I'd gone back for her. Would things have turned out differently?

What's done is done. I can't change that.

She wanted to explain at the office, but I don't know if I want her to. What if she says things I don't want to hear? What if I could've had her?

I flick off the lights in the gym and head for a shower, knowing I probably won't sleep again tonight.

———

Days have passed.

I tried to call Jenna a few times and it keeps going to voicemail. I don't want to leave a message in case her husband checks her phone. If her evidence is any indication, I wouldn't put it past the dude. Abusive husbands are always controlling and do shit like that. I should've passed her case off like I said I would. It's too personal.

But, I just—can't.

I don't know what to do. Do I drive out to her place to check on her? Pretend I need her to sign paperwork? I don't want to tangle with her husband but I'm worried. What if he knows she was here and he did something to her?

I can't sit here not knowing.

Knocking on Weston's office door I let out a breath. He isn't going to like this shit at all. I never let personal feelings get in the way of a case, but this is different.

It's Jenna.

"Got a minute?"

"Sure. Come in."

I take a seat across from him and just dive in head first.

"Remember the time I got drunk back in college and told you about the girl?"

"The one you were pussy-whipped over that left you behind? Yeah, how could I forget?"

I stare off at the wall. "I wasn't *that* bad."

"Your life was a country song." He laughs. "What about her?"

"She came in yesterday."

"Damn."

I sigh. "Yeah. Hadn't seen her in thirteen years."

"You okay?"

I should lie. I look weak as fuck right now. I can't, though. Weston's the only one of the assholes in the office I'd trust with this. If anyone understands, it's him. Especially now that he's settling down. "Honestly…" I blow out a breath and run a hand through my hair. "I don't know. She's petitioning for divorce. It's bad."

His eyes narrow. "And she sought you out for counsel?"

"Yeah."

I lay out the story for him about the files she brought in.

"I don't like it. Won't end well for you. Telling you this as a friend and a colleague. You're too invested emotionally. You'll be tempted to step in and play hero. I don't want you working it."

"I can handle the shit." It's a lie. We both know it. Fucking Jenna. She has me lying to my best friend and partner.

He eyes me for a few seconds that feel like forever. "You're not going to take no for an answer, so I won't waste my breath. You didn't come in here to ask, you came in here to apprise me of facts, and I appreciate that even if I think it's stupid."

"It's not—"

"Don't interrupt me. Anyone else I'd tell to fuck off right now. *That* says something about you. It's your decision. You know it's personal, but I trust your judgment. Keep me informed."

"I need to check on her. She hasn't answered my calls. I need to see her. I think I should move her into the empty apartment on my floor to keep her safe."

He glares across the table. "Jesus, how bad did this woman fuck you up? Are you insane?"

"What?"

"She could be fine. Could just be another client. What are you going to do? Drive to her house? Kick the shit out of her husband? We're not twenty-one anymore. Fuck. You need to grow up."

"Of course I'm not going to go in swinging. I can make something up if he's there."

"This is just—fucking stupid. Are you listening to yourself?"

I rub my face with my palms and stare right back at him. "I have to do this. I *need* to know she's not hurt."

"Fucking hell." He stands up and starts pacing. "Did you stop to think maybe she changed her mind. It's not uncommon. She's a battered woman. A lot of them never have the courage to leave."

"Even more reason for me to go."

"Oh, bullshit. You're not a professional at helping abused women. You can't force help on someone like that. They have to want it."

"She filed for divorce."

"And if she did it willingly, she'll be in touch."

"I'll talk to her. Fuck, I'll get Brooke to talk to her. She deals with that stuff."

"You're not bringing my wife into this shit. If you need to see her go do it, but man—you can't put your career on the line for her. She dumped you. Remember? You just saw her once, for the first time in thirteen years. You wouldn't do this for another client without all the information up front."

I know that shit. I don't need fucking reminders. Maybe I'm being an idiot, but I'll never forgive myself if something is wrong.

I should've already gone. I won't make that mistake a second time.

Chapter Ten

JENNA

It's gone. I burned it to ashes.

There's nothing left but the frame and a few walls. They ruled it an accident.

I didn't do it on purpose, even though I'd thought about it. When I lit Leonard's stuff on fire the wind blew the flames back on the house. I was extremely lucky. It happened after I went to sleep. I can't believe I was that stupid. I drank a little too much and passed out before putting it out. Several hours later I woke with the roof already threatening to fall in.

Fortunately, a neighbor saw the blaze on his way home and called for help. I've been in the hospital for two days from the smoke inhalation. They've treated me with oxygen and an IV. There are a few first-degree burns on my left arm, but other than that I came out pretty much unscathed.

Revenge nearly killed me.

A cab dropped me off about an hour ago. I'm sitting on a stump, pondering my life. I need to find somewhere to stay. We had insurance but I'm sure Leonard will find some way to get the money.

I wonder what my mother would think of all this. God, I wish she was here. I could really use one of her hugs.

Leonard doesn't know about the fire. Has no clue. I don't want to deal with him yet.

I should probably call Jaxson. He's my attorney, after all.

Just as I think about it a black SUV pulls in the driveway and Jaxson gets out.

God, he's beautiful in his suit. I probably look like a hot mess. I know I feel like one.

My hair needs brushed, and my clothes smell like smoke. I'm wearing the same thing I wore to his office. I was lucky I left my purse in the car and the important paperwork in the fireproof safe.

So many things rush through my mind right now. I'm scared.

I really want Jaxson to take me in his arms and tell me everything is going to be all right. I just want to be held for a few minutes. Forget about the world for even a second.

"Jenna." Nothing in the world sounds better than my name on his lips right now.

There's something about him that just makes me feel—safe. Protected.

"Over here." I wobble a little when I stand up and didn't realize how lightheaded I was.

He stares at the charred shell that was once my house. "What happened?"

I fight against the tears. I don't want him to see me like this. "Long story."

"I've got time."

It's hard to be strong with him staring at me the way he does, but I don't want to look weak. I'm *not* weak. Not anymore. "Walk with me?"

He holds out an arm for me to take. I accept it without even thinking.

He has no idea how much I need his support right now, but I refuse to beg for anything.

We walk around the house and I confess everything. I know it was stupid, but he doesn't seem to judge. It's like the old Jaxson is back, not the hard-ass lawyer. It's hard not to smile. Jaxson gets me like no one ever has.

When we walk past the barn Jaxson stops in his tracks and looks inside. "We spent a lot of time up there." A fleeting smile flashes across his face for a split-second.

I take his hand and lead him to the ladder.

He stops in front of it and shakes his head. It's like he's holding back everything. Like he's pushed our past way down inside and doesn't want to open that box. "I don't know." He shakes his head, slowly.

"Please?" I give him a long, hard stare, and step onto one of the rungs.

"I just—"

"I've never seen you at a loss for words before."

"I'm not sure this is something I want to revisit."

"I just want five minutes."

"Look, you don't owe me—"

"Jaxson?"

"Yeah?"

"I need this. Please?"

Something about the way he stares at me, the whole situation—I can't fight back the tears any longer. They stream down my cheeks.

Jaxson moves at lightning speed and wipes the tears from my face. "Okay." He nods lightly and holds the old wooden ladder steady. "Okay."

He follows me up once I reach the top.

The hayloft is empty other than a few old boxes.

I open one of them and find an old horse blanket, then spread it on the dusty floor.

His suit is dirty, and he has a smudge on his cheek, but seems oblivious.

"This is how I remember you." I wipe the dark line away.

His smooth fingers grasp my hand. "What happened to us?" His gorgeous brown eyes lock onto mine.

I lose all train of thought as he just stares.

"Jenna?"

I blink. "Sorry. Just—sorry."

"Maybe we shouldn't do this."

No! I have him up here and I may never get another opportunity. I look away and start the story before he can change his mind. "That night ruined my life." I wipe a tear from my cheek. "There are things you don't know. Things I've been ashamed to tell anyone. Especially you."

"I'm in a hayloft. There's not really anywhere for me to escape. Just tell me what I did."

I shake my head and cup a palm over my mouth. "You d-didn't do anything."

He grabs me by the hand and leads me to the blanket so we can sit.

I try to smile through all the pain and rub my thumb over his knuckles. "Your hands used to be so rough." I miss the callouses on his hands from days of working the ranch and mending broken fence posts. "Things didn't turn out so bad for you, right? You're doing well for yourself, like you said you would. I'm so proud of you."

"Jenna?"

"Yeah?"

"We both know that's not why I'm up here."

"Right." I shake my head to try and snap out of the daze that forms around my brain any time he's around. "I wanted to go with you so bad." My voice tries to crack. I hate this. I hate crying. It's not me. But with Jaxson it's just—different. "I was waiting. I was right over there in my room, staring out the window, waiting." I burst into tears.

"What were you waiting for?" He takes my hands in his. "Just breathe for a second. Take your time."

"I was waiting to sneak out my window. We were so close. So close to the life we wanted."

"So why didn't you come?"

"My mom. She came to the door and said Dad wanted me in the office."

Jaxson's head angles to the ground and he just stares at the floor, silent.

"He knew. He knew what we were doing."

Jaxson's face holds no emotion as I tell him everything that happened.

After a few long seconds that feel like an eternity, he shakes his head and looks up at me. "Jesus." He stands up and laces his fingers behind his head, pacing around the loft. He keeps looking at me and then out toward where the house was. "You should have told someone."

Tears roll down my cheeks. "I know, but I was scared. He was going to throw your family on the street. They would've had nothing."

His jaw clenches and he stares. "That wasn't a burden meant just for you. You had a phone."

"I-I..."

"No, Jenna. That's what caused all this. You made me hate you. The woman I loved more than life. All the evil thoughts that drove me for years. Yeah, your old man was a prick for what he did. But we could've figured something out. I would've waited for you. I would've done—something."

"I know." I stand up and try to get him to look at me. "You were stronger than me. It's why I wanted to follow you anywhere. You always were."

He sighs and seems to loosen a little.

"I can't fix that. But I need help now and you're the only person I knew to turn to. You saw the pictures I'm sure. He'll be back."

Jaxson whips around with rage on his face that I've never seen. "He *won't* touch you again."

"I just need to be divorced and done with him."

Jaxson stalks over and grips my hand. "You won't see him again unless I'm in the room. I have an apartment next to mine. Fully furnished. You'll stay there until this is done. There's security at all hours."

I shake my head nervously, but I'd be lying to myself if I wasn't screaming on the inside for him to take me there right now. Jax has always been protective and assertive. He's just, *it* for me. "You don't have to take care of me."

"This is happening. I won't lose you…" He looks away and catches himself for a moment.

I want to melt into his arms, but I can't. Not until this is all behind me.

"History isn't going to repeat itself. You're going."

"There was no way for you to know. It wasn't your fault. I was just doing…"

"It *was* my fault. I should've come back. I should've known something…"

Brushing his thumb over one of the scars on my arm, he bends his head down and kisses the raised skin.

Looking into his eyes, I feel transported back in time to the last time we were in the loft. He still stares at me the same way he did then.

Chapter Eleven

JAXSON

I want nothing more than to kiss Jenna so hard that she agrees to my demands. "I'll be there for you this time."

"Jax…"

"We both know what's going to happen." I slant my mouth over hers and claim what should've been mine all these years. I tell her with the kiss that she's going with me and there's nothing she can do about it. I won't have her homeless, running around like a target for her ex. It's not gonna happen.

"Okay." She breathes out the word after our lips part.

I take her by the hand. "You'll love the place. It's comfortable and secure."

She gives me a brief nod like she's ready to leave this nightmare behind.

I just want her to feel safe, protected. We walk outside, and I guide her into the car and buckle her seatbelt. "I'll have someone come for your car."

She nods again.

I walk around to the driver's side and glance over at the charred house. I just shake my head and try to fight back a snicker.

I can't believe she burnt the fucking house down.

She'd always seemed to love the place growing up. Hell, I loved it too, but only because it was *her* place. I guess after what she's gone through in there, the feelings can easily change.

I take her hand in mine as we pull away. My fingers brush over her knuckles just to see her smile for even a brief second. I can't remember the last time things felt so—right.

"What's this?" I glance down.

She has my class ring on her finger.

"Found it the other night." She half blushes and looks away. "Sorry, I don't know. It's silly."

"Why's it silly?"

"I put it on and it just felt right. I know I'm married and everything, but…"

"But what?"

"Come on, Jax." She shrugs and stares out the window.

"What?"

She turns slowly toward me. "I've never stopped loving you."

Her confession sends all kinds of emotions coursing through my body. I should've known she'd have never stayed behind and married some asshole. Left me hanging high and dry. It makes sense that she'd still be holding onto things.

I'm not sure what this will look like. I have a certain lifestyle. I'm a different person now, and I don't know if I can just morph back into the kind of man I was. There's no way she'll approve of the man I've become, no matter how much money or power I have.

When she first walked into my office I didn't expect any of this. I don't know what I want anymore. I'd convinced myself I was happy, but now that she's back in my life I feel differently. It's like I'm ashamed. She always made me want to be better—a good person.

If I know one thing in the moment, it's this—I still love her.

I've never felt *this* for anyone else.

She shakes her head. "You don't have to say anything in return. I know it's crazy." Her fingers twirl my ring around on her finger.

"This whole thing is complicated."

Her head angles toward the floorboard. "I know."

"Look, Jenna, I…"

"You don't have to say anything in return. Seriously. I didn't expect you to be waiting around on me or anything. You don't owe me anything."

"Hey." I grip her forearm.

She glances over at me.

I turn briefly from the road to face her. "I still love you too. I never stopped."

"Really?"

"Of course. What we had doesn't just go away."

"I know, it's just been so long."

"Look, you're married and I'm your lawyer. It's all crazy right now."

"Nothing can happen. Got it."

I shake my head. "Will you just sit there for a second and let me speak?" I smile to let her know I'm halfway joking.

She pretends to zip her lips with one hand. It's adorable. She's beautiful even when she's been through a housefire and hooked to IVs.

"We need to keep our distance and let this play out. You have to be smart. You've been through a lot."

She starts to say something but I hold a finger up to stop her.

"It doesn't mean that I don't want to explore things further. But right now… It's too much too fast for you. One thing at a time. You don't need extra complications."

"May I speak now, sir?"

"Be careful how you say things like that. I only have so much restraint."

She grins. "I get what you're saying, but you have no idea how long I've waited for this. For you. If there is one certainty in my life, it's that I want to be with you. I always have. I always will. Time won't change how I feel about you."

"We'll have to wait and see what happens."

My cock grows rock-hard thinking about taking her to my apartment building. Her being right down the hall. I want her heart. I want her mind. I want her body.

I want *her*.

Goddamn, I've never wanted anything so much in my life, but we have to do this the right way. My knuckles turn white as I grip the steering wheel trying to stay in control. Right now I want nothing more than to pull the car over and fuck her in the backseat.

We were always good together, but we were kids. I'm a grown man now and can't even imagine what it would be like to fuck her. Make her come on my cock over and over again. Press every one of her buttons until she can't walk.

There's a tense silence the rest of the drive. It's like the air is charged with pure sex. Every strand of DNA in every cell in my body screams for me to claim her. Take whatever I want from her body. The worst part is she'd let me have it all. She'd give me whatever the hell I wanted and probably more. If I don't get her into that apartment and get some space, I'm going to come inside her pussy over and over. I'm going to bite, suck, lick, and mark every square inch of her skin to let the world know that she's mine and they can fuck off.

I steal a glance at her as I park the truck. Her pearly whites graze her bottom lip as she watches every move I make.

Fuck me. Everything she does makes me want to groan.

Every flick of her hair over her shoulder has me adjusting my cock when she looks away.

My balls practically scream at me, just aching for release.

The entire walk into the building she keeps glancing at me. Batting eyelashes. And not in a flirty way, just a Jenna way. It's just her. She's everything.

I'm a gentleman and hold doors. I ask her if she needs help. I try to do everything for her.

I don't do that shit for anyone. Nobody.

Every step I take next to her is pure torture.

The second we're in the elevator and the doors close, my hands are in her hair and my lips are on her mouth.

Way to take it slow.

I practically crush her mouth with my kiss. My tongue shoves against the seam of her lips, demanding entrance. She willingly opens up for me. Her tongue sweeps across mine as we battle for control. She only does it to work me up more, though. She still remembers exactly how to kiss me, and exactly how to shift every gear in my body.

I'm like a starved animal.

It's pure primal, raw instincts. I growl against her neck and tear at her clothes. I'll shred anything in my way to get my cock inside her.

I need her—now. More than anything I've ever needed in my life.

The ding of the elevator saves her from being fucked senseless.

I snap out of my sex-induced stupor long enough to realize what I'm doing and try to straighten our clothes up.

I want to take her to my place. To my bed. But if I do, I'll never let her leave it. I need to be smart. She's in a horrible marriage.

She may want me now but what happens when she finds out who I really am? She might regret this. There's so much life she hasn't experienced because she's been chained to her husband. She deserves to get to live on her terms for a while.

I've had time to experience life. I've fucked too many women to count. I've traveled and started a business and been to black tie events and penthouse parties.

"You're overthinking. You always did."

"You can't read my mind." Yeah, she can. She's always been able to. She's always known—me.

"I want you. I always have."

I push us against the hallway wall and press my forehead to hers. "You don't know what you want right now."

"You're wrong."

"No, I'm not. You need to put your life back together…"

Her hand slides down to my cock. "I want you to fuck me."

I unwillingly push her hand away. I've never turned down pussy in my life and my cock doesn't know what the hell is going on right now. If I didn't love her we'd still be banging in a parking lot somewhere right now. But, I just can't do this to her. She's not in a good place. "No." I shake my head at her.

"Is there someone else?"

I scoff. "No. It's because…" I lower my voice because I realize I'm talking way louder than I usually do, almost yelling. "I want to do things right. You don't know me anymore. Not the guy I've become. You might not like him."

"So, you're a bad boy now? Maybe I'll like that."

I pin her arms above her head against the wall and press against her, hard. Then I lean down next to her ear.

Her breath hitches and she gulps.

I was never rough like this with her when we were younger. "Let me take care of you. I have to do this the right way."

She starts to say something, and I exhale down her neck.

A light sweet moan parts her lips and I have no idea where all this fucking self-control has come from.

"I love you. But not now. There will be plenty of time for fun later. Or you may run for the hills."

"Okay." She nods, breathless. "But I'm not going anywhere."

"Good."

I press away from her and grab all her stuff I dropped on the floor when I shoved her against the wall.

She leans back, staring at me with a light grin on her face.

"What?"

She shakes her head. "Nothing. You're just—hot."

I smirk. "Damn right I am."

I unlock the door to the apartment next to mine.

Her eyes grow wide when she sees it. I give her a quick tour of the place and pretty much watch her fall in love with it.

"It's beautiful. Thank you, for everything."

"It's no problem. You'll be safe here, and we'll get you back on your feet."

She smiles as she walks over and stares out the window.

I keep my distance across the room. I already know I won't be able to control myself, living next door. But I'll do everything in my power not to fuck things up for her. Despite the urge to fuck her all night long, then call in to work and fuck her all day tomorrow, I want her happy. It's all I've ever really wanted.

"I need to do some work. Make yourself at home. I'm next door if you need anything. I'll order lunch. If you make a list, I'll have my housekeeper go shopping for you. Clothes, whatever you need. There are towels and everything in the bathroom. There may even be clothes. Claire stays here sometimes."

"Your sister?"

"Yeah."

"I haven't seen her since your dad took her away."

"I moved them closer as soon as I was able to."

She nods.

"So, I'm going to…" I throw a thumb back toward the door.

"Okay."

As soon as I leave the apartment I'm on my phone making calls to get eyes on her husband. I want that cocksucker out of her life for good. We have all kinds of PIs and security that do work for the firm. Dudes nobody wants to fuck with. "You keep that asshole in your sights at all times."

"I'm on it, boss. If he pisses sideways, you'll know the direction."

"Good."

Leonard Reyes put his hands on what's mine. He's going to suffer for every goddamn time he put his hands on her and pay her every fucking nickel he took from her.

I'd kill that motherfucker but if I go to prison I'll lose Jenna.

He's done hurting her. He's done existing.

I'll have that bitch buried in the desert with a goddamn cactus tombstone.

I send a text to Weston, so he won't worry.

Jax: I'm back. She's here. All under control. Be back in the office Monday.

Weston: Sounds good. Handle your shit. Let me know if you need anything.

Jax: Can you keep this between us for now? I don't want the husband finding out where she is.

Weston: Is he a cause for concern? How bad is it?

Jax: Under control. Don't worry. I have eyes on him. He won't get near her. But I want it to be as difficult as possible for him to even make an effort.

Weston: I hope you know what you're doing. You should give me the case. You know I'll roast his nuts on a fire.

Jax: I appreciate it, but I need this. I want to bury him with the shovel myself.

Chapter Twelve

JENNA

Being next door to Jax is surreal. I've been numb for so long I don't know how to feel. Overwhelmed—that's a good word for it. Jaxson's the dream. He was out of reach for so long and now I'm next door. He's right on the other side of the wall. When he kissed me I thought I might die. Part of me always held onto a hope that we'd be together again, but I always thought Leonard would kill me before it came to fruition.

I'm a mess—need a shower. Thinking about Jax kissing me while I smell like a rotten ashtray makes me cringe.

I walk to the master bathroom and start the shower even though I'd love to soak in the tub. I need to wash this filth away first. The last thing I want to do is sit in a tub and marinade in it. A bath can wait.

As I wash off the grime from the past few days, I feel rejuvenated. My mind clears like the water swirls everything down the drain. I'll do whatever it takes to win back my Jax and keep him for good. After seeing his smile and tasting his lips I know I can't live without having him.

I love him so much it hurts.

I want to look into his eyes every day. I want to see him look like the boy he once was, not the man I turned him into.

I just need to rid myself of Leonard first.

Walking from the bathroom, I wrap a towel around my body and put my hair up with another. I didn't even think to look for clothes. Thoughts of being clean trumped everything else.

I stroll into the master bedroom and look for something to wear but all I find is a t-shirt. I slip it over my head and it hangs down to my thighs. I'll have to make do with washing my one pair of clothes until I can go shopping.

The laundry room sits just off the kitchen connected to the pantry. I start a load, the only thing I really still have in the world, and search for a pen to make a list of things I need. Looking around, I can't help but smile a little at the fact that he really did go after his dreams. He did it. All on his own. It makes him even more attractive. I never would've imagined him in this posh building wearing a suit and tie every day, but I'm not surprised that he found success.

I don't expect him to take care of me or buy me anything. I can handle myself. It's sweet that he wants to, but I can't let him do it. He's done enough already. I brought all this on myself. I can tell he wants to take the blame for some of our past, but it was me. I thought I was doing the right thing, but now, I'm not so sure.

I'm bent over the counter writing when Jaxson walks in carrying a bag of takeout. His eyes instantly brighten when I look at him over my shoulder. I forgot the shirt is probably riding halfway up my ass.

"Jesus. You trying to give me a heart attack?" He places the bag on the dining table and crosses the room in three strides so that he's right behind me.

His hands go to my ass and shivers immediately dance up my spine. He peppers kisses along my neck. "I brought food." His fingers dig into my hips. "Think I found a better menu, though." Sliding a hand around to my stomach he presses his hard cock against me. Heat pools between my thighs and I know I want him. There's nothing stopping us from being together.

I'm only married on paper. Not in my heart. Jaxson owns my heart. He always has.

"And I'm hungry." Spinning me around to face him, he lifts me onto the counter. With one knee he spreads my legs forcefully, and then kneels down.

I watch him, wondering how this will compare to when we were younger. He's all man now.

A growl leaves his throat when he feels how wet I am for him.

I have no shame. There's no hiding how much I want him. His torturous lips meet the sensitive skin of my inner thigh. He teases the spot I want him most, rubbing his finger over my clit just enough to make me purr.

It's been so long since I've been loved by a man who actually cares for me.

He's the only one.

Ever.

His mouth latches onto my pussy as he hums against my clit. He watches every single one of my reactions to his touch, then slowly slides a finger inside me.

Tangling my fist in his hair, I hold on as he finger-fucks and licks me. It's better than I remember, and I'm already on the edge. He's improved his technique. I want to be jealous that he's been with others, but all I can think is that he's mine now.

"Fuck, your pussy is so damn tight, Jenna."

"I haven't been with anyone in years."

"How long's it been since someone made you feel good, baby?"

I arch my back when he hits the spot deep inside me just right.

A devilish grin spreads across his face.

I gasp when he does it again. "The-the last time I was with you."

"I'm going to make it up to you every goddamn day. I'll give you an orgasm for every day we've been apart."

He flicks his tongue across my clit.

"Holy shit." I nod at him. "May take a while."

"I've got time." He speeds up his fingers and tongue, to the point I'm squirming on the counter ready to explode.

He works his fingers in and out while his thumb circles my clit. "You ready?"

"For what?"

"To come all over my face." He dives back between my legs and takes my clit between his teeth, sucking and pulling.

My head flies back. "Oh my God, Jaxson." Fireworks go off behind my eyelids and waves of pleasure roll through my limbs.

It's the most intense orgasm I've had in my life.

Chapter Thirteen

JAXSON

W hen I walked in and saw Jenna's sweet ass it was game over. I knew I was going to make my move. Then she confessed that I was the last and only man to get her off and I nearly lost it. The need to get her off was so intense I couldn't stop.

She stares up at me after just coming all over my mouth.

I have to have her. I want to bury myself in that tight, hot cunt.

Her eyes grow wide when I throw her over my shoulder and haul her toward the door.

"Jax!"

I smack her on the ass and smile. Part of me is rock-hard knowing I'm about to be balls-deep inside her, but some other feeling invades my stomach. It just feels right, the way it was always supposed to be.

I stop when I open the door and glance down the hallway. Coast is clear. I haul her into my apartment because she belongs in my fucking bed, forever.

Once we're in my room I drop her on her back and make my way between her legs again with my face. She writhes and squirms as I taste her once more.

So. Fucking. Sweet.

Fuck keeping my distance. I want her. I fucking need her like I need water or air.

I can't get enough of her taste on my tongue. I want her coming every minute of the day. The more pleasure I bring her the more she seems to come back to life. It's what she deserves. It's what she's always deserved.

"I want you inside me."

I grin deviously. I used to love bringing her to the edge and letting her dangle before I'd allow her to come. I slide two fingers into her and curl them right up to her sweet spot.

There is nothing that compares. Nothing better than seeing Jenna naked in my bed.

Her warm skin pressing against mine. Her moaning my name over and over. I know sleeping with a married woman is wrong, but she was never his. Jenna Jacobi has always been mine.

The urge to fuck her is too great and I replace my fingers with the head of my cock.

She hasn't been with anyone in a long time. It may hurt her.

I ease into her even as her heels dig into my ass, trying to take me harder.

"Am I hurting you?"

Her body tenses as I push in farther, but she bites her bottom lip and shakes her head slightly. Her nails rake down my back.

Fuck she feels good. Her pussy stretches to fit me perfectly, the same way it did when I took her virginity.

I dip down and take one of her nipples into my mouth. She arches her back up into me.

"Fuck me. I want it." Her nails dig harder into my back.

"Oh, I'm going to fuck you." I push deeper, vowing to myself that I'm going to love her. I'm going to cherish Jenna. This is our second chance and I won't screw it up this time around. "Every goddamn day." I shove into her harder.

"Oh my God."

I brush her hair back from her face and look her in the eye. "Are you on the pill?"

"No. I was on the shot for years but stopped taking it."

"Good." I growl the word with a desire I've never felt before and plow into her. I want to tie her to me in every way possible. It may sound crazy and unhinged, but I don't give one single fuck. I want everything I thought was lost. I know I said she needed time and space to heal after the hell she's been through, but I want to be that for her. We've lost enough time already. I'm going to give Jenna the world.

I want my kid inside of her. I want what Weston has with Brooke and what Brodie found with April. I had it before all of them and lost it. We rarely get second chances at something amazing in life, and I'm not going to fuck it up again.

She sucks my thumb into her mouth as I stare deep into her eyes.

I'm going to fuck her every way possible for the rest of her life, but right now, it's the most emotional sex I've ever had in my life. Shifting my hips, I thrust slowly, wanting to savor every second I'm inside her. Show her how much I love her with every thrust. It's like we're one person, completely joined, and I don't want us to ever be apart.

Jenna's so damn beautiful. I can't stop staring as I quicken my pace.

She moans beneath me.

I lean down to her ear and whisper, "Come on my cock, Jenna."

She tightens around me and nods.

The harder I thrust, the more unraveled we both become. Before long I'm pistoning in and out of her and she's crying out my name over and over. When she clamps down on my cock I can't hold back any longer. I thrust to the hilt so hard it slams the headboard up against the wall and knocks down a picture. I keep my cock buried and blow in the depths of her. Wave after wave I thrust a little harder with each one, completely claiming her pussy, marking her as mine.

I stay inside her until I'm satisfied she took every single drop, and I hope she gets pregnant immediately.

Rolling off her, I put a hand on each of her thighs and keep her ass tilted up.

"What are you doing?" She has a bewildered look on her face.

I look at her pussy and there's a small amount of my come trying to make its way out. I push it back inside with one of my fingers.

"Marking you as mine." I grin. "Putting my baby in you."

"Jax…"

"Things will be different this time around."

Chapter Fourteen

JENNA

I've been in Jax's bed all morning. It all seems too good to be true. I know I should probably get my phone out of my purse and charge it. I'm sure someone has contacted Leonard about the fire.

I can't move, though.

Right now, I'm in the arms of the man I've always loved, and I just don't care. Maybe it's because I know when I get up I have to get back to the real world. To my real problems.

Jaxson wants to build a life with me. He looks dead serious every time he talks about it.

The life we were meant to have.

I want nothing more than for that to happen. I mean, the man is determined to put a baby in me. We've made love twice today. At first, I thought he was being silly, but he really is adamant about making it happen.

I can't tell if we're both still crazy in love, or just crazy. Maybe both.

His phone rings and wakes him up from a nap.

I sit back against the headboard and ogle his back and ass as he bends down to answer it.

I want to pinch myself, because this is all too good to be true.

Sitting on the edge of the bed he swipes his finger across the screen.

"Shit," he mutters under his breath.

"Everything okay?"

"No. I mean, umm, yeah. I gotta go to the hospital. My friend, one of the partners at the firm—they're having a baby."

"So go. I'll be here when you get back." I try to hide my disappointment that he has to leave. I keep forgetting that he has a life I know nothing about.

"I'm not going without you."

"I don't have anything to wear." I drop the sheet revealing my naked torso.

He moves toward me. "Don't tease me like that."

"I'm being serious. My clothes are in the washer at the other apartment."

Jaxson doesn't say anything else. He puts his phone to his ear and starts barking orders at someone and says something about half an hour.

I sit there and stare at him, partially in shock. He must have more money than I thought. Not that it matters. It doesn't. I just want him.

Twenty minutes later there's a knock on the door and a man wearing a suit enters. He's armed with several bags of clothes.

I shake my head at Jax. "What'd you do? This is too much. Way too much."

He grabs one of my forearms and pulls me close to him. "I told you. I *will* take care of you."

I know he will do what he says. I just want him to be mine.

My man.

I go over to the other apartment to grab my makeup from my purse, so I don't look like crap the first time I meet his friends. What will they think of me? Will they accept me? Will they think I'm a terrible person or a whore because I'm technically still married?

It was a marriage I never wanted. That has to count for something.

I plug my phone in to charge while we're gone. With my makeup on I feel more human and not so washed out.

I want to make a good impression, so I wear a green dress and a pair of black heels.

The green looks great against my hair color. Jax has always loved me in green.

"You ready?" He pokes his head through the bathroom door.

"Yeah." I let out a breath and pray this goes well.

His friends sound important to him so that makes them important to me. The man who brought my clothes drives us to the hospital.

Jaxson's hand grips my thigh possessively, and his fingers inch up under the hem of my dress. When he realizes I'm not wearing panties a low growl catches in his throat. "Jenna…." His tone is a warning as he slips a finger inside me.

I gasp.

"Do you know how crazy you make me? Then you pull some shit like this?"

"I didn't have any."

He pumps his finger faster and my breath hitches. I'm sore from earlier but it's a good ache to have. One I've missed.

"We'll have to talk about your punishment, later." He has a devilish grin on his face.

My nipples go hard, and he stares down at them.

"No bra either?"

I shake my head.

The car comes to a stop and Jax rolls down the dividing window between us and the driver. "Get out." He practically barks it at the guy.

The driver exits the car without even glancing back at us.

My eyes widen at Jax. "That was rude."

"I don't give a flying fuck. I need to be inside you right now."

I can't help but chuckle at what must be a joke. "Here? Are you crazy?"

"Crazy about you." He pulls his finger from my pussy and takes it to his mouth, licking it clean. "Tastes like someone is a little crazy about me too." He pushes the skirt of my dress up over my hips and undoes his zipper, then yanks me onto his lap. "Put that cock inside you and ride it."

He's so much more demanding than I remember, and there's something insanely hot about it.

Straddling his thighs, I sink down and grind on his cock, loving the way it fills me. As hard as I'm rocking against him the car has to be visibly shaking from the outside.

"That's it. Ride that dick." His hand snakes up the front of my dress to palm my breast.

I whimper a little when he tweaks my nipple. He grins at my reaction and follows suit on my other breast. His lips sear the skin on my neck as he trails kiss after kiss until he reaches my mouth.

His tongue brushes against mine and I moan into his mouth.

He knows he owns me. He has to. I'm banging him in the parking lot of the hospital and I'm so lost in him I don't even care.

It doesn't take long for me to find my release. Right when I do it must be too much for Jax to bear. His cock kicks inside me and hot spurts of come fill me to the brim. He grunts a few times and then holds me in place, refusing to let me move an inch until he finishes.

His lips brush over mine once more. "I love you."

W alking into hospital—Jenna on my arm, my come deep inside of her—it's perfect. All eyes in the hallway turn to us as we approach. There isn't time for introductions as Brodie brings his kid out and hands him over to Weston. Maxwell gives us an odd look, but I brush it off. I don't need him giving me shit. Not today.

I only plan to stay for a few minutes to avoid any awkward conversations. I know Weston has mixed feelings about the situation, but I'm seeing this through. I'm never letting Jenna get away again.

She is it for me.

We all make our rounds doting over the new baby. His face is red and his head is surprisingly round for a new baby, but he's perfect.

I glance over to Maxwell. "Claire get you her resume?"

"Yeah, not that I needed it. She's hired."

"As an employee. That's it." I raise an eyebrow.

He holds up his hands but grins at the same time. "I know."

"I'm not joking, bitch."

Brooke shoots me a glare as if to say, *language, bitch*.

I hold up two hands at her. "Sorry." I pat little Charlie on the head softly. "Sorry, little buddy."

Maxwell flips me the bird when nobody is looking.

I say my goodbyes after a brief introduction of Jenna to everyone.

Weston approaches us as we make our exit. *Shit*. I don't want to hear one of his lectures right now, especially in front of Jenna, and he's notoriously blunt.

"Gonna grab dinner. Join us?" Judging by his expression and his cold tone he isn't really asking.

I give Jenna a quick glance. "Hungry?"

"Whatever you want to do, but I am pretty hungry. We didn't have lunch."

I turn to Weston. "Where?"

I don't want to go. I want to take Jenna home, but she's hungry and I don't need Weston giving me a bunch of shit. It'll be easier to just do this and be done with it.

"Milago's?"

"Pizza?"

"Brooke's been craving one of their deep dishes."

I don't miss the look Brooke gives him and I have to wonder if there's something they aren't saying.

"Sounds good."

"We'll meet you there." He looks at Jenna. "Nice meeting you. See you soon."

"Nice to meet you both."

———

Brooke and Weston beat us to the restaurant and already have a table. Weston already ordered me a beer and a water for Jenna.

"We weren't *properly* introduced back there. I'm Weston and this is my wife, Brooke."

"Jenna." She accepts his offered hand.

"It's a pleasure to finally meet the woman who crushed this guy."

"Hey." I give him a stern look.

"Take it easy." He takes a sip of his beer, grinning the whole time.

"Are you guys a thing?" Brooke turns to Weston. "I thought you said she was a client?"

"It's complicated." I need to change the subject. "You guys order yet?"

Jenna squeezes my hand under the table. Her fingers spider-walk toward my cock and I let out a cough when she then squeezes.

"Waiting for you guys. So, Jenna, what do you do?" Brooke looks like she's happy I finally have a woman she gets to talk to.

"Unemployed at the moment. It's complicated."

Weston raises an eyebrow at me when he hears 'complicated' and I flash him a stare that says *don't*.

Jenna continues stroking my cock and doesn't miss a beat on the conversation. "I'm hoping to revive a charity my mom ran. It was called Walker's Hope. It focused on abused horses."

"The ranch would be a perfect location for that." My words come out funny, probably because I'm getting a fucking handy under the table.

It's amazing and at the same time surprising. Jenna was always more of a good girl when we were younger. It's nice knowing she wants me so bad she can't wait until we get home.

"I have to deal with, umm, insurance and all that stuff first."

Brooke is shaking like she can't wait to get a word in. "I have an amazing idea. I work for a nonprofit too. I handle legal cases for abused women. Anyway, if you started the foundation again, maybe we could work together with some of the women looking to get back on their feet."

And just like that the two of them are off in their own conversation. Jenna's hand leaves my cock and I glare at Brooke, even though she has no idea what she's done. I turn to Weston. Great. No handjob and I get to talk to his ass.

Weston loosens up once the food comes, and I can see that Jenna is growing on him. I knew she would. Jenna is amazing. The more her and Brooke talk animatedly about their big plans to get her foundation running again the more Weston begins to smile.

They eventually go off to the bathroom together like women do. I don't know what it is about them traveling in packs, but it never fails.

Weston immediately stares at me when they're out of sight. "Okay, I like her. She's nice and ambitious and my wife loves her. I can tell you two are still insane about each other. It's a little disgusting." He grins. "I just don't want to see you get fucked in all of this."

"I love her, man. I know it may sound crazy because she only came back into my life a few days ago but she's *always* been the one."

He shakes his head, grinning his ass off. "Kryptonite pussy."

"Exactly." I hold up my beer and we clink the glasses together. I grin, and my mind immediately goes back to thinking about fucking her. I'll have to get her home soon before my cock explodes from her stroking me under the table.

We part ways after Brooke devours a piece of chocolate cake. I'm almost certain she's pregnant but I don't press the matter. They'll announce it when they're ready. Maybe they don't want to steal Brodie's spotlight with the birth of his son.

When we get back to my place Jenna's cell phone keeps vibrating on the countertop in the kitchen.

She picks it up and her face turns pale as a ghost.

My hands ball into fists at my sides. I'm pretty sure it's him.

"Leonard?"

She nods. "Voicemails."

I hold my hand out. "Give me the phone."

She shakes her head. "I need to handle this."

"I'm your attorney. It's my job to handle it. You're not speaking to him." The thought of her calling him has rage coursing through my blood. I'll rip that motherfucker's balls off and shove them down his goddamn throat.

I hold out my hand. "I want to hear the messages. We need to record them for evidence."

The voicemails start to play.

"My account is empty I need you to wire more money."

"Where the fuck are you? I have been calling all morning. Pick up the phone."

"Goddamn it! You better have some fucking money waiting when I get back to Texas."

"You better pray you're dead from that fire. Tony just called."

"I just got in town. Pick me up at the airport."

"The hospital says you were released. You fucking cunt. Wait until I find you."

My fingers grip the phone tighter with each message, and my jaw clenches so hard I think my teeth might shatter. I set the phone down and try to push the rage deep down, but I can't.

I punch the fucking wall so hard it puts a hole in the drywall.

Jenna jumps back and covers her mouth.

Fuck, I shouldn't have done that in front of her. But she's not going anywhere near that guy.

I turn to her slowly and my face has to be blood-red. "Sorry you had to see that."

"I'm just, umm, afraid to ask what he said."

"I'm sure you have a pretty good idea."

She turns and looks out the window, almost like she's terrified to go outside again. I can't believe she's had to live like this for so long. For a fucking decade. What makes some men think it's okay to beat and terrorize their spouse? Prison is too good for this motherfucker.

I'm going to bury him.

Jenna's arms start to tremble. I walk over and do my best to console her.

"These messages will work in our favor. It's terroristic threatening. When I file the petition for divorce I'm filing a restraining order."

Her eyes wander up to mine and practically say, *like that will stop him.* She looks away again and shakes her head.

I cup one of her cheeks in my palm and turn her to face me. "He will *never* hurt you again." I pull her in close to my chest and never want to let go of her. I know she feels safe, the way she should feel with a husband.

The tears start to flow from her eyes and she buries her face in my shirt. "O-okay."

Looking down at her, it just makes me hurt. Jenna is fucking tough. She's one of the strongest women I know on this earth, and this son of a bitch has turned her into this.

Not on my fucking watch. If I have to kill this bastard and go to prison so that Jenna can live her life without worrying about him, I *will*. It's not preferable, but I don't care. I'll do anything for her to be safe. Anything to protect her.

Jenna finally walks to the freezer and tries to ice my fist when she comes back, but I refuse. I'm fine. I only wish the wall had been Leonard's fucking face. "Don't even think of calling him back."

Jenna stays quiet, and I wish I knew what she was thinking.

She nods.

I don't know if I believe her. She's independent. She's not good at having someone take care of her.

She needs to get over that for now. She can have whatever she wants when this ordeal is through. But I have to make her listen to me on this.

I force a smile on my face to try to lighten the mood. Anything that might make her happy. "Let's forget about him for now and go to bed."

"Okay."

Chapter Sixteen

JENNA

I spent the weekend being spoiled by Jax. He surprised me with breakfast in bed and took me shopping for a few extra things I left off the list last time. It was nice to escape life for a little while and just hang out with him. Today, however, we're back to reality.

Leonard won't stop harassing me through voicemail and text messages. I don't respond to any of them like Jax said.

Jaxson has a contact at the judge's office who owes him a favor and he's trying to expedite the process to get the restraining order filed and the petition for divorce served while we know he's in Texas.

Jax is calling in a lot of favors for me. I'm lucky to have him back in my life, and at the same time I feel horrible for other women in my situation who don't have someone to handle all this stuff for them.

I still can't believe I waited this long. For years I've felt worthless, like I had no options. I lost my sense of self when I was forced to marry him.

When Dad died, everything changed. Something inside me snapped and all the pieces fit together. I wanted to fight for myself for the first time in years. This is all so surreal, like I'm living a new life. I forgot how to be me, and how to let someone love me. Now, I remember what it's like to be desired and cherished by a real man.

Jaxson loves me so much. I can see it in his eyes and in every action.

I'm excited to get Walker's Hope established again but I don't want to get too far ahead of myself. Brooke volunteered to help me in any way she can. I get the feeling we're going to be great friends. I like her a lot.

I was a bit surprised to learn that Jaxson owns the building with all his partners at the law firm. Not sure why it surprised me, but it did. I'm glad they're all so close, like a family in the same building. Part of me is a little jealous that they were able to share in all of his success and be close to him all these years while I missed out.

I lost any friends I had after two years of being married to Leonard. He made sure to cut off any contact with the outside world. Anyone who might've talked some sense into me he made sure to get rid of. I was in a dark place after what I'd been through and then with losing my mother the way I did. I'd like to think she's smiling down on me now, happy I've gotten my act together and found my way back to the man I was meant to be with.

Jax hasn't told Claire we're back together. I'm not sure how she'll feel about it. I'm sure his family was pissed at me for a long time, since I never really had a chance to explain. And I was close to all of them too. I shut everyone out, afraid to face them after Jaxson left. I didn't need any reminders of what I'd given up.

I can only hope she'll forgive me when she finds out what happened.

A knock sounds at the door but the housekeeper beats me to answering it.

A woman walks in with a rolling table.

I shake my head at the way he's pampering me. It's nice, but still a little much. Apparently, Jax ordered me a personal massage. I've been pretty tense since the messages started rolling in, and the right kind of sore from all the sex. A massage does sound incredible.

———

"How's it going?" Jax smiles when I walk through the doors of his office. I need to sign paperwork. Part of me thinks he just wanted to see me during the day.

"Great." I make a show of stretching my arms above my head. "The massage was perfect. Thank you."

"Good. He's being served tomorrow morning. Staying at a hotel not far from here."

"Does he know where I am?"

"No, and the judge was more than happy to grant our requests when he heard the messages."

I run over and wrap my arms around his broad chest. "Thank you. For everything. I mean it. You are so good to me."

He puts his palms on each of my cheeks. "I want this over with, so we can move on with our lives. Make your dreams reality."

"What about you?" I smirk. 'What's your dream?"

"I'm looking at it." He grins.

"You know there is one thing you always wanted that I never gave you."

His eyebrows raise. "What's that?"

I move closer to him and kiss my way along his jaw until I reach his earlobe. I suck the delicate skin between my lips and caress it with my tongue.

"Better close the blinds first."

He smirks. "Naughty little girl."

I wait for him to walk over and lower them, but he has a shit-eating grin on his face. He picks up a remote off the desk and hits a button. All the blinds come down at once.

I shake my head at him. "You just have a perfect response for everything, don't you?"

"The circumstances were fortunate. I had to take advantage. Now tell me about this gift of mine."

Jaxson sits back in his chair, already knowing what I have in store for him. He leans back with his fingers intertwined behind his head.

"Unzip your pants."

He smirks at my command. "That's your job, babe. I'm receiving a gift, remember?"

"Don't pretend you don't like it when I'm bossy." I walk over and go to my knees in front of him. "Is this what you want?" I bat my eyelashes. "A good little girl that'll do whatever you tell her?"

He winks. "Now, you're getting it."

I pull his thick cock out of his pants and eye it curiously. "Maybe I'll be a good girl and just tease the tip a little. Go really slow."

"You can be a little naughty if you want."

I lean over and lick him from the base to the tip, staring up at him. "Yeah, that's what I thought, motherfucker." I take him as far in my mouth as possible, so hard I gag myself.

He nearly lurches forward he's so surprised and his legs tremble next to me. I smile around his cock and bob up and down fast for a few seconds, then take him out of my mouth.

He stares down at me, eyes wide, shaking his head. "Jesus Christ, woman. Fuck, I love you." His mouth curls up into a devilish smile. "Maybe you are a naughty little bitch."

"Don't stop talking dirty to me like that. It makes my pussy wet." I go back down on him, working his shaft while taking him in and out of my mouth.

His fingers eventually snake into my hair and he makes a fist, guiding me up and down on him.

He's made me feel so damn good these past few days, I want to return the favor. I'm on a mission to give him the best damn blowjob of his life.

"God, you're sucking that dick like a dirty little slut."

My pussy heats up at his filthy mouth. We never did anything like this back when we were younger, and I have to say that I love it.

"Mmhmm." I hum the word around his cock, then pull him out of my mouth and lick both of his balls. He's trimmed and neat. What a relief that was, the first time he pulled his cock out. Jaxson definitely grooms himself well. It might've worried me a few days ago, but now, I know it's all for me.

I feel like I'm doing pretty well for my first blow job.

The way he groans confirms that he likes what he's receiving.

Warmth pools in my belly and between my thighs as I continue to explore every inch of his big cock with my tongue. With every stroke and lick I take him farther into my mouth. I suck my cheeks around him. His hand tightens in my hair and his hips start a languid pace as he slides his cock back and forth between my lips, fucking my mouth harder with each thrust.

"Fucking hell, Jenna."

My mouth hurts but I don't give up. I want to do this for him, give him what he wants, make him feel good. I want him to own my mouth, my pussy, my heart—I want to give him everything.

"Jesus. Fuck." He grunts as he nearly hits the back of my throat. Tears well up in my eyes but I fight through it.

My hand has a mind of its own and I unbutton my pants then shove my fingers in my panties and circle my clit.

His pace quickens. He pops free of my mouth and strokes his shaft in front of my face. "Goddamn, you naughty little bitch. Couldn't resist touching *my* pussy, could you?"

I take one of his balls into my mouth in response to his question.

He hisses and a white pearl forms at the head of his cock. I can't resist the urge to taste it.

He groans again when the tip of my tongue meets his dick. "Pull your fucking panties down, now."

I do what he says without even thinking. It's like he has me in a trance.

He yanks me to my feet. His hand still strokes his cock, and his face is strained when he bends me over the desk.

Jax kicks my legs apart. One hand grips my hip and he shoves his cock to the hilt.

I let out a moan that rips through the office and echoes off the walls.

When he thrusts into me, he lets out a grunt and his cock practically explodes inside me. He thrusts two or three times, each with a hot spurt of come that follows.

I turn back to try and get a look at him, completely spent and satisfied, as he collapses against my back. He drops kisses along my neckline and collar bone, before raising back up.

I try to stand up when he slips his cock out of me, but he splays his fingers across my back and keeps me pinned against his desk. I glance back to the side to see what he's doing, and I barely make out him stroking the remaining come from the end of his cock. I feel him rub around the edge of my pussy, collecting any stray come, and then he presses his fingers into me and leans up next to my ear. "I *will* put my baby in you."

"Holy shit." The wooden desktop next to me fogs up when I exhale the words against it.

Without my feet touching the floor, he rolls me over to my back and holds my legs up in the air so that nothing can spill out of me.

I lay there, staring up at him with a wide grin spread across my face. He looks like a man who's possessed but has a wry grin on his face at the same time.

His head angles down and he looks right at my pussy, his stare already heating me up again. He licks his lips and his eyes roll back up to meet mine and smirks. "My turn."

Chapter Seventeen

"Y ou know there's something else I've never done." There's a sparkle in Jenna's eyes as we walk into the apartment after dinner.

"What's that?" I lead us toward the bedroom.

I watch her as she ponders her words, then loosen my tie as she kicks off her shoes.

"Actually, there's a list."

"A list huh?" I wrap my arms around her from behind, kissing her neck while I pull her ass up against my already hard cock. She drives me crazy. I can't get enough of her. When I'm not fucking her, I'm thinking about fucking her. "Think we need to check a few things off it tonight."

I get the feeling she's nervous, and I don't want her to hesitate telling me what she wants. Whatever she wants, she gets. Bottom line.

I spin her around so that we face one another, and she blushes.

"What is it? I want to give you whatever you want. You can ask for anything."

"This is just new to me. I feel inexperienced."

I take her by the hands. "I'd try anything for you. *Anything.*"

She looks away. "I don't know."

I lead her to the bed and kiss up and down her neck. "Say it. Tell me what you want."

"So, I was reading this book and the guy tied her up."

"Is that so?"

"Yeah. I don't know." She shakes her head with a smile, then turns back to me. "I just thought it sounded really hot."

I pull her to me and kiss the side of her head. I don't have much experience besides handcuffing someone to the bed, but I'll learn every goddamn thing about it if that's what she likes. I'll read books, take notes, whatever. "Okay."

I pull my tie over my head and grab her wrists, then wrap my tie around them.

"What are you doing?" Her eyes widen.

"Practicing." I slant my mouth over hers and push her down onto the bed with my kiss.

The knot isn't tight. She could break free if she wanted but she definitely likes it when I take control.

It's not something I've ever had a problem doing.

I slide her pants down to her ankles along with her panties and she kicks them onto the floor.

Taking my time, I kiss my way up her smooth legs, teasing around her pussy but never making complete contact. I lick, suck and bite everywhere but there.

When I get to her torso I pull her shirt up over her eyes, leaving her nose and mouth clear to breathe.

"Jaxson?"

I ignore her plea. This was her fantasy and I'm giving it to her.

I slowly tease around her nipple while she writhes and squirms before taking it between my fingers. Tiny goosebumps break out all over her tits and her hips start to buck, her pussy needing attention. I make her wait and apply the same attention to the other breast before alternating sucking each one into my mouth.

Her tight body rubs against me, searching for any friction she can get. Kissing my way back down between her legs, I exhale warm breath across her clit and watch the rest of her skin pebble with goosebumps.

"Jax, please. God, I need to come."

"Patience." I drop a single kiss on her clit.

I enjoy this even more than I thought I would. Taking my time and making her squirm. I could get used to this shit every day.

I spread her pussy lips with my fingers and lick her long and slow from ass to clit.

Her hips lift from the bed and she pants with the shirt still up over her eyes and her hands tied together.

Fuck, she tastes so goddamn sweet on my tongue. My cock aches pressing against the seam of my pants. I could probably come immediately if I shoved into her, but I'm taking my sweet-ass time with this.

Every time I get close to where she needs me the most she raises her hips and gives me a perfect view of her tight little asshole. I haven't gone there yet, but that's about to change. Using her arousal, I rub my finger over her puckered ass, applying the smallest amount of pressure as I tongue her cunt. Her legs begin to tremble around my face and her body starts to flail. Warmth coats my tongue and I know she's right on the verge of release. I stroke her clit even faster with my tongue and slide my pinky finger into her ass.

She stills for a brief moment then her hips buck up against me, trying to take my finger deeper. I clamp down with my mouth on her clit, suckling it between my lips as my tongue goes wild over it.

"Oh, god." She practically screams out, and her entire body tightens and convulses. She seizes up and I don't give her one second of reprieve.

I keep my mouth latched onto her and ride out her entire orgasm as she comes all over my face.

After a few seconds I lean up and pull her shirt back down from over her face and unwrap my tie from around her wrists.

I smile down at her. Jenna pants, completely speechless, gasping for air as she comes down from the clouds.

Her eyes flutter like she's about to fall asleep, and she lets out a low moan of approval.

I can't have her passing out, though.

My cock's far too greedy for that. I unbutton my pants and push my cock into her hot velvet cunt. Her pussy is still spasming from her orgasm, and I know it's only a matter of time before I claim her ass.

I'll work her up to that slowly, but it's mine. All of her belongs to me.

Her legs wrap around me as I thrust into her over and over.

It doesn't take long for my balls to tighten and I blow inside her again without spilling a single fucking drop.

Chapter Eighteen

JENNA

"I can't move." I stretch my arms above my head and let out a long yawn.

"Sleep well?" Jax smirks knowing damn well he fucked me to sleep.

"Mmhmm." Wow, last night was amazing. I'll never hesitate to tell this man what I want ever again.

"Good." He gives my ass a playful smack.

I yelp. "Hey."

"Breakfast is being served on the bar. Bring your appetite."

"I'll be down in a few minutes. I need to shower. And I'm not sure I can get up."

He smirks that sexy damn smirk of his. "Let me know when you're out of the shower and I'll carry you."

"You don't—"

He cuts me off. "Big day at the office and I told you breakfast is on the bar top." He stares down at my pussy. "So shower up so I can eat before I go."

I squirm just thinking about what he has in mind, and I want to be sexy for him. I feel so relaxed around him now, and my personality doesn't feel as constrained. "That's quite an appetite you have."

"You have no idea." He grabs my arms and tugs me up out of the bed then maneuvers me to the bathroom. "I'm fucking starving. Can't get enough."

When I step into the shower the warm spray of water feels like tiny pricks on my sensitive skin. I'm going to have to hit the gym if I'm going to keep up with him in the bedroom. I go through the motions quickly, eager to please him, skipping washing my hair until later.

I haven't heard from Leonard at all and I hope it means he's been served and will give me the divorce without a fight. Nothing has ever been easy with that man, though.

I slip on my robe and head down, wondering why Jaxson wasn't waiting to carry me like he said.

I turn the corner and turn pale as a ghost.

"Oh my god!" Claire squeals in the kitchen. "Jenna."

"Hey." I give Jax the stink eye for not warning me. What if I'd walked down completely naked?

He shrugs, mouths the word 'sorry', and holds up a bagel at me. "She wanted to bring her big brother breakfast."

I can't help but smile because it reminds me of them when we were younger.

"I'm going to put on some clothes and give you two a minute." I'm glad to see that they're still close, and I head back to the bedroom.

As I put on what I'll wear for the day, I hear them arguing and I already know it's because of me. It was all a show earlier.

"Don't you think this is fast? Shouldn't you let the ink dry on her divorce papers before you move her in?"

My heart sinks into my stomach. I definitely don't want to drive them apart or cause problems with their relationship.

"Claire, I love you. You know that."

"Yeah?"

He shakes his head. "Don't come in my house and tell me how to live my life. I love her. I don't need my kid sister telling me how to manage my shit."

"Sorry. I really am happy for you. I just don't want to see you get hurt again. Don't you remember last time?"

"Thanks for the concern, but I'm a grown man. She's not going anywhere. Get used to it."

"Okay. I can respect that." She takes a step toward the door. "I'm gonna go. Tell Jenna I'm glad she's back but if she hurts you again I will track her ass down."

"Understood." I see him smirk as he says it while I hide around the corner.

I wait for the door to close before I join Jaxson in the kitchen. I don't know if he knows I heard them or not, and I take a bagel and spread some cream cheese across it.

His eyes flick up to meet mine. "You're being quiet."

I let out a low sigh. "I was thinking that I should start looking for a place soon."

The knife he was using clangs on his saucer.

"What are you talking about? You live here with me."

"For now, but we're moving too fast. I should get my own place and we can date."

"You're not going anywhere. I just got you back. You're probably carrying my child already."

"Claire made a good point. I'm not even divorced yet. How will that look to the judge?"

"You heard all that?" He glares toward the door like he's looking for Claire.

"Yeah." I nod. "And don't get all pissed at her. She's looking out for you."

"I know, but she doesn't need to say shit like that. It's none of her business."

"Just calm down a little." I take a bite of the bagel.

"I put your address down as the apartment next door. For the judge. No one will know unless you want them to. I know how to be a lawyer. What's this all about?"

"I just hated hearing you two fight because of me. I don't want to cause you stress with your sister."

"She'll be fine. She likes you. Don't worry."

I know he's right, but I still have a sinking feeling in my stomach. "You know I love you."

"I love you too. What are your plans today?"

I sigh at him changing the subject, but it's probably for the best. "Need to get the insurance company on the phone and see where we stand on the claim on the house. Make a few calls about the charity and what I need to do to get it up and running."

"Sounds good." He walks over and kisses me only the way he can. "I'm gonna head to work."

I already miss him when he walks out the door.

———

I've made a few calls, and everything is going much better than expected. The claim for the house is all in order and they're going through the usual steps before anything gets paid out. I talk to Brooke for a little while on the phone and make a few other calls about the charity.

I stand there, staring out the window and taking in the Dallas skyline. My life feels like a fairytale coming true. The whole time, though, my stomach churns—just twisted up in knots. I can't shake the feeling that life is never this easy. Not mine, anyway.

Every time I think I have the world in my palms, I get crushed. Maybe it's the years of Leonard's constant abuse. Beating me down relentlessly, physically and mentally, telling me I'm worthless. Not worthy of dreams or success.

I wish I wasn't this way. I wish I could enjoy the amazing path my life has taken, all because I finally got off my ass and did something about it. Jax assures me all the time that I'm brave. That I'm worth something to the world.

It's hard to take in, though. Some people just have a way of affecting you that I can't even explain. It's like my brain knows Jax is right, but I'm incapable of processing and believing it. I just have to take a deep breath and get through things one day at a time.

I walk to the counter and pour another cup of coffee. The smell wafts into my nose and gives me a little mid-day boost that's desperately needed. It's hard to stay motivated to get things done when you live in a penthouse, surrounded by beautiful things and so many options to be lazy.

I refuse to be someone like that. I need to be working, doing, going. I need purpose, and this charity will give me that. My phone rings and it's a number I don't know. Against my better judgment, I answer it, even though it may be Leonard.

"Hello?"

"Mrs. Reyes?"

"Yeah?"

"This is Detective Brighton with the Dallas Police Department."

My hand instinctively covers my mouth. What can this possibly be about? What did Leonard do or say?

I start to say something but he cuts me off.

"A process server was found dead earlier this morning. We believe he was serving your husband with divorce papers. Have you seen Leonard Reyes? Or have you heard from him?"

"Oh my God." I stumble back a little and catch myself before I fall over. It's like a million knives to the stomach. Would Leonard kill someone? He would hit me, but he would never explode. It was always cold and calculated, psychological manipulation. He made every hit count when he would beat me.

"Mrs. Reyes?"

"Yeah, sorry. No. Haven't heard anything since the messages Weston gave the police. That was the last communication."

"Okay. If you hear from him, we need to know immediately."

"Absolutely."

"You need to get to a safe place. We're sending some of our guys your way to watch the building. If you need anything else, please let them know."

"I will, thank you."

"We'll be in touch."

The second he hangs up the phone, it hits me. I smell it.

A hand grips the phone in my hand the second my brain processes that it's Leonard's breath. Cold steel presses against the back of my head, and he slowly spins me around to face the barrel of a gun.

He smiles wide, and I feel like I might vomit. Nausea, anxiety, everything horrible a person could feel rushes to the surface. Cold sweat breaks out along my forehead, and my throat grows warm and salty.

He doesn't look mad. Doesn't look angry. He's actually grinning at me the same way he did the night my father sold me to him.

His eyebrows waggle. "Honey, I'm home."

Chapter Nineteen

JAXSON

I'm out the door of the firm the second I get the call from the detective. Yeah, they might be sending people to watch the building, but I don't give a fuck. Jenna's mine, and nobody can protect her the way I can.

That motherfucker.

I know he killed John. He's been serving clients for the firm for years. He's a great guy, family man, has three kids. Dead, because of this piece of shit, worthless prick. Weston chases after me, clearly alerted by my reaction, but I hop in the Lexus before he can get to me and haul ass out of the parking lot in a cloud of smoke.

The detective said he spoke with Jenna and she was fine. The apartment isn't far from the firm, but my blood boils with every second that passes. I don't have a fucking gun in my car. They're all locked in my safe in my bedroom.

I just want to get there and hold her in my arms. She has to be so scared right now.

The tires squeal on the pavement when I slide into my parking spot and I'm through the front door. Our usual security guy isn't there, which is really odd. I have to punch in my code.

When I make it through the door, I take a glance over the counter. He's on the floor with blood dripping from his temple. He wasn't shot, it just looks like he was pistol whipped.

Fuck!

I hop over really quick and check for a pulse. He has one.

I dial 911 on my way up the stairs. "Get an ambulance here, fast."

I rattle off the address, hang up, and stare at the elevator and the stairs. I have no clue which way he would take her. I'd think he'd want to be inconspicuous after just knocking the guy unconscious at the front. There's a rear exit out of the stairwell. The door only goes one way.

I just have to pray that he hasn't gotten Jenna out of the building yet.

I take the stairs two at a time, practically running, but staring up and listening for echoes. When I get to my floor, I ease the door open slowly. How the hell did he even get through the front door?

Jenna told me how manipulative he is. Who knows, he may have faked an emergency. Jim had all the information about Leonard— pictures, height, weight. Maybe he wore a disguise? Jim's not a cop, I guess. I'll get answers about it all later. Right now, there's only one word racing through my mind.

Jenna.

I peer around and don't see anything happening.

I step inside and head toward my apartment. There are two entrances to my place, so I head toward the front to see if I can listen in. The last thing I want to do is get her killed by announcing my presence. I have to stay calm, despite the fact my hands are squeezed into tight fists and my face has to be blood-red.

Jenna is mine.

I just got her back.

I'll be goddamned if I lose her forever to this psycho.

When I get to the door there's no sign of forced entry, but the door is cracked a little. I hear voices in the front room. It hits me.

If he swiped Jim's keys he'd have access to the apartment. How could I have been so stupid? I should've paid for extra security. I should've been more careful.

If I lose her it'll be all my fault.

I push those thoughts deep down inside. They won't help me right now.

I have to be calm and in control of the situation. Losing my shit won't save her. Being smarter than that cocksucker will. It's hard to tell myself this when every second is another bit of time he has to kill the love of my life.

I ease through the back door and into the guest bedroom. The voices grow louder. I try to get closer to assess the situation.

When I get to the kitchen and peer around the corner I can see and hear everything. Jenna sits in a chair in the middle of the room clutching her face while he paces back and forth with a gun in his hand.

"You think you can play me?" He tilts her chin up to him with the barrel of the gun and laughs right in her face. "You're nothing, Jenna. You're shit, and you'll always be shit. Your own father sold you to me because you're worthless."

"Please, just stop. I'll do whatever you want. I can get you money. Please."

He laughs again and heat rushes to my face. I'm going to kill the fuck out of this guy. He's going to pay for every ounce of fear he's put into her. It doesn't look like he's going to kill her right now. This is his game. He wants to see her suffer.

"This is a nice place you have with your rich-ass boyfriend. I didn't think you'd have the balls to cheat on me."

"It wasn't cheating. We were never together."

"Got that right. Your pussy was more worthless than your brain."

"What are you going to do, Leonard? You killed a man. You're holding me hostage."

Goddamn, I wish she'd stop talking. She's going to say something that pisses him off and there's no telling what he'll do.

"Just making you sweat it out. We'll be leaving soon, and you'll be getting me my goddamn money. I always have a plan, baby. That's what smart people do."

"I'll get you whatever you want. Just please, let me go."

I have to do something before he makes a move. I crouch down and make my way over behind the island in the kitchen about ten feet away from them.

I lean my head out to look around the corner of the cabinets right when he smacks her across the face.

He covers her mouth right when she tries to cry out and the muffled scream lands in his palm.

Fuck this.

I get on the balls of my feet, ready to charge after him when my phone goes off loud as fuck.

Motherfucker!

Weston's face pops up on the screen. The ringtone blares through the room.

"Ohh, the boyfriend is here. Come on out, Mr. Hunter."

I stand up.

He trains the gun right on me.

I glare back at him. "I'm going to kill you with that."

He laughs. "That so?"

I have to be in control of this shit. Distract him long enough for Jenna to make a run for the door. She's not tied up. I'll take a bullet for her. I'll do anything for her.

"Goddamn right it is. Right after I take this phone call."

He waves the gun around, grinning. I don't look at Jenna. I don't want to do anything that'll make him do something crazy. This has to be unemotional until it's over. If being in a courtroom has taught me anything, it's that.

"You're a cocky motherfucker. It might be admirable if I wasn't about to blow your fucking head off."

"Yeah, yeah. I've heard worse threats on a Tuesday. And they all end up getting fucked in prison. Hope that's your thing." I take my phone out and decline Weston's call. I don't even look up at Leonard. My heart thumps a million-miles-an-hour in my chest, but I know what I'm doing. Reading people is my job. It's what made me rich. I just have to trust my instincts.

The lamps behind him in the living room are connected to my phone. I pull up the app and take a silent breath. The seconds slow down to minutes. I press the button.

Chaos.

That's what follows.

It all happens so fast, I don't even know if I'm in control of my body. At the same time everything halts like we're in slow motion. Nothing but raw, primal evolution takes over. Fight or flight, and I'm not much of a flyer.

Leonard turns his head when the lights click on behind him. I plant on my back foot and explode off it. His head slowly turns to the lights and it's like his brain clicks on and he realizes what's happening.

Fuck trying to rationalize with this guy. I don't negotiate with anyone who wants to kill the woman I care about. It's them or me, and they're the one that's going to die.

He tries to turn back around, and the barrel of the gun hovers in Jenna's direction. I dive for him like I'm back in high school playing football. A perfect form tackle.

My right hand smashes into his forearm and jars it backward. A loud boom sounds through the room and the bullet slams into the drywall.

I keep my momentum moving through him. I'm bigger, but not

by much. My shoulders crash into his stomach and I try to drive him through the fucking wall.

Jenna screams.

It echoes through the room. It almost sounds deep like her voice has been slowed down on a record player.

The gun falls to the floor and I hammer Leonard through the huge television and entertainment center. My whole body flies into him and we both crash. There's an explosion of glass shards and plastic.

He wheezes underneath me from where I knocked all the air out of his lungs, and I come up onto my knees, all in one smooth motion. I have his shoulders pinned down and my fists rain down on his face with right and lefts from the sky.

The bones in his face crunch against my knuckles and I don't feel anything but adrenaline-fueled rage.

I can't stop hitting him, even after he goes limp.

After ten or fifteen hard punches in a matter of seconds, a pair of hands grip me and yank backward. Small, petite hands that have to be Jenna's.

My body naturally reacts, and I whip around with my fists still in the air until I see her face.

She's okay.

She's safe.

Blood covers my face, but I know it's Leonard's from the onslaught of blows I landed. Blood oozes from his nose and mouth.

I jump to my feet and wrap Jenna in my arms and hold her close. She cries into my shoulder, the tears soaking my shirt. I cup her head in my hand. I can't let go of her. Ever.

"I'm so sorry. I'm so sorry." She cries the words over and over.

I hold her out at arm's length. "*No.* No more."

"No more what?" She sniffles.

"No more apologies for that piece of shit. It's not your fault." I stare around the room. I want this asshole tied up until the cops get here. He's not going anywhere. I've seen enough movies to know him lying there not moving isn't good enough. "Get the gun. I'm tying him up." I sprint to the closet where I think there's some rope or a belt or something.

Right when my hand hits the handle I hear it.

Boom!

Boom!

Over and over. My ears ring and I can't hear anything after the second one, but I can feel the shockwaves.

I spin around.

Jenna's standing there, the gun smoking while she empties the entire magazine of lead straight into his chest.

She pulls the trigger three or four times after it's spent. It just keeps clicking and clicking. She's screaming and crying. I'm not even sure if she's using real words. I can't make them out at first while my ears still adjust.

I haul ass over to her.

She screams at him the entire time as I grab her by the shoulders. "You motherfucker! I hate you! I hate you! You stole my life from me! I hate you!"

When I spin her around so she doesn't look at him anymore, she drops the gun at her feet and starts apologizing over and over. She cries in my arms.

"What did I do? Jax? Oh my God, what did I do?"

"Nothing." I stroke her hair. "You did nothing wrong. It's okay. I promise."

She shakes her head. "I just wanted him gone. I didn't want to worry about him the rest of my life. I'd have nightmares, even if he was in jail. I'd never know—"

"It's okay."

"No, it's not. I'm going to go to prison. I'm going to—"

I kiss her as hard as I can. A kiss that tells her everything is going to be fine. That she did nothing wrong. A kiss that's a promise to protect her always, and that she'll always be safe in my arms.

When our lips finally part, I cup her cheeks in my hands. "It's going to be fine. I'll take care of this."

"How?"

"Just do everything I say. We don't have much time."

"What? How? What?"

"Jenna?" I give her a quick little shake because I need her alert and not rattled for the next five minutes.

"Yeah?"

"I'm the best fucking attorney in Dallas. It was self-defense. *We* will fix this. Nothing will happen to you."

She nods, the tears still flowing down her cheeks. "Okay."

I grip both of her wrists and hold them in front of me. "We got this."

Chapter Twenty

JAXSON

Three months later

I watch Jenna, smiling the entire time in front of the huge ribbon. She deserves every second of this. She worked her ass off to make her dream come to life. It's the grand opening of her charity Walker's Hope.

Brooke left her job at her firm to be Jenna's partner.

Weston fiddles with his watch next to me while we watch them cut the red ribbon. Jenna's old ranch has been totally rebuilt and renovated.

The Hunter Group invited all our top clients to raise money for additional funding even though the firm already made a sizeable donation.

Jenna and Brooke want to work with battered women and children. Give them somewhere to go to get away from their troubles while finding work. The horses are all service animals and it gives the women an activity and a new bond.

The future couldn't look better for us.

A round of applause erupts as the ribbon falls to the ground and they're swarmed with people offering congratulations.

Jenna looks so damn happy and it's good to see her smile. She's been going to counseling to deal with everything. Personally, I think the ranch and the charity is the best therapy for her, but it can never hurt to get extra help.

As far as I'm concerned, Leonard got exactly what he deserved. He'll never hurt anyone again.

I've had to watch Jenna closely. I know the guy put her through hell, but it's just complicated all around. She's always been someone who cares about people, even if they're a despicable human being. I want to make sure she doesn't blame herself for what happened to him. Assure her constantly that it wasn't her fault. Fact is, I was relieved when she did it.

Weston got there right before the police. I told him exactly what happened. We told the police that I tackled him. The gun fell to the ground. I got away and Jenna unloaded on him. It wasn't technically a lie. It really was all in self-defense from the beginning, as far as I was concerned.

Charges were never brought.

It's a relief every day to just put it one more day behind us.

Maxwell leads my sister off. I don't like the way that bastard looks at her, but this isn't the place to confront him. I know they have something going on, though. I'll find out what it is.

"You notice it too?" Weston grins at me.

"I'll talk to him. Not here, but it'll happen. I might kill his ass."

"Go easy on him. I think he's in love. I think Claire is his kryptonite—"

I whip my head over and point a finger, but halfway smile at the same time. "Don't you dare say it."

He laughs. The prick will have too much fun with this shit.

I leave Weston to go find Jenna.

They're giving tours of the property to all the people. Showing them what their money will go toward.

An office building now sits where the main house was.

They're building even more new stables so they can house more horses. Many of the horses are rescues. They have an entire area for training the new arrivals, making sure they're ready to pair up with one of the women staying there.

I see Weston grinning as he catches up to Brooke and places his hands on her ever-growing baby bump. I knew they were expecting but Brooke wanted to wait until she was past the first trimester before announcing it. She suffered a miscarriage a few months into their marriage and was scared.

I can't blame her there.

It had to have been a hard ordeal.

We just found out Jenna is pregnant a few days ago. Seems my methods of putting a baby in her worked. Of course, like an idiot, I announced it immediately. I couldn't keep that to myself. Was too proud and excited. I don't think Jenna minded at all. She's just happy to be free and have a life now.

I find her by one of the stables talking with a potential donor.

I wait off to the side, just watching her shine. She's so in her element and happy. This is her big moment and she's handling it like a pro. It's all just—perfect.

I planned a surprise of my own today.

When she's done, I grip her lightly by the hand. "Walk with me?"

"Okay."

I'm quiet as we walk along the property. Nerves swell up in my stomach and my heart races. My hands grow a little clammy and I hope she doesn't notice. I'm a cool customer. Always good under pressure. Jenna's the only one to ever make me nervous about anything.

When we get to the old barn Jenna gives me a stern look. "Please tell me you're not sneaking me off for a quickie in the middle of the grand opening?"

"Get your mind out of the gutter." My fingers brush up against the box in my pocket. "Come on." I take her by the hand.

"Okay." She draws out the word and gives me an interrogative side eye.

I didn't want her climbing the ladder to the loft while she's pregnant, so I had everything set up on the ground level.

I open the doors to the barn.

There's a table in the center with fine linens and candles lit. Servers rush around, smiling.

"Jaxson, what is this?" She turns to me.

"Congratulations, babe. I'm so damn proud of you. All that you've overcome. All that you've accomplished. We've already been through so much. I can't wait to start a family with you. But, there's one thing I haven't done yet." I go down on my knee and pull out the box, opening it up and holding it up in front of her.

She gasps and covers her mouth.

"I've never been a man who asks for things. It's not my style. I always know what I want, and I go after it until it's mine."

Happy tears stream down her cheeks and her face flushes bright pink.

"And what I want is for you to marry me and be my wife." I shake my head. "I won't take no for an answer. I'll go after it every day for the rest of my life if I have to."

"Jaxson!" She's practically trembling as she nods and pulls me to my feet. "Yes. Of course, yes!"

I claim her with a kiss and a round of applause erupts behind us.

Weston had gathered everyone up and brought them over to witness the proposal.

My hand roams down to her belly, the main place it stays these days. My other hand grips the back of her neck and pulls her even harder into the kiss. Our foreheads meet and for a moment we're alone, just us, eyes locked onto one another.

I stare into her eyes and I see everything. My whole life right there in her irises. "Mine." I growl the word at her.

"Always." She smiles back.

Then I drop to my knees and both of my hands go to her belly. I don't give a shit who's watching us. This is my family. Mine. And I will protect them at all costs. I drop kisses on her stomach over her top. "You're mine too. Got it?"

Jenna whispers down at her belly. "You'll get used to how bossy he is."

"Got that right." I smile at my baby and then up at Jenna.

We may have taken an unconventional road to get to this point but there's no other woman out there for me. None. Jenna is it. I can't wait for the wedding day to make it official in the eyes of the law, even though it's been true our entire lives.

I get back to my feet and wave everyone off behind us. "Sorry to cut things short, guys. But I need to have a meal with my fiancé and my kid." I smile at Jenna. "A family dinner."

Everyone walks away, and I lead Jenna over to the table and pull the chair out for her.

"You spoil us."

I smirk. "Get used to it, future Mrs. Parker."

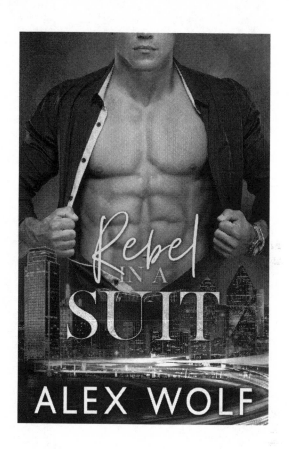

Rebel
IN A
SUIT

ALEX WOLF

I'm a rebel in a suit.

Relationships bore me.

I've been burned once and that will never happen again.

Left the drama behind me in California.

Now, I'm a partner at a high-powered law firm in Dallas.

I murder the opposition in the courtroom during the day and bang whoever I want at night.

I'm a kinky bastard and keep that part of my life safe and compartmentalized.

A man can never have enough money, power, and respect—and I have enough for a hundred lifetimes.

When my best friend Jaxson suggests a new assistant I know it's a bad idea.

I don't mix work with pleasure.

She's smoking hot with her skirt constantly riding up her thighs while I attempt to concentrate.

She drives me crazy e
I'm a rebel in a suit.

Relationships bore me.

I've been burned once and that will never happen again.

Left the drama behind me in California.

Now, I'm a partner at a high-powered law firm in Dallas.

I murder the opposition in the courtroom during the day and bang whoever I want at night.

I'm a kinky bastard and keep that part of my life safe and compartmentalized.

A man can never have enough money, power, and respect—and I have enough for a hundred lifetimes.

When my best friend Jaxson suggests a new assistant I know it's a bad idea.

I don't mix work with pleasure.

She's smoking hot with her skirt constantly riding up her thighs while I attempt to concentrate.

She drives me crazy every second of the day, chewing on the cap of her pen or asking me if I need anything else from her.

The way she says my name—*Mr. Bass.*

There's only one problem.

She's Jaxson's little sister.

I shouldn't touch her.

I should find a reason to fire her.

But, I can't.

I can fight it all I want, but I know she's going to end up beneath me, begging for more.

I have to have her.

I *will* have her.

She was *mine* before she walked into my office.

Because I'm Maxwell Bass, Attorney at Law.

Chapter One

MAXWELL

I'm on the verge of closing a multi-billion-dollar deal for a client. The largest of my career. What the hell was I thinking when I agreed to take on Jaxson's bratty sister as my new personal assistant? I don't have time to train her. I don't need drama she'll bring with her little prick of a boyfriend. She's always running to Jax with all her problems.

Asshole.

I bet he did it to pawn her shit off on me. Well played, but I never lose at anything.

As I step out of the elevator, I notice her desk is empty. Late on the first day. Beautiful. I don't need this shit. I'm not a fucking babysitter. Only two things matter in my world—power and pussy. And I already get pussy whenever I feel like it.

I don't have time to fetch my own coffee. I don't have time to answer phone calls and write down appointments and shit.

I walk into my office, oblivious to my surroundings, totally focused on how to fire Claire before she even starts, when my eyes land on a red pair of fuck-me heels attached to tan legs that would wrap perfectly around my waist, if they weren't attached to…

"Claire." I breathe out her name as I stand there wide-eyed. It takes a lot to shock me, but goddamn.

Gone is her usual messy bun and university sweatshirt. Her dark hair hangs longer than I would've thought, cascading over her shoulders in loose waves. Her hazel eyes brighten as her mouth curves into a smile.

"Good morning. I got coffee for you and a water. Went ahead and checked your schedule for today and pulled files for all your meetings. I found your last PA's notes in my desk and tried to figure out everything I could."

"Yeah, that's umm, great." This is going to be trouble. Now I need to fire her for an entirely different reason. There's no way I can fuck Jax's sister, but my cock doesn't seem to process that information.

She has on makeup but not too much. Red lipstick stains her lips and I can't help but think how good it would look painting a ring around my cock.

I thought for sure she'd be incompetent, late—fuck off on the internet when I needed shit. Apparently, I was wrong, but I'll never tell anyone that. I only hired her as a favor. Seemed important to Jax.

There's an awkward silence for a moment.

She stands there awaiting my orders. I don't give her any yet. I can see that I make her nervous, and it does something for me. I like it a lot.

Her eyes stay locked on me as I take a sip of my coffee. It's shit, but I need caffeine.

I won't crush her on the first morning and tell her it tastes like Chewbacca's asshole.

Truthfully, I like the ways she looks standing by my desk. I move past her and take my seat. It'd be easy to reach over and run my palm up her leg. As tempting as the thought is, I refrain because I notice Jax strolling past my office. When he looks through the glass and sees us, he pokes his head through the door.

"Off to a good start?"

"Don't need you checking up on her, Dad." I give him a shit-eating grin.

He glances around and flips me the bird, then walks off.

Keeping my hands to myself won't be hard. All I have to do is look at Claire and see the resemblance to Jax. I shudder a little at the thought. But, as I stare up at her, she doesn't look like him at all. *Damn*.

I was hoping I could picture him in a wig and make a connection, trick my mind. I blink and return my gaze to the mountain of files awaiting my attention.

Fuck, I didn't think this through. Jax is going to be all up in my business all the time now too, dropping by, asking how she's doing.

Since she doesn't look like Jax, there's only one other option—be an asshole and work her to death. She'll either quit or all my work will get done in record time and she'll hate me so much she wouldn't fuck me anyway.

Sounds like a plan.

"I have some dry cleaning that needs dropped off. When you're done with that, I'll be ready for lunch." I reach into the top drawer of my desk and hand her the keys to my apartment. "Almost forgot. You need a company phone and laptop. Go see Camillia in HR. She'll get you set up and do all your paperwork too. Once you know your phone number, I'll need you to program it along with your personal number into my phone."

"Yes, sir."

"Don't look so nervous. They're simple jobs. Only an idiot could screw it up." I flash her a wide grin.

I wave her off and get busy on the stack of files while I wait for reports from the team I have working on a property value.

Chapter Two

CLAIRE

I t feels weird hitting the button for Maxwell's floor when I walk into the building where all the partners live. I've never been to his apartment before. I don't even know what he needs dry cleaned or where to find it. His words play over and over in my head.

"Only an idiot could screw it up."

When I unlock the door, it isn't much different from Jax's as far as layout, but their styles are definitely like night and day. Jax's taste is highly sleek and modern, but Maxwell's apartment looks more like a beach house. The living room has a shelf with seashells, and photographs of him surfing.

My cheeks flush at the sight of him in nothing but low-cut swim trunks. His body is definitely not hard to look at.

Tiki masks hang on the walls along with more photographs of the beach. If Maxwell loves the ocean and surfing so much what in the hell is he doing in Dallas? He should be living in Malibu or something. I walk around downstairs looking for the clothes I need to drop off but don't see anything.

Making my way upstairs I find his bedroom first. The bed is unmade, and there are dirty clothes strewn everywhere. There's a camera mounted on a tripod. I know I shouldn't touch it, but I can't help but be curious. If he has a security camera in here I'll definitely be fired.

I hit play and my brain immediately screams for me to shut it off and sprint from the room, but I can't look away. Maxwell is on his bed with one arm behind his head. He's completely naked stroking his huge cock with the other.

What the hell is wrong with him? Why would he video himself jerking off?

How am I ever going to look him in the eye again? Some things you can't unsee.

Run!

I can't look away, though. It's like a car accident on the side of the road. A beautiful, muscular, car accident with a giant dick. My thighs squeeze together and I curse them silently in my mind. His fist glides up and down as his eyes close. Suddenly, two women climb onto the bed and join him. They block the view and I don't know what it is, but I find myself wanting to claw their eyes out. It's too much. I have to get out of here. One of them takes him in her mouth while the other makes out with him.

It's so…filthy.

Run!

Warmth spreads through me as I hear a groan of pleasure erupt from his mouth.

I don't know what comes over me, but my fingers move down through the V of my shirt and into my bra. I tweak one of my nipples, watching Maxwell and his filthy threesome. My other hand moves up the bottom of my skirt, rubbing my clit over my panties.

Brian, my ex, liked to watch porn. But none of the guys in the movies were Maxwell. This is all so—wrong.

I push thoughts of that bastard away. He dumped me when I refused to put out. We fooled around a lot but never went all the way.

I know what I'm doing right now is wrong, but Brian never made me wet like I am right now watching Maxwell. The thought scares me. I have a job to do. Jax would murder both of us if he knew what I was doing right now, or that I fantasized about his friend.

I flip the screen around to face the bed unable to resist what my body needs.

Fuck it. I've never done anything wild in my life. I deserve this. Get it out of my system and get back to work.

I pull my skirt up over my hips and push my panties to the side as I sink two fingers in my pussy. My eyes stay on the screen while one woman sits on Maxwell's face and the other rides him. I can't help but wonder what it would be like to be one of those women, taking that thick cock. *Jesus, he's beautiful.*

I imagine his hands gripping my hips.

My thighs quake as I imagine riding him. Having him all to myself. I pull my fingers to my mouth and lick them clean before pushing them back in.

I can't take my eyes off the screen. Max is now behind the woman that was on his face, taking her hard and fast. Her face is buried between the legs of the other woman.

I watch as the muscles in his back flex with his movements. The sound of their bodies slapping together is interrupted when my phone goes off from my purse up on his dresser.

I ignore it and allow myself to finish what I started. I rub my clit faster as I smell the strong scent of his cologne on the sheets.

My orgasm rolls through my hips and my fingers sink deeper into my pussy, hitting my most sensitive spot. My thighs squeeze as my walls clamp around my fingers and I ride this incredible wave of pleasure.

I look back to the screen and see Maxwell slapping his dick on both of their asses as his come spurts out all over them.

Jesus, the man is hot and clearly knows what he's doing in the bedroom. How am I going to work for him?

The phone starts ringing this time, and I know I need to get out of here.

I scramble around the room picking up any dirty clothes I can find. Hopefully, by the time I return to the office I'll have scrubbed these images from my mind.

When I get out of his apartment I notice he sent me a text.

Maxwell: I want a footlong hot dog from Hayward's

I nearly choke as I read the message.

Jesus. Get your mind out of the gutter.

I'm sitting in my car still trying to catch my breath and come down from my release when another message comes through on my new company phone.

Maxwell: You okay?

My heart goes into panic mode when my brain processes the words. I know he's just checking on me, but I immediately feel guilty. Does he know what I was doing in his bed? Is he fucking with me? What if he tells Jax?

I take a drink of water and try to calm down before replying.

Claire: Do you want sides? Something to drink? Toppings?

The phone rings and I see it's him.

I don't want to answer but I know I have to if I want to keep the job. How would I explain myself to Jax if I don't make it one day?

Right now, my first instinct is to leave and just keep driving. I can't believe I just went to town on myself on his bed. I want to just disappear.

I shake my head and clear my throat before I swipe the screen.

"Hello?"

"Find my suit?"

I gulp. "Mmhmm."

"Why were you ignoring me? I don't like to wait for shit. Get it done and meet back here. We'll eat then."

"Okay." My finger practically cracks the screen I punch it so fast with my finger to end the call.

Chapter Three

MAXWELL

It dawns on me I didn't tell Claire what she needed to get from my apartment for the dry cleaners. I start to text her, but I have a better idea. I pull up the security feed for my place on my personal laptop.

I watch as she examines my apartment. Probably thinks I'm a slob. They all do.

She smiles to herself as she picks up a picture from the mantle. I follow her as she walks up the stairs, swaying her hips, making my cock hard. One could argue that it's wrong to spy on her, but it's my fucking apartment and I do what I want.

With every step she takes, her skirt rides up her thighs a little more and I see a little more of her ass. I wonder what color her panties are? I bet she wears white cotton. Pure and innocent.

Jaxson always brags about what a good girl she is. It almost seems like she's his own daughter sometimes. I always roll my eyes. He never shuts up about her. I think he forgets she's in her mid-twenties.

I blink a few times when I see what's happening on the screen. Apparently, she's a curious woman. I lean toward the computer when she examines the camera I have set up at the foot of my bed.

Well, this just got entertaining.

Her fingers run along the buttons…tempted to spy on her boss. My cock grows a little harder and I zoom in on her.

Go ahead. Push that button, Claire. Don't be shy.

I grin to myself.

Well, fuck me—she just hit play.

But here's the real question—will she run away or stay and watch?

I have a healthy sexual appetite. I love pussy and I'm a kinky bastard. Sweet Claire isn't even scratching the surface with this video. It was just a routine Monday night. I should put a stop to this but when I see her touching herself I can't bring myself to do anything but watch. In fact, being the bastard I am, I close the blinds to my office and sink down in my chair.

"Oops. How'd that happen?"

Somehow my cock is out of my pants. Better take care of that. Must be a sign from up above.

My cock aches, just hard as a fucking rock, when she moves to my bed and sits on the edge with her skirt hiked up.

You naughty little bitch.

Her panties are sexier than I'd guessed. I never dreamed she'd be turned on watching me fuck two other women, but she is. I figured the second she hit play I'd be getting slapped when she returned.

I zoom in closer and watch her stuff her fingers in the pretty little pink pussy. I grip my cock, stroking myself as I watch little Miss Innocent ride her hand. Her head flies back, dark hair fanned out on my sheets. Her thick lips part and she brings her fingers up and sucks them into her mouth, moaning as she tastes herself.

Christ, she's fucking sexy.

I jerk my cock harder and faster imagining her lips wrapped around me, sucking me to the back of her throat.

Fucking her would be poetry. I'd love to look into her eyes while I feed her my dick.

Jesus, I'm about to blow already.

A shudder travels down my spine and my balls tighten before I blow all over my hand. Wave after wave. I'm still busting into my hand when I text her with the other. She's fucking with my stuff, so it's only natural I should fuck with her. She needs to be punished for making me jerk off on my hand like some teenage boy.

Claire looks up when the phone goes off, but doesn't stop pleasing herself on my sheets. It takes everything I have not to drive over there and finish the job for her.

I start calling and she ignores all of them.

It pisses me off. My jaw ticks as she finishes up then races around my room in an orgasm-induced haze.

I finally get her on the phone. Even her goddamn voice nearly has me hard again. I need her back in the office now.

I'm fucking starving, but not for food. I want my cock in her tight cunt as soon as possible.

I grab a tissue from my desk to clean up.

Then I wait.

Chapter Four

CLAIRE

I've been sitting in the parking garage for ten minutes. I know Max's food is probably getting cold. I can't bring myself to go in there after what I did. My brother would die of shame if he found out. I don't know what came over me, but the worst part is…I liked it. I want more. I want Maxwell. I want him to take me like he did those women and show me how a real man fucks.

I've never been with a man before. I've only dated boys. Max is tall and commands respect with his dangerous blue eyes. He has a surfer's body and can wear a suit like he belongs on the runway.

My phone pings.

Maxwell: better have my food on my desk in five minutes.

My first response is to ask what happens if I don't, but I think better of it. He's been short with me ever since I walked in the office this morning. Maybe it's because I'm Jax's sister. I grab the bag of takeout from the passenger seat and make my way to the elevator. The blinds in his office are pulled down so I knock on the door.

"If you aren't lunch go away." His loud voice booms and I bite the inside of my cheek.

He's angry that I've made him wait for his food because I'm a chicken shit. If I want to start standing on my own and stop living off Jax's allowance, I better pull myself together.

Squaring my shoulders back, I open the door and walk in like I own the place.

His head snaps up. "About damn time."

"Sorry, caught up in traffic."

"Rule number one. If you're going to work for me, don't bullshit me. You can't bullshit a bullshitter. Number two. If you're running behind, let me know. Number three. Never waste my time. Time is money."

"Yes, sir."

I offer him a weak smile as he snatches the bag and takes it over to a seating area in the corner.

"Well…" His eyes sear into me. "Gonna join?"

"I uh, don't like hot dogs." I do but there's no way I can eat right now. I need out of this room, fast.

His brow quirks up. "Can't handle twelve inches?"

"What did you just say?" There is no way he just said what I think he did. Did he?

Before he can reply my brother throws the door to the office open.

Maxwell scowls in his direction. "Don't you knock?"

"Just coming by to see if Claire had lunch yet? Why are your blinds down?" His tone is accusatory.

"I don't want assholes bothering me while I eat." Maxwell smirks. "Why do *you* think they're closed?"

Jaxson rolls his eyes then turns to me. "Claire, lunch?"

"Sure." I glance over at Maxwell. "That is if you don't need me for anything else, sir."

His lip twitches when I call him sir, and I swear my body heats up another twenty degrees.

Maxwell pretends to mull it over.

I think he's really just trying to piss Jaxson off.

"It's fine. You can go."

I scurry out of his office. He's making me crazy and it hasn't even been a full day.

I follow Jax to the company cafeteria and get a salad.

"Aren't you eating?" I smother the lettuce with ranch dressing, suddenly feeling starved now that I'm out of the office.

"Already did. Wanted to see how things are going."

"Good. I think it could be a good fit."

No you don't. This is a horrible idea. You've seen how the first day has gone.

"Glad to hear it. If he gives you shit, let me know."

"He's fine." I wave my hand around and dig back into my salad.

"I need to get back upstairs."

"Go. I'll see you around."

When I get done with my food I head back upstairs and take a seat at my desk. I look to my left and feel the heat of Maxwell's stare scorching into me and notice the blinds are open once again.

I smile at him and he gives me a hard stare through the window.

Did I do something wrong?

I chew on the tip of my pen, a lifelong habit I can't seem to break. There's no way he knows what I did. Even if he does have some voyeur cam set up—which I wouldn't put past him—he couldn't have seen it yet. He's been working all morning. The thought of him finding out has my stomach in knots.

I need to focus on work to take my mind off it.

But, no matter how hard I try, I can't. I squirm in my seat remembering the look on his face when he came. His mouth was partially open, his square jaw clenched. He looked relaxed, not like the smug asshole mean-mugging me from the other room.

My company phone pings with a text.

Maxwell: My office. Now.

Jesus.

I expected him to be bossy, but he takes it to a whole new level. I put the pen down on my desk and scoot my chair back. I stand up and fix my skirt. It keeps riding up my thighs as I walk into his office.

"Close the door." He practically growls at me.

I do as he says.

He points to the chair across from him. "Sit."

"Did I, umm, do something wrong?"

His blue eyes pretty much pin me to the seat.

"Do you have a dress?"

What the hell? "Yeah. Why?"

He smiles, rubbing the pad of his thumb across his chin before leaning across the desk. He looks so dominating in his gray suit.

"Got an invitation while you were at lunch. I need a date. Someone professional but hot enough to distract the man standing between me and a multi-billion-dollar deal."

"I don't know." I fiddle with my hands in my lap. "I don't think I'm the one for something like that."

"Of course you are. I can't get a damn thing done today with you wearing that skirt halfway up your legs. It's about an inch away from flashing me those black panties you're wearing."

Heat spreads across my face and flushes down my neck to my chest. How in the hell does he know what color…?

Shit! Triple shit!

"Look at me." His brows narrow.

My eyes immediately obey his command. "You saw?" My words come out on an exhale.

"Goddamn right I did." He licks his bottom lip. "Had to close the blinds and fuck my hand just so I could focus."

"I'm sorry." I look at the floor.

He stalks around his desk until he's standing in front of me, then leans back and folds his arms across his chest. "What are we going to do about this?"

I should feel ashamed, but the way he's staring me down in his suit with those hard blues—I might get off just looking at him.

"Please don't tell my brother."

He smirks. "Why the fuck would I tell him?"

I shrug and dare to look up at him.

He licks that bottom lip of his and rakes his stare up and down my body. "Fuck, you'd be a perfect submissive. After this charity event I'm taking you somewhere."

"What?"

"Shh." He leans over and trails his index finger down my lips, then leans next to my ear. "I saw you watching me on that camera. Saw what you did in my bed. Saw everything. So don't play dumb, okay?"

"Look, I may have gotten carried away, but that's all it was."

He leans back and snickers. "I know what you need. You're curious. I know someone who'd be perfect for a girl like you."

For some reason my confidence kicks into overdrive. Confidence or stupidity. "Why not you?"

A grin spreads across his lips. "Promised your brother I wouldn't touch you." He sighs. "God knows I want to. So, I'll just have to watch someone else." He pulls a black card from his pocket. "Get a dress. Shoes…whatever you want. Classy but sexy. It's black tie."

He waves me out of his office before I even know how to respond. What the hell is he even talking about?

He did get one thing right, though. I am curious.

Chapter Five

MAXWELL

This is a terrible idea. I'm already in over my head.

Jaxson will kill me—well, he'll try. I smirk to myself. What he doesn't know won't hurt him. Claire's like a ripe virgin sent here to torment me. A forbidden fruit I should stay far away from.

I don't mix fucking and business. That's a good way to ruin everything I've accomplished. The guys all know I love to fuck around and I'm into some crazy shit, but they don't know I hold membership to an elite club for people with—eccentric tastes. Shit you can't do with some one-night stand you take home from the bar.

The club is my best kept secret. It's mine, and only mine. Something special to me.

Getting pussy is easy. Always has been.

I don't do relationships. I like to fuck, and I like… other things. That's why I find the club so appealing.

Watching Claire have the balls to rub one out on my bed while watching me bang two women—I bet she'd love it there.

I can see it written all over her. She needs to be fucked. She needs a man. Not that little bitch she brought to the last Christmas party. I could mold her into a perfect sub, but if Jaxson ever found out…it would ruin the company.

I can't wait to see what she gets.

I told Jaxson I sent her to pick up a new suit.

I'm already lying to him and imagining how she'd look wearing a collar with my name on it.

A girl like Claire needs to be owned. She needs to be mine. It's an absolutely terrible idea, and I have no clue why I'm excited about sabotaging myself and one of my closest friendships.

There's just something about her.

Once I get in the privacy of my car, I pull out my phone and bring up Claire's personal number.

Maxwell: you get a dress?

Claire: yeah

Maxwell: I want to see it

Claire: what?

Maxwell: send me a picture

Claire: you can't be serious

Maxwell: I watched you finger fuck yourself on my sheets. I think a picture will be fine.

A few minutes pass and eventually the dots start bouncing on the phone. The picture comes through as I'm typing out a message for her to hurry the fuck up. My cock stands at attention as I wait for it to load.

As soon as it finishes, I feel the need to throw my phone through the window. It's hanging in a fucking closet.

Nice one, Claire. Think you're funny?

I can't even see what it would really look like.

Maxwell: you alone?

Claire: yeah. why?

Maxwell: I need to swing by and pick up my card. Text me your address.

She sends it and I relay the information to the driver.

Knowing she's probably pacing back and forth, nervous as hell—it feels fantastic. Toying with someone as innocent as Claire is my idea of fun.

When I arrive at her building, my face screws itself up. Why in the hell is she living in this building when there's an empty apartment next to her brother? I can practically smell the shit from the sewer. I don't like it. Her living here.

I don't even know why I care. She isn't special to me. No one is.

Made that mistake once with a girl in California. She fucked my best friend. Last I heard they got married and have three kids.

I made sure to send them a wedding gift. It was a custom dildo molded from my cock. At least they'll always have that to remember me by.

I was a bitter bastard when it all went down but now I don't give a flying fuck about either of them. It's why I left town. Put all the bullshit behind me. I took the job here and started over.

I walk straight into the building and the main door is unlocked. Of course it is. I stare around at the shitbox of an apartment complex. What was Jaxson thinking letting her move in here? I want to kick him right in the pecker.

When I get to her apartment on the third floor I knock.

Her soft voices calls out, "It's open."

My jaw clenches. I knock again, harder this time.

Why the fuck would she just invite someone into her apartment without checking to see who it is? Jesus.

I listen for her footsteps. When I hear her approach, I step off to the side. She needs to learn a lesson in safety.

I know they grew up on a ranch where they could probably sleep with their doors unlocked, but this isn't a fucking hamlet out in butt-fucking rural county. This is a big city.

The door opens, and she pokes her unsuspecting head out. The moment I catch a glimpse of her dark hair as she looks the opposite direction I make my move and grab her, clamping my hand over her mouth.

Her fight or flight instincts kick in and she struggles against me. Her tight ass rubs over my crotch and my whole body tenses at the sensation.

"What the fuck were you thinking." I growl the words in her ear and let go of her.

She takes a swing at me on instinct.

I won't give her an F, because it's pretty impressive.

She still doesn't pass, though. Fucking hell, I'm going to have to talk to Jax.

"What are you doing?" Her eyes widen, then narrow in on me. Relief washes over her face, but she still looks pretty pissed.

"A favor. You live in a piece of shit neighborhood and didn't even bother checking to see who was at the door. What if I was a rapist or serial killer?"

Her face turns red and she folds her arms over her chest. "I knew it was you. You said you were on your way over."

"Doesn't matter. You always check. You're a single woman. Your brother should've taught you better than this." I glance around. "The fuck are you doing living here anyway?"

She sighs. "I like it here. It's got character."

If by character she means bad insulation, rats, and shitty fixtures, then by all means, it has character.

I follow her inside, closing the door behind me, unsure of what I'm really doing here. Playing with fire. That's exactly what I'm doing. I don't need my card or whatever excuse I gave her.

"Can I get you a drink? All I have is juice, water, milk, or tea."

"No. I shouldn't even be here." I look around her apartment feeling like I stepped back into college. Mismatched art on the wall. Her couch is a futon for fuck's sake. It reminds me how young and off limits she is.

"Why? Because you're my boss or because of my brother?"

"Both."

"Well, I have your card. It's in my purse. Give me a minute. I was getting ready to make coffee. You can sit or whatever."

She's changed from her work clothes and her t-shirt rides up as she stretches to retrieve something from a cabinet.

I catch a glimpse of a daisy tattooed on her hip.

"Out of the way, shorty." I reach past and grab a coffee mug for her.

Her fingers brush over mine, warm and inviting. An invitation I try to ignore.

Saying and doing are two different things though.

"I'd like to see what I bought. Go put on the dress."

She cocks her head to the side as she pours water into the coffee maker. Her teeth graze her bottom lip.

"You want me to put on the dress? Here? Now?"

I take a step toward her. "Look, Claire. I don't like repeating myself. And I don't say shit that I don't mean."

Chapter Six

CLAIRE

Holy shit.

Maxwell is in my apartment. The man is temptation walking. God, he smells nice. Not overpowering or too musky. He has a clean smell, like fresh linens when they first come out of the dryer. But there's a hint of something more. Something I can't put a finger on. Attraction. Raw sexual chemistry hangs in the air between us. I inhale a breath and the air seems thick.

It's like he's sucking all the oxygen from my small apartment. I know he thinks my place is beneath a man like him, but I got it on my own without my brother paying my way.

He wants me to move into the apartment next to his, but I refuse to accept it. He has done so much for me. I want to show him I can stand on my own two feet even if it is paying rent on a crappy apartment.

Sure, he got me a job, but it's not permanent. I don't want to go to law school. My passion is writing. I view working at the firm as inspiration. Maybe I'll get a juicy story idea from one of the cases or from people I work with. I could write some dirty stories with Maxwell as my muse.

The man is seriously sexy. The way he looks at me right now has me thinking things I shouldn't. He's my boss, but after today, I think we're past that.

I don't think either of us wants anyone knowing what happened.

Maxwell could be a stepping stone. The man to get me over stupid Brian.

I leave him alone in the living room/kitchen to go try on the dress. I wasn't even going to consider it, but the saleswoman insisted. She said this dress was made for me.

I'm nervous about the plunging neckline and not being able to wear a bra with it but she assured me I would knock everyone off their feet.

I've never owned a dress like this, but I'm a woman, not the little girl my brother still likes to pretend I am. It's time for me to grow up and act like it. No more chasing stupid boys who aren't going anywhere. I'm ready for a man. A man who takes what he wants. A man who can give me what I need.

Pulling my shirt over my head, I stare at my body in the mirror, taking in the plain white bra. I need to invest in something sexy. Something that will make me feel like the woman I want to become.

I quickly shimmy my pants off.

I slide down the unflattering panties I put on earlier and kick them under my bed. I don't expect anything to happen but there's nothing wrong with being prepared. I laugh to myself thinking about how my grandma used to tell Jax and me never to leave the house in dirty underwear in case we were in an accident. I think the same logic can be applied to going on a date with a sexy man. Is it even a date? I shake my head and convince myself it's just for business purposes.

Pulling the black dress from the hanger, I step into it but when I go to pull up the zipper, I can't reach it. *Stupid short arms and legs.*

I maneuver to my bedroom door and holler for Maxwell. "Can you give me a hand in here? I can't reach the zipper."

I hear him clear his throat. "Yeah." He starts down the short hallway, and I feel like the walls are closing in on me. His tall and broad-shouldered frame heat me up as he stalks closer. His eyes burn into mine, and I have to look away. I don't know what this man is doing to me, but he's making me want things—for him to touch me.

Twisting around, I turn my back to him.

A shiver courses up my spine when his knuckles graze along my skin right above my ass.

With a gentle tug, he pulls upward. "There." His strong hands grip my shoulders and I can't breathe, let alone get out the "thank you" lingering on the tip of my tongue.

I remain still as he leans closer. His fingers brush my hair aside and his soft lips touch the base of my neck. The warmth of his tongue sweeps over me as the tip darts out and gives me a lick, tasting my delicate skin halfway between my ear and collarbone.

I turn my head slightly on instinct, wanting to get a look at him. Our eyes lock before he looks down over my shoulder, getting a view down the front of the dress.

"Are you bare underneath?" His lips are practically right next to mine.

"Yes." *Please kiss me and put me out of my misery.*

Chapter Seven

MAXWELL

The urge to kiss Claire is too damn tempting.

I can't resist.

Sliding my fingers down her arm, I turn her body into mine. The dress has a deep V that runs the same length down the front and back—sexy and sinful. She looks fucking incredible.

It's a paradox. I want to stare at her beautiful body in this gorgeous dress, and at the same time I want to shred that fucking thing to pieces to get to her sweet little pussy.

Coming here tonight was a mistake, but I've lived a life full of them. What's one more?

I can't change who I am. I do things I shouldn't to get what I want. I need to leave before this goes too far, but I need one kiss. One fucking taste of her lips. The temptation is too great.

Claire looks up at me, and I dip my head down ready to claim her mouth. She smells of cherries and vanilla. Sugary sweet and pure temptation. I stroke her cheek with one finger, moving it along her jawline and down her slender throat, taking my time.

No need to rush perfection. She's meant to be experienced, not devoured. I look over and catch our reflection in the mirror. Her head reaches the top of my chest as she pushes up on her tiptoes and places a hand on my shoulder.

I love how short and petite she is. I could do unspeakable things to her in all kinds of positions. She's already the perfect height to kneel in front of me.

"This dress—" I trace a finger down her ribs to the top of her hip. "This dress is trouble."

She smiles.

A strong smell of coffee comes from the kitchen, but she doesn't budge.

"Good girl," I whisper in her ear and close the distance between our lips. I press my mouth to hers and Claire surrenders to me completely.

Fuck, she's so submissive. Even in a kiss I can tell that about her, the way she opens up immediately, doesn't fight for control.

A soft moan leaves her throat as I continue to dominate her mouth. Slipping my hand inside the dress, I cup one of her breasts. Not too big and not too small—just fucking perfect and natural.

There is nothing better than the feel of a real woman. I'm not a fan of fake tits and other kinds of implants and shit. I want to feel her the way she was made.

My phone vibrates in my pocket, breaking the moment.

"I should get this."

"Yeah, I need, umm—coffee."

Pulling my phone from my pocket, the notification is nothing that can't wait. I should make up an excuse to leave and end this but now that I've had a taste I need more. So much more.

I want that dress on the floor.

I'm not naïve. I understand my own brain very well. I know exactly what I came here for, and it wasn't to pick up my credit card. I want to fuck Claire and get this little fantasy out of my system. It's a terrible idea.

"I need to go."

"Oh, okay." She walks around the corner. "I'll see you tomorrow. Here's your card."

I can't help but notice she stares at the ground and looks sad that I'm leaving. That makes me smile on the inside.

I take the card and leave without another word. As I walk down the stairs I pass that pussy ex-boyfriend of hers, Brian. I forgot he lives in the same building. That's going to be a problem.

I want to slam him against the wall and dare him to knock on her door, but I don't. Instead, I give him a smug grin that says *I just fucked the shit out of her*.

Then I hide around the corner and wait until I'm sure he didn't go to her place. I give a thank you nod to the sky, because I don't know what I would've done if he did. It wouldn't have been pretty.

She works for me now. She's mine.

———

When I get to my apartment, I go straight to the bar for a drink.

I can't stop thinking about that piece of shit being in the same vicinity as her. What if he left his apartment when I was gone and went over to her place?

I down a rocks glass and fill it up again, then take the new drink upstairs with me. When I walk into my room I can't stop picturing Claire on my bed earlier. I walk by and run my fingers over the sheets where she fucked her hand. I set my whiskey down on the night stand then crawl over to right where she was.

I press my face into the sheets, and I can still smell her hot cunt on them. My cock aches, it's so fucking hard. I stick my tongue out and press it to the sheets, just to try and taste her for even a microsecond.

I wish she were here now spreading her legs for me.

Fuck, smelling and tasting her is so intoxicating.

Regret stings in the walls of my chest. I should have stayed and fucked her brains out. Let Brian hear the truth through her screams on the other side of the walls. Let her whole fucking apartment complex know. *She's mine.*

Well, she should be. If I didn't respect Jaxson she'd already have that snug pussy wrapped around my dick.

My phone buzzes from my pocket again.

My friend Jacob is at the club tonight. Has a new pet he wants to show off.

I fire off a text that I will be there.

I need to shower, but I have something else to do first—relieve the hard cock tenting my pants. I bunch up the sheets that still smell like Claire's aroused pussy, and I wrap them around my cock and fuck my hand until I come all over them. For some reason I imagine blowing inside her, and I get off in seconds.

Seconds!

How is that even possible, and why do I want to come inside her so bad? Why do I want to mark her as mine and growl at anyone that looks at her?

I've never been jealous in my life, and right now I want to go yank her out of that shitty apartment, move her in our building, and fuck a hundred orgasms out of her.

Christ, what's this woman doing to me? Yeah, I need to go to the club. Get some shit out of my system.

———

The club used to be a hotel. Now it's a place for people like myself with desires and urges that can't always be met by one partner.

I sign in at the front desk and head to the bar to see who's here.

I spot Jacob immediately with a busty blonde sitting at the bar.

"Maxwell." He shoots me a grin and introduces me to his new sub in training.

She's beautiful and exactly his type. I've never seen Jacob without a skinny blonde with huge, fake tits. But, she's the exact opposite of what I enjoy—usually.

"She has a friend, you know?" He raises an eyebrow at me.

"Not interested. Thanks, though." I nod to the bartender for my usual and look around the room.

Sandra is here. She was my first sub in Dallas. We parted ways a few years ago when we both realized our relationship was holding us back. We're still good friends, but I don't know if I want to introduce her to Claire right away. I'm conflicted. I think Claire would love it here, but I just don't know. Some people have a hard time wrapping their mind around a place like this.

I wink at Sandra when she waves.

"Maxwell." She kisses me on the cheek when she walks up.

"You attached tonight?"

Her eyebrows rise. "What?"

"I need a friend to talk to."

"Oh. Okay, let's go."

I smile at Jacob and follow Sandra upstairs.

———

"Sounds like a disaster waiting to happen."

I shake my head. "I can't get her off my mind. You don't understand."

"There is only one cure for that." She folds her arms across her chest and stares. "You'll fuck her and ruin her. You and I both know this is a terrible idea. If you bring her here are you ready to see her with another man? If she's here unclaimed she'll be fair game."

I sigh. She doesn't have to remind me of the rules.

Chapter Eight
CLAIRE

When another knock sounds at my door I wonder if Maxwell changed his mind. I'd be lying if I said I wasn't disappointed when he left, but I know it's probably for the best. I can't hook up with my boss who happens to be one of my brother's best friends.

Max scared the crap out of me earlier when he grabbed me, but it turned me on at the same time. Him grabbing me and scolding me. It's obvious he cares about me and wants me protected, and I've never had anyone act that way besides my brother.

I walk to the door with butterflies in my stomach and an uneasy feeling sinks in when I see it's Brian.

I open the door. "What are you doing here?"

His eyes scan my entire body before he says anything. "Damn, baby, this dress. Wow." He lets out a heavy breath.

"I'm not your baby. What do you want?"

"Can I come in?"

"No."

"Come on. I miss you and we should talk."

"We broke up. What's there to discuss?"

His brows knit in confusion. He hooks his thumb over his shoulder. "Who was that guy that just left. You seeing someone already?"

"It's none of your business." I know I shouldn't be rude or stoke any flames but it's nice to see him jealous. He never really acted like he ever wanted me before. It's too little, too late now.

His jaw ticks. "I want you back. I made a mistake."

"Right." I stare off at the wall and shake my head. "It was a mistake when you told me you weren't in love with me and thought we should see other people. What did you think I would do? Mope around and wait for you to come back? You did me a favor. I realized you were right. We *should* date other people. I was saving myself for you but when we broke up I did a lot of thinking… You let me go pretty easy. I figured a man who loved me would've fought a lot harder than you did."

"That's the problem, Claire. You wouldn't have sex with me. I have needs." He takes a step toward me.

I take a step back, but he presses faster and cups my cheek in his palm.

I'm not with Maxwell. I shouldn't feel like I'm betraying him, but I do. This all feels—*wrong*.

His foot moves to kick the door shut behind him.

"We belong together. I'm sorry."

The words I wanted to hear last week are meaningless this week.

I put a palm on his chest and push him back. "You should go. I don't want you back."

He stares at me, dumbfounded, like he can't believe he was just rejected.

I lean up to give him a kiss on the cheek, to try and let him down easy, but he turns into me and mashes his lips against mine.

His tongue probes at the seam of my mouth, demanding entrance.

I push back against him, trying to get away but he's way stronger. His arms wrap around me and he picks me up and carries me toward the bedroom.

"What the hell? Get off me! Let me go!" I punch and claw at him, but he laughs it off. He walks me into the living room and slams us down on the couch. He pins me down by the shoulders and hovers over me, glaring.

"Did you fuck him?"

I try to look away, but he grabs my chin.

"You're hurting me." Tears form in the corners of my eyes and I try to pull my head away.

"Answer me!" I've never seen this kind of jealous rage from him before.

I try to fight as I twist and claw at him. The full weight of his body crashes down on me and he grabs the center of my new dress and rips it down the middle of the V.

"You fucked him, didn't you?" His hand whips across my face.

"Yes!" I don't care if it's a lie. I scream through my tears. I want him in as much pain as I'm in right now. "I fucked him and loved every minute of it. Right before you got here, and his cock is *way* bigger than yours."

His fist rears back but my neighbor pounds on the wall and screams for us to keep it down.

Brian looks down at me and must realize what he's done because he falls back on his heels. Guilt washes over his face. "I'm sorry. Claire. I didn't mean…fuck. I'm sorry."

I scowl at him. "Just go. And don't come near me again or I'll call my brother and have you thrown in jail."

He pushes up from the bed and runs a hand though his dark hair. "I'm fucking sorry."

I try to hold back the tears as I pant. I don't want to give him the satisfaction, but they won't stop. I've never been so scared in my life. "Please go, now."

He finally turns and slinks out of my apartment.

Once he's gone I jump up and lock the deadbolt. I run to my bedroom and bury my face in the covers. I just want to disappear as I cry into the sheets. I'm so scared.

I never thought he would be *that* guy. The type of guy who would hit a woman.

And he lives in my building.

The worst part is he got what he wanted.

He rattled me.

And now my dress is ruined, along with my heart.

I have to get out of this apartment.

Chapter Nine
MAXWELL

I jump in my car to leave the club when Claire's name pops up on my phone. I debate sending her to voicemail. We're on a path to destruction. A car crash waiting to happen, but I can't stop myself. I've never wanted a woman the way I want her.

I answer after the third ring. "Hello?"

"Hey."

Something's wrong. I can hear it in her voice.

"What's wrong?"

"I-I don't know why I'm calling you, but something happened."

I think about that prick, Brian, heading up the stairs. I knew it. I fucking knew it, that motherfucker did something. I could see it in his eyes when he saw me.

"What happened?" The question comes out harsher than intended.

"I don't want to be alone right now."

I'm surprised she called me. She usually runs to her brother for this shit.

"I would go to Jaxson's, but he has company…"

"Where are you?"

"Your apartment."

Fuck me.

"Be there in a few minutes."

When I walk into my place, Claire's in my kitchen eating pickles. The sight of her so at home in my place hits me in the chest. Maybe a relationship is what I'm missing in my life. After talking to Sandra about everything I think maybe she was right. I'm going through the motions in all areas of my life. It's becoming boring and routine—monotonous. Even sex with random women is unexciting. I need something. The deal I've been brokering has me stressed. On edge.

"I hope you don't mind." She waves the dill spear in her hand at me. She slides the pickle between her lips slowly and all I can think about is how I want to smack it out of her hand and replace it with my dick.

"It's fine." I walk toward her, and she backs up a step.

She's on edge. Instinctively shying away. Something happened.

I'm going to kill that motherfucker.

Claire has on a pair of leggings and an oversized sweatshirt. Normally her hair would be piled up on her head when she's dressed like this but it's down and she keeps turning that side away so I can't see.

Rage courses through my veins, but I have to be calm and collected. She doesn't need me blowing up in front of her. I have to stay calm—until I see that bitch, Brian, again.

"Show me."

"Show you what?" She moves around the island, keeping it between us. She smiles, but there's pain in her eyes.

I'd recognize it anywhere. "Don't play games."

"I don't understand."

"Show me what he did to you."

Her smile falters. "I don't know what…"

"Claire?"

"Yeah?"

"It's okay. Let's see."

Her eyes well up again. "Please promise me this stays between us." Her voice cracks.

I nod.

"Jaxson will kill him. He has enough going on right now."

I can't help but notice she's worried about her brother right after she's been assaulted. You can't buy that kind of love and loyalty. I respect the shit out of it, but that little shit isn't going to get away with what he did.

"Fine. I'll kill him. Show me."

She sits down on a barstool and pushes her hair back off her shoulder. I stalk over to her and tilt her face toward the light. The skin on her cheek is swollen and red. I brush my thumb over the mark and she winces.

"He's fucking dead."

"Max?"

I shake my head. "No. If I see him, he better fucking run. What happened?" I continue to stroke her jawline, unable to pull my hand away.

"We were already broken up." She looks away at the wall and tells me everything that happened.

I want to smile at the fact she told him I fucked her with my huge cock, but that'd be poor form in the moment. She could've been hurt way worse.

"I'm sorry this happened to you. And that I caused it."

"It wasn't your fault."

"I know. But, I complicated things for you."

"He ripped the dress." Another tear rolls down her cheek.

I catch it with my finger and brush my thumb across her face to wipe it away. "Claire?"

"Y-yeah?"

"It's just a dress. We'll get you another one."

"I shouldn't have come here. I was just so scared and knowing he was on the other side of the walls..."

I pull her into a hug and stroke her hair. "It's fine. Don't apologize for wanting to be safe. You're safe here." Without thinking I drop a kiss on the top of her head. Fuck, her hair is so soft. I want to bury my nose in it.

She sniffs. "Thank you. I know you're busy and have a lot going on. You shouldn't have to deal with my issues."

She's not wrong. This bullshit is why I didn't want to hire her. The girl always has drama going on, but this is acceptable. She has a right to feel safe and not have some cocksucker assaulting her.

And there's another thing I can't get off my mind—the fact that I like her being here. It feels, right.

I let out a long sigh.

Fuck.

I need two things. A buzz and pussy.

It's a bad idea but fuck it. She looks like she could use a drink too.

"Let's go out to the balcony." I kick my shoes off and grab a joint and a bottle of liquor.

She follows me out the sliding glass door and takes the seat opposite mine and pulls her knees up to her chin.

Even slightly bent she's beautiful as she gazes at me from under her lashes. She's so small and petite. I'd look like an idiot trying to sit that way, but it just looks natural for her.

Putting the joint between my lips, I spark a lighter in front of it.

I take a hard pull and inhale the smoke until I feel I can't breathe.

Extending my hand, I offer a hit to Claire.

Jaxson would have my ass for this, but it'll mellow her out. We both need it. It's been one hell of a night.

Willingly, she accepts it and takes a few small puffs.

A welcomed silence stretches between us as we smoke and stargaze, both seemingly lost in our own thoughts.

I keep feeling her stare penetrate my skin.

"How do you feel?"

"Better."

"Wanna feel even better?" *Jesus, I'm higher than I thought.*

Buzz—check.

Pussy—in progress.

Her head nods slightly.

I put the roach out in the ashtray and go down on my knees in front of her.

"Do you trust me to make you feel good?"

She nods again and her eyelashes flutter and close when my hand slides up her leg. "Please."

Chapter Ten

CLAIRE

"Good." He smiles up at me. "I want to taste your sweet pussy."

I must be blazed out of my mind because there's no way he just said that out loud.

I hope I remember his words tomorrow because it's so going in my book. Gently, he slides my leggings off.

"What if someone sees us?"

He stares right at my pussy and his eyes heat it to a billion degrees. "I don't give a fuck."

Jesus.

My head falls back against the chair. It's been a rough day, and this is exactly what I need.

Greedily, his fingers massage my thighs and he's getting dangerously close to where I want him. I can't help but smile as I sit here like a queen on a throne being worshiped at the altar.

He looks like a man on a quest, looking to conquer something. God, he's so powerful and sexy and just—fucking hot.

Max forces my legs farther apart.

I want to touch him but I'm hesitant. As if he can read my mind, he takes my hands in his and brings them to his hair.

The strands of blond hair are silky to the touch as I caress my fingers over his scalp.

His massage soon turns to kisses along my legs, teasing me more and more every time he gets close, then he backs away.

I'm about to come undone already.

He brushes his thumb lightly across my pussy, nothing but a thin layer of fabric separating our skin. "I'm going to kiss you here."

"Please." I pant as he teases me, rubbing his finger in a lazy circle over my clit.

God, I don't think I've ever been so wet in my life.

He tugs the white cotton to the side, exposing me. I feel like I might combust. I gasp when he licks the entire length of my seam, his tongue landing on my clit. He flicks his tongue across it and up to his top lip, staring into my eyes the whole time.

"Claire?"

"Y-yeah?" I practically moan my word at him.

"I've never tasted anything sweeter than this pussy."

"Oh my God. Please don't stop."

I tilt my hips up, needing more of his lips on me. I want his tongue inside me.

He glares at my panties like they're standing in the way of what he wants. "These are in my way. I want you bare." His fingers tug on the waistband of my white briefs and rips them in half. Then he repeats it on the other side and pulls them off me in tatters. I don't miss the fact that he shoves them in his pocket.

"I'll make a note of that, Mr. Bass."

His eyes roll up to mine and there's a spark of excitement in them. "Make a note of this while you're at it."

He slides a finger into me as his tongue flattens across my clit and then sweeps back and forth over it.

My fingers tighten in his hair and pull his head closer. I try to moan but it comes out as a gasp of gibberish. I've never felt anything like this in my life. My entire body is electric and it all pulses straight down onto his tongue.

A firm hand grips my hip and his fingers dig in, holding me right where he wants me with my legs over his shoulders.

He works another finger in and explores the depths of me. He curls his fingers up and hits my spot just right. Another gasp comes out of me.

"There it is." I feel his lips curl into a smile on my pussy.

He's learning me. Analyzing everything. Watching every reaction.

Not that he needs to. My brain won't stop screaming what a fucking god he is for pressing every erogenous button in my body with ease.

He keeps his tongue working back and forth then circles as his fingers slowly stretch me out.

"So. Fucking. Tight."

I forget where I am. Everything fades away. The motherlode of all orgasms is building in my core, and it won't be long before I give in.

To hell with the weed. His tongue is a drug I could get addicted to.

Using the arms of the chair for support I arch my back needing him deeper.

"I'm so close." My words come out on a pant as the sweet ache pulses between my thighs.

He keeps his fingers working as he stares up at me. "Come all over my fucking mouth then."

Before I can respond, his tongue is on me again, stroking my clit harder and faster than before.

Max's fingers damn near fuck me into a coma when his mouth latches onto my clit and he hums all over it.

The man eats my pussy like it's the last meal on earth. Like a ravenous dog. I can hear him growling against my sensitive skin.

It's too much to hold back. I follow his orders exactly as instructed.

A whimper escapes my lips as my whole body tenses, and I squeeze around his fingers. I convulse, shake, and rock. My fingers dig into his scalp and I can't stop saying his name over and over as the orgasm rolls through me in waves.

Once my body relaxes, I can barely breathe as he gets up and pulls me to my feet.

"Let's get you into a bath and then bed." His voice is smooth like whiskey as he sweeps me up off my feet and into his arms.

He carries me the entire way. Upstairs in the massive bathroom with a tub big enough I could swim in, Max sits me on the edge while he starts running the water.

I don't know what it is about him. Maybe it's the buzz or the orgasm but I don't feel self-conscious. I feel cherished.

Special.

Once the tub is halfway full I watch as he strips down to nothing. The camera didn't showcase how good he looks in person. It's a hundred times better live. A tribal tattoo covers the expanse of his broad chest and travels down his side.

I can't stop staring at him. His cock juts out, hard and rigid.

Max smirks when he sees me lick my lips.

"See something you like?"

I'd usually blush in a situation like this, but I don't for some reason.

I reply by pulling my sweatshirt over my head, revealing I'm not wearing a bra. Two can play at this game.

Chapter Eleven

MAXWELL

I'm in the tub with Claire. She's right here between my legs while I massage her shoulder. My cock has never been so hard in my life. I ache to be inside her. After what that asshole put her through she deserves to be pampered and treated like a queen. She should feel safe and cherished, and not have one ounce of fear in her body. A real man takes care of what's his. When I'm with someone special they get everything they need. When I enter into a relationship it isn't just about sex. It's about building trust.

Not that this is a relationship, but there's something special about Claire. I want her in ways I haven't wanted a woman in a long time.

I haven't wanted to trust anyone in forever. The shit my ex-girl-friend and ex-best-friend put me through fucked with my head for a long time. Sandra helped me work through it and for that, she'll always be a great friend, but spending time with Claire shows me I need more. I *want* more than I've wanted from a woman in the past.

It's crazy though. Claire and I are nowhere near that territory. I don't know what the fuck I'm doing with her. She was supposed to be an assistant, not be *mine*. I don't even know how she'll react when she finds out what I'm into. What I need. I can already imagine her wearing my collar around her slender throat.

How fucking sexy it will be to chain her up and fuck her ass.

Jesus. I shake my head even thinking about how absurd it is.

How will she react when she finds out? I never get nervous. But my stomach twists in knots when I think about it—her. *I am who I am.*

But, for the first time since I can remember—I'm worried.

She rests her head back on my shoulder and stares up at me. "Thank you for tonight."

"Not a problem at all." I press my lips briefly to hers and she turns to straddle me. Her hot little pussy is rubbing over the head of my dick and I want nothing more than to impale her.

Every cell in my body screams at me to take her, but my brain tells me I shouldn't—even if it kills me. I know when I fuck Claire there will be no turning back. I'll get lost in her. If there's one thing I know for a fact, it's that I'll fall for her.

Her hips roll as she grinds against me, teasing the tip of my cock with her pussy lips.

Her hands rest on my shoulders as she stares into my eyes. The tip of my cock is right against her entrance, and she pushes herself so that it parts her slick folds.

Claire goes rigid and grimaces.

I close my eyes and a groan catches in my throat. Fucking hell, she's so damn tight. I may be high, but I know virgin pussy when I feel it against my thick cock.

"Claire…" I grip her shoulders and pull away. "Are you a virgin?"

Her teeth graze over her swollen bottom lip and she nods.

My ass hammers against the backside of the tub as I push myself away. I shake my head at her. "No. Not like this."

Her jaw clenches. "I want you. I want this." She moves closer and I hold her away with my hands. "I don't expect anything in return, or after or whatever. I just, want to be with you."

Every muscle in my body tightens, and I sit there and stare at her, naked in my tub. Fuck, she's so pure and innocent. Everything I'm not. I can't do this, and yet I've never wanted anything more. I could claim her. Be the first and only.

The devil on my shoulder keeps telling me if I don't do it she'll run out and fuck some assbasket just to get it over with. Or to get over me. Christ, she's perfect.

I have to do this. We're like magnets, pulling each other together no matter how hard I resist.

The angel on my other shoulder doesn't say shit because Claire rolls her hips and rubs her tight cunt over my cock. I close my eyes.

God, forgive me.

I'm powerless to resist.

"Please." She inches herself onto me.

My eyes spring open and I can tell she's in pain already. I place my palms on each side of her face, and nod. "You ready?"

She returns my nod.

I kiss her. Not like a normal, passionate kiss. A kiss that is sweet and sensual and tells her that everything will be okay and she can stop whenever she wants. My tongue sweeps over hers as I thrust a little harder into her.

She sucks in a huge breath and a whimper catches in her throat.

I stroke her hair back behind her ears and keep kissing her with my hands on her face as I push all the way in.

I groan when she squeezes around me and think I might pass out. It's so hot and tight and she's so perfect. Tears spring up in the corners of her eyes, but she's smiling. I kiss them away and I rock back slow and easy, not wanting to hurt her any more than I have to.

"Are you okay?" I press my forehead against hers.

She nods against me. "Yeah. Perfect."

I can't remember ever fucking a woman like this. It's because I'm not fucking her. I'm making love to her, something I never do. It's emotional sex of the highest form, and God help me if I don't feel my heart pinching a little with each thrust, knowing I'm giving her more of myself than I've ever given anyone.

Guiding her hips, I control the pace, taking her slow and easy no matter how bad I want to rut into her.

Fuck, I need to have her in my bed—under me. I want her to come on my cock and remember this night forever.

"Come on."

After toweling our bodies off faster than humanly possible I spread her legs, naked on my bed.

I should be careful and be safe, but I want nothing more than to mark her. I want to come inside her virgin pussy.

As I join her in bed I can't help but notice her staring at my camera.

The thought of being able to watch this later makes my cock grow another inch. "Want it on?"

"Yes."

I move from the bed long enough to press record. Then I walk back toward her slowly, stroking my shaft. Claire watches every single movement.

Her fingers twitch and I know she wants to touch herself but she's nervous. Goddamn, I'm going to enjoy helping her explore her sexuality.

"Touch yourself, like you already did in that same spot." It's a command, not a request.

Her hand slides between the valley of her breasts. At a leisurely pace she runs her fingers over her nipples. They harden under her fingers and I stroke myself harder and faster.

I watch as she lets go and her hand moves lower to her clit, rubbing it in a lazy circle.

The bed dips under my weight as I lay next to her.

I take her hand by the wrist. "Now touch me." I guide her hand to my aching cock. Her dainty fingers can barely wrap around me, and they slide up and down, slow and steady.

Then I say something I've never told another woman in my entire life. "You're in control. Show me what you'd have done if I'd walked in on you."

Her mouth curves into a smile and she sits up on her knees. Good girl.

Her tongue starts just above my balls and she licks up the length of my shaft. Electricity pulses through my limbs at her touch. Her sweet mouth is tight as she suctions her lips over the head of my cock.

Fisting my hand in her hair I push her head down and pull it back up, helping guide the pace. Knowing that I'm her first does something to me. A warmth blooms in my chest.

Her hand moves in time with her mouth as she gets a rhythm going. As good as she's getting at giving head, I need in that pussy. I can't take it any longer.

I slide my cock out of her mouth and roll her onto her back.

She writhes under me like she can't take another second without me inside her. Cock in hand, I rub the head along the seam of her tight pussy, teasing her, coating myself with her arousal.

Chapter Twelve

CLAIRE

My body is on fire with raw desire. Max makes me crave wicked things. The way my body comes alive under his touch—the way he kisses me—it's intense. I never knew a man could make me feel this way.

When he asked me if I wanted him to film this I knew without a doubt I did. I want to know that he'll watch it and think of me because I want to do the same. If all I ever have of him is this one night, at least I'll have something to remember it by.

There's something about him that makes me comfortable.

I feel safe.

His lips claim mine and I'm lost in the moment again. The weight of his body presses down on me as he lines his thick cock up with my entrance. His tongue plunges into my mouth tasting and exploring. Before I know what happens, he fills me again, and I suck in a huge breath. There's pain, but nothing but pleasure follows it. My pulse hammers in my ears as our bodies are joined once more. My whole body trembles beneath him. I've never felt so—alive.

My arms hook around his neck, clinging to him as he pins my knees up to my shoulders and fucks me with precision, hitting my sweet spot with every stroke. I'm falling apart at the seams—unhinged as my nails scratch down his back.

"Fuck, Claire. So tight."

I love knowing that I drive him crazy.

That this man wants me as much as I want him.

Max pulls out to the tip then slides back in, driving into my body as the headboard bangs against the wall.

"Oh, fuck. Max." My eyes roll back in my head as another orgasm cascades through my body.

He pumps into me three more times and I feel his cock kick deep inside me.

He pushes in as far as humanly possible and lets out the manliest grunt I've ever heard in my life. Hot jets of come shoot into my pussy as he shudders above me.

I put my palm on the side of his face as he spills into me. He's so beautiful and everything about it feels just—perfect.

Collapsing next to me, he lays his head on my chest and sucks my nipple into his mouth. His fingers move between my legs, gathering some of his come that spilled out. I shudder as my body greedily reacts to his touch, but I'm too tired to move.

Rubbing his fingers along my slit he slides them farther back until they're pressed up against my ass.

His thumb teases at the sensitive skin, pressing deeper. "Soon I'll be the first to take this too."

My body tenses at the thought of him fitting his big cock in my ass, but I do enjoy the way his fingers and thumb feel.

Eventually, we both drift to sleep.

———

I wake the next morning alone in his bed. My body is so stiff I don't think I can move.

I ache in the most delicious of ways but I'm ridiculously sore everywhere below the waist.

Slowly, I make my way from the bed to the bathroom and clean myself up.

My head pounds as I wash away the evidence of the night we shared. His smell is still on my skin and I breathe it in. It's such a horrible idea the more I think of it. He's my boss. My brother's friend. But I don't know how we can go back to the way things were after last night.

It was amazing.

After showering I help myself to one of his shirts. My panties are history and my pants are probably still on his balcony.

I start to go downstairs in search of Max when I overhear him talking to someone else in the room.

"Jesus, must've been a good night. You look like shit." It sounds like Brodie, one of the other partners at the firm. I can't be sure but I'm almost positive it's him.

"You have no idea." I can practically hear the smile in Max's voice and I feel all giddy inside.

"Who is she?"

"No one you'd know. Random pussy." He laughs and my heart sinks.

I can understand him keeping it a secret, but something about it hits me in the stomach like a sack of bricks.

"Anyway, I need you to go over this contract for a merger. I'd do it but I'm swamped with the baby and everything."

"No problem. I'll try to have it on your desk after lunch."

"Appreciate it."

I wait until I hear the door close. When I'm sure Max is alone I go in search of my pants so I can get the hell out of here. *Asshole.* How could I have been so dumb?

The sex was amazing, but him, not so much the morning after.

I rush past him as he starts up the stairs.

"Hey."

"I need to go." I don't dare to even look at him because I don't want to be tempted again. He'll have some excuse. Lawyers can talk their way out of anything.

"Can I give you a ride home or something?" I can hear the confusion in his voice, but I shake my head and go out on the balcony trying like hell not to cry.

He follows me out.

I just have to hold it together for five minutes and I can be done with this.

Some first time.

Claire has frozen me out for three days.

Three days.

Nobody does that shit to me. I've been tempted to bend her over my desk and spank the attitude out of her a few times, but I've been too damn busy helping Brodie so we can secure the deal I've been working on. Not to mention Jaxson watches me like a damn hawk at the office. I don't do childish games.

I thought she was different. But if she expects me to play along, she has analyzed the situation incorrectly. The only games I play involve roles and I don't see her wearing a nurse's outfit in my bedroom.

One way or another I'll get the truth, even if I have to fuck it out of her.

I'm not a patient man.

I know what I want.

I know what she needs.

But not now. Work is time for business, not bullshit.

I return to the office after a court date when I spot a vase of red roses on her desk. It's the third time she's gotten flowers this week.

Being a nosy bastard, I pluck the card from the arrangement.

Claire,

You will never know how sorry I am. I won't stop trying to win you back.

All my love,

Brian

My hands ball into fists and I think about hurling that shitty-ass cheap vase through the window. Instead, I return the card to where it was.

I stomp to my office and loosen my tie.

I don't like feeling jealous. I don't do jealous. Claire isn't mine, but she will be. I know it, and deep down, she does too. Brian can eat shit and die. He'll probably do both the next time I see him, and I'll be sure to let him know I did fuck her first. I'll always be her first and he'll never touch her again.

I send a text.

Maxwell: Where are you?

Claire: On way back from lunch. Is there something you need?

Oh, there is plenty I need. Her over my knee.

Maxwell: I need you in my office five minutes ago.

Claire: Getting off the elevator now, sir.

The sir at the end has my cock warring with my zipper.

I wait not-so-patiently for her.

The elevator dings and the door opens.

I nearly lose my shit.

I'll be goddamned if Brian isn't standing next to her. She brought that piece of shit into my office. I swear to God it's like this woman wants me to hulk out on the world.

I march out of my office daring him to step off the elevator. My eyes drill lasers into his fucking skull. I don't care if it makes a scene. He isn't welcome here. Even if it means outing Claire's secret and telling Jaxson what he did.

When Brian sees me he doesn't even step off the elevator. Just sinks back into it like a good little bitch, with his finger hammering the button to get him out of there.

Claire looks at me and her face pales.

"My office. Now!"

She jumps when my words echo off the walls. "Yes, sir." She gives me a mock salute.

I don't know if I've ever been angrier in my life than I am at this moment. So many thoughts run through my head. This is why I didn't want to hire her. This shit right here.

I close the blinds and lock the door once I have Claire alone in my office.

"What are you doing?" She glares at me as I pace around the room, making sure nobody else can see or hear what's happening.

"What were you doing with him?"

Folding her arms over her chest she pushes her cleavage up. "He wanted to talk."

"Jesus, I thought you had a fucking brain. Don't go near him again."

"Don't tell me what to do. You're my boss at work. You have no say over my personal life."

My jaw ticks as I undo my tie.

I stalk over toward her. Is this what she wanted? Attention? She's got it. I lean down in her ear. "I'm your boss *all* the time."

I take her wrists into one of my hands.

"What are you doing?" She struggles against me as I lead her to my desk.

"You want to act out to get my attention? You got it, Claire." I bind her hands with my tie behind her back and bend her over the desk.

"Max." I hear humor in her tone. She loves every second of this, even if she pretends not to. She wants to fight, but she won't. Claire can deny it, but I know what she needs. What she craves.

Pushing her skirt up over her hips, I stand back to admire her sweet ass.

God, I can't wait to fuck that too. I'm going to own every inch of her body.

"You're mine, Claire. Stop trying to deny it."

"I'm not anyone's."

"Why were you with Brian?"

"I told you, he wanted to talk."

I massage her right butt cheek.

"Don't lie to me. I'll always know when you're lying."

Crack!

She jolts when my hand makes contact with her ass cheek. I rub the pink outline of my handprint and she wiggles under my fingers.

Spreading her legs farther apart, I graze my hand over her panties feeling how turned on she is. Just as I knew she would be.

"This sweet pussy tells me the truth about everything. It's much more reliable than the words that come out of your mouth." I tease her slick cunt and her legs start to quake.

"Max, we shouldn't. Not at work." She pants the words as I slip one finger in.

"Shouldn't but we are. You should've thought about that before you brought that bitch to my office. Now you have to be punished." I thrust a second finger in.

"Now, I want to know what this bullshit attitude is. You've been this way ever since I fucked this pussy the other night."

"I…"

I twist my finger upward and she moans.

"You what?"

"I heard you." She can barely get the words out because she's about to come all over my fingers.

I keep the same pace, pumping her tight cunt. Her hips start to buck against me, like she can't get enough.

"That's it, ride my hand and tell me what you heard." She squeezes against my fingers and her body shudders as her orgasm begins and I pull my fingers out, denying her.

I yank her up by her bound hands I rub my cock against her ass. "You'll get off on my cock if I decide to let you, but first I want to know what happened."

"You said I was no one special."

"Oh, so you heard me talking to Brodie." I bring my hand around to her front and push my palm up her shirt to tweak her nipple. "You should've known better. It was to protect what we have here."

A gasp leaves her lips as I bend her forward again and undo my zipper.

Before I enter her, I bring my laptop out of sleep mode and hit play as I angle the screen so she can watch. It's our video. I've been watching it non-stop since we made it.

Easing her panties down her thighs, I rub the head of my cock along her entrance.

"See how good we look together?" I slide inside her and the feeling nearly takes me to my knees. Her heat wraps around me and nothing else matters but driving my cock in and out of her.

Chapter Fourteen
CLAIRE

"Jesus, you see what you do to me?" Max whispers in my ear as he presses me down on his desk fucking me so hard I may be seeing stars. "This pussy belongs to me."

He pulls out and rubs his cock over my ass. I can feel him spelling out his name as he comes all over me.

"You're mine." This time he growls it in my ear. "Tonight, I'm going to introduce you to my life." He pulls my panties back up and my skirt back down over his come that spells his name on my ass.

I don't know why it's so hot, but I already want him again. Going to see Brian was maybe the dumbest thing I've ever done in my life. I feel so stupid for doing it, but something about Max—I wanted to hurt him as much as his words hurt me. It was ridiculous. I'm not that girl—ever.

His lips brush over my temple and he unbinds my wrists.

"Now go get me a coffee." He smirks as I try to regain some composure.

My face is flushed as I smooth my hair and catch my breath.

Brian apologized for last week. I told him I forgave him. Not for him but for me. I'm not sure whether I believe that or not, but I need the freedom to close that chapter of my life and possibly move forward with Maxwell, as crazy as that sounds.

The man makes me insane. He's dominating—powerful, and the way he makes my body feel is out of this world.

Being with him has made me see how much of my life I was

wasting chasing meaningless relationships. Dating him was like practice. Like he was a starter boyfriend. Not that I think of Max as my boyfriend, but I enjoy what we're doing right now.

I understand why he said what he did to Brodie, but it stung hearing it even if he didn't mean the words. There were a million things he could've said instead of that.

I finish pouring his coffee and as I walk back through the office I can feel eyes on me. Do they all know what we were doing?

His touch is still fresh on my skin. I can smell his cologne on me. His come is drying against my ass right now. I smell just like him.

"Your coffee, sir."

I bend down sure to show him my cleavage as I place the mug on his desk. I'll never look at his office or ties the same again.

"I've had your dress for tonight delivered to my apartment. We'll get ready at my place."

I'd forgotten all about the event he wants me to attend.

"What about my brother? If he sees me at your place…"

He waves me off. "He's too busy with Jenna to notice what we're up to. I told him my date canceled and you're filling in. You know the deal better than any date I could bring anyway." He grins and takes a drink of his coffee. His lips twitch as though he has something to say but doesn't.

"I need to get my makeup and stuff, so I'll still need to go by my place."

His jaw tightens. "Already handled. I have a stylist coming over. You'll be pampered."

I know he's doing this so I won't be near Brian. I'm really starting to adore this cocky asshole.

———

We leave the office in separate cars. I don't want to draw any unnecessary attention to us. I feel guilty keeping this from my brother, but it could be disastrous.

My brother has been my rock and always been there for me. I don't want to hurt him or disappoint him. Right now, Max and I are fucking. Having fun. My brother doesn't need to know about my sex life. If it doesn't work out, then there won't be hard feelings between them over me. If things get serious, I'll tell him.

True to his word Max has not only a stylist but a makeup artist and hairdresser at his apartment to do me up for tonight.

I'm so nervous. The only events I've been to are office Christmas parties to support Jax. This is different.

Once the fashion team is done with me I'm afraid to move. Afraid I'll somehow ruin the look. I don't even recognize my reflection. Dark red lipstick stains my lips and the dress matches. It has a sweetheart neckline and falls a few inches under my ass cheeks. I don't know how I'll sit down without giving everyone a show. I hope I'm not expected to dance.

Max steps up behind me looking so damn hot in his tux. His blond hair is combed back from his face and he just shaved. God, he smells amazing too. He looks like he stepped out of a GQ magazine cover. Or off the set of People's sexiest man alive.

"I have something for you. Two things actually." He places a necklace around my throat. It's diamond and platinum and looks like it costs more than I'd earn in two years.

"Max...it's too much."

He leans in next to my ear. "Beautiful necklace for a beautiful woman." His lips brush along my skin as he fastens the clasp. There's a small heart pendant in the center and I must admit it really *is* stunning. It's more of a choker than a necklace.

I smile at him through the mirror. "What's this other thing?"

"Lean forward. Palms on the sink."

"Max!" I gasp when his cold hands run up the backs of my thighs. He lifts the bottom of my dress over my now-exposed butt cheeks.

"No panties."

I feel his breath on my neck as he growls the words. "Can't have the lines."

He reaches around me and takes something from a drawer. "Do you trust me?"

"Yes." I breath out the word and keep my eyes on him, but he disappears in the mirror when he lowers himself behind me.

His lips kiss my right ass cheek then he bites down on it. "God, I love your perfect ass."

"Why thank you." I try to twist around to look at him, but he digs his fingers into my hips and holds me in place.

"Stay still."

Suddenly his finger is rubbing some kind of gel on my asshole and pushing in slightly. I gasp at the pressure from the sudden intrusion. Next thing I know he inserts something into me and it feels strange but good. I do my best to relax, but it all feels so—foreign.

"I'm going to have a lot of fun with you." He kisses my butt and nips me with his teeth again before fixing my dress. "You look so gorgeous." His hands rest on my shoulders momentarily as he stares at us together in the mirror. We really do look amazing, like a couple. His hand moves to his pocket and whatever he put inside me vibrates, sending a wave of pleasure coursing through my legs.

"Does it feel good?"

"Yeah."

"Good. Let's go." He takes me by the hand.

He can't be serious. I can't go to the party like this. How will I even walk?

Chapter Fifteen

MAXWELL

It takes her a moment to get used to the plug, but before long she's walking along at a decent pace. When we get in the backseat of the car and the driver pulls out onto the road, I push the vibrate button on my phone. I smile like the devil when she shudders and her eyes close. Claire becomes mine tonight. She doesn't know it yet but the necklace I gave her is my collar.

I will have her. I can't fight this shit any longer. One taste of her pussy and I knew I was gone. Fucking kryptonite pussy. She has it.

"Max...It's too much. I can't..." Her fingers dig into my thigh.

I start to think maybe she's not cool with it.

But, her eyes roll over to mine. "I need you right now."

Goddamn right you do, forever.

"Later." I smirk and turn the plug off.

Her face scrunches up. "You suck."

"Oh yeah. I will suck." I lean next to her. "On your clit later."

We make it to the event and when we step out of the car a photographer takes our picture for the Dallas society page in the newspaper.

I give her a quick glance. "Don't fidget."

Her fingers move away from her collar.

"Sorry. It's just so gorgeous and expensive. I'm afraid of losing it."

"You won't." I grin, knowing the clasp only opens if I unlock it with a special key.

We make our entrance and there are so many eyes on Claire. I glare at any of the men, so they know who she's with. They can look but never touch.

She's mine and only mine.

I'm fucking eager to get this party over with and get her to the club, so I can show her a brand new world. *My* world. The world I want to share with her. I'd be lying if I said I wasn't nervous. I don't know how she's going to react, even though I think she'll love it.

"Mr. Bass. Glad you could make it. And who is this?" Carter Wilkes raises his brow and grins at Claire.

I have to force a smile. I can't fuck this up. "This is Claire."

"Wow. You look like an absolute angel." The old fucker stares at her tits and I can tell it makes her uncomfortable by the way she shifts.

I knew he'd be a little ridiculous. He's onboard with the deal, but his younger brother is a real asshole.

Claire offers him a weak smile and I take her farther into the room. Their family owns an art collection that my client wants to buy for a museum he plans on opening. If I negotiate this contract well, I stand to earn retirement-type money.

Claire stiffens as I hand her a flute of champagne.

"What's wrong?" I didn't turn the plug back on.

"At the bar." She takes a hefty drink.

I expect to see her brother or something, but no, it's that motherfucker Brian. Anger bubbles up but I *have* to keep my cool. I can't afford to make a scene.

I'm going to kill this piece of shit. Soon.

"What's he doing here?" It's more rhetorical. I don't expect an answer. I don't really care. All I know is he's a dead man walking.

He spots Claire and starts in our direction. I shoot him a cold look and he turns the other way and nearly rams into a table like a fucking douche.

Thank God she never fucked him. I cringe at the thought.

"Come on. We have a few other people to meet."

She downs the rest of her champagne and I tell her to slow down. I don't want her wasted.

It isn't long before dinner is served, and Brian takes a seat across from us next to Carter's sister.

The old bitch stares up at us. "Claire? I thought you were dating Brian. He's my grandson."

Everyone at the table turns to Claire. She stares at me like she had no idea, and I believe her, but we still have to get through this bullshit.

"Grandma. Now isn't the time." Brian gulps when he sees me glaring at him.

I'm sure he doesn't want me telling his family how he put his hands on her.

"Claire is *my* date this evening, Mrs. Wilkes."

"Eleanor, please. And what a shame. I really thought you two were going to get married." She turns to Brian.

I don't know how much more of this shit I can take. Fuck it.

Claire coughs and I press the button for the vibrator. She pushes back her chair abruptly.

I grin.

"If you'll excuse me. I need to use the ladies' room." Her eyes narrow into slits as she looks at me.

"I hope it wasn't something I said." Eleanor looks clueless.

I'm having way too much fun with this as Claire walks away.

I wait a few minutes and excuse myself as well.

I pull my phone and send a text to Claire.

Maxwell: You better not be removing the plug.

I turn up the intensity as I stand outside the bathroom. I hear her yelp and can't resist going in. She doesn't see me as I ease the door shut. I crank the plug up a little higher.

"Oh God." She grips the bathroom sink.

"Close."

Her head whips around to me. "Max. I can't. Please."

I lock the door and stroll over to her. "Not much longer. I promise. But for now. I spin her around and push her dress up on her hips. I have to bite back a groan at the sight of her pink swollen pussy, just aching for my mouth.

I go down on my knees and give her clit a kiss. Her legs tremble when my mouth presses on her.

"Please." She lets out a deep exhale. "I need you."

"I know exactly what you *need*. Soon." I turn the plug off and pull her dress down. "Patience is a virtue."

Claire glares at me and I discreetly exit the bathroom.

When she returns to the table I smile and the band starts to play.

"Dance with me." I don't ask her. I tell her.

Her hand finds mine and I lead her to the floor. Pulling her body close to mine I want nothing more than to take her right here. I can practically smell her pussy under the thin layers of fabric on her dress.

"The things I want to do to you right now." I growl in her ear and nip at the shell. "You are so fucking sexy, Claire."

A tap on my shoulder pulls me out of our moment. "Make an old man happy and let me cut in," Carter says. "My brother is ready to hear your proposal."

I eye him up and down, and look at Claire, letting her know I'll be right back. "Excuse me." I turn to Carter and give him a stern look. "Hands to yourself."

"Of course, son."

I laugh and make my way to where Bill waits alone.

Chapter Sixteen

CLAIRE

Nothing says uncomfortable like dancing with an old man with a butt plug shoved up your ass. I swear to God if Max turns it on while I'm dancing with Father Time I may kill him. He won't have to worry about what my brother will do to him. Thank God it wasn't Brian who asked to dance.

"I hear you dated my great nephew."

"I did, but it didn't work out." *Jesus, this is awkward.*

"Between me and you. I'm glad. I never liked that ungrateful little shit."

I try to suppress my laugh but can't.

Carter smiles at me.

"I like you, Claire. I like Mr. Bass too. You make a nice couple. The way he looks at you reminds me of the way I looked at my late wife, Coral."

"I'm sorry for your loss."

"Oh, that was a long time ago. She died young and I couldn't bring myself to marry again after I lost her." He has this sad faraway look in his eyes and my heart aches for him. "Thank you for the dance." He brings my knuckles to his lips.

"Thank you. It isn't every night I get to dance with a true gentleman."

Carter smiles faintly and wanders off. I glance around the room in search of Max but don't see him. I hope he's closing his deal so we can get the hell out of here.

I head over to the bar for a drink to kill some time. I'm tempted to go to the bathroom and take this damn plug out, but I don't know what Max will do. He's having way too much fun with it, but part of me knows I love it too. Hopefully, it pays off in all the ways he's promised.

I feel ready to burst I want to orgasm so bad. I might pass out when he finally gives it to me.

My ass vibrates and my head whips around the room. I see him grinning at me from a table near the back where he must be talking to Carter's brother.

The vibrating stops and he gets back to business.

Asshole. I smile at my dirty thoughts.

"Having a good time?" Brian scoots into the empty seat next to me.

"Yep." I pop the p.

"Want to dance?"

"Nope." I do the pop thing again.

"Because of your boyfriend?"

"He's my boss. I'm here for work. Don't mess this up for me like you already did once, Brian. I told you we're over. Leave me alone."

"I get it. I screwed up. I'm only asking for a dance. That's it."

"Brian…"

"You want me to make a scene?" He takes me by the hand and leads me to the center of the floor. I don't know what to do. If I resist he might fuck this up for Max. If I go through with it, Max will be pissed. I can't win. Everything is like a whirlwind of doubt I wasn't prepared for.

I steal a look in Max's direction knowing this won't end well. He's deep in conversation and not paying attention. Maybe I can get this over with fast before he even notices. I don't want to ruin this deal he's worked so hard for.

A slow song comes on.

Fuck!

Brian pulls me in close, and I try to fight to keep distance between us.

"I wish I could go back and make things right."

I close my eyes. "Brian…please. I don't want to do this."

He presses his body against mine. "We fit together nicely." I can feel the erection tenting in his pants.

"You need to stop."

His face grows red. "Why? Because you're fucking that guy?" He raises his voice and people around us take notice.

"Please." I practically beg him to stop.

His jaw tenses. "Remember? You told me you fucked him and his huge cock." He shakes his head. "What a little slut. Fucking your way to the top, huh?"

His hand moves lower on my back and he grabs my ass.

Tears well up in my eyes. "Please don't do this."

"You owe me, Claire. I waited months to fuck you and the moment we break up you run off and bang some asshole who gives you a little attention." His hand moves up under my dress. "He dressed you up like his whore."

"You're drunk." I shove his shoulders to get him away from me, but he yanks me back against his crotch.

Everything seems like it happens in slow motion, but at the same time I don't have time to react.

Max rips him away from me and blasts him in the face.

Brian tumbles to the ground and blood gushes from his nose.

"Don't put your fucking hands on her again!" Max towers over him and glares.

Brian paws at his face. "Fuck you! Both of you. She's nothing but a little whore. You'll see."

Max goes after him again, but I grab him by the shoulders.

"Please stop!"

The music halts and everyone stares. I hold my hand over my mouth trying not to cry. I probably ruined the deal for him. This will cost him and the firm so much money.

"I'm sorry." I whisper against his chest as it expands and contracts with each of his deep breaths.

"I don't give a shit about the fucking deal. He had his hands all over you. You're mine. Nobody touches you. *Nobody*!" His forehead comes to rest against mine. Breathing hard he kisses my lips briefly, and his palms move to my face. "Are you okay?"

I nod against his touch. I want to get lost in it, disappear from this place.

The man he was talking to walks over to us.

Max leans up and bows out his chest. "Apologies for this, but…"

The man cuts him off. "I never liked that little shit." He holds a hand up. "He's had it coming. Call me on Monday. I'll do the deal. You've got balls, Mr. Bass. I like that." He grins.

"Thank you, sir." Max extends his hands and they shake on it.

When we get outside Max starts laughing. "Did that really just happen?" He hooks his thumb over his shoulder.

"It did." I lean up against him.

He takes me in his arms. "You're sure you're okay? He didn't hurt you?" He inspects my entire body, his eyes raking up and down.

I grip his hand. "I'm fine. And I'm so happy for you."

He picks me up and twirls me around. "Woo!" His word echoes off into the night.

We get in the back of his private car and Max pulls me onto his lap. My dress pushes up my stomach as I straddle him. and his head lands between my breasts. I can tell he's still amped up on adrenaline and I'd love for him to put that energy to good use.

Freeing his cock from his pants I need him inside me now. I can't wait a second longer.

I grind my pussy against his dick. I'm so wet for him.

He pushes upward and shoves his thick cock into me. It's not making love this time. It's primal and raw and ridiculously hot.

Max pushes the straps of my dress down, exposing my tits. "God I love being inside you." His mouth caps over my nipple and he bites down as I grind on him, rolling my hips from side to side.

He wraps my hair up in his fist and tugs my head back as he thrusts up into me.

A moan parts my lips, and his cock pressing up against the plug in my ass has me about to lose my mind. I'm so close to orgasm when the car suddenly stops.

"We're here." He pulls out of me and grins.

"Gotta be fucking kidding me right now?" My whole body is about to combust. I contemplate coming all over the leather upholstery.

I get my shit together and fix my clothes, not without letting him know I'm unhappy with my orgasm situation.

He runs his fingers through my hair and combs out the tangles. "Soon."

Chapter Seventeen

MAXWELL

I lead Claire inside the club and her eyes widen. "What is this place?"

"My best kept secret."

I sign into the book and lead her to the bar.

"Tonight is Hedonism night. Anything goes."

She looks around the room nervously. I can't believe I ever contemplated bringing her here to fuck someone else. I think in my mind, I knew it was just a reason to get her here so I could fuck her myself.

Claire's mouth is agape, and she catches herself and closes it as she stares around. Couples are engaging in all sorts of crazy shit. Everyone's naked, even the staff.

"Relax. I'll order us some drinks for our room."

"You have a room here?"

"I'm a member." I take her by the hands. "We need to have a serious talk. I want tonight to be fun for you. And I want you to have this part of me. But, it's up to you. You don't have to do anything you don't want to."

"Okay." She clings to my hand and nods.

A wave of doubt and anxiety rushes out of my body. I don't know if I thought she'd storm out and never want to see me again, or what. But, she seems to be open minded which is a win in my book.

"Someone will bring the shit to us. Come on. There's someone I want you to meet."

Sandra has been dying to meet Claire since I talked to her. She wants to meet the woman who has my heart and earned my collar.

We find her in the purple room. One of the owners is obsessed with Prince and the room is her homage to him.

Sandra leans back in a chair while some guy sucks on her toes.

"Enough." She shoves at his head, and he kneels by her chair. "So, it's true?" Her eyes focus on the collar around Claire's neck. "She's young. Beautiful too."

"Sandra this is Claire. Claire this is Sandra. She's an old friend."

"Hi." Claire gives her a small wave.

"Please join." Sandra holds her hands out, motioning to the empty seats.

I nod at Claire, letting her know it's okay, and pull her forward and into my lap as I take a seat next to Sandra.

She dismisses the man.

It leaves the three of us alone.

A server brings a tray of drinks in and exits quickly. I give Claire a shot and take one for myself. Sandra declines.

My cock presses against her ass and I slide my hand around and finger her pussy, continuing what we started on the way here.

Claire lays her head back on my shoulder and moans.

Sandra leans over and kisses Claire on the mouth. I can feel Claire's pussy heat up around my finger. I would never share Claire with another man, but she's been fantasizing about a threesome since she watched that video of me in my room. The video that started all of this. I reach into my pocket and turn the plug back on.

Claire jolts and moans as Sandra claims her mouth.

Sandra and Claire continue to kiss as I finger her pussy and she grinds her ass against my cock. Fuck I want her ass while Sandra eats her sweet cunt.

I pull the vibrator out and Sandra goes down on her knees in front of us. She spreads Claire's thighs apart and strokes her fingers over her pussy. I lift up on her hips and unzip my pants. My dick springs free and I line the head up with Claire's sweet puckered ass. Thank fuck the plug was in there all night, getting her used to this. I grab some lube and push it into her and spread it around. Her muscles all stiffen at the initial intrusion, but she relaxes almost immediately.

Sandra licks on her clit and tongues her sweet cunt taking her mind from the pressure of my cock as I ease her down onto it. Fuck it's even tighter than the first night I claimed her pussy.

Now, all of her is mine. Nobody can ever take that away from me. *Nobody*.

Pushing the straps of her dress down, I roll her nipple between my thumb and forefinger, pinching and pulling as she grinds on my dick.

My other hand trails down her throat, loving the feel and sight of my collar.

I can feel Sandra's fingers against my cock as I fuck Claire's sweet ass. Sandra's mouth is latched onto her, tonguing her clit.

It won't be long before Claire loses it. She's been holding it all day like a good girl. She deserves this.

My cock buries in her tight ass and she moans and pants, her eyes closed.

"Oh god, I'm so close." She breathes out as I bounce her tight ass up and down on my dick. Sandra comes up and kisses her mouth, letting her taste her sweet arousal. It's hot as fuck and I might blow in her ass soon.

Claire contracts and squeezes as her orgasm rocks through her. I've never seen her come like this before. Her arms shoot out to the side and her whole body quakes. Her ass squeezes my cock so hard I think I might faint from the euphoria.

Sandra goes back down and licks the cream from her cunt, sucking her clit into her mouth.

Never in my life would I have thought Claire would be so kinky, and that she'd be mine.

But she is.

I want to give her everything she wants.

Anything she wants.

It's hers.

Chapter Eighteen

CLAIRE

Maxwell and I are in his room at what he refers to as the club and I'm still recovering from the earth-shattering orgasm he and his friend brought me to. I'm sure they have history. It's a history I'm not sure I want to know. Maxwell is different to say the least. But I love every second of it. He is who he is, and that's who I want.

I don't want him to try and change for me, and I'm so curious about all of this. Something about it just feels—right, like I should be here too.

I get to learn so much I didn't know about Max and it only makes me want him more. He has this whole secret lifestyle nobody knows about, but it turns me on and I want more. I want to experience that again. I just don't want to share Max with anyone else. If he'd fucked her I probably would have gotten jealous. I might have even walked out. Maybe that makes me a hypocrite, but I can't bear the thought of him with anyone else.

I would never be with just a woman without Max. I don't want anyone but him, but I have to admit what we just did was a lot of fun.

He hugs me to his chest and fingers the choker around my neck. "Do you know what this is?"

I shake my head.

"It's not just a random piece of jewelry. It means you belong to me. That you're mine. It only comes off with a special key."

I swallow hard. I had no idea. I thought it was just a necklace to wear to the event. No wonder he took such care when he put it around my neck.

"I wanted to ask you to be my submissive, but I want more than sex with you, Claire. I want to get to know everything about you. I want to share our lives together. Opening up like this…" He sighs and then trains his eyes on mine. "It doesn't come easy for me. But I'm willing to try for you."

This is all happening so fast. "You're asking a lot. This is all so…I mean, you don't even know me. Not really. We have amazing sex but other than that…"

"I know that you make shit coffee, but I drink it anyway because *you* made it. I know you want to be a writer. I see you working on your manuscript in your down time at work when you think I'm busy and not watching you. Claire." He places his index finger under my chin and tilts my head up to meet his eyes. "I'm always watching you. I can't stop thinking about you and being with you. I know you're worried about what'll happen with your brother if he finds out, but if he's a good brother he'll want to see you happy. I'm an asshole. But, I'm a good man for you. I want to be yours the same way I want you to be mine."

"You do?"

"Absolutely." He pulls me into a kiss.

I break free for a second and smile. "Is my coffee really that awful?"

"It tastes like Voldemort's asshole." He laughs.

I swat at him. "You should've said something."

"I don't want anything but Voldemort coffee. Every fucking day."

I nuzzle into his neck. "So, if you're going to be my man what does that mean exactly? Will you still come here and be with other people?"

His face hardens. "Absolutely not. I don't want anyone but you. There will only ever be you. We can come here to try different things…if you want."

"Can I tie you up?"

A devilish grin spreads across his face. "Let's not get carried away." He kisses my forehead.

"Am I allowed to be with other people?"

He tenses. "Is that what you want?"

"No…but Sandra was fun. Have you guys…?"

He sighs. "A long time ago, but we're friends. I knew you'd be comfortable with her and I wouldn't be jealous of her because I know I'm the one you'll go home with."

"So we agree? No fucking other people?"

"Yes."

"Good because if you stuck your dick in her I may have cut it off."

His palms land on my cheeks. "I will never hurt you. But if at any time either one of us has desires, we'll speak about them first. Always."

"Okay."

"Speaking of discussing things, I don't like you living in that apartment. And I don't want that prick anywhere near you."

"What are you suggesting?" If he asks me to move in I may hurt him because that is moving way too fast.

"Move into the apartment next to your brother's place. It's closer to work…"

"And closer to you?"

"Exactly." He rolls over top of me. "Are you mine, Claire?"

"Yes." I let out a huge breath. "But you have to tell Jaxson."

"Let's not tell him yet. He has stuff going on."

I shake my head. "Okay, but you know the longer we wait the madder he'll be."

He plants a kiss on my forehead. "Let me worry about that."

"If you say so."

"I do." He runs his hands along my thighs and settles between them.

He licks the length of my pussy. "Fuck, I love how you taste."

For a minute I thought he was going to say he loves me. I don't think either of us are ready for that.

Not yet, anyway.

Chapter Nineteen

MAXWELL

For three months Claire and I have kept our relationship a secret. I know I need to come clean to Jax. I'm sure he suspects something is going on. Everyone does. I hear the whispers at the office. There's even a pool going on about how Jaxson will react when he finds out. It's funny how they don't think I know things.

The timing to tell him is never right and now with Brooke and Jenna opening up their foundation I don't know when that time will come. I've enjoyed having Claire all to myself and not having to share our relationship with anyone else but I'm tired of not being able to kiss her whenever I want or hold her hand in public.

I'm tired of not having her in my bed at my apartment. Tired of sneaking off to the club to fuck my girlfriend.

This is it. I need to tell him today because I know I'm in love with Claire and I want to ask her to move in with me.

She doesn't know that I love her, but I do. I'm so damn crazy over her I can't sleep at night unless she's in my arms. I want to wake up and see her sweet ass naked in my bed. I want to shower with her before I go to work and see her makeup cluttering up the counters in my bathroom.

There's nothing better in this world than her smile, except maybe her coming on my cock or my face but still. I want her with me.

My phone pings with a text.

Claire: you still going with me to the big opening?
Maxwell: On my way down.

Claire: K

God, I hate when she responds with a single letter like that. It's a waste of a damn message. Why bother to reply at all if that's all she's going to send? I sigh and shake my head. I swear she does it so I'll take her over my knee and spank her pretty little ass. I must admit it does make me hard when I see her skin glowing with my fingerprints.

When I knock on her apartment door she answers wearing nothing but a towel.

Fuck me. The towel she has wrapped around her body doesn't cover anything. Her perfect tits are popping out of the top and her ass cheeks are hanging out the back.

I steal a look in the direction of her brother's door.

"Don't worry. They left hours ago. No one is around but me." She pulls me inside by my tie.

"We're going to be late."

"We have time." She yanks on my belt and unzips my pants as the towel falls to the floor. I scoop her up in my arms and place her on the kitchen counter.

"Naughty girl."

"Yeah, I am. You're a bad influence." She reaches out and strokes my cock that's now hard in her palm.

I move between her legs and she wraps them around my waist as I bend down to take a nipple in my mouth. I suck until it hardens and then do the same thing to the other.

"Fuck, you're perfect." The words *I love you* hang on the tip of my tongue, but I hold them back. I'm not sure if she's ready to hear the three words that will change our relationship. I rub my cock up against her pussy. "Look how wet my little cunt is for me." I slap the head on her clit, and her head flings back, her gaze angled up toward the ceiling.

We've been having fun, but I want more. I want her to be in my life permanently. Part of me is afraid I'm fast-forwarding the relationship. Trying to go from point A to point B too fast. I'm her first and only sexual partner, other than fucking around with Sandra, but she doesn't count. I'm the only man to ever fuck her and I want to keep it that way. I just hope I'm enough for her. That what we share is enough.

She's close to finishing her novel and has been in contact with an agent. She has to go talk to them. The agent is in New York. There's a big publisher interested in her story. What if she gets a big book deal that takes her away from me? I would never tell her not to pursue her dreams, but I don't want to lose her to that either. I won't be the guy who stands in her way, but I do love her. I love her more than I thought could be possible.

I thrust inside her, feeling at home, like we are a perfect fit. As we make love on the kitchen counter I realize that if she goes, I'll follow her.

It would kill me to leave the firm and Dallas behind, but I would for her. I'd do anything for her.

Chapter Twenty

CLAIRE

The whole time we have been at this opening event Max has been acting strange. Nervous even. Every time I talk about New York he gets closed off and it sucks. I think he's afraid I'm going to get a big book deal and become famous or something and leave him behind, but I won't. Dallas is my home. Max is in Dallas. So is my brother and Jenna. When she first came back into his life I was worried, but things seem to have worked out great for them. They're starting their life together. The one they were always meant to have, and I only hope my brother will be as accepting when he finds out that I'm with Max.

Because I love Max. I've been wanting to tell him for a few weeks now, but I've been afraid of pushing him away. I know I'm the first real relationship he's had since his last girlfriend cheated on him with his best friend.

Some people are shit, but not everyone.

With my brother off doing his special surprise he planned for Jenna, I take Max's hand in mine. I'm tired of hiding.

"Hey." He smiles looking down at our entwined fingers.

"Hey." I look down at the ground.

"What is it?" Usually, Max is the most confident man I've ever met. But sometimes when he thinks something is wrong with me, he looks so boyish. I love that about him. I love everything about him.

"I don't want to do the whole sneaking around thing anymore. I love you and I want everyone to know that we're together."

He stops and his face pales. "Wait...what did you just say?"

My heart pinches. What if I just fucked everything up? "I'm tired of sneaking around."

"No, I got that part. The other thing."

"That I love you." I smile.

He yanks me into his arms and kisses me something fierce. It's a happy kiss. My body floods with happiness.

His tongue glides along my lips as I open for him.

"I love you too." He pulls back a little and brushes my hair behind my ear. "I've loved you for a while now."

I exhale a huge sigh of relief. "Thank God it wasn't just me."

He grins. "There's something else that I've been wanting to ask you."

I suck in a breath. If he proposes I may be the one spanking his ass.

"Move in with me?"

I look up at him, happy and surprisingly, somewhat disappointed that he didn't pop the question. Though, deep down I know we aren't ready for that step.

I nod and smile. "Okay." I kiss him again.

Then it happens.

A throat clears behind us.

We both turn slowly to see April, Brodie, Weston, and Brooke gaping.

"You owe me a hundred bucks, bitch." Brodie punches Weston on the shoulder.

Weston stares at us, wide eyed, almost catatonic. His eyes never leaving us as he takes his wallet out and hands Brodie a hundred. I shoot them dirty looks and they all start laughing.

"What's so funny?" Max growls.

"Brodie can be the one to break the news to Jaxson that Claire is his kryptonite pussy."

Brooke smacks his chest. "Hey."

"Hey what? It's true." Weston shoots me a wink.

"I don't think I like any of you." I'm halfway joking and trying not to laugh at how awkward this is.

"As long as you still like me." Max kisses me again.

"Okay that's enough of that." Brodie pulls Max away from me just as my brother and Jenna come from the barn.

They're all smiles.

I don't even want to know what they were just doing in there. Jenna has straw in her hair.

"Good, you're all here." Jax straightens up in front of us.

"I said yes!" Jenna squeals and holds out her ring finger.

Max gets this mischievous look on his face, like he's up to something. He walks up to Jaxson with me next to him. "Congratulations, man. I'm really happy for you. And speaking of being happy. I hope you'll be happy for us too." Max pulls me to his side. "Claire and I are moving in together."

Jax's eyes get big as hell, and Brodie and Weston are covering their mouths trying not to lose it.

Jenna winks at me. I may have told her about me and Max like two months ago. I needed someone to confide in and I knew she'd never rat me out.

Jax's face turns red and glares at the two of us quietly for so long I'm afraid he is in shock.

Jenna squeezes his hand. "Honey, you're worrying me. You love Max. They'll be neighbors and we can all hang out."

"Fucking wonderful, babe." His jaw flexes, but it's obvious he's trying to hold it together. Jaxson takes a deep breath and pinches the bridge of his nose.

He finally shakes his head and turns to Max. "If she's happy, fine." He takes another deep breath. "If she comes to me crying over your sorry ass I will..."

Max slaps a hand on Jaxson's shoulder. "You'll try." He grins.

Jax doesn't grin back.

"Take it easy, man. I love her. She's the best thing to ever happen to me."

"Yeah. She's his kryptonite pussy." Brodie laughs. Jaxson pops him in the nuts like they're all back in their college days.

Brodie bends over at the waist, nearly hyperventilating.

Weston points at him and laughs until Brooke smacks him in the chest.

"Damn. Fucking hell." Brodie stares up at Jaxson, half-laughing, half in pain.

"That's my sister! Stop talking about her pu..." He takes a deep breath. "Can we all just get on with our day now?"

"Sorry, man." Brodie grins at me and Max, and all I can do is shake my head.

Even grown men will act like boys sometimes.

"So, did Max buy you that pretty necklace you're always wearing?" Brooke traces a finger over my heart pendant.

"Yeah, he did." I smile.

"It looks so expensive. Reminds me of a fancy cat or dog collar though."

My cheeks heat and the guys go silent.

"You put a collar on my sister?" Jax pushes at Max, and Weston and Brodie get between them.

"Jax, will you just stop. Max and I are adults. What we do behind closed doors is between us. I'm not a kid."

He nods and runs his hands through his hair, seething for a few seconds. "I know." He gives me a hug and kisses the top of my head then he shakes Max's hand reluctantly. "You better take care of her."

"I promise, man. I love her."

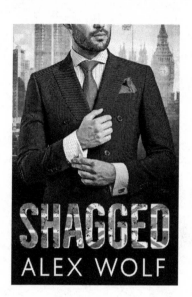

CHAPTER 1

Matthew Spencer was a man who had it all.

He woke up to the sound of fake birds chirping and artificial sunrise creeping up his wall. It was a program on his phone, designed specifically for that purpose.

He ran a rough, calloused hand through his hair and sighed contentedly. His eyes blinked open, focusing on the golden sun that slowly climbed to his left.

Another beautiful day of being me.

The rich aroma of his morning coffee wafted into his nose and he sniffed, then rolled over in bed, feeling quite rested and rejuvenated. Matty knew his morning routine by heart. He would get up at his own leisure, have a cup of coffee, eat a healthy breakfast prepared by his personal chef and nutritionist, and then maybe he'd consider starting work. *Maybe.*

His phone switched on using the same system that handled his alarm routine. It buzzed with an influx of text messages and missed calls.

Matty Spencer was a popular man. He was a loved man. But he was also a busy man, and he was not about to leap out of bed for anyone.

They knew his phone was off all night. If it was important, they could come to him. They didn't *need* his attention. They just wanted it.

Although being loved was a rewarding feeling, to Matty, it was also very tiring. He was not a machine, made to constantly please others. He was aware of how desperately they clung to him for his wealth and connections.

The phone lit up again and rattled against the nightstand. He sighed and tensed up. It was as if he were under attack.

He glanced at the phone and decided to scroll through. His mother and a couple of friends had tried to call him. The jingling-coins ringtone told him that he'd received a message from one of the countless gold-digging sluts on his booty-call list. He snickered at that.

They all thought he was unaware of their intentions. He laughed at how foolish they were, knowing that he could play people the way they tried to play him. For all the people he despised and had to be polite to, there were hundreds more willing to grovel at his feet. He knew it was wrong to enjoy this, but he didn't care. Why should he put up with all the responsibilities of being wealthy and popular if he couldn't enjoy the perks?

As his body acclimated to the day, he rose and scrolled through more of his messages. Thank God he kept separate phones, one personal and one business. He couldn't imagine digging through the pile of shit trying to find an important memo from a client or partner.

Good morning texts from countless numbers who didn't even have names attached to them came through like clockwork. Sexts from three different girls—two with pictures. He didn't ignore those.

A message from his mother consisted of three hundred emojis and a cat picture. A few were friends begging for handouts. And, of course, one girl throwing a hissy fit because he'd rejected her the previous night.

It wasn't his fault he wasn't always in the mood for her. Sometimes he wanted someone else.

If there was one thing that Matty Spencer knew, it was the fact that he was an asshole. He wasn't so deluded as to believe that everyone liked him, or that he couldn't try harder—that he shouldn't be better, but at the end of the day, he knew he didn't have to be. It was good enough to be a billionaire, have every girl he reached for, and to be respected and admired.

When he was younger, he'd often cared what others thought of him. He'd done everything he could to please them. It'd only taken being ripped off twice to realize that you couldn't be a pushover in this world. From then on, he'd lived only for himself. At thirty-one, that philosophy had yet to fail him.

He dropped his phone on the floor and walked to the window, pressing a button and watching the screen roll up. A beautiful view of the London skyline appeared in front of him. He nodded and smiled, pleased with the day, before wandering over to the other side of the room where his coffee would be ready.

He sipped it. Perfect aroma, perfect taste, and perfect temperature. Modern technology was a wonderful thing, coordinating his mornings for him. He streamlined everything in his life to suit his needs. And to think that he'd funded and co-developed all the programs which made his house run so seamlessly. No doubt his shower would be ready to begin, his chef would've just received the message to prepare his breakfast, and his maids received an alarm telling them his bed would need to be made. Most mornings he didn't even have to think actual thoughts until eleven or twelve. It was beautiful.

His business phone rang, interrupting his thoughts. A loud tone, immediately associated with one person. His secretary at his office. She knew not to contact him unless strictly necessary. Sighing, he called out to his robotic assistant on his phone. "Mia, answer call."

Emilia Hernandez's voice came through crystal clear as though she were standing next to him in the room. "Sorry to bother you, Mr. Spencer. I'm sure it's some misunderstanding, but—"

"It's fine. What is it?" He took another sip of his coffee.

"The partners from Watanabe Corp are here. The agenda does say you have a meeting with them."

"When? It's not on my planner." He scrolled through his daily tasks.

"About an hour ago. I tried to get hold of you, but it went straight to voicemail."

"Shit, I must have synced it with my personal one." Matty groaned. "I don't see any appointment listed."

"Well, they're in the office, and they're pretty angry. I can try and stall, but it's probably best if you get down here."

He groaned and straightened up. "Tell them my cat died this morning. I'm distraught. They'll buy it." Matty snickered to himself. Even the rich were idiots sometimes.

"Of course. Anything else?"

"Nope. Mia, end call."

As soon as the phone shut off, Matty said, "Mia, call Mr. Johannes. I need to rearrange some things."

He grabbed his clothes as Mia connected him.

This inconvenience perturbed Matty. He was a busy man—not a rushed-off-his-feet, nine-to-fiver. He didn't have to get up at six, and had no desire for a morning commute—but he was busy all the same. The thought of an eight-hour workday vexed him to no end. He'd carefully structured his life to avoid these types of circumstances, and his foolproof system had failed him.

He ran a vast company selling smart-home solutions, about to enter trade with one of the biggest app developers in the world, and his own system had let him down and caused him to be late.

"Yes, Mr. Spencer," said Mr. Johannes, as soon as he picked up. "How may I help you?"

Matty shrugged on his button-down and moved to the mirror, running a pre-warmed brush with a light layer of gel through his hair. "Is Terrence here? I'm running late for a meeting. I need a ride."

"Terrence has the day off, Mr. Spencer."

Matty's jaw clenched. He didn't enjoy inefficient conversations. When he made a statement, he expected a solution. Not a fact. "Well, who is on duty?"

He could practically feel Johannes wince on the other end of the line.

"Nobody, I'm afraid, Sir. There are no chauffeurs available until tomorrow."

Matty scrubbed a hand through his hair and thoroughly disheveled it. He swore under his breath and ran the comb through it again. "We're in London. I'm positive there is someone in this city that is capable of driving."

"Of course, Sir. I shall call in a new chauffeur immediately. We should have one by twelve."

"Twelve?" Matty groaned and his fingers tightened around the brush. "A fucking taxi would be faster than that. I needed to be at the office an hour and a half ago."

"I shall call Terrence and pay him triple to come to work right away. But that will nevertheless take at least forty minutes. Considering your present predicament, a taxi may be the fastest option."

Matty paused.

Could he wait for a taxi? Or for Terrence to arrive? No. This deal was important. Not vital, but important. It would help his company. It would make an exorbitant amount of money. Fuck it, he'd drive himself. "I'm driving. Leave the keys to the Lambo by the front door."

"Of course, Sir. Anything else before I attend to that?"

"Nothing."

"Very well, Sir."

Matty took a quick glance in the mirror, flew down the hall, and out the front door. Standing in the street, holding his keys, he glanced around. It didn't take a genius to realize something was seriously wrong.

His car was gone. Nowhere to be found. "Goddamn it!" He looked up and down the street once more. Had someone moved it? Had he accidentally stopped it down the road, in front of a neighbor's house?

No such thing. His eyes landed on a bright yellow sign.

A no parking zone? Seriously? And they hadn't even knocked on his door to let them know they were towing away a fucking Lamborghini?

This wasn't some shitty little suburb or quaint country town. This was an area entirely inhabited by the elite, living in urban mansions worth tens of millions of pounds. Which councilor with a stick up his ass had approved a no parking zone?

Matty took a deep breath. It would be fine. He had plenty of other cars. He'd just waste another minute, go inside, and get one.

The limo would be too ostentatious, but he had a Ferrari that would be quick and look nice and sleek as it pulled into his private garage beneath the building.

He folded himself inside the low-lying vehicle and backed out. At last, on the road. He flew around a few corners, the engine a low growl. Matty wondered how other people did this every day. He *loved* driving. Adored it. How could you not when you had a car that was so sleek, powerful, and beautiful? But on this busy, smoggy road? Surrounded by these imbeciles? It was like sitting on a golden throne in the pits of Hell. Torture from a luxurious seat was still torture.

A blue light flashed behind him and left him with a sinking sensation. *Please let it be an ambulance.*

Police.

Shitfuck.

He pulled over and rolled his window down as the officer approached from behind. "I don't have fucking time for this."

"I can see that. It's why you're getting a speeding ticket." The officer strolled up next to the window.

"A ticket? Are you not aware who I am?" Had he even broken the law? He'd been in a rush, but he hadn't thought he was speeding.

"Someone who can afford a ticket, Sir. Let's not make it into something worse."

Matty nodded and stared at the whites of his knuckles as he gripped the wheel. "Sure, just—let me have it, and I'll be on my way."

With the ticket firmly wedged in his pocket, he drove swiftly, but not too swiftly, to his office building, parked, and tried to balance the urgency of the situation with the need to look professional, and composed. It wasn't like a few more minutes would make much of a difference.

I need to sort my life out.

He walked up to the desk where Emilia waited with a sympathetic smile, her warm brown eyes and full face fell somewhere between motherly and matronly.

"Can you call and see if there is a human we can hire to organize things? A babysitter for adults, perhaps?" Matty asked.

"Can Mia not handle things, Sir?"

Matty shook his head. "I'm afraid not."

"I was just thinking of the company image."

Matty nodded. "Understood." He paused and let out an exasperated sigh. "I need you to keep quiet about this for that very reason. But, I need an actual person to tell me where the fuck I'm going wrong."

Emilia nodded and smiled. "I'll look into it while you attend the meeting, Sir."

"You're a star." Matty breathed a sigh of relief. Now, all he needed to do was survive this bloody meeting.

———

Despite the initial setback, he managed to appease the Watanabe partners, and it looked as though a long-term relationship between their companies would be beneficial enough for them to overlook the morning's near disaster. They seemed to buy the cat story, which amused Matty to no end. However, the adrenaline quickly settled, and the need for a fresh coffee arose as he waved goodbye from the hallway.

The elevator doors slid closed and he turned around to face Emilia. "Any luck then?"

"Well, I did remember that your friend, Mr. Arvin, suggested a PA last time he was here. *And* that you laughed at him. But I thought maybe you would have reconsidered, so I contacted him and asked for her name." She handed him a small appointment card.

"Not storing it on Mia this time?"

Emilia shook her head. "Not because of that. I thought if someone were to remotely access your planner they might—"

"Smart move. Maybe you could organize my life for me instead?"

Emilia shook her head once more. "Sorry, Sir. I only really handle times and dates, names and places. And from what Mr. Arvin said, Ms. Smith is a little more thorough."

"She will be here tomorrow?" Matty twirled the card between his fingers thoughtfully. All it had was a name, a phone number, and a time scribbled on it. "Five p.m.?"

"*Today* at five p.m., Sir. I said it was a matter of urgency, but to be discrete. She will see you at your home."

Matty nodded. "Perfect. I suppose I'd better head back. Unless there are any other appointments I'm unaware of?"

"None, Sir." Emilia stared anywhere but at Matty, avoiding eye contact.

"Hey."

Her eyes moved up and met his.

"I don't blame you for any of this, just so you know. You're the warden of this nuthouse, but I won't hold you responsible for the meltdowns."

Matty didn't enjoy being bothered with trivial nonsense, and it usually perturbed him to no end. But, he'd learned long ago, not to piss off the help. Emilia was a valuable asset to him, and a loyal one at that. It served him well to keep her happy.

His company's automated system had fucked up his day for the last time, though. It was time to bring in a professional human, and let them do the job.

"Grateful to hear that, Sir. Oh, and Mr. Arvin said, please pardon my language but these were his exact words: 'Look out, she knows what she's doing and she's great, but she can be a total bitch.'" Emilia smiled as professionally as always.

Matty nodded. "I'll bear that in mind."

"Is there anything else, Sir?"

"No, that'll be all. Thank you."

———

Approaching Matthew Spencer's house, Christina Smith knew she was dealing with a very wealthy client. The mansion looked new and extravagant, like it'd been ripped out of Hollywood and dropped in the middle of a London suburb.

Sandy walls framed the place, and the gate was wide enough to fit a tank through. The gardens were full of exotic plants, dotting the greenery with splatters of reds, pinks, yellows, and blues. It was also the only garden on the street which hadn't been carefully manicured that morning. Couldn't he afford to pay someone to come landscape the house?

He'd called for her to come at once. Seemed more likely it was a breakdown in communication. He definitely needed her services if he couldn't even keep his lawn mowed.

She walked up to the front gate and noticed that the intercom had a two-way video option.

Christina flipped open a mirror and made sure that her hair was still firmly tied back, and her makeup was clean and professional. The more money these guys had, the more perfection they demanded. When she'd first started, she'd assumed her work would speak for itself. That'd been a mistake.

Her skin had to be flawless, her lips cherry red, and the lines of her makeup sharp. Her wavy brown hair had to be pulled and twisted until there wasn't a single stray hair sticking out. Her dress was tailored, dry cleaned, pressed, and she wore perfume that was two hundred pounds an ounce.

If she was not perfectly dressed and on point, how could they trust her to organize everything for them?

Reassured that she looked okay, she pressed the button on the intercom. It came to life, and an older man in a dark suit stared back at her on the screen. "Good afternoon, please state your business."

"Umm, I'm Ms. Smith. I have an appointment with Mr. Spencer. Five o'clock. I'm a few minutes early."

"Very well. Do come in."

There were no subtle options for entering the estate. Not unless you were a servant, it seemed. Everyone was forced to go through the main entrance.

The gates creaked open slowly with a slight squeak. She could see the older man already waiting at the door. She was used to places like this and knew many of the people in these houses actually lived paycheck to paycheck and were up to their eyes in debt. By now, she'd learned to have a nose for money. And judging by what she'd seen so far, this guy—like his friend Mr. Arvin—was loaded.

There were little signs of extravagant wealth woven through the place. There were also many signs that these things were seriously neglected. A unique sculpture sat near the porch. It didn't look like it'd been cleaned anytime recently. Many of the exotic plants were beginning to wilt without any reason for it. A solid gold knocker hung on the door. It was just for looks. Nobody would ever use a damn knocker. Whoever she was helping was someone that never thought before buying.

No wonder he needed her help.

The older gentleman welcomed her in, guided her to a main living area and asked her to wait there for Mr. Spencer. She walked around the room, scoping it out. The inside was as much of a mess as the outside.

She spotted a pile of unopened mail on the table by the window. An overdue bill was up on the mantlepiece when she strolled over. A dirty coat was out in the hallway, on the floor. All normal things in a normal house, but very out of place in a mansion with a ton of employees to keep the place running. Finally, she sat down in one of the chairs and waited.

"Good afternoon, you must be Ms. Smith?" A rich, baritone voice came from the hallway the second she'd taken a seat.

She whipped around to face the man. "Yes, Sir. Are you Mr. Spencer?" It couldn't be him. This guy was too young to have this kind of money.

"I am." He walked over to the chair across from her but stood instead of sitting down.

"It's nice to meet you." She stood and held out a hand.

He waved her off without shaking. "Do sit back down."

It was always hard to tell how these wealthy people wanted her to act. Even social interactions were like games to them. They always had to be in control. They always treated employees like they were less than them and showed off their power any chance they got. Most of the time, it was telling her to do the opposite of whatever she was doing. But she always played along. It didn't hurt anybody. She sat down and waited for him to explain why she was there.

Her game was thrown off for a second, and she had to regain her composure. She wasn't used to having clients that didn't have gray hair. He was also one of the tallest, strongest looking men she'd ever seen. Breathing became difficult when she got a good look at him. He could've easily been a movie star or a musician. In fact, he probably was. She just hadn't recognized him because she didn't pay attention to celebrities and gossip magazines. It was rare for someone under sixty to live in a place like this, and Mr. Spencer looked like he was pushing thirty at the most.

"I'm sure you get asked this a lot, but what is it exactly that you do?" He walked around her chair and then over to the window, where he shuffled through the letters, clearly not sure where to begin.

The man didn't even know why he was hiring her. That wasn't surprising. "You should put them into separate piles for bills, personal, circulars, and business. Then work through them by date."

He glanced at her. "I see."

"That's what I do. I show you how to manage your home. I make sure you have all the staff you need, line up all your schedules. Help you get more organized."

"Like one of those automated solutions?"

"No way. Those things are a disaster. The technology isn't there yet. Unlike a computer, I can actually reason and make decisions on the spot, as opposed to depending on how someone coded a computer." She thought for some kind of analogy she could use. "I guess you could think of me as a sort of modern Victorian housekeeper, or a personal business manager."

"I'm still none the wiser." His words had an edge to them, like maybe she'd offended him somehow. "But I suppose it's worth a chance." He put the letters down and stalked back over to her chair. "Do you want me to explain the problems to you?" Mr. Spencer sat down in front of her.

She shook her head. "If you knew the problems, you would've solved them by now."

He let out an exasperated sigh. "I'm pretty sure I know what's wrong with my own house."

"Sorry for being forward, but you know the consequences of the problems, not the problems themselves. It's like being sick. Everyone knows their symptoms, but they still go to a doctor to be diagnosed and treated. I'm here to diagnose your life and prescribe a treatment for it."

"That makes more sense to me. You're analyzing the situation. At the end, would my life be cured of its ailment?"

"I've never left a patient ill." She paused with a slight smile. "Now, sometimes clients stop treating their condition and symptoms return, but if you follow my plan, you shouldn't have to see me again."

"Are you sure that none of your clients let the symptoms return purposefully?" His eyes raked down to her heels and back up.

Christina nodded. She knew exactly what he meant. "I'm sure it happens. That's up to them."

"You're prepared to start immediately?"

She nodded. "Absolutely."

"Great. Once you've been shown around just do whatever it is you do. And if you need anything, don't hesitate to ask the other members of the staff."

"Will do. Thank you, Mr. Spencer." And just like that, she had a new job.

"One last thing."

"Sir?"

His voice lowered. "I'm not sure how much Emilia told you about my business, but, we need to keep this all *very* quiet."

"Your secretary didn't tell me anything about what you do."

"I'm actually the owner of Mia, the smart-house."

She realized why he was frustrated a few moments before. "Umm, you designed Mia?"

"In a way. Not on my own, obviously, but yeah." He shrugged.

"Sorry for what I said earlier." Shit, that could've cost her the job.

He shook his head. "No. Between you and me, Mia's a disaster."

It all made sense at once. The owner of a company that sold smart-home solutions was living in complete disarray. He needed a human professional to fix his personal life. No wonder he was so evasive and probably embarrassed. And he was so desperate he'd made an appointment with her.

She smiled. "No worries. We can fix this."

"I bloody well hope so. Let's have a tour of the house."

She stood up and his eyes burned through her. He may not have noticed her figure before, but he definitely did now. It didn't take a genius to realize he was checking her out. And why wouldn't he? She was petite, with perfect, full curves that had been squeezed into a tailored dress—along with impeccable hair and makeup. Christina knew most men thought she was hot. Her male clients all looked at her the same way.

It was definitely clear that Matthew Spencer liked her. Everything about him changed as they walked from room to room. The way he carried himself, his tone of voice. Not to mention the fact that he was personally showing her around.

His hand fell on the small of her back as he guided her to the next room. She figured he was also a man who didn't know what it was like to be rejected. This could either be fun or torture. She wasn't sure. But there was no way she would reciprocate.

She had a personal rule of not sleeping with clients, and her work made dating impossible. She spent weeks at a time living in strange men's houses, flying around the world to fix their personal lives. She was fortunate Mr. Spencer lived in the same city as her. She was always busy. And she had to be a cold bitch to get the respect she deserved. Otherwise, these men would walk all over her.

Trying to ignore the way he placed his hand on her back, she took in her surroundings.

Everything was perfectly clean, but out of place. Lights were on in rooms with large, bright windows, and turned off in dark hallways. Shit was strewn over tables and chairs, as though someone had set it down and then forgotten it was there. As he walked, Mr. Spencer explained all his problems. Missed appointments, employees not coming in on the right days, contractors not being called in for repairs, or none of them were coordinated right.

He was just spending, spending, spending, like a boy with his father's credit card. Every time something went wrong, he threw money at it until it went away. A rough calculation told her he was spending about five times more money than he should.

She'd worked for men with the same issues, but Matty Spencer was taking it to the extreme. The place looked like it'd been decorated by a frat boy. At least the place wasn't too cluttered, and he had servants to keep the place clean, but, the decorating was all nudes and edgy pop art, or expensive cars—classical sculptures, and original prints from famous artists. The aesthetic was what she would expect in a Harvard dorm room.

From the sound of it, the rest of his life went the same. He'd see something he wanted to do, and he would just go and do it. He'd just whip out the credit card at anything he wanted to buy. Anyone else would've been in trouble by now, but not Mr. Spencer. She figured he'd coasted through life on a combination of wealth and quick wit, and only now was he starting to feel the effect of it.

"You like the décor?" He smiled as he caught her staring at a large sculpture of a naked woman on a horse.

She nodded and faked a smile. "You have unique taste." She definitely had an opinion, but she wasn't there to improve his decorating skills.

Despite his atrocious sense of style, she couldn't help but be jealous. She made a decent living, but she'd never earn a fraction of what he spent in a year. She was desperately saving for a dream house back in Kentucky, for her father. She lived completely frugal. Only spent money on absolute needs and items she had to have for work. He could probably buy that modest home with his weekly paycheck. She couldn't imagine living somewhere like this.

It was one of the perks of the job, though, living vicariously through her clients. She could enjoy beautiful houses during the day, and at night when she traveled. Many of her clients had guest houses and didn't want to foot the bill for her to stay in a hotel.

Even with her local clients, she could usually get away with working a few hours every morning and then kicking back for the day. She was that good. Then she could sit back and enjoy expensive wine and whatever entertainment the home offered.

It would be a few weeks before she could do that here, though. This guy needed a lot of work. And the work always came first.

———

Fuck me!

Christina was one of the hottest—no, *the* hottest woman Matty had ever seen. In all his years of dating models, actresses, even porn stars, he'd never seen a woman so perfectly proportioned with her hourglass frame. She was sensual in every movement. She was—exactly his type. He never even thought he had a type before, other than "hot", but looking at her, he knew Christina was it.

Every little thing about her was breathtaking. She had brunette hair and sharp brown eyes. The way her tailored dress hugged her figure, clinging to her firm hips and tight waist. The sharpness of the painted lines on her face, the boldness of her lips, the way her eyeliner drew you into a mesmerizing gaze. The way she masterfully strode in skyscraper heels. Stilettos so tall that no woman should be able to get away with wearing them, yet somehow clinical and stern like the rest of her. Heels that took her from a petite Hispanic woman to a powerful goddess who could look men of his stature in the eye without needing to peer up like a child.

Normally he would mock or chastise women like her. She was cold. She was collected—a professional. She embraced her femininity only in as much as to announce her sex, and rejected every hint of softness, fragility, or humility foisted upon her. She was a woman, but a clean-slate, aseptic, robotic woman. All the female and none of the feminine. All the woman and none of the human. But goddamn, she wore it well.

Her look inspired confidence in him. On the one hand, he knew it was carefully crafted for that exact purpose. But on the other hand, any woman who could put herself together so perfectly, so sharply for an interview, and then hold that look, that character together— she was a walking advertisement for her own composure and order. And composure and order were precisely what he wanted to buy from her. Her presence in his home would be a pleasant little perk, of course. But she had a job to do first and foremost.

"I need you to start work as soon as possible." He guided her into his office. "I'm ashamed to admit, but everywhere I look I see nothing but disorder. This needs correcting. It's humiliating for a man in my position, in my industry, to be living in such disarray. If someone were to notice, the whole premise of my company may be called into question."

Christina made eye contact.

He could see the look in her eye, judging him, probably wondering why he was creating these products if he knew nothing about them.

"I can start today. If that's what you want."

He studied her for another moment. How could she talk without a hint of emotion on her face? Was she even a woman at all? Perhaps she really was a robot?

He wondered what shaped her and molded her into the way she was. Perhaps she grew up in an emotionless environment, or some trauma trained her to hide all her feelings. It didn't matter, though. He would hire her. She would whip the place into shape, and he'd go on living the way in which he was accustomed.

"I would like you to start immediately. I have a backlog of four weeks of paper letters. I hate them. I prefer emails and video calls. So they're completely unread. You can go through and organize them so I can manage them in the future."

"You know what I cost, right?" She raised an eyebrow.

"Haven't a clue."

She sighed. "It is nine hundred poun—"

"Don't care." He brushed her off with a flippant hand. "Just bill my secretary. No, my housekeeper. I can't have you connected to work."

Her face canted to the side. "You don't even need to think about the price?"

Matty stared at her, confusion written all over his face. "I don't care if it's nine hundred pounds a day, or an hour. Just send the bill." Surely, she was not so dense as to think he needed to budget.

"Mr. Spencer, this is the sort of attitude that got you in this position. How you got by in life until now is beyond me."

Matty smirked. "These amounts aren't material enough to warrant close attention. Thank you for the concern, though."

"Well, one day when the money runs out. You'll be glad you hired me."

She began collecting the piles of papers and letters from the various shelves, open filing cabinets, and low tables around the room. He watched, wondering how she got by so far in her job with her snarky attitude. Usually, it took a few weeks for someone to hate him. This was a new record.

He fussed with his shirt cuff and watched her work. "Is the attitude part of the service or complimentary?"

"What do you mean? Am I supposed to call you 'sir'?"

"Well, you are my employee now."

Christina shook her head. "You hired me, but I'm not your servant, or an employee. I'll call you Mr. Spencer."

"Does this bluntness earn you many repeat customers? I don't recall asking for this attitude to be a part of the contract." He sat down on the edge of the coffee table, completely amused.

"If you had to work with children every day, your question would answer itself. I work with a lot of men in your position. I know how I *need* to speak to you."

Did she just compare me to a bloody child?

He knew for a fact he was at least five, maybe even ten years older than her. She couldn't be but what? Twenty-five? This was new. He couldn't figure out if he should laugh or become angry.

Matty scoffed. "You know, I'm not sure I've ever been spoken to like this, requested or not."

"I said need, not want." She moved the stack of letters and papers onto the desk. "Nobody *wants* to be told the truth. But it's what my clients need. If I soften my words, trying not to offend anyone, then clients only hear what they want, and they ignore the actual message. Suggesting and implying things isn't good enough." She flashed him a clearly fake smile.

"It's more ladylike," Matty said. "Saying things so bluntly is not ladylike at all."

"I'm not a lady. I'm here to get results." She didn't even look up from the papers she was shuffling around to get just right. "Ahh, better." She sat down at the desk and began scrutinizing the letters.

He ought to be angry with her, fire her immediately. In all regards, he should probably hate her. She was everything he hated in a woman.

Yet somehow, every one of her actions drew him more to her, like some kind of addiction. Normally, he liked his women passive, submissive, sweet and girly. But not Christina. She was—different. Perhaps that's why he currently enjoyed her company.

She lightly pressed the pen to her plump lips as she pored over a sheet, tapping her mouth gently in the manner of someone who used to chew pencils in school, but had since learned not to.

Drawing in a sharp breath, he realized that a heat stirred inside him. He needed a drink. Something stiff to ease his mind and prevent additional stiffness.

"Care for a brandy?" He moved toward the cabinet.

"I don't drink on the job. I have to stay focused to give you the best work possible."

Matty shrugged with a grin. "I've never found a little sip at work to do any harm." He slowly selected one of the three aged brandies from his vast liquor cabinet. Christina stared at him as if he were an animal who should spend more time organizing the post than choosing a drink.

"Maybe that's why you had to call me."

He wanted to reply but could not think of anything. Damn, she had a sharp wit for a young woman. And an equally quick tongue. She was like the mind of a no-nonsense matron in the body of an American fairytale creature. Where was she from, anyway? His guess was South America. He didn't know much about the culture there. Maybe this was normal. It was a delightful challenge. How had she wound up crunching numbers and sorting post for anyone? Sure, it was better to be doing such menial tasks for a man like him, but he knew so many talent scouts who would whisk her off her feet in a heartbeat. How had she remained so undetected?

"I'm amazed a beautiful woman like yourself, working in this part of the country, is not something like a model, or an actress." He poured himself a drink.

"There are plenty of beautiful women who work in business."

Matty shook his head. "I've never, in my entire life, seen a woman as pretty as you who does not make a living off her looks. Especially not an unmarried woman. Do you not want to be a model? To be famous?"

Christina shook her head. "Nope."

"Too good for it? Too smart to make money off your looks?"

"Nope. Many models are smart. I know one or two myself."

"Did a model break your heart? Is that why you chose your current line of work?" He was genuinely baffled and couldn't help himself trying to break through her cold exterior. She was this attractive and knew models and had no desire of becoming one?

She paused her current task to stare up at him. "Beauty fades, sensuality expires. Being good at business doesn't." She stared up at him. "An intelligent model who knows how to play the system and become a recruiter might be able to make a living off it for her entire life. But I'm not good at that. Some of *us* would rather do what we're good at, instead of doing something we find fun."

That last bit was definitely another jab at him. Tommy Arvin hadn't been wrong. This woman *was* a total bitch. How she could treat her employer this way was beyond him. If she were anyone else he would have kicked her out, or started placing higher demands on her already. But he just smirked and sipped his brandy as she worked. He would *not* give in first.

Why did he like her so much? That was the issue that troubled him the most. She was precisely the sort of woman he avoided like the plague. The sort of woman he scoffed at, and who his friends would suggest suffered from lack of sexual activity. It was as though she had heard that men like feisty girls and decided, "Hey, that's cute, now let me show you how it's done." This was just pure cruelty.

But simultaneously, it was kind of nice. Her cruelty excited him, made him yearn for her even more. Despite being his social subordinate and an employee, she was somehow standing above him, on a pedestal. And he wanted to knock it out from under her, and show her who really was the boss.

Christina Smith was sort of an enigma. He should not like her. But he did. He wanted to break her down, to control her, to possess her mind, heart, and body. She was a challenge. And he was more than prepared to rise and meet her defiance.

"Perhaps I ought to make you a model. I cannot believe that any woman has at no point desired to be famous and admired for her beauty."

"I didn't say I never imagined being a model, or an actress, or a singer. But many people are afraid of blood and dream about being doctors, and a lot of people fear flying, and dream of being a pilot."

He shook his head. "Are you saying you wouldn't make a good model? You don't strike me as someone with such low confidence, but I suppose it's a possibility. Or do you mean to say that you fear failure? That would be odd for a businesswoman—"

She paused and put the papers down.

Matty came alive on the inside. Had he finally cut to her core? Put a chink in her armor?

"What I mean is that a dream is not necessarily connected to the reality of the world. What little girls picture when they dream of modeling isn't reality. Dreams aren't real. They don't come true. To put it bluntly, they're a waste of time."

That was one of the saddest things he'd ever heard anyone say. He actually pitied her in that instant. Everyone had dreams. Even he had things he aspired to do someday, that were beyond his reach. No matter how much money you had, there was always something you didn't have the time, the energy, or the connections to do. And he had an entire life plan mapped out to achieve his dreams.

"So, you gave up on all of your dreams? Just like that?"

She shook her head. "They're not my dreams anymore. I know how the world works, and I don't have what it takes to succeed in that environment."

"I have the means to make sure that you could succeed. And you most certainly have the beauty."

Why was he doing this? He was under no obligation to help her out. But he felt a dual impulse. On one hand he wanted to help her, and on the other to get her under his thumb—which motivated him to offer her everything he had at his disposal.

She glanced over at him. "Are you a model?"

He shook his head. "I know a few directors of agencies, and I've dated enough models in the past. I'm sure they'd be able to help you."

"Maybe we should just stick to what we know best." She held up the disheveled papers with a curt smile.

To continue reading Shagged tap HERE!
FREE in Kindle Unlimited

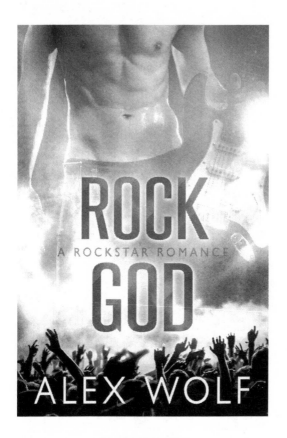

ROCK GOD

A ROCKSTAR ROMANCE

ALEX WOLF

Coming July 6th!

Chapter One

BRISTOL

I walked through the door of my apartment, sweaty. My backpack felt like it was trying to tug my shoulders to the ground. It was a long day at school and I still needed to work on a paper due next week. Valerie, my best friend, came down the hallway with a wide smile on her face just as I dropped my bag.

Her pale blonde hair was up in a messy bun with the new pink ends hanging over her face. "How's it going?"

I shot her a skeptic glance. I could already tell she was up to something.

"Exhausted. Been in class since eight and still have a ton of work. I'm *really* looking forward to graduation." There had to be circles under my eyes as I wiped them and probably smeared mascara all over the place in the process. I didn't care.

"No, you're not." She used her annoying singsong voice as she clapped her hands.

"Huh?"

She sat on the couch next to my backpack. "I scored free tickets to the Nine Muses concert tonight. They're opening for The Years. You have to come!" Her dark brown eyes pleaded with me to agree with her.

I frowned and shook my head. "No way. I have a paper to work on. I don't even know their music." I dropped onto the arm chair that faced the couch, pushed a hand against my bobbed hair, and sighed.

Valerie was going to push this until I agreed. She'd been this way

since middle school. "You need a night out. You study too much."
She leaned forward. "Come have a few drinks. Check out the band.
Loosen up for once." She waggled her eyebrows. "I'll make you
coffee."

I was too tired to argue, but not too tired to surrender completely.
"I don't know." I looked at my watch. It was just past five. "What
time's the show?"

"Eight. I have great seats and Miller can't go. He's covering a shift
at the bar."

I rolled my eyes.

"He's a huge fan." Valerie shrugged with a smile, not looking too
upset about it. Her and Miller weren't serious as far as I could tell
but they were definitely more than friends. "Please?" Her big, round
eyes practically begged.

I blew out another exasperated breath and stared at my bag then
back at her. "*Fine*. But I'm not staying out all night. I want to go
running and work on my paper tomorrow. Okay?" I stared at her.

Valerie nodded dramatically, barely holding in her enthusiasm.
"Deal." She stood up and smiled. "Want me to make that coffee? We
can grab dinner before the show."

"I'm going to take a shower." I grinned. "But, yeah. Coffee
sounds amazing."

I knew Valerie would want to help me get ready and make a
whole production of tonight. Sometimes, I wished that I was more
like she was. I preferred to go to the movies or maybe a coffee house,
even stay home.

I walked down the hallway and into my bedroom, yawning half
the way. I stripped my sweats and t-shirt off and stared in the mirror,
hating my pale skin that highlighted every sign of exhaustion. I took
way more classes this semester than I should have.

Valerie got us the apartment. While I paid some rent, she covered
most of it with her parent's help. I'd be eternally grateful for that and
told myself to suck it up and go out. It was the least I could do. I
turned on the water and stepped in, letting the steaming liquid sluice
over my sore back.

I loved showers. They were relaxing and one of the few times I
was alone. The stress practically flowed out of my body. I washed up,
wrapping a towel around my head and drying off before I pulled on
my robe and tied it in a knot. I brushed my hair quickly and headed
out to the kitchen, inhaling the fresh aroma of the coffee.

She always made it strong and a little sweet, just the way that I liked it. I slipped into one of the barstools and reached for the cup as she slid it across the marble countertop.

"Thanks."

She smiled and nodded. "I'm going to shower too. Then we can get ready." She grinned once more before going back to her room.

I took a long sip. I hadn't had coffee since this morning before class. It was a miracle I made it through the day. Come to think of it, I hadn't eaten anything more than a protein bar either. My stomach growled, and I grinned as I set the cup down and went to get another one to hold me over.

Valerie hollered when she was ready, and I headed into her room. She was blow-drying her thick, straight hair in her bathroom. Music blared through her Bluetooth speaker.

"Is this one of the bands?"

She nodded, looking into the mirror. "Nine Muses."

I had to admit, they had a great sound and his voice was raspy in that sexy way. I was a sucker for good music, but I didn't see bands too often. I just used it as background noise if I was working on something.

"Aren't they great?"

"He's got a nice voice."

She flipped her hair up to run a brush through it and smirked into the mirror.

I smirked back.

Valerie dried my hair and used her straightener to give it a sleek look before glancing at the make up on the counter.

"Sit." She smiled.

Within the hour, I looked like a different girl with black liner in a pointy wing and heavy mascara. She added some shimmer to my face and slipped a dark pink lippie into her purse for later.

I wore a black dress with cute cap sleeves and a ruffled skirt that ended mid-thigh. Valerie insisted that I wear some of her chunky Mary Jane shoes as she slipped into a gray dress with thin straps and a loose skirt that flowed around her thighs. She was gorgeous, I had to give her that.

I smiled at her again before I glanced into the mirror. I looked good but knew tomorrow it would all be nothing but a reminder of the work I didn't finish.

We left the apartment and took her car to a little bistro down the road for a quick bite. It was decent and affordable for my budget from tutoring.

My parents paid for school and a small part of the apartment, but they couldn't afford to give me a lot of pocket money. My brother started college this year in San Diego, so they had to make sure we could both get an education.

Valerie was always generous. I was lucky to have her. Her parents had a lot more money, and she was their only child—a spoiled one at that.

I sipped a dollar margarita as we waited for our food, listening to her talk about the night before with Miller.

"Are you really just friends?"

She nodded. "Yeah. We like to hang out. It works." Miller worked nearly every night at a bar, so they rarely spent an entire evening together. "It's fun. Maybe you need a 'friend' too. Work out some of that stress." She laughed when I raised an eyebrow at her.

"I'm good. I'll save that for after graduation." I had too much to do to even consider something like that, though there were times that I missed sex. It'd been a while. My second year at college with a guy I briefly dated. Not very memorable.

"Whatever you say."

The waiter set our plates down.

I was starving and dug right in.

She stared at me and shook her head while I inhaled everything on the plate. Once it was cleared I looked up at her half-eaten meal.

"You done?"

I shook my head and slid a middle finger up at her.

"Come on." She laughed and paid the waiter.

The venue was just a block over, so we joined the other people on the sidewalk heading that way. There was a crowd wrapping around the side of the building and down the street.

We did what we always did. Waited and people watched. Valerie looked around at everyone. It was mostly college students and a few older couples.

I leaned against the wall, already tired and ready for a nap after the big meal.

We got to the front and Valerie handed the tickets to the man before they searched our bags. Once through security, we walked inside and figured out where our seats were before getting drinks at the bar.

The older theater was charming, and I loved the vibe as I glanced around. There was enough light to make your way through, but it was dark enough to feel the excitement. I followed Valerie into the main room. Everyone took their seats as the place filled with voices and laughter. Valerie led us to our seats just to the right of the center of the stage, two rows back.

"I'm impressed. Where'd you get these tickets?" I had to lean in close to hear her over the crowd.

"A girl in my business law class had them but was going home this weekend. I bought them since I've been wanting to see these guys. She gave me a great deal." She beamed as people wandered across the stage to set up.

I sat back and sipped my drink, taking everything in. Usually, if I treated myself to a concert it was in the nosebleeds or far away from the stage.

This was definitely better than working on a paper at home.

The lights went out.

Screams and cheers boomed through the room.

I shivered and looked around when Valerie gripped my hand. A blue light came on that barely lit the stage and silhouettes appeared like shadows moving through the haze. I tried to see more as I leaned forward. A slow drumbeat started as a light shone on a guy behind a large set and the blare of guitars filled the room. When the man behind the mic began singing, I recognized his voice from the song playing at the apartment. It was even raspier and sexier in person. The lights came on all at once.

There he was.

A tall lean body filtering through the smoke.

And then his face.

I couldn't look away, like I was caught in a tractor beam.

I stared at the tall, muscular man behind the microphone.

My breath hitched, as I looked him up and down slowly, longing to get my hands into his tousled brown hair. It was that look that was messy but perfectly styled. A look that few men could pull off.

He wore faded jeans and a thin white t-shirt as he leaned forward, singing something about a girl with turquoise eyes. She sounded beautiful the way he described her, and I smiled as I tried to see his face in the light. He had tanned skin and a great body. It stirred something deep inside me.

He grew more interesting with every song. His voice had a huge range from low to high, and you could feel his emotion in every word. I was a shaking mess by the time the set ended and leaned back as I took a deep breath. I looked over at Valerie, who was giving me a knowing smile.

I laughed and leaned over to her. "I'm getting a drink. Want anything?"

"Yeah. Whatever you're having." She had to scream for me to hear her.

When I got back, we watched the headliner. They were a good band but lacked the soul that Nine Muses had. I'd never been to a show where the opener overshadowed the headliner. Jesus, his voice and the music haunted me, and I imagined him in my head the rest of the show. When the lights came back on, I let out a slow breath and grabbed my purse to leave.

Val raised her eyebrows at me. "I know what bar they hang out at. Wanna go?"

My exhaustion was replaced with a low hum of energy flowing through my veins and I slowly nodded. She smiled and stood, slipping her purse over her body before walking to the door leading to the street.

My heart thumped in my chest as we joined the other people spilling out of the venue, wondering if I'd have a chance to see him again—or maybe even meet him.

Valerie shoved through a large crowd milling on the sidewalk, tossing a big smile over her shoulder.

I hurried to catch up.

Chapter Two

DAVID

I stood against the wall sipping a beer as I looked over the people that came backstage to hang out. There were more women than men.

They were all drinking and laughing when I felt eyes on me. I glanced toward the door and noticed a curvy blonde smiling my direction. She shifted her hair over her shoulder, looking like they always did.

I took another swig and glanced toward the other guys in the band. They were caught up with some groupies and I assumed they'd be occupied for a while.

They were trying to get me to go to a club, but I just wanted to go to our usual spot—the local bar I'd been hanging out at for years. A dive with pool tables and booths scattered around. A place where I could get some privacy.

In the beginning the attention was awesome. It grew old fast.

Basically, I just wanted calm. With the way we were soaring up the charts, the days of dive bars were going to be gone soon. I wanted to hold on to what little I had left for as long as possible.

I was rich from a trust fund my grandparents left me when I was eighteen. I didn't need the money we were going to be earning soon, but the fame was something we all wanted for the sake of our music.

It wore me down, but the women were a perk. Being the lead singer, I was the mysterious guy—the one everyone saw first—the face of the band. The other guys had plenty of game, but I could look like Steve Buscemi and still get laid whenever I wanted.

I walked across the room and nudged Jake, our drummer. He looked up at me with a curious smile.

"Let's get out of here. Hit Frank's for a beer." I spoke in a low voice, so no one would hear us.

All it took was one of these chicks to get wind of where I liked to hang out and it'd be ruined forever.

Jake stood and told the others we'd see them tomorrow.

They all knew where Frank's was if they wanted to show up. We made our way out of the room and into the crowded hallway. Women stared at me as we passed. I was still riding the high from the show, but I wanted to hang out with my best friend tonight. I didn't want the attention and to hear their stupid questions and ridiculous giggling and shit. Half of them couldn't name most of our songs. They just wanted to fuck a rock star.

We walked through the back door and I led the way to the side-walk. Frank's was just down the street and I tugged a beanie over my head as we moved away from the theater. It seemed as though the crowd was too busy to notice us as we walked, and I breathed out slowly. "That was a great show!"

"Yeah. Awesome crowd." Jake looked ahead to see the small run-down building. "You're going to be headliners soon."

"Looks that way." I walked up to the doors and pulled one open. We went inside and looked around.

I breathed out a sigh of relief.

It felt like home.

I strode up to the bar, looking around the half-full room as I tugged the beanie down a bit lower. I took a seat and Jake joined me after ordering a round of beers. My eyes roamed to the TVs scattered around the bar, catching some highlights from the hockey game earlier. When I looked at the other end of the bar, there were two women were sitting at a booth. One had blonde hair with bright pink ends that hung down her back. She was pretty, but it was the other one that caught my attention.

A pale redhead with smoky eye makeup and a dark lipstick. She looked away when our eyes met. Maybe she was shy, but fuck, she was beautiful. She tucked a strand of hair behind her ear.

I caught myself leaning toward her before straightening up. I didn't know what it was about her. Maybe it was because she was different. She didn't look like the typical groupies that hung around the band.

I looked away so I wouldn't stare, but my cock strained against my zipper. My eyes rolled back over to her. It was impossible to look away.

She glanced up and blushed when I caught her. Whispering to her friend, they both looked over with nervous smiles and Jake let out a groan.

"What was that about not being recognized?" He shook his head.

I shrugged. "It's two girls, not a fucking gaggle."

"The ginger's hot."

My face tensed, and I ground my teeth. "Try again."

Jake sipped his beer. "Staking a claim?"

I turned to him slowly. "Yeah."

He snickered. "Of course you are."

"Let's send them a drink." I waved the bartender over.

He leaned toward us, and I asked him to take the girls two of whatever they were drinking. I slid a twenty over.

He got to work and delivered the drinks, then nodded at me as he went to help another customer.

The girls smiled and held up their glasses in thanks as I stared the redhead down for a moment. I was a bit surprised.

She hadn't walked over and thrown herself into my lap like most girls did.

Good. A challenge for once.

Finally, after several exchanged looks, I had to break the seal and headed to the bathroom. When I walked out, I wasn't paying attention and crashed into a warm body. I stumbled and pressed her up against the wall with my chest.

"Jesus, what the fuck." I pushed myself away and looked down to see the redhead, flushed pink and gripping my arms. "Oh."

"You don't have to be an asshole."

I backed up a step and reached for her forearm. "You okay?"

She yanked it away and scoffed. "Fine. Thanks for the drink."

She started to walk away and I grabbed her by the arm and spun her back to me. "I said I was sorry."

Her eyes were deep green and big as she stared back at me. I didn't want to move. Just breathed her in. There was a hint of cherries like body wash or something.

She stared down at my hand then back up at me. "I need to go. Nice show." She started away from me.

"You a fan?"

"My friend took me. Hadn't heard of you before." She looked into my eyes and then at my lips.

I considered kissing her. Just to see what she'd do. I smirked. It was going to be fun fucking with her. She was shy and sassy, and I figured she definitely had a wild side to her.

The quiet ones always do.

The one thing that intrigued me about her—she didn't fawn all over me.

"Have a drink with me." I nodded toward a booth.

Her eyes widened then she shook her head. "I don't think so."

Really? Interesting.

I backed away from her slowly. "I get that you're afraid of having fun. Probably have some studying to do anyway."

Her face tightened.

Struck a nerve there. Better keep it up.

She looked around like she was searching for someone to rescue her. Probably so she could run back to the library. I could tell by her type. Studious and responsible, the kind that shouldn't have anything to do with a guy like me. But, I was her fantasy. She was into me and didn't like that she was.

She was a Rubik's Cube, and I decided right then that I was going to fuck her tonight.

"It's just a drink." I leaned down to her ear. "It's not like I'm going to fuck you on the table."

Her heartbeat sped up on her neck and a slight gasp parted her lips. "One drink. Only because my friend will kill me if I say no." She glared up at me. "Nothing will happen, though."

I grinned. "Sure it won't."

I gestured for Jake to join me as I walked to the booth. Her friend practically tripped over her feet running over to meet us.

I slid in next to the redhead and her attitude.

Jake took a seat by the blonde.

It was going to be too easy. The blonde was practically jizzing her pants looking at Jake. She was the key. It'd happen in three simple steps: I talk her into something, she gives Red shit about it, I'm balls deep in Red.

That was the key to my evening being a success.

We introduced ourselves to them and the blonde informed us that they knew who we were before giving us their names. The blonde was Valerie and the snarky one next to me was Bristol. They were roommates and local college students, both graduating in a few months.

I pressed my leg against Bristol as we chatted. She moved away every time I did it.

Jake and Valerie flirted back and forth.

They seemed occupied, and I slipped an arm around Bristol's shoulders as I smiled down at her.

She glared straight ahead but didn't move my arm.

I breathed in the cherries again. I wondered if her sweet little pussy tasted the way she smelled. She couldn't get rid of me now if she tried.

"What song did you like best?"

She let out an exasperated sigh.

It was a test. Most fans would tell me that they liked the latest hit, or they'd make up some bullshit because they didn't even know the songs. Maybe she'd be different.

"There was one about a friend that you had to say goodbye to. That one. You actually looked like you felt something when you sang it."

I raised an eyebrow. She became more attractive every second. Most people didn't like that song, and it was my favorite too.

I looked away, still surprised by her choice. "Wrote it when a friend died a few years ago. It was brutal."

"Sorry. Didn't mean to bring up old wounds." Bristol was a girl that actually looked like she meant things when she said them. It was an endearing quality.

Most people wanted something from me. She seemed to want nothing to do with me after the hallway incident.

"It's okay." I changed the subject and traced a finger slowly over her shoulder. "What are you studying?"

She shrugged my hand away. "Elementary education."

"You have to study for that?"

"Jesus, you're an asshole."

I laughed. It was so easy pressing her buttons. "What? It's a legit question. How hard can it be to break a graham cracker in half?"

She didn't respond.

Good for her.

She looked across the table and blushed as my gaze followed hers. Jake and Valerie were full on making out at the table.

"I need to go." She slid up against me and I didn't budge.

I just sat there and smiled my ass off.

This was the moment where I would shine. "Well, if you have to go. We better get going too. Come on, Jake."

Valerie's head popped out from the tangle of bodies across from us. Just as I'd planned.

"You can't go, Bri. We're having fun tonight, remember?"

Bristol glared at me. I shrugged like *what can you do?*

She fell back in her seat and stared daggers at the two of them.

I leaned down in her ear. "You could at least pretend to enjoy being here."

Her eyes shot to mine. "I just thought you'd be different. The way you sang tonight doesn't match the asshole I'm talking to."

I slid a hand down her thigh. "I think you like it."

She moved my hand. I let her.

"I think you're full of shit."

"I think you're afraid to have a little fun. Let me tell you something, Bristol. I'm going to be completely honest."

"What's that?"

I leaned over in her ear and whispered, "I think your pussy's wet right now. The way I'm talking to you. And even if you leave, you're going to touch yourself tonight and imagine it's me."

"You're so fucking cocky. You take it to a whole new level."

"You didn't say I was wrong."

She sat there in silence, heart racing, breaths growing shallow.

"You should at least treat yourself to the real thing. Have some fun for once." I ran my hand over hers on the table and whispered, "My cock is so much better than these fingers."

"Shit." Her eyes were closed when she breathed out her response. They widened at once and she looked at me like she wasn't sure if she'd heard herself say it or not.

"I need to go."

I shrugged and moved from the booth, inviting her to leave.

She stood up, defiant, hot as fuck. Maybe I pushed too hard, but I didn't care. Getting my dick wet was never an issue.

She stood there and stared at me, then over at her friends making out, then back at me.

I shrugged and glanced down at my cock then back up at her. "Last chance?"

"Thanks for the drink. I think I'm just going to go home."

"No." Valerie poked her head out again. "And you can't walk home by yourself. It's dark."

I grinned. "No worries. I'll walk her home."

Jake raised an eyebrow. "Really?"

"Not gonna happen." Bristol brushed her palms down her skirt.

I wrapped an arm around her. "It's late. There could be ruffians about. I insist."

She grinned at the word ruffians, almost smiled, then scowled again.

I felt a thrill rush through me, because she hadn't stormed out yet. I'd have never said the things to her I did if I didn't think she was into it. She definitely was.

Her eyes darted around, and she stared at me. I told her with my gaze I wasn't taking no for an answer.

"Ugh, fine."

"Yay!" Valerie went right back to making out with Jake.

Too easy.

He looked over at me with a curious smile and nodded.

I held out my arm for Bristol to take. "Shall we?"

She scoffed and walked right through my shoulder on the way to the door.

I'd win her over. No problem.

This was going to be awesome.

ABOUT THE AUTHOR

Alex hails from the Midwest and currently resides in New Orleans. He enjoys writing steamy romance but more importantly he enjoys the "research" required to produce the steamy scenes. If you like filthy-mouthed, possessive alpha heroes and steamy romance, then he's the author for you!

Sign up for my newsletter and receive EXCLUSIVE content throughout the year
subscribepage.com/alex-wolf

Where you can follow me

facebook.com/authoralexwolf

bookbub.com/profile/alex-wolf-e6b843b5-de8a-4be9-8e94-f8076a9113f1

twitter.com/AlexWolfAuthor

instagram.com/authoralexwolf

goodreads.com/authoralexwolf

Made in the USA
Lexington, KY
26 November 2018